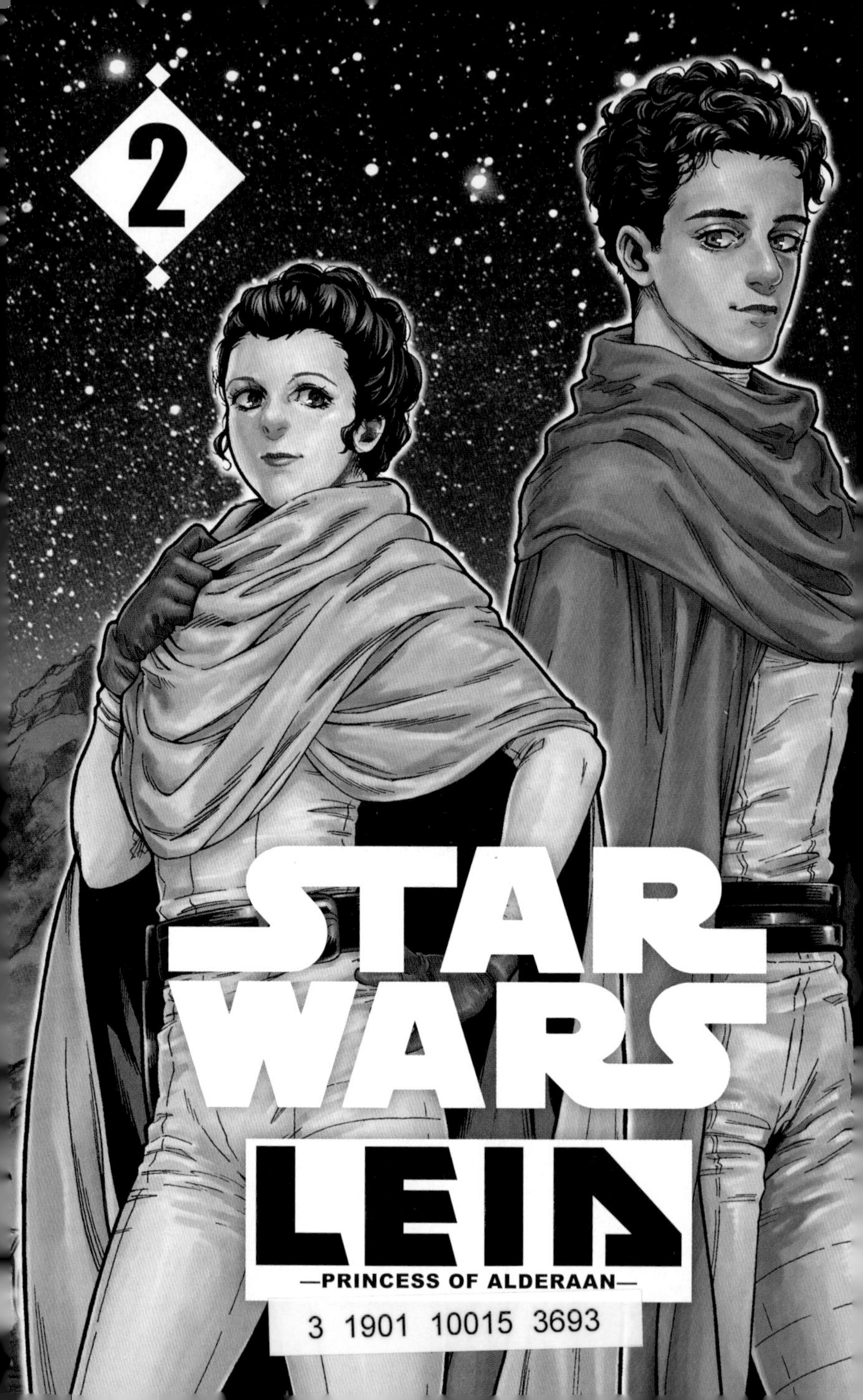
2
STAR WARS
LEIA
—PRINCESS OF ALDERAAN—

STAR WARS LEIA
—PRINCESS OF ALDERAAN—

2

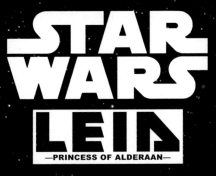

CONTENTS

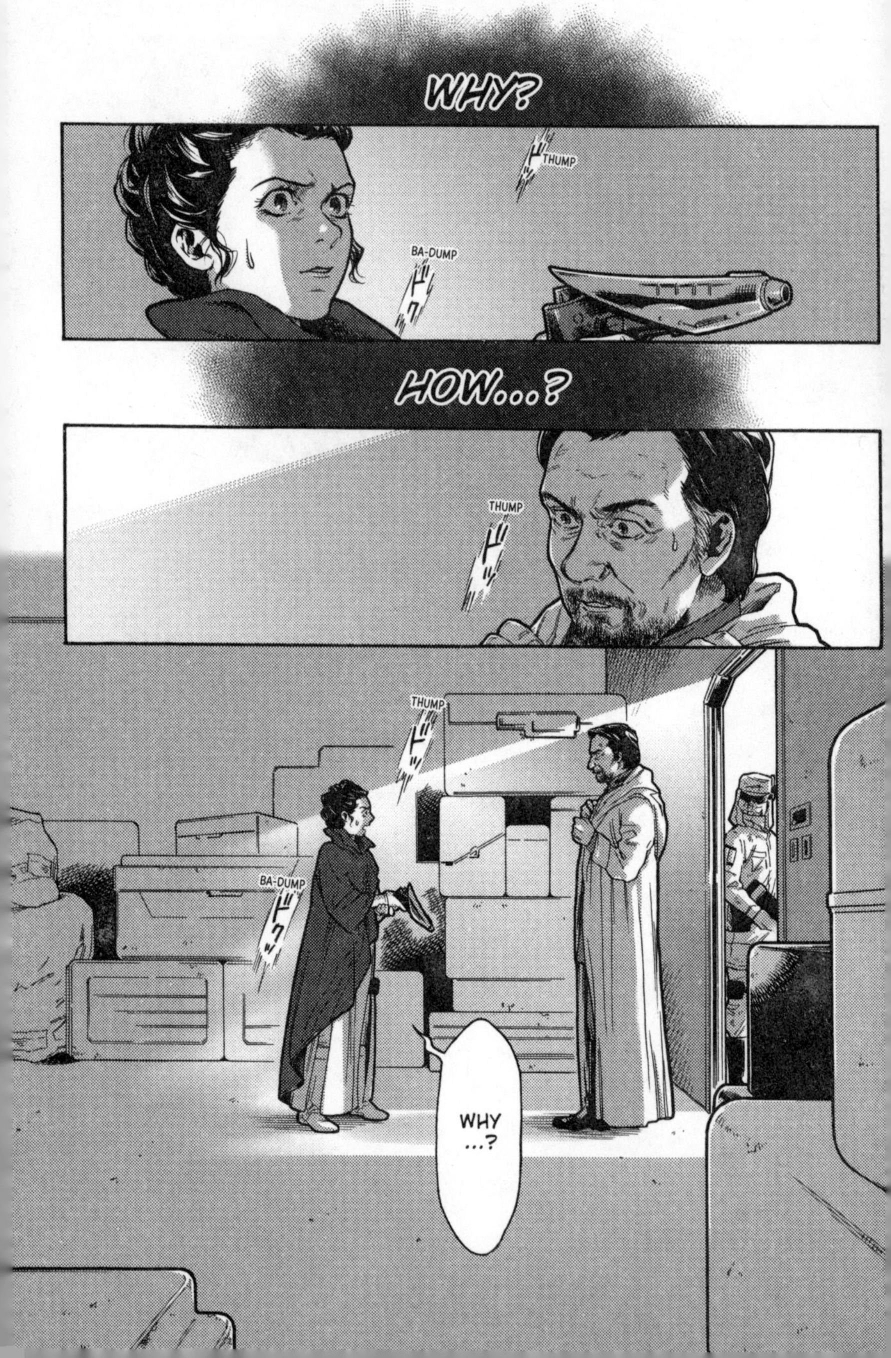
WHY?
THUMP
BA-DUMP
HOW...?
THUMP
THUMP
BA-DUMP
WHY ...?

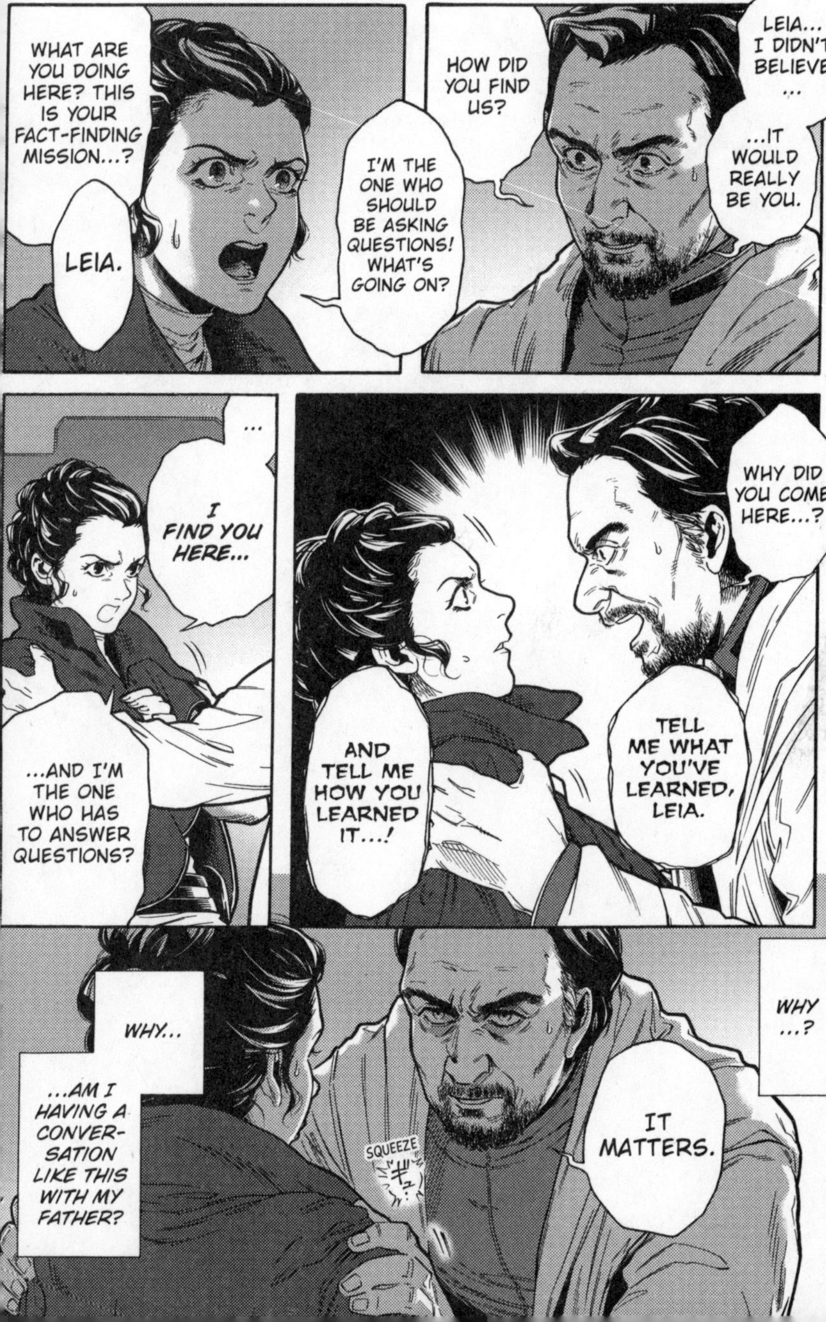
LEIA... I DIDN'T BELIEVE ...
...IT WOULD REALLY BE YOU.
HOW DID YOU FIND US?
I'M THE ONE WHO SHOULD BE ASKING QUESTIONS! WHAT'S GOING ON?
WHAT ARE YOU DOING HERE? THIS IS YOUR FACT-FINDING MISSION...?
LEIA.
WHY DID YOU COME HERE...?
TELL ME WHAT YOU'VE LEARNED, LEIA.
AND TELL ME HOW YOU LEARNED IT...!
...
I FIND YOU HERE...
...AND I'M THE ONE WHO HAS TO ANSWER QUESTIONS?
WHY ...?
IT MATTERS.
SQUEEZE
ギュ
WHY...
...AM I HAVING A CONVER-SATION LIKE THIS WITH MY FATHER?

episode 5 Wavering

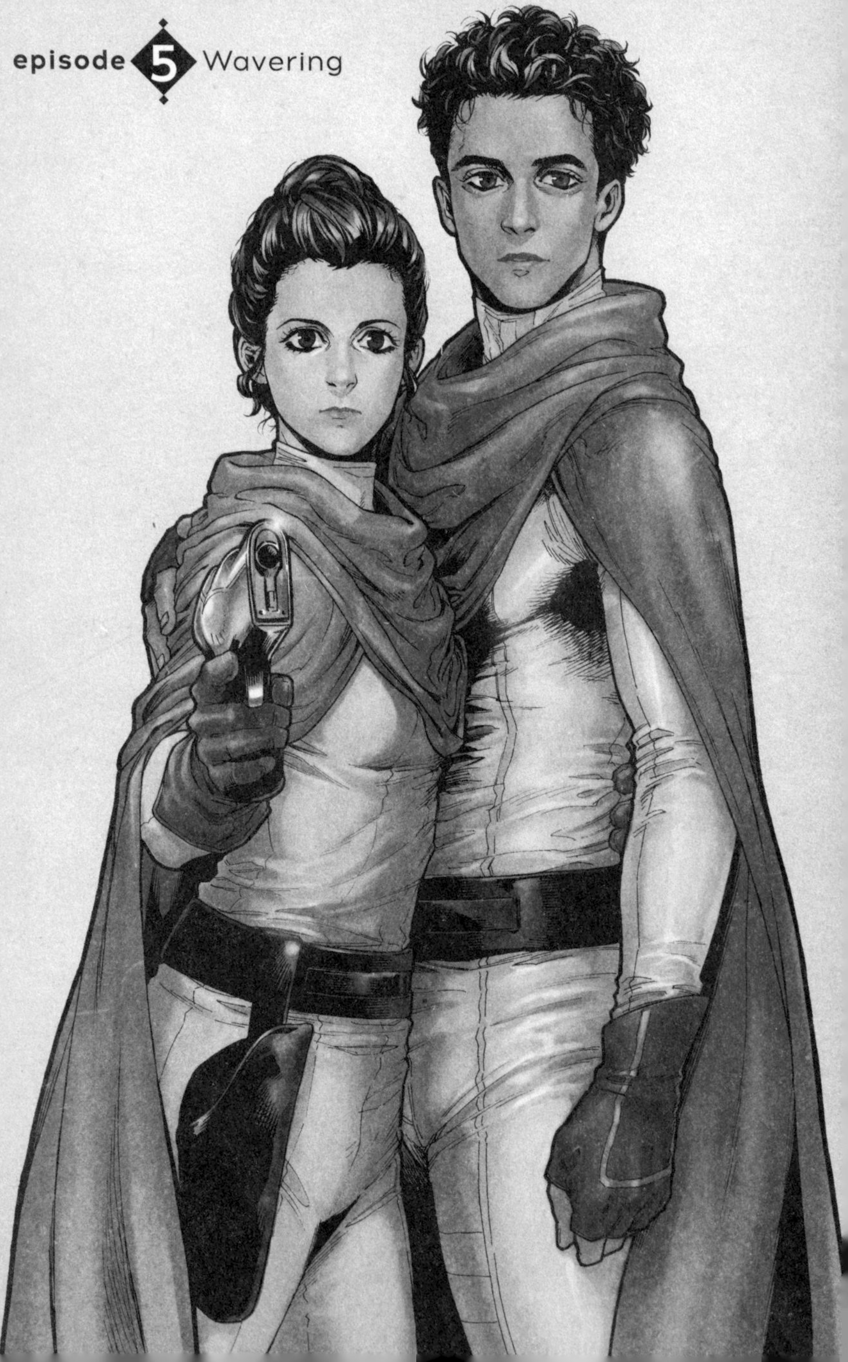

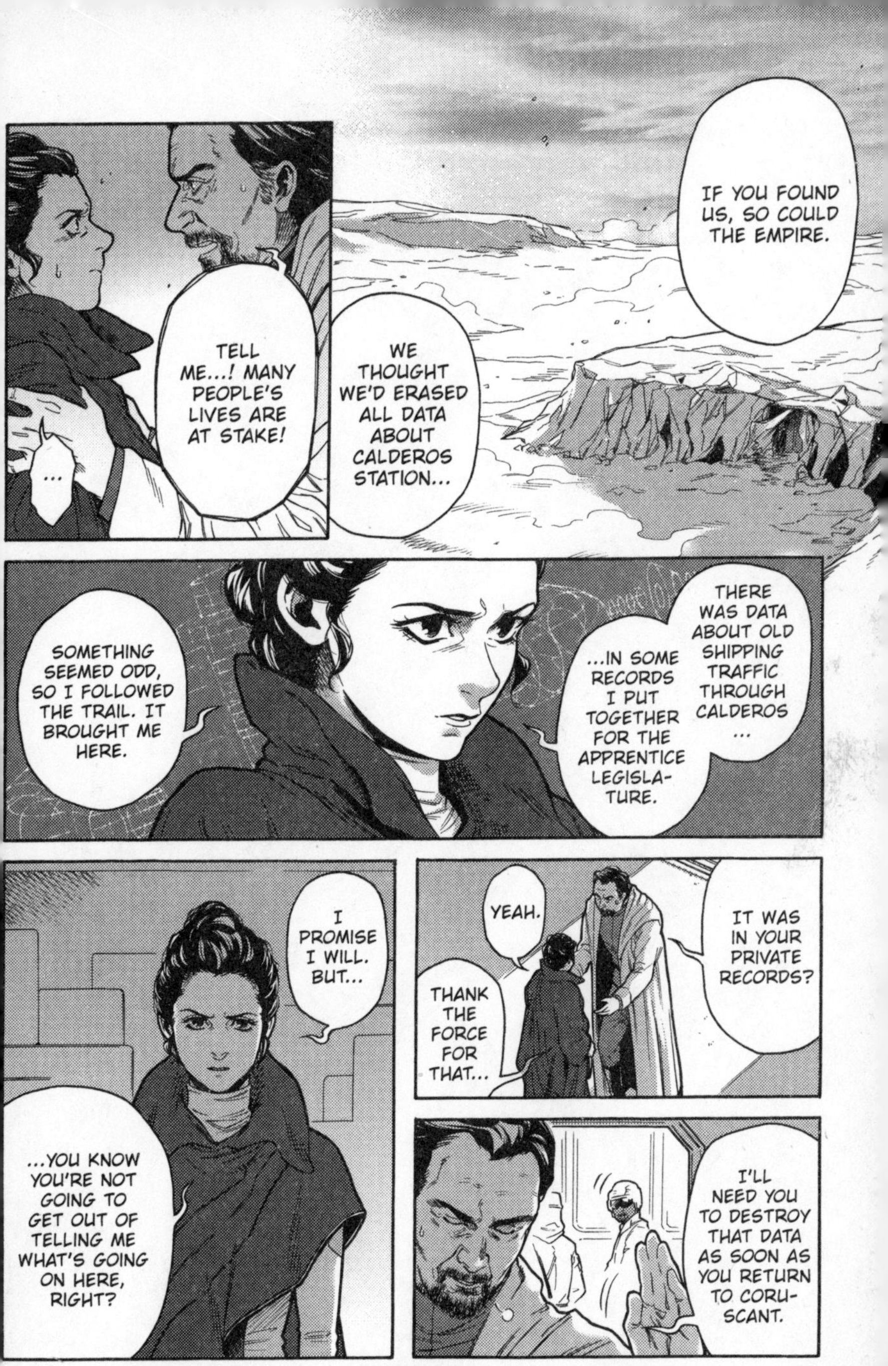
IF YOU FOUND US, SO COULD THE EMPIRE.
WE THOUGHT WE'D ERASED ALL DATA ABOUT CALDEROS STATION...
TELL ME...! MANY PEOPLE'S LIVES ARE AT STAKE!
...
THERE WAS DATA ABOUT OLD SHIPPING TRAFFIC THROUGH CALDEROS ...
...IN SOME RECORDS I PUT TOGETHER FOR THE APPRENTICE LEGISLA-TURE.
SOMETHING SEEMED ODD, SO I FOLLOWED THE TRAIL. IT BROUGHT ME HERE.
IT WAS IN YOUR PRIVATE RECORDS?
YEAH.
THANK THE FORCE FOR THAT...
I'LL NEED YOU TO DESTROY THAT DATA AS SOON AS YOU RETURN TO CORU-SCANT.
I PROMISE I WILL. BUT...
...YOU KNOW YOU'RE NOT GOING TO GET OUT OF TELLING ME WHAT'S GOING ON HERE, RIGHT?

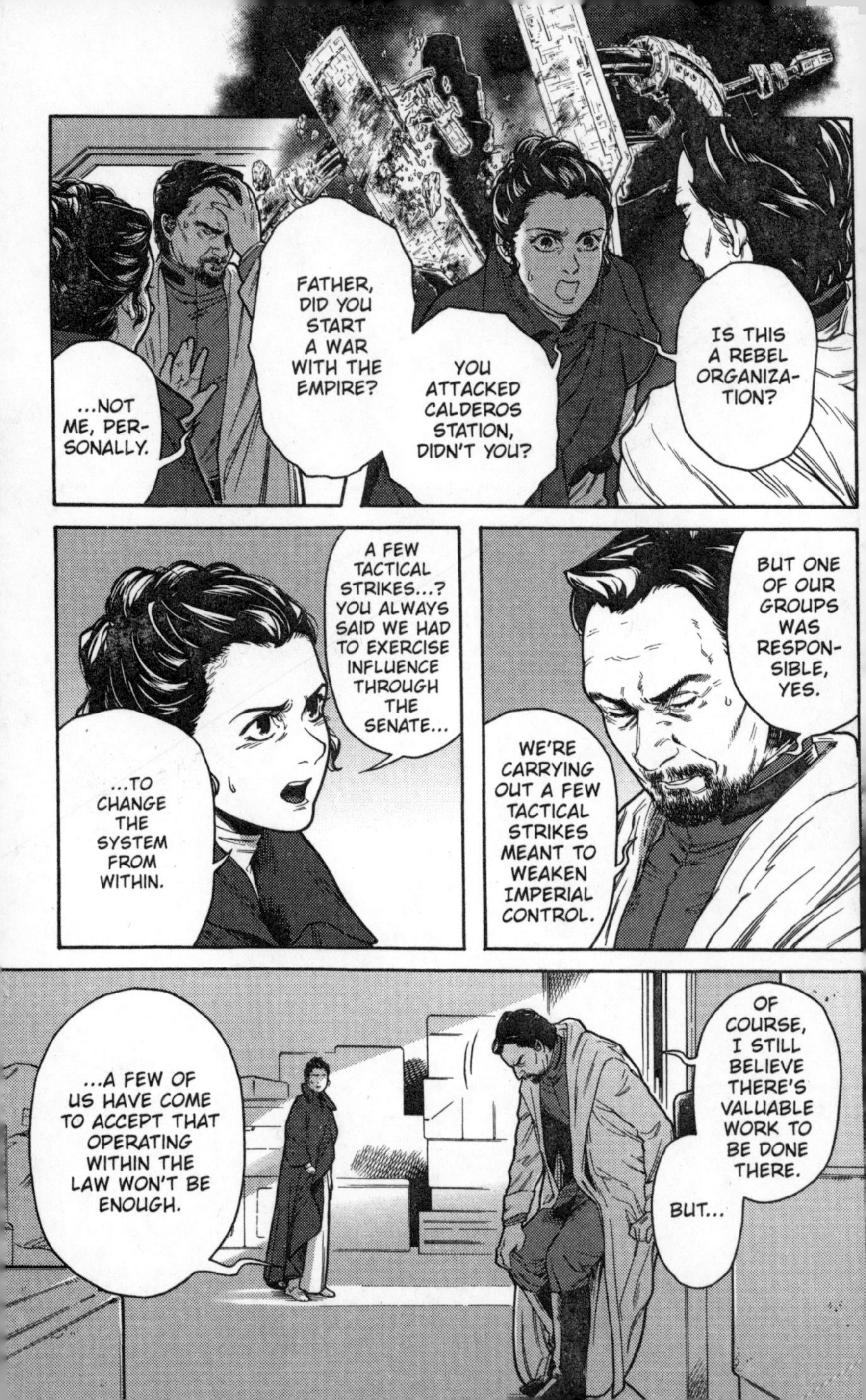
IS THIS A REBEL ORGANIZATION?
YOU ATTACKED CALDEROS STATION, DIDN'T YOU?
FATHER, DID YOU START A WAR WITH THE EMPIRE?
...NOT ME, PERSONALLY.
BUT ONE OF OUR GROUPS WAS RESPONSIBLE, YES.
WE'RE CARRYING OUT A FEW TACTICAL STRIKES MEANT TO WEAKEN IMPERIAL CONTROL.
A FEW TACTICAL STRIKES...? YOU ALWAYS SAID WE HAD TO EXERCISE INFLUENCE THROUGH THE SENATE...
...TO CHANGE THE SYSTEM FROM WITHIN.
OF COURSE, I STILL BELIEVE THERE'S VALUABLE WORK TO BE DONE THERE.
BUT...
...A FEW OF US HAVE COME TO ACCEPT THAT OPERATING WITHIN THE LAW WON'T BE ENOUGH.

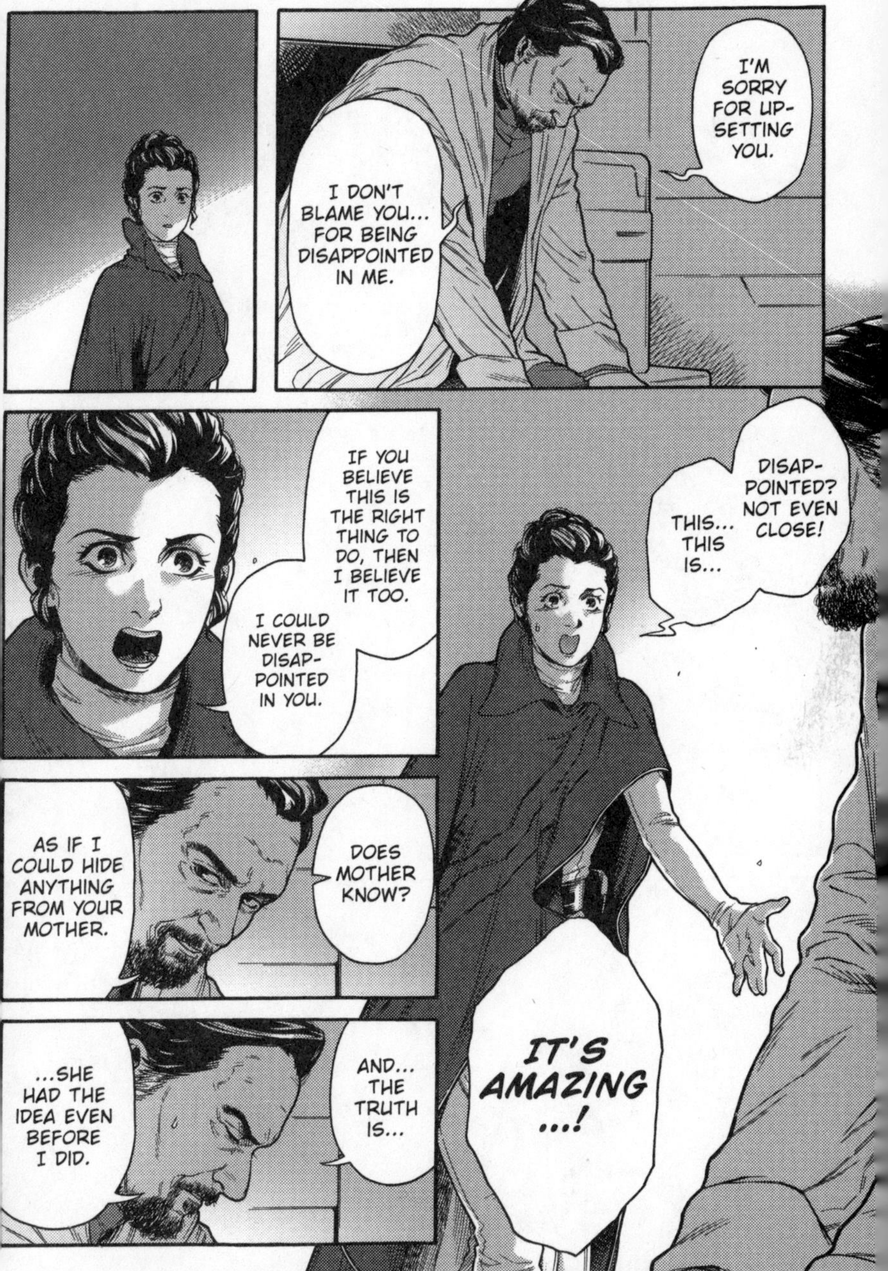
I'M SORRY FOR UP-SETTING YOU.
I DON'T BLAME YOU... FOR BEING DISAPPOINTED IN ME.
DISAP-POINTED? NOT EVEN CLOSE!
THIS... THIS IS...
IT'S AMAZING ...!
IF YOU BELIEVE THIS IS THE RIGHT THING TO DO, THEN I BELIEVE IT TOO.
I COULD NEVER BE DISAP-POINTED IN YOU.
DOES MOTHER KNOW?
AS IF I COULD HIDE ANYTHING FROM YOUR MOTHER.
AND... THE TRUTH IS...
...SHE HAD THE IDEA EVEN BEFORE I DID.

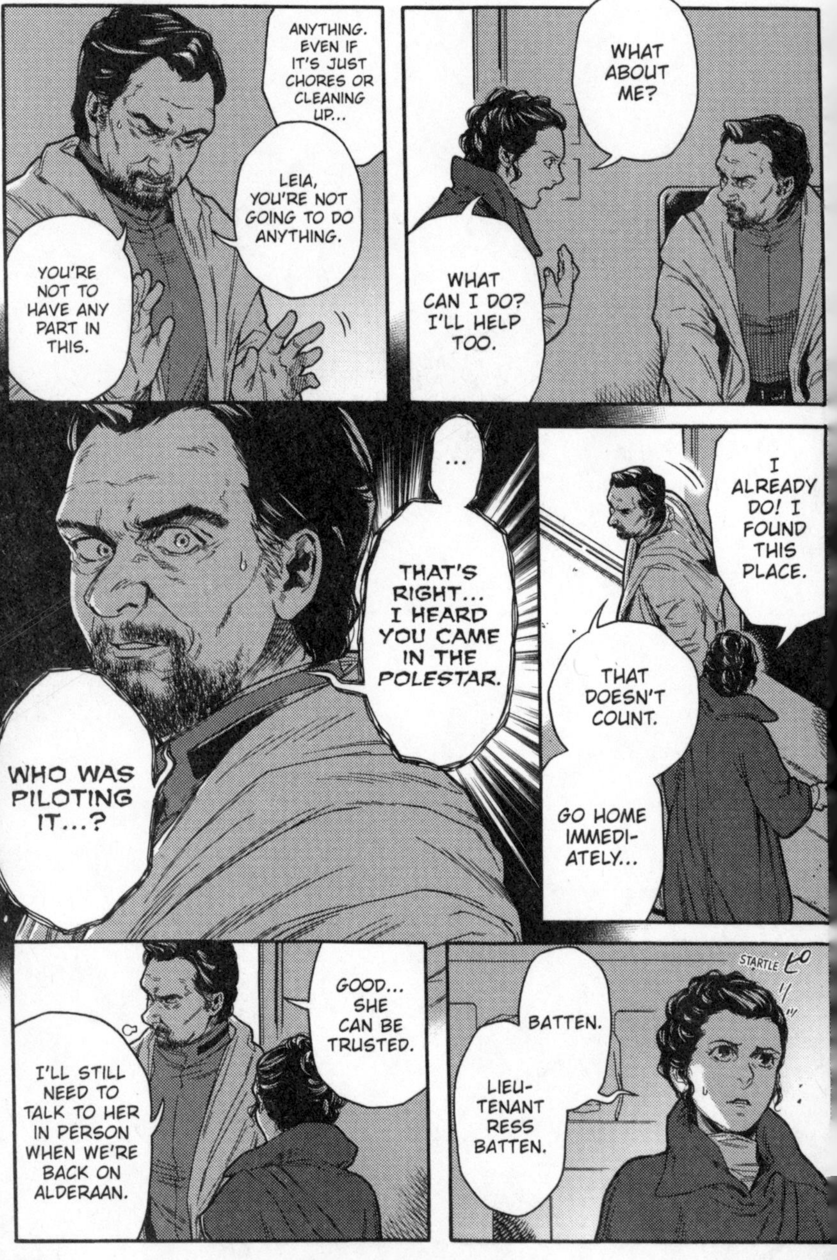
WHAT ABOUT ME?
WHAT CAN I DO? I'LL HELP TOO.
ANYTHING. EVEN IF IT'S JUST CHORES OR CLEANING UP...
LEIA, YOU'RE NOT GOING TO DO ANYTHING.
YOU'RE NOT TO HAVE ANY PART IN THIS.
I ALREADY DO! I FOUND THIS PLACE.
THAT DOESN'T COUNT.
GO HOME IMMEDI-ATELY...
...
THAT'S RIGHT... I HEARD YOU CAME IN THE *POLESTAR*.
WHO WAS PILOTING IT...?
STARTLE
BATTEN.
LIEU-TENANT RESS BATTEN.
GOOD... SHE CAN BE TRUSTED.
I'LL STILL NEED TO TALK TO HER IN PERSON WHEN WE'RE BACK ON ALDERAAN.

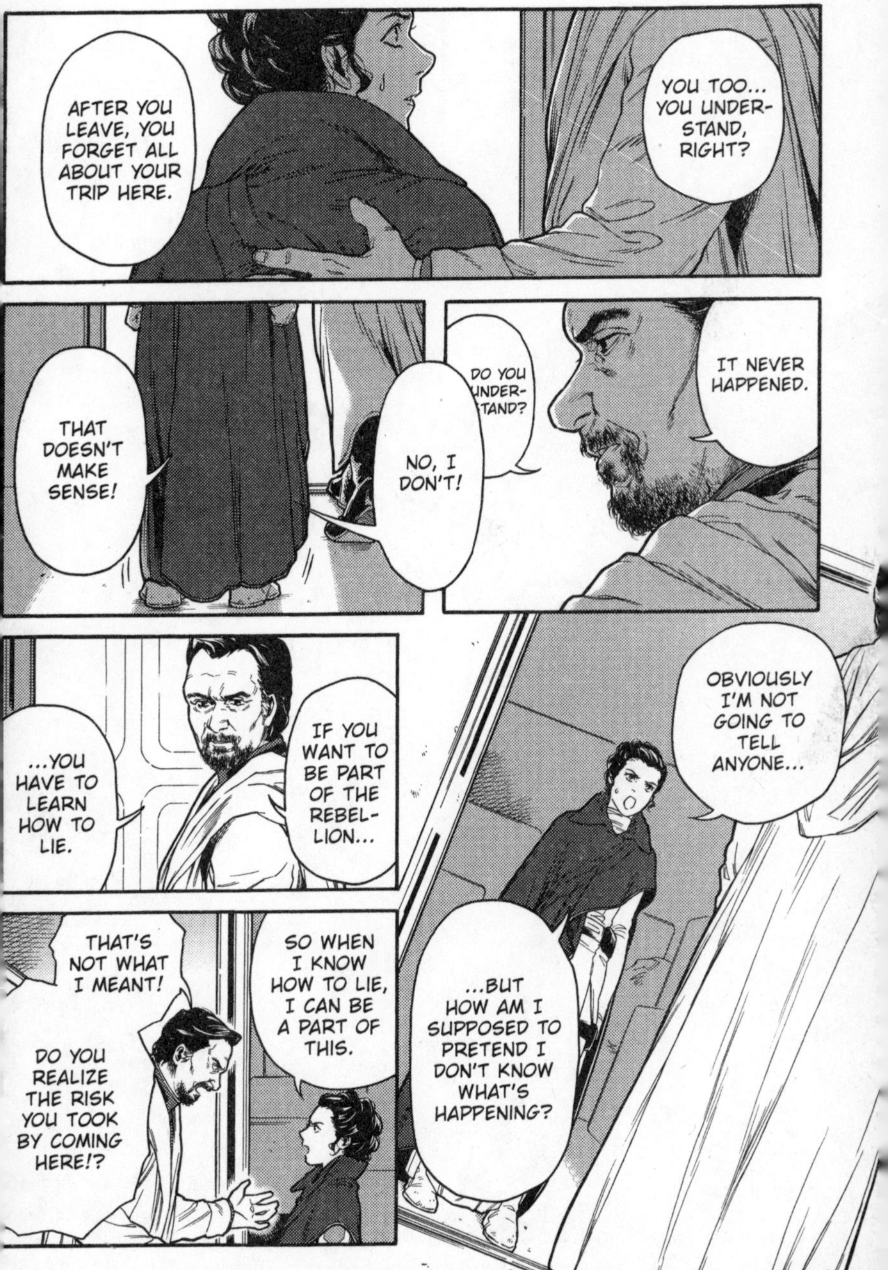
YOU TOO... YOU UNDER-STAND, RIGHT?
AFTER YOU LEAVE, YOU FORGET ALL ABOUT YOUR TRIP HERE.
IT NEVER HAPPENED.
DO YOU UNDER-STAND?
NO, I DON'T!
THAT DOESN'T MAKE SENSE!
OBVIOUSLY I'M NOT GOING TO TELL ANYONE...
...BUT HOW AM I SUPPOSED TO PRETEND I DON'T KNOW WHAT'S HAPPENING?
IF YOU WANT TO BE PART OF THE REBEL-LION...
...YOU HAVE TO LEARN HOW TO LIE.
SO WHEN I KNOW HOW TO LIE, I CAN BE A PART OF THIS.
THAT'S NOT WHAT I MEANT!
DO YOU REALIZE THE RISK YOU TOOK BY COMING HERE!?

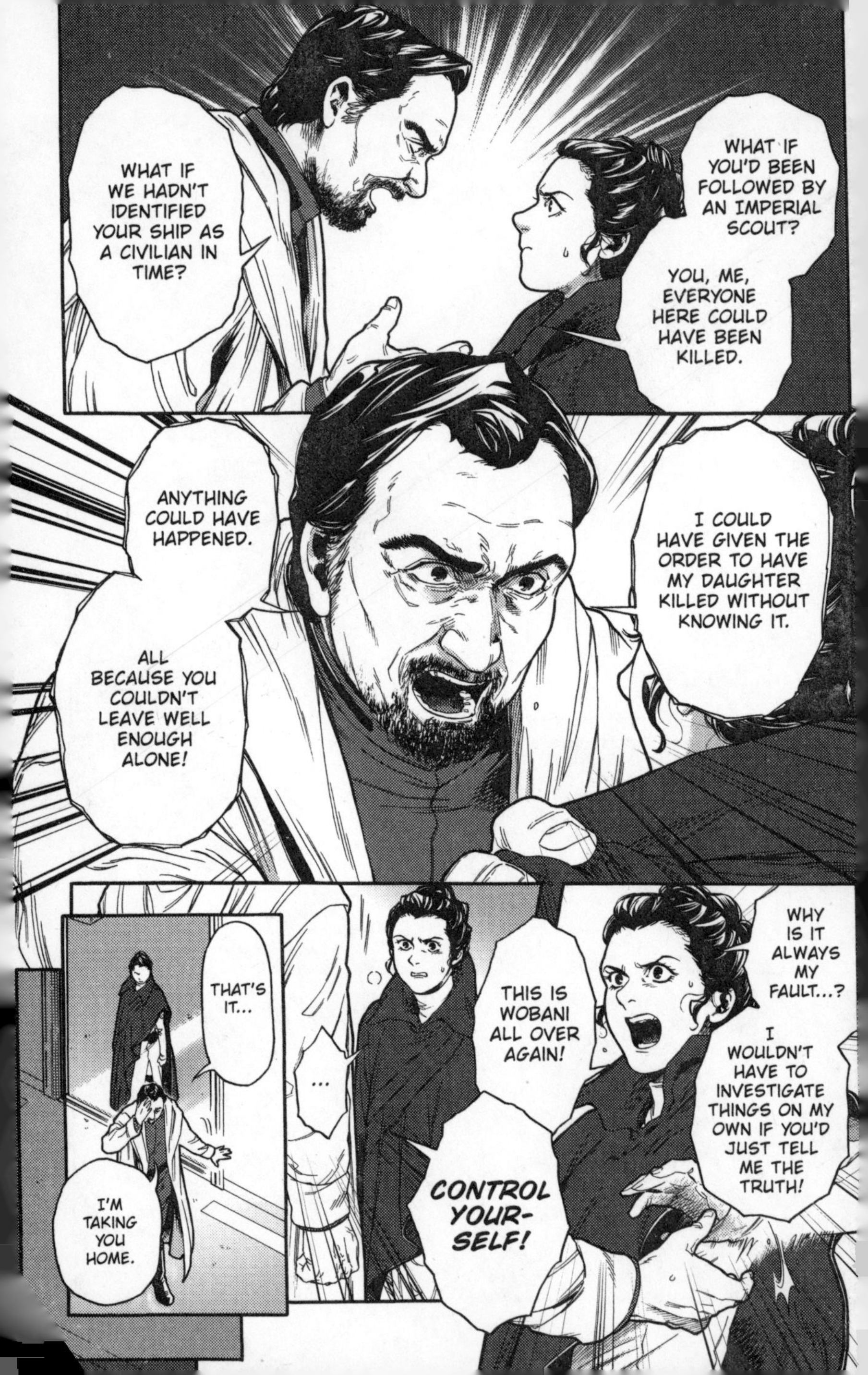
WHAT IF YOU'D BEEN FOLLOWED BY AN IMPERIAL SCOUT?
YOU, ME, EVERYONE HERE COULD HAVE BEEN KILLED.
WHAT IF WE HADN'T IDENTIFIED YOUR SHIP AS A CIVILIAN IN TIME?
I COULD HAVE GIVEN THE ORDER TO HAVE MY DAUGHTER KILLED WITHOUT KNOWING IT.
ANYTHING COULD HAVE HAPPENED.
ALL BECAUSE YOU COULDN'T LEAVE WELL ENOUGH ALONE!
WHY IS IT ALWAYS MY FAULT...?
I WOULDN'T HAVE TO INVESTIGATE THINGS ON MY OWN IF YOU'D JUST TELL ME THE TRUTH!
THIS IS WOBANI ALL OVER AGAIN!
CONTROL YOUR-SELF!
...
THAT'S IT...
I'M TAKING YOU HOME.

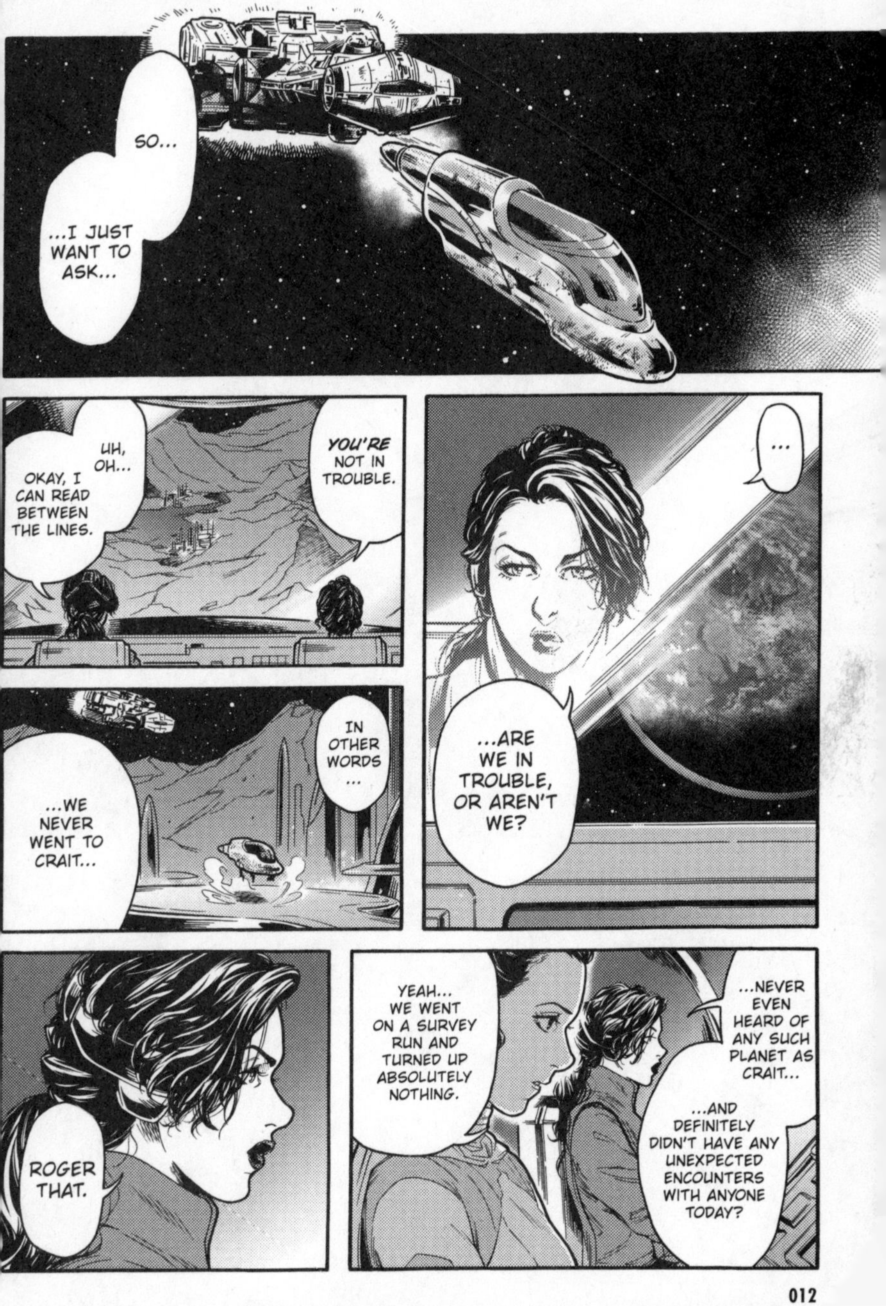

SO...
...I JUST WANT TO ASK...
...
...ARE WE IN TROUBLE, OR AREN'T WE?
YOU'RE NOT IN TROUBLE.
UH, OH... OKAY, I CAN READ BETWEEN THE LINES.
IN OTHER WORDS...
...WE NEVER WENT TO CRAIT...
...NEVER EVEN HEARD OF ANY SUCH PLANET AS CRAIT...
...AND DEFINITELY DIDN'T HAVE ANY UNEXPECTED ENCOUNTERS WITH ANYONE TODAY?
YEAH... WE WENT ON A SURVEY RUN AND TURNED UP ABSOLUTELY NOTHING.
ROGER THAT.

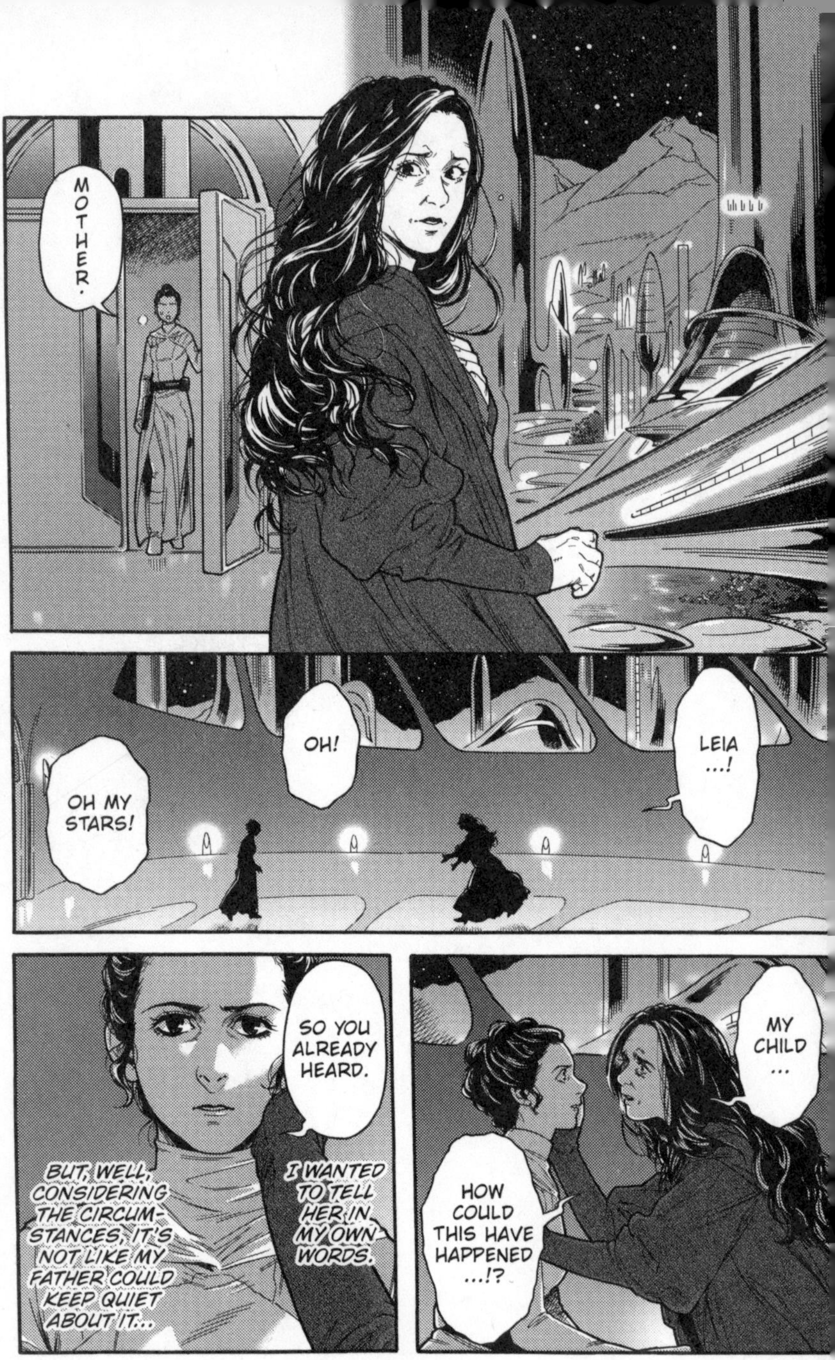
MOTHER.
LEIA ...!
OH!
OH MY STARS!
MY CHILD ...
HOW COULD THIS HAVE HAPPENED ...!?
SO YOU ALREADY HEARD.
I WANTED TO TELL HER IN MY OWN WORDS.
BUT, WELL, CONSIDERING THE CIRCUM-STANCES, IT'S NOT LIKE MY FATHER COULD KEEP QUIET ABOUT IT...

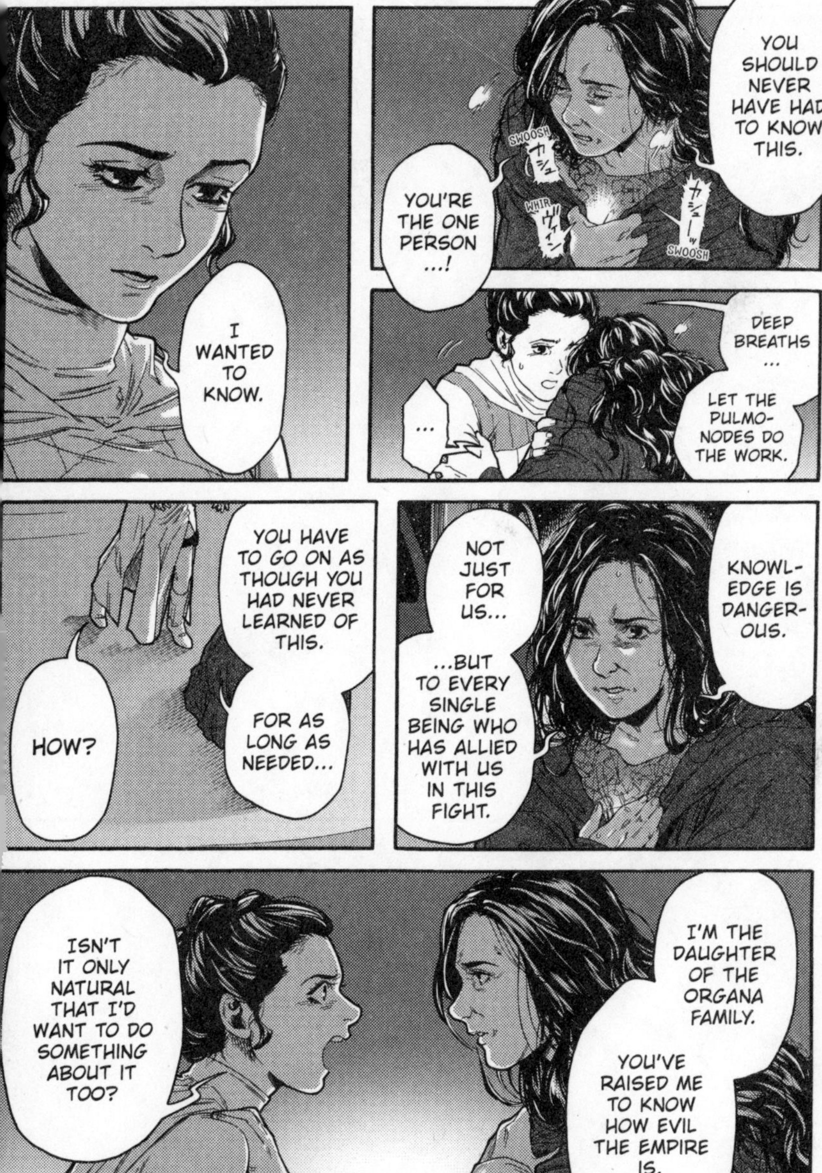
YOU SHOULD NEVER HAVE HAD TO KNOW THIS.
SWOOSH
WHIR
SWOOSH
YOU'RE THE ONE PERSON ...!
DEEP BREATHS ...
LET THE PULMO-NODES DO THE WORK.
...
I WANTED TO KNOW.
KNOWL-EDGE IS DANGER-OUS.
NOT JUST FOR US...
...BUT TO EVERY SINGLE BEING WHO HAS ALLIED WITH US IN THIS FIGHT.
YOU HAVE TO GO ON AS THOUGH YOU HAD NEVER LEARNED OF THIS.
FOR AS LONG AS NEEDED...
HOW?
I'M THE DAUGHTER OF THE ORGANA FAMILY.
YOU'VE RAISED ME TO KNOW HOW EVIL THE EMPIRE IS.
ISN'T IT ONLY NATURAL THAT I'D WANT TO DO SOMETHING ABOUT IT TOO?

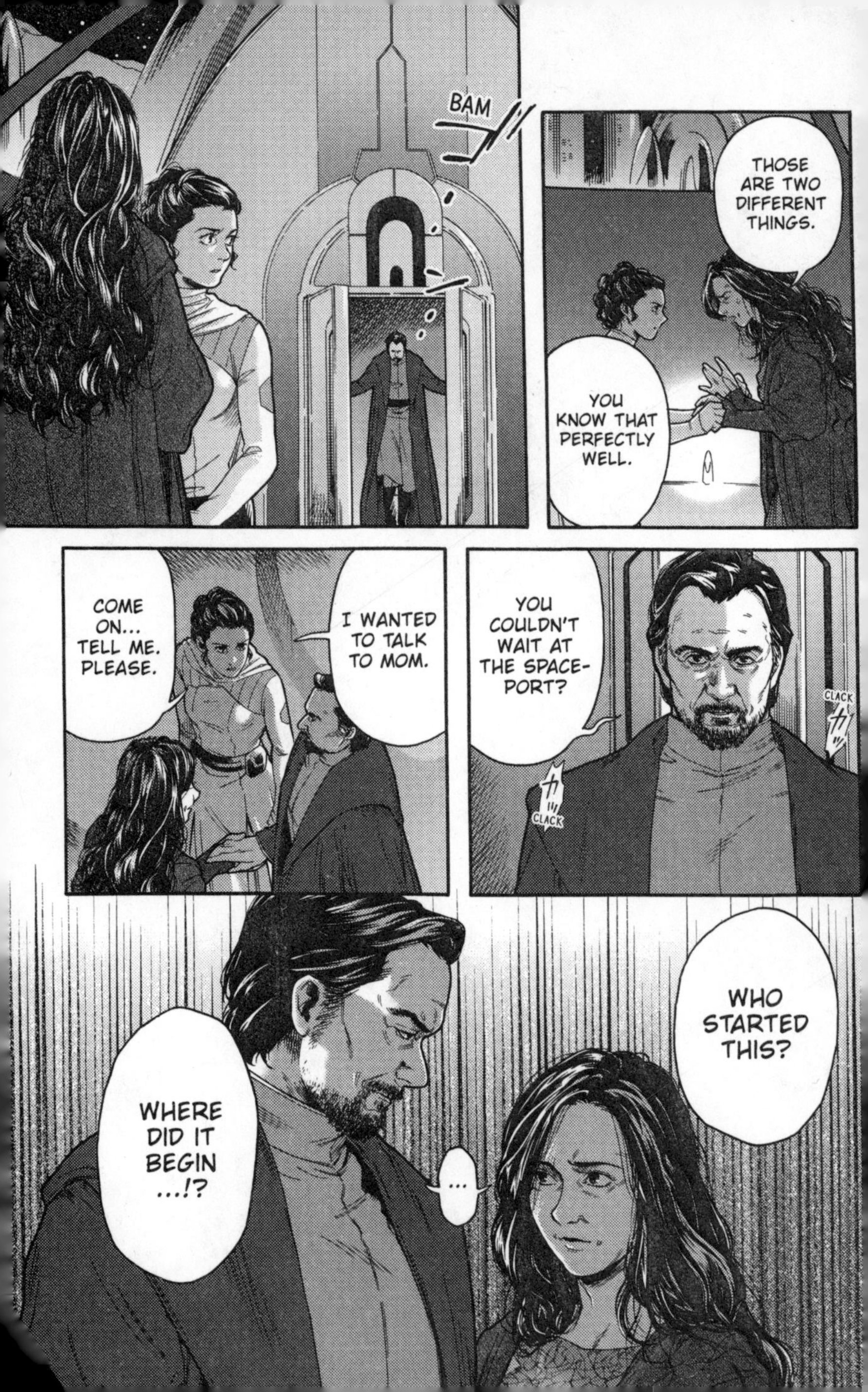
THOSE ARE TWO DIFFERENT THINGS.
YOU KNOW THAT PERFECTLY WELL.
BAM
YOU COULDN'T WAIT AT THE SPACE-PORT?
CLACK
CLACK
I WANTED TO TALK TO MOM.
COME ON... TELL ME. PLEASE.
WHO STARTED THIS?
...
WHERE DID IT BEGIN ...!?

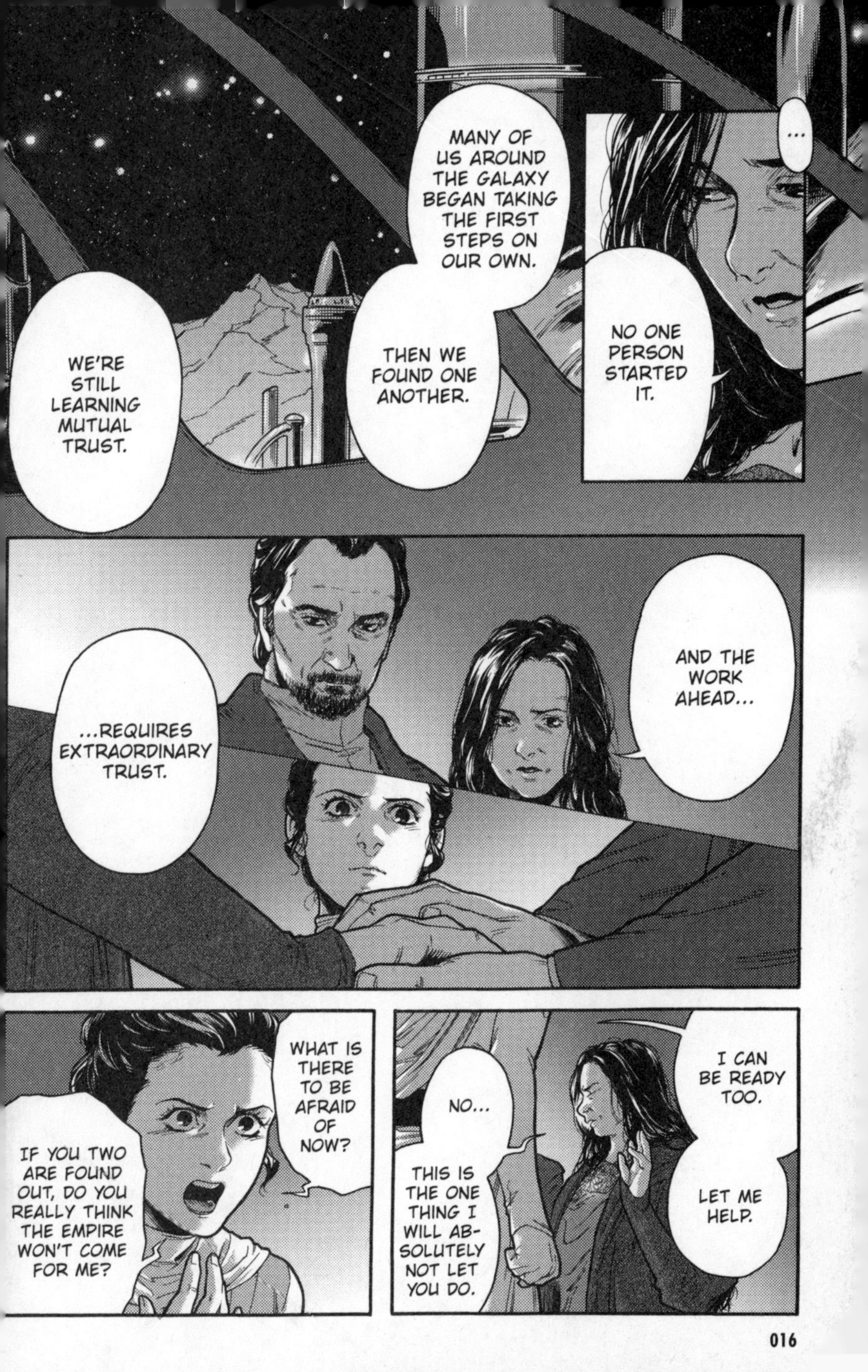
...
NO ONE PERSON STARTED IT.
MANY OF US AROUND THE GALAXY BEGAN TAKING THE FIRST STEPS ON OUR OWN.
THEN WE FOUND ONE ANOTHER.
WE'RE STILL LEARNING MUTUAL TRUST.
AND THE WORK AHEAD...
...REQUIRES EXTRAORDINARY TRUST.
I CAN BE READY TOO.
LET ME HELP.
NO...
THIS IS THE ONE THING I WILL ABSOLUTELY NOT LET YOU DO.
WHAT IS THERE TO BE AFRAID OF NOW?
IF YOU TWO ARE FOUND OUT, DO YOU REALLY THINK THE EMPIRE WON'T COME FOR ME?

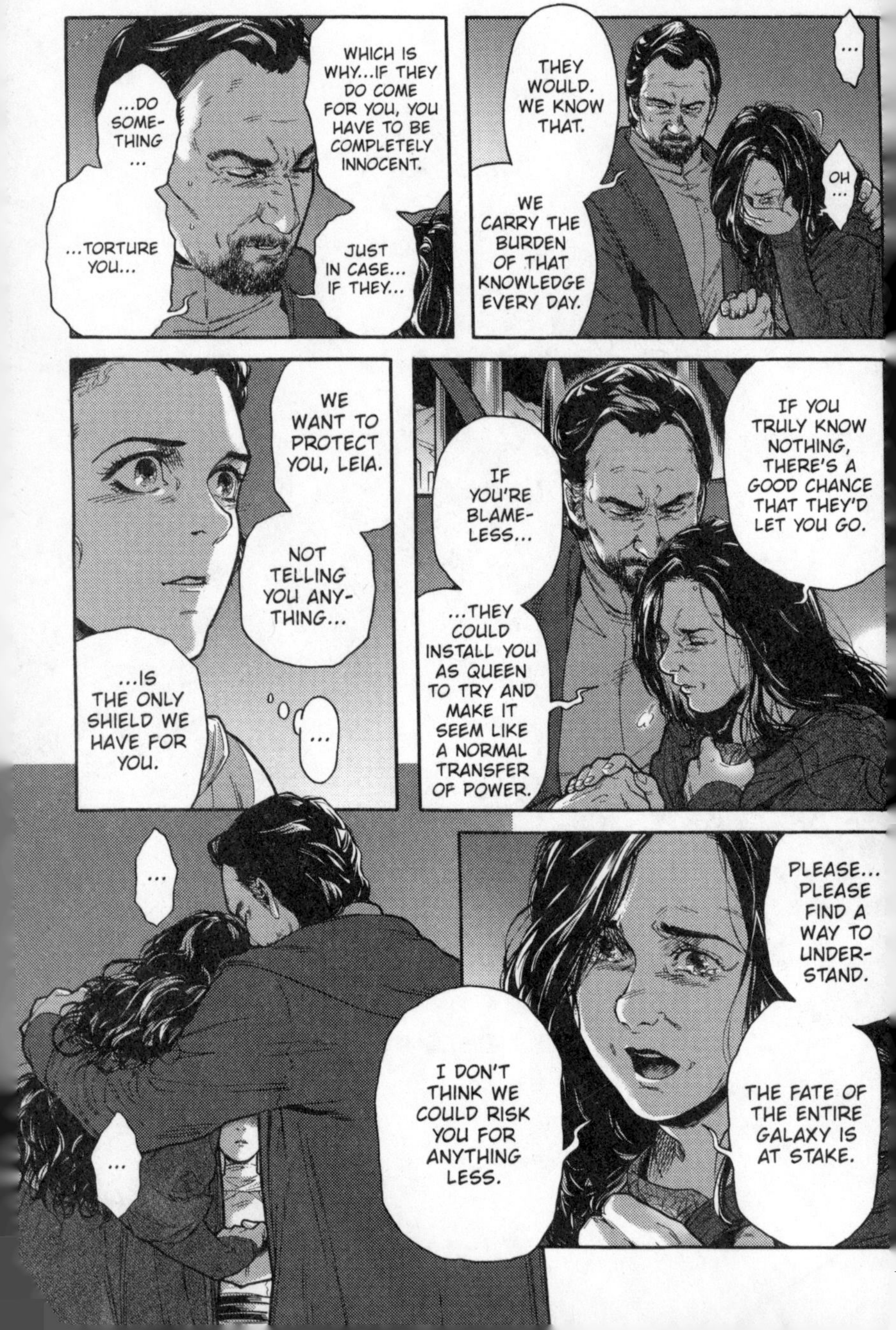
...
THEY WOULD. WE KNOW THAT.
OH...
WE CARRY THE BURDEN OF THAT KNOWLEDGE EVERY DAY.
WHICH IS WHY...IF THEY DO COME FOR YOU, YOU HAVE TO BE COMPLETELY INNOCENT.
JUST IN CASE... IF THEY...
...DO SOMETHING...
...TORTURE YOU...
IF YOU TRULY KNOW NOTHING, THERE'S A GOOD CHANCE THAT THEY'D LET YOU GO.
IF YOU'RE BLAMELESS...
...THEY COULD INSTALL YOU AS QUEEN TO TRY AND MAKE IT SEEM LIKE A NORMAL TRANSFER OF POWER.
WE WANT TO PROTECT YOU, LEIA.
NOT TELLING YOU ANYTHING...
...IS THE ONLY SHIELD WE HAVE FOR YOU.
...
PLEASE... PLEASE FIND A WAY TO UNDERSTAND.
THE FATE OF THE ENTIRE GALAXY IS AT STAKE.
I DON'T THINK WE COULD RISK YOU FOR ANYTHING LESS.
...
...

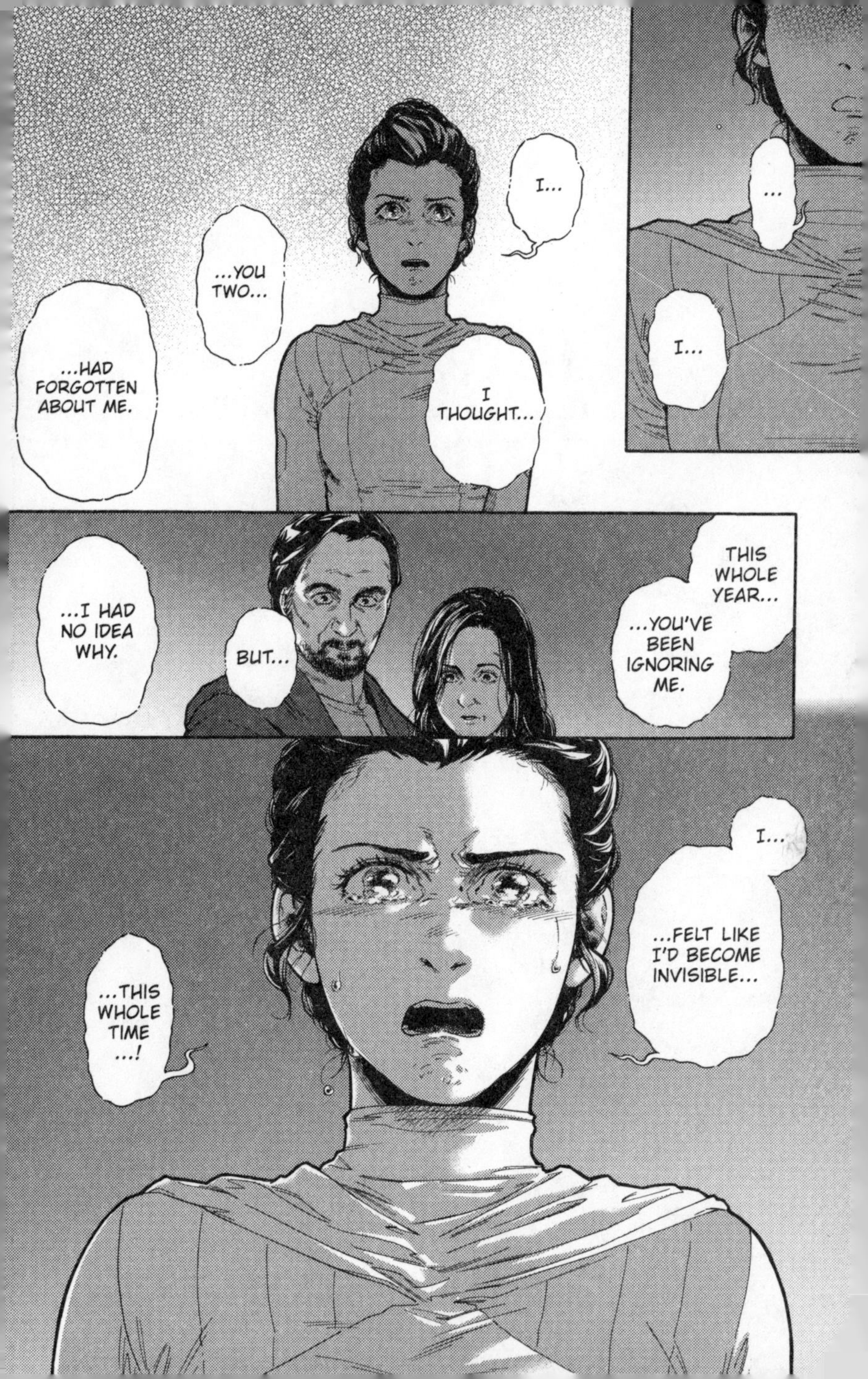
...
I...
I...
I THOUGHT...
...YOU TWO...
...HAD FORGOTTEN ABOUT ME.
THIS WHOLE YEAR...
...YOU'VE BEEN IGNORING ME.
BUT...
...I HAD NO IDEA WHY.
I...
...FELT LIKE I'D BECOME INVISIBLE...
...THIS WHOLE TIME ...!

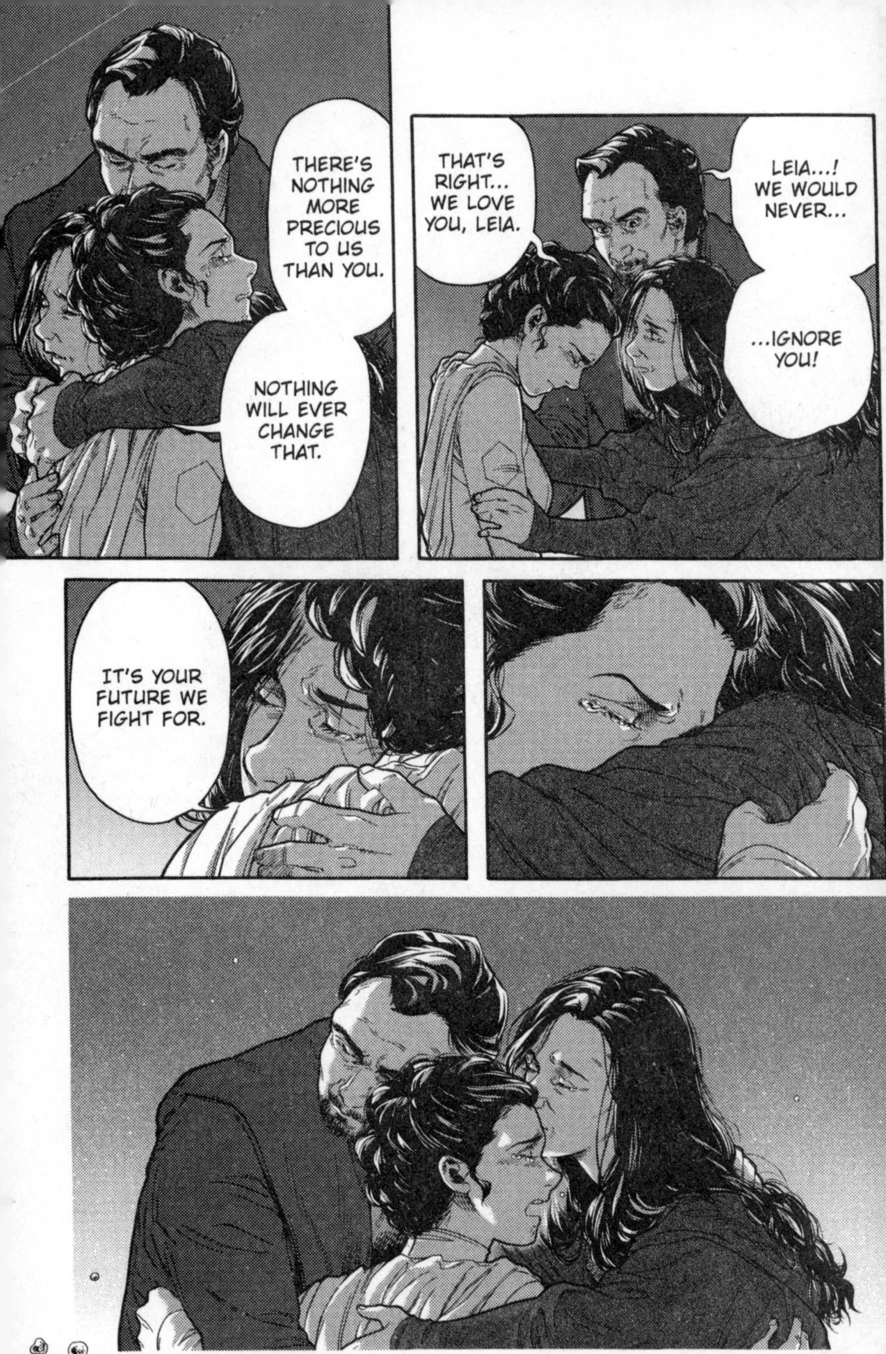
LEIA...! WE WOULD NEVER...
...IGNORE YOU!
THAT'S RIGHT... WE LOVE YOU, LEIA.
THERE'S NOTHING MORE PRECIOUS TO US THAN YOU.
NOTHING WILL EVER CHANGE THAT.
IT'S YOUR FUTURE WE FIGHT FOR.

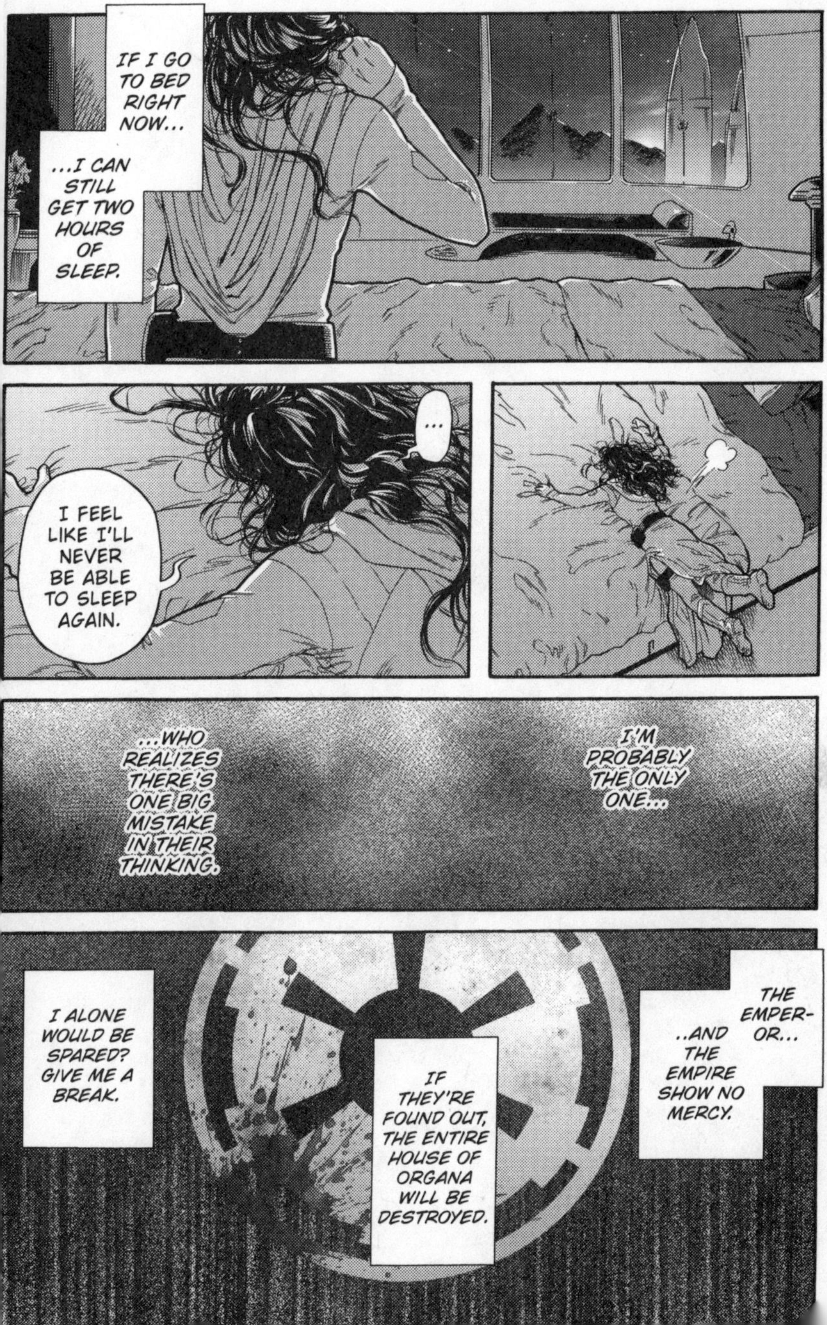
IF I GO TO BED RIGHT NOW...
...I CAN STILL GET TWO HOURS OF SLEEP.
...
I FEEL LIKE I'LL NEVER BE ABLE TO SLEEP AGAIN.
I'M PROBABLY THE ONLY ONE...
...WHO REALIZES THERE'S ONE BIG MISTAKE IN THEIR THINKING.
THE EMPEROR...
...AND THE EMPIRE SHOW NO MERCY.
IF THEY'RE FOUND OUT, THE ENTIRE HOUSE OF ORGANA WILL BE DESTROYED.
I ALONE WOULD BE SPARED? GIVE ME A BREAK.

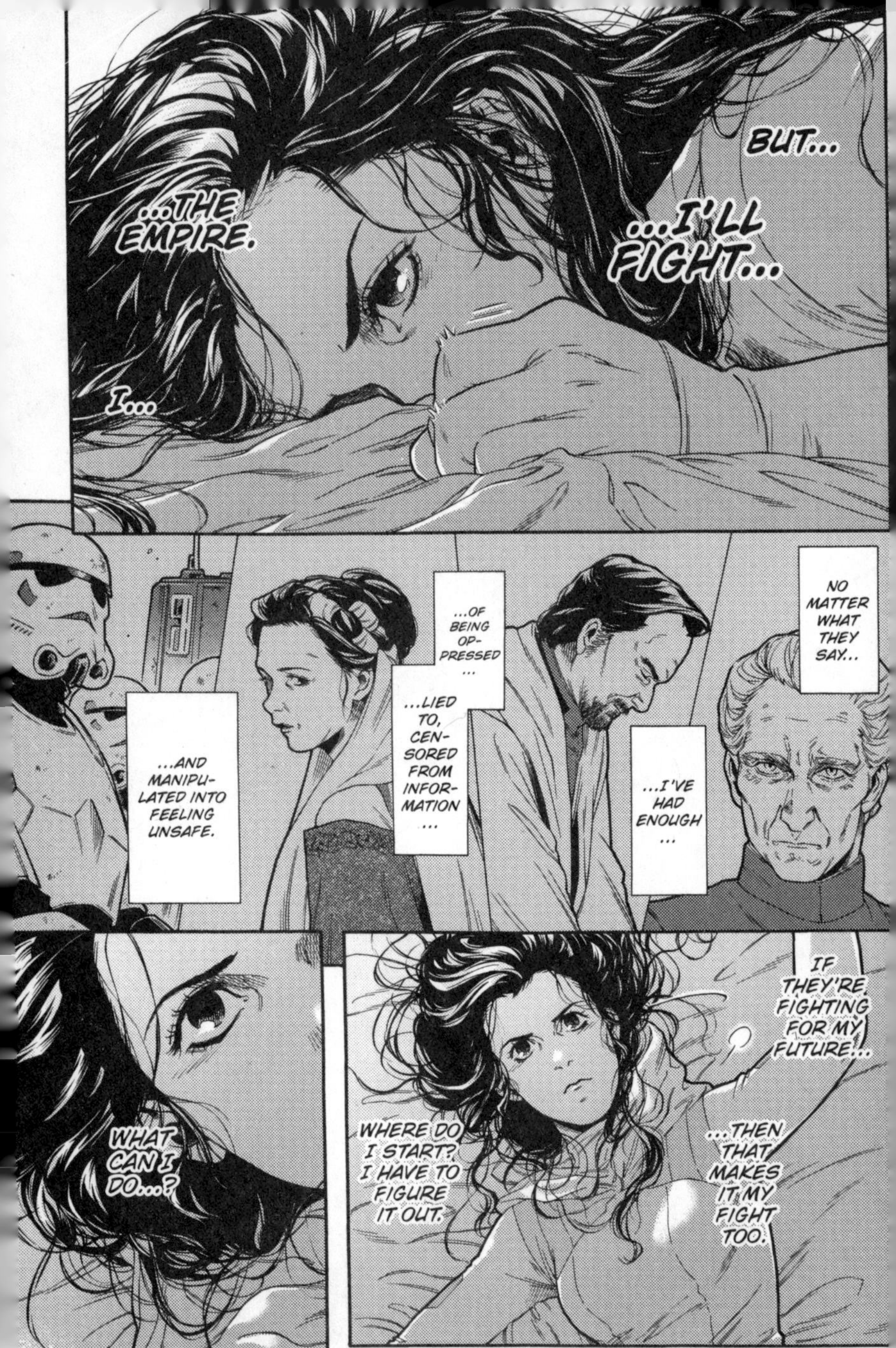
BUT...
...I'LL FIGHT...
...THE EMPIRE.
I...
NO MATTER WHAT THEY SAY...
...I'VE HAD ENOUGH...
...OF BEING OP-PRESSED...
...LIED TO, CEN-SORED FROM INFOR-MATION...
...AND MANIPU-LATED INTO FEELING UNSAFE.
IF THEY'RE FIGHTING FOR MY FUTURE...
...THEN THAT MAKES IT MY FIGHT TOO.
WHERE DO I START? I HAVE TO FIGURE IT OUT.
WHAT CAN I DO...?

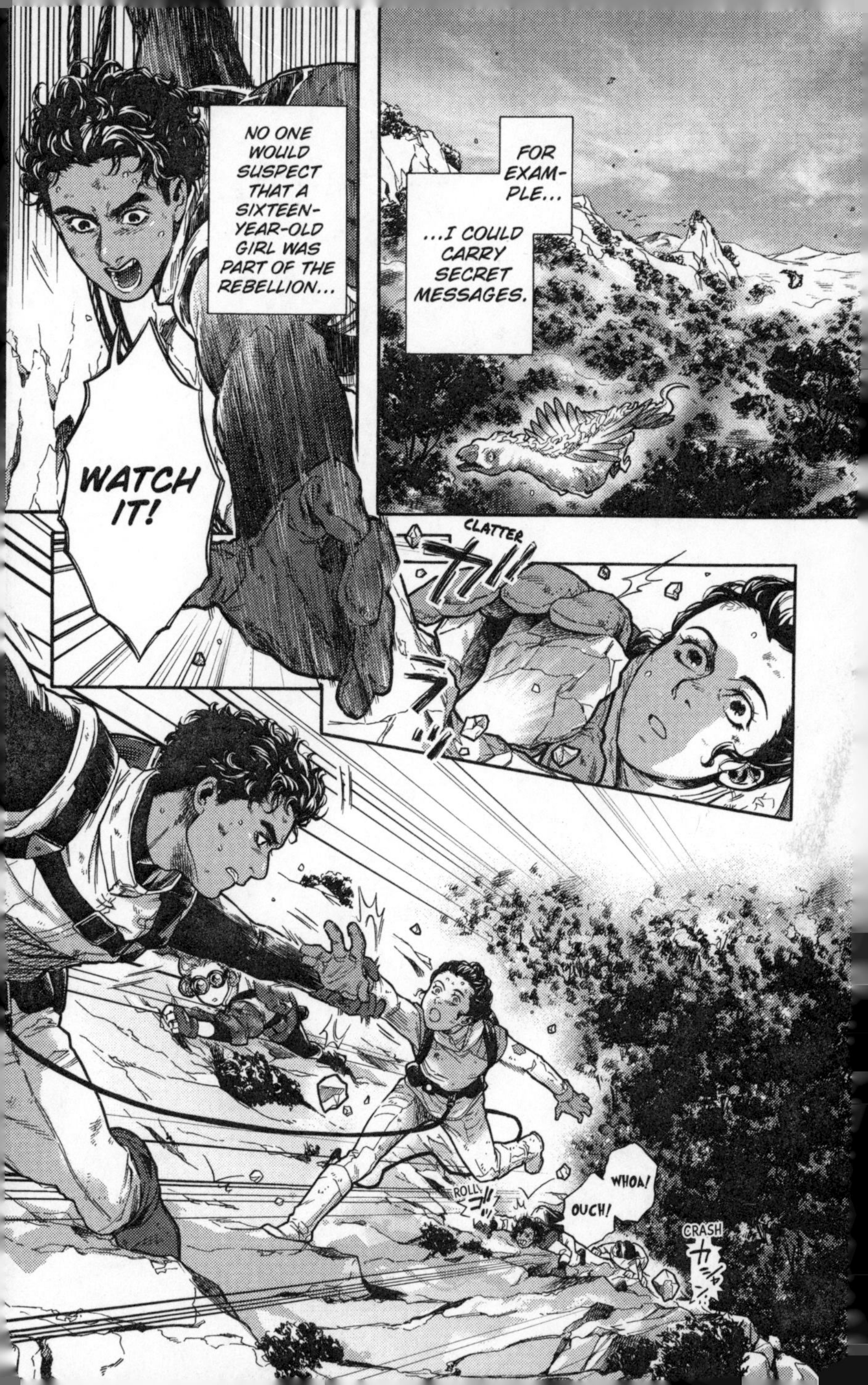
FOR EXAMPLE...
...I COULD CARRY SECRET MESSAGES.
NO ONE WOULD SUSPECT THAT A SIXTEEN-YEAR-OLD GIRL WAS PART OF THE REBELLION...
WATCH IT!
CLATTER
WHOA!
OUCH!
CRASH
ROLL

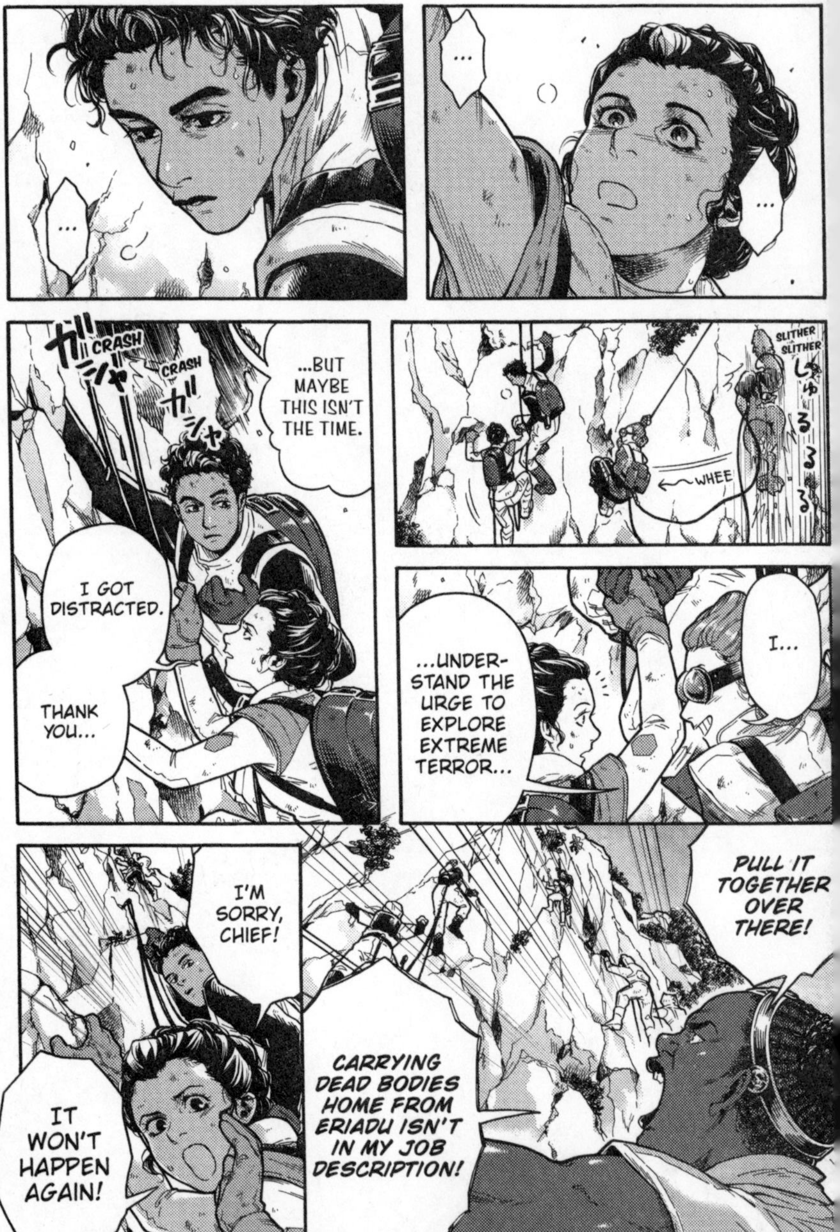
...
...
...
SLITHER SLITHER
しゅるるる
WHEE
I...
...UNDER-STAND THE URGE TO EXPLORE EXTREME TERROR...
ガシャ
CRASH
ガシャ
CRASH
...BUT MAYBE THIS ISN'T THE TIME.
I GOT DISTRACTED.
THANK YOU...
PULL IT TOGETHER OVER THERE!
CARRYING DEAD BODIES HOME FROM ERIADU ISN'T IN MY JOB DESCRIPTION!
I'M SORRY, CHIEF!
IT WON'T HAPPEN AGAIN!

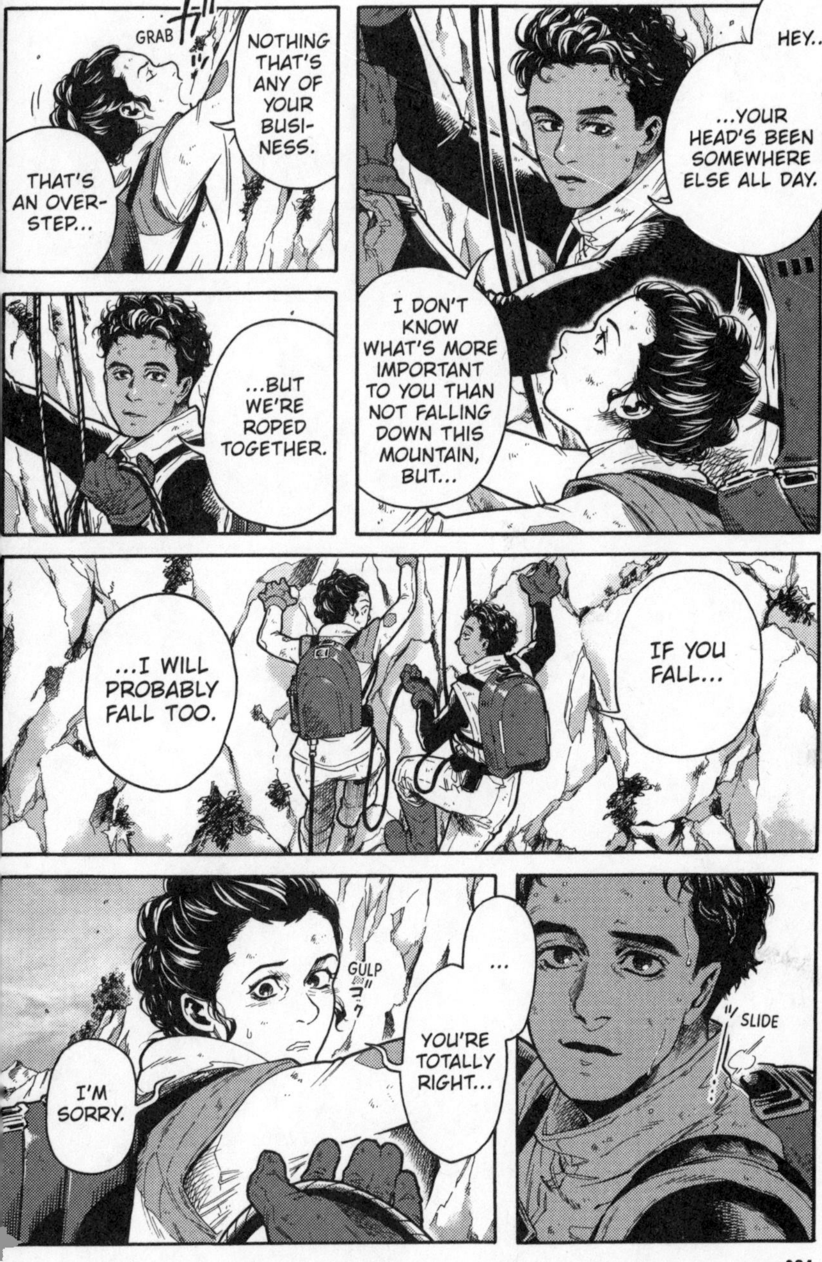
HEY...
...YOUR HEAD'S BEEN SOMEWHERE ELSE ALL DAY.
I DON'T KNOW WHAT'S MORE IMPORTANT TO YOU THAN NOT FALLING DOWN THIS MOUNTAIN, BUT...
GRAB
NOTHING THAT'S ANY OF YOUR BUSI-NESS.
THAT'S AN OVER-STEP...
...BUT WE'RE ROPED TOGETHER.
IF YOU FALL...
...I WILL PROBABLY FALL TOO.
SLIDE
...
YOU'RE TOTALLY RIGHT...
GULP
I'M SORRY.

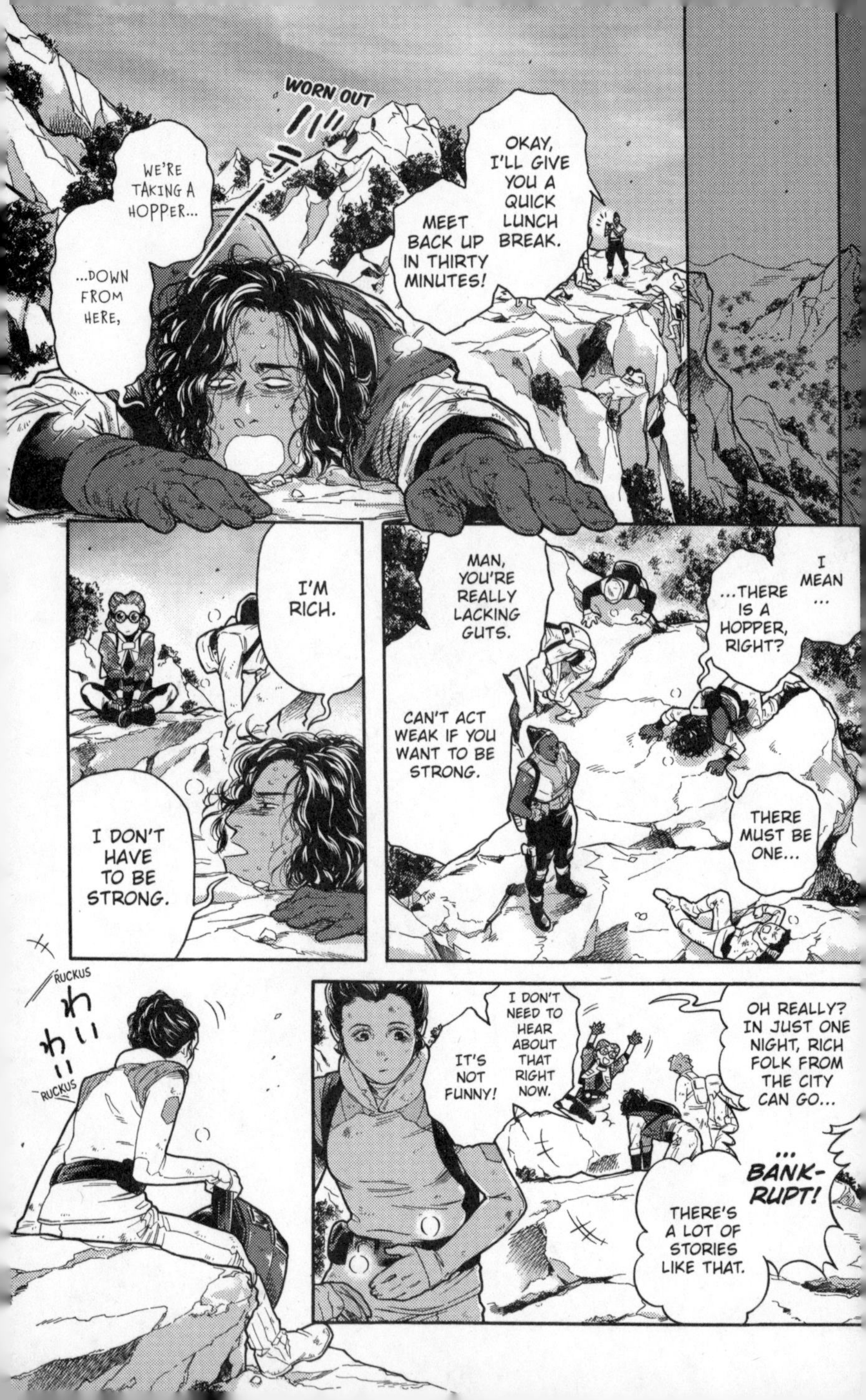
OKAY, I'LL GIVE YOU A QUICK LUNCH BREAK.
MEET BACK UP IN THIRTY MINUTES!
WORN OUT
WE'RE TAKING A HOPPER...
...DOWN FROM HERE,
I MEAN...
...THERE IS A HOPPER, RIGHT?
MAN, YOU'RE REALLY LACKING GUTS.
CAN'T ACT WEAK IF YOU WANT TO BE STRONG.
THERE MUST BE ONE...
I'M RICH.
I DON'T HAVE TO BE STRONG.
OH REALLY? IN JUST ONE NIGHT, RICH FOLK FROM THE CITY CAN GO...
...BÄNK-RUPT!
I DON'T NEED TO HEAR ABOUT THAT RIGHT NOW.
IT'S NOT FUNNY!
THERE'S A LOT OF STORIES LIKE THAT.
RUCKUS
RUCKUS

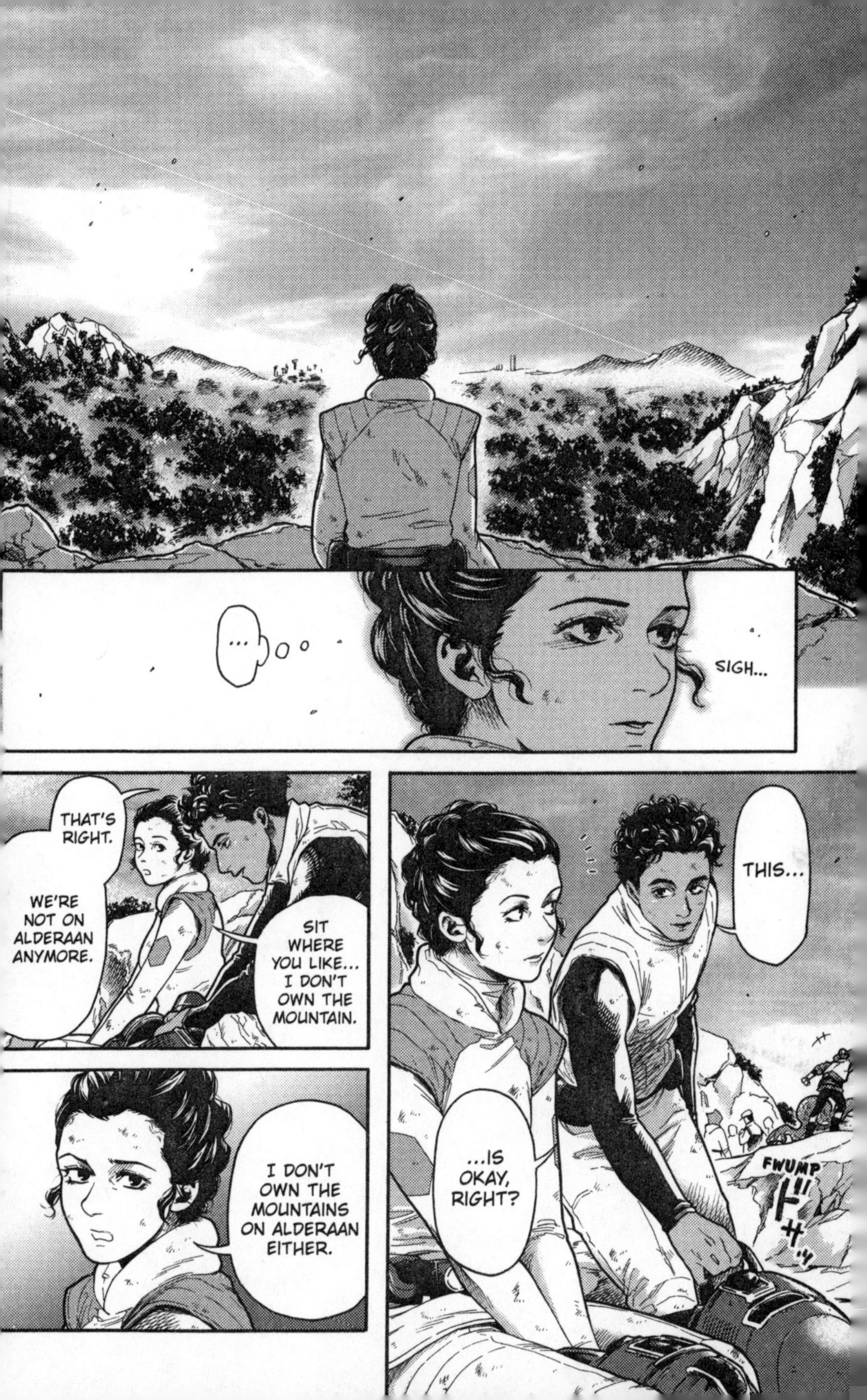
SIGH...
...
THIS...
...IS OKAY, RIGHT?
FWUMP
SIT WHERE YOU LIKE... I DON'T OWN THE MOUNTAIN.
THAT'S RIGHT.
WE'RE NOT ON ALDERAAN ANYMORE.
I DON'T OWN THE MOUNTAINS ON ALDERAAN EITHER.

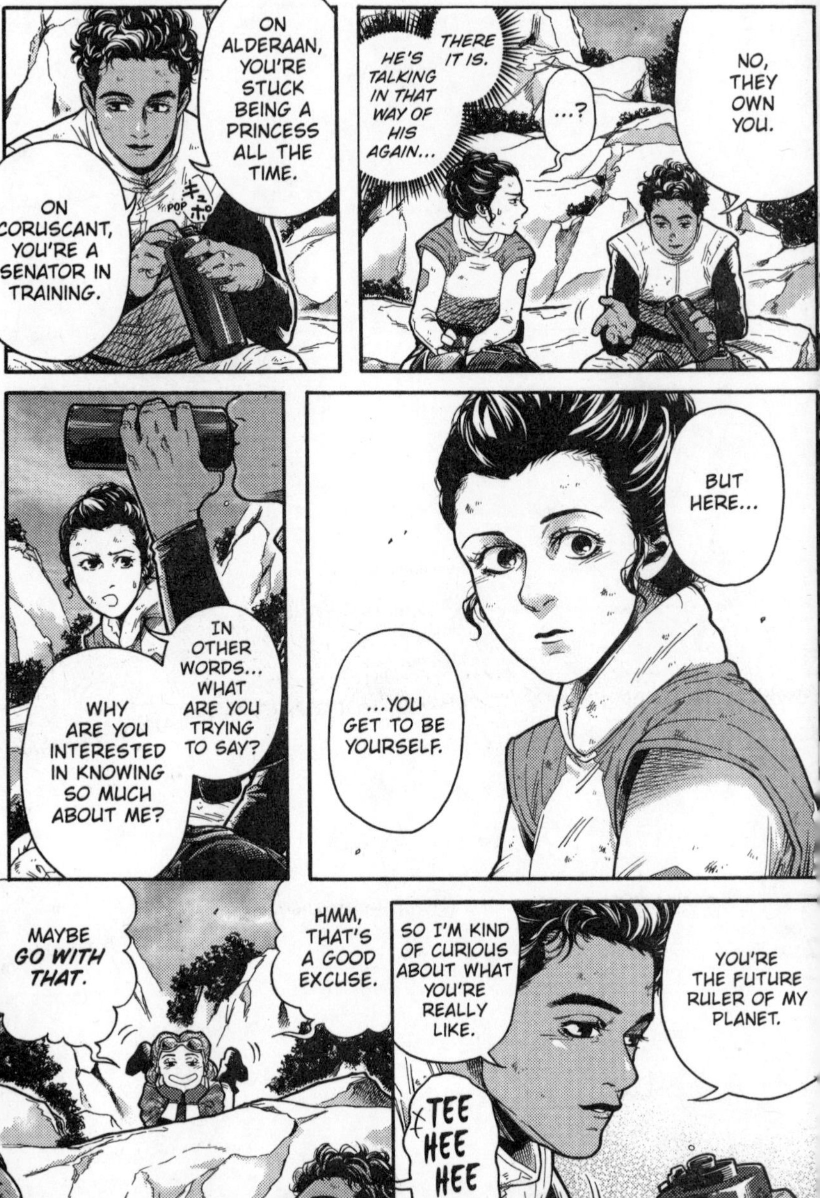
NO, THEY OWN YOU.
...?
THERE IT IS.
HE'S TALKING IN THAT WAY OF HIS AGAIN...
ON ALDERAAN, YOU'RE STUCK BEING A PRINCESS ALL THE TIME.
キュポ POP
ON CORUSCANT, YOU'RE A SENATOR IN TRAINING.
BUT HERE...
...YOU GET TO BE YOURSELF.
IN OTHER WORDS... WHAT ARE YOU TRYING TO SAY?
WHY ARE YOU INTERESTED IN KNOWING SO MUCH ABOUT ME?
YOU'RE THE FUTURE RULER OF MY PLANET.
SO I'M KIND OF CURIOUS ABOUT WHAT YOU'RE REALLY LIKE.
TEE HEE HEE HEE.
HMM, THAT'S A GOOD EXCUSE.
MAYBE *GO WITH THAT.*

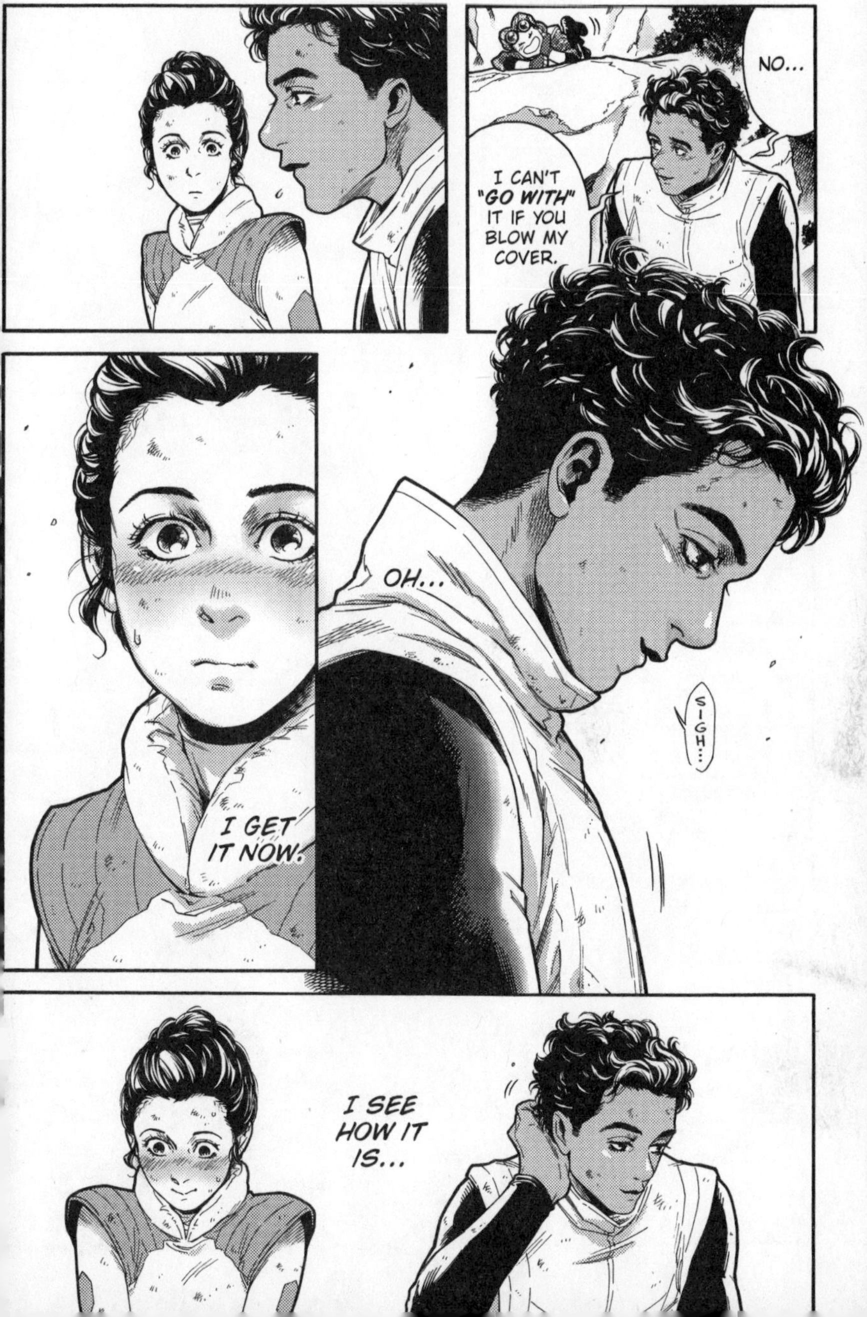
NO...
I CAN'T "GO WITH" IT IF YOU BLOW MY COVER.
OH...
SIGH...
I GET IT NOW.
I SEE HOW IT IS...

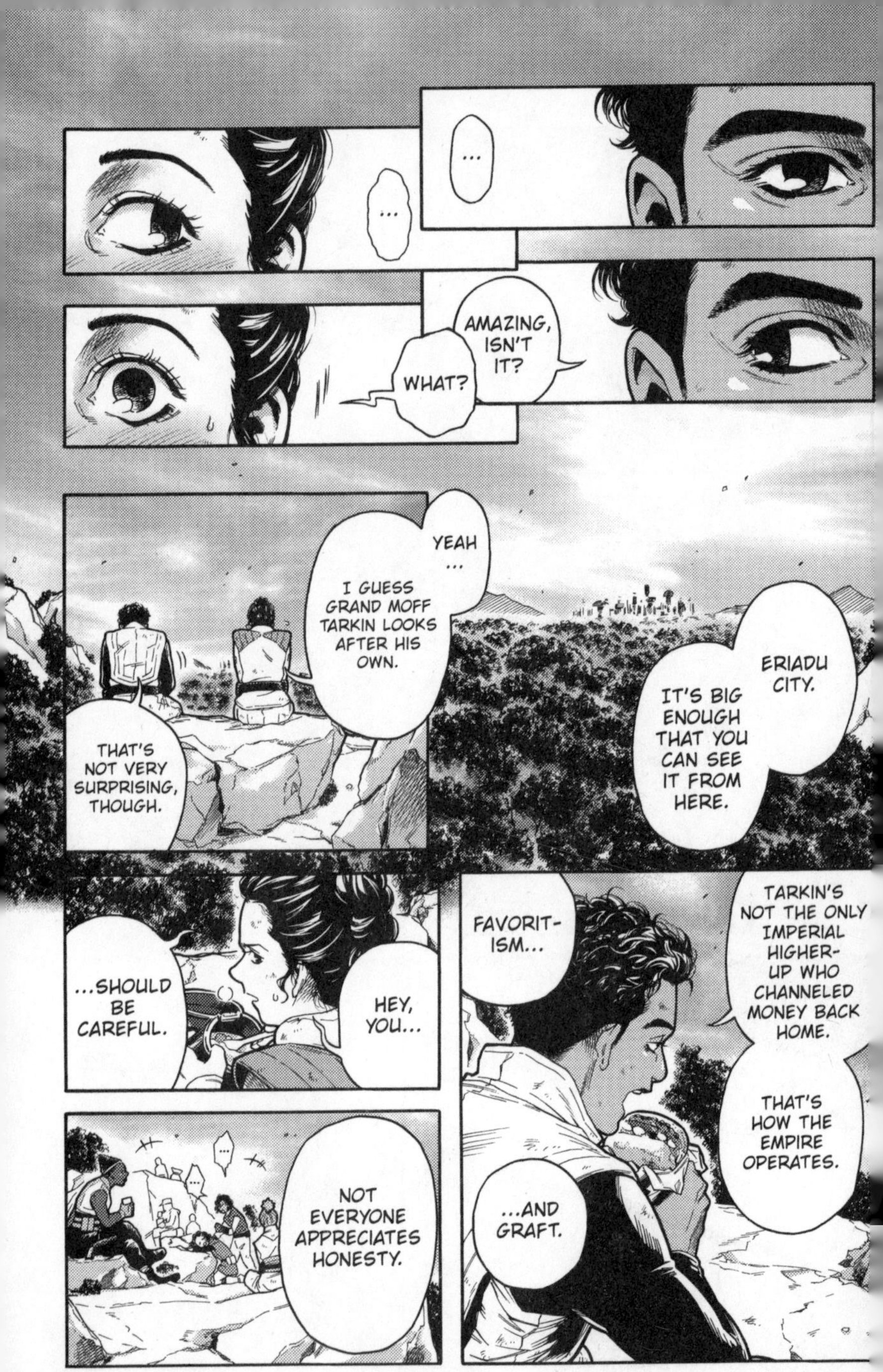
...
...
AMAZING, ISN'T IT?
WHAT?
ERIADU CITY.
IT'S BIG ENOUGH THAT YOU CAN SEE IT FROM HERE.
YEAH...
I GUESS GRAND MOFF TARKIN LOOKS AFTER HIS OWN.
THAT'S NOT VERY SURPRISING, THOUGH.
TARKIN'S NOT THE ONLY IMPERIAL HIGHER-UP WHO CHANNELED MONEY BACK HOME.
FAVORIT-ISM...
THAT'S HOW THE EMPIRE OPERATES.
...AND GRAFT.
HEY, YOU...
...SHOULD BE CAREFUL.
...
...
NOT EVERYONE APPRECIATES HONESTY.

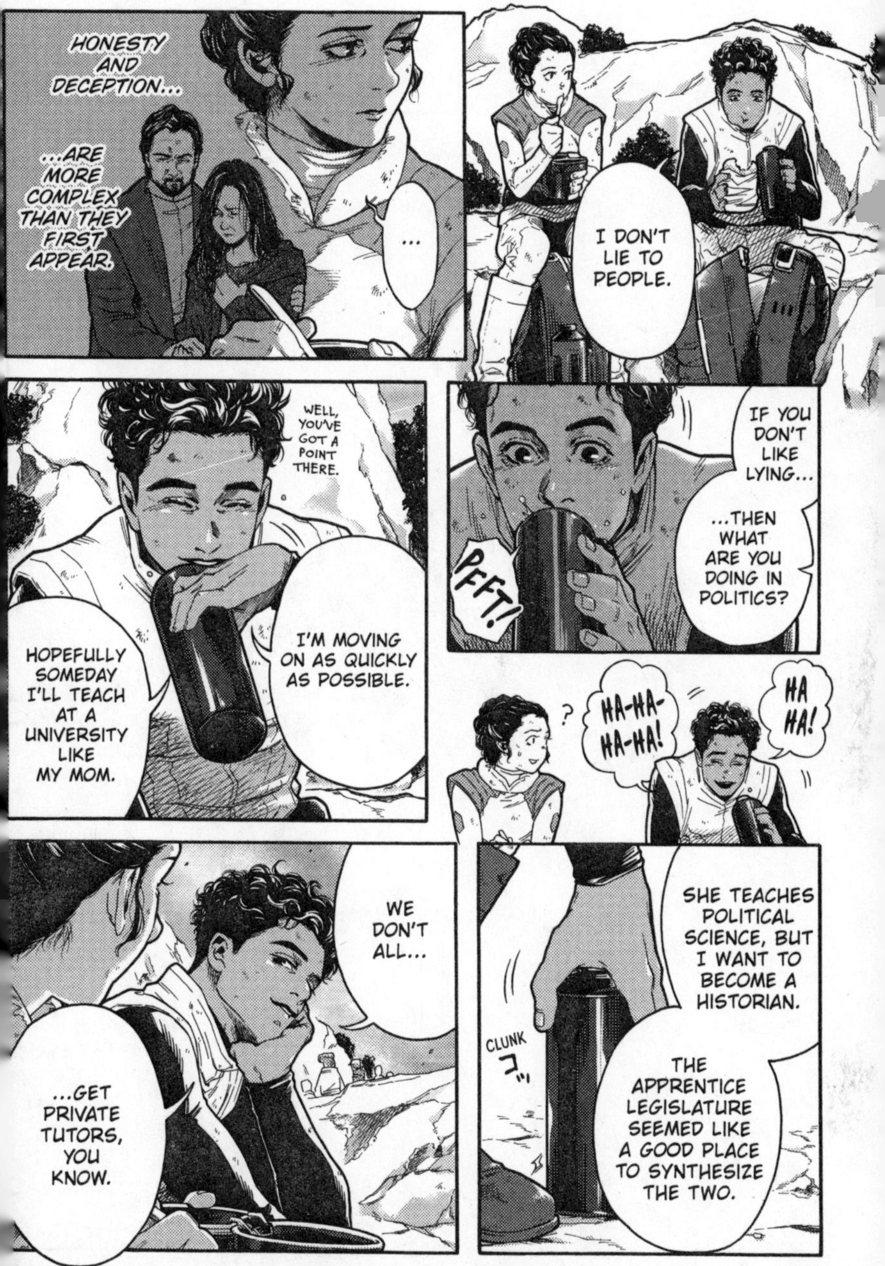
I DON'T LIE TO PEOPLE.
...
HONESTY AND DECEPTION...
...ARE MORE COMPLEX THAN THEY FIRST APPEAR.
IF YOU DON'T LIKE LYING...
...THEN WHAT ARE YOU DOING IN POLITICS?
PFFT!
HA HA!
HA-HA-HA-HA!
?
WELL, YOU'VE GOT A POINT THERE.
I'M MOVING ON AS QUICKLY AS POSSIBLE.
HOPEFULLY SOMEDAY I'LL TEACH AT A UNIVERSITY LIKE MY MOM.
SHE TEACHES POLITICAL SCIENCE, BUT I WANT TO BECOME A HISTORIAN.
THE APPRENTICE LEGISLATURE SEEMED LIKE A GOOD PLACE TO SYNTHESIZE THE TWO.
CLUNK
WE DON'T ALL...
...GET PRIVATE TUTORS, YOU KNOW.

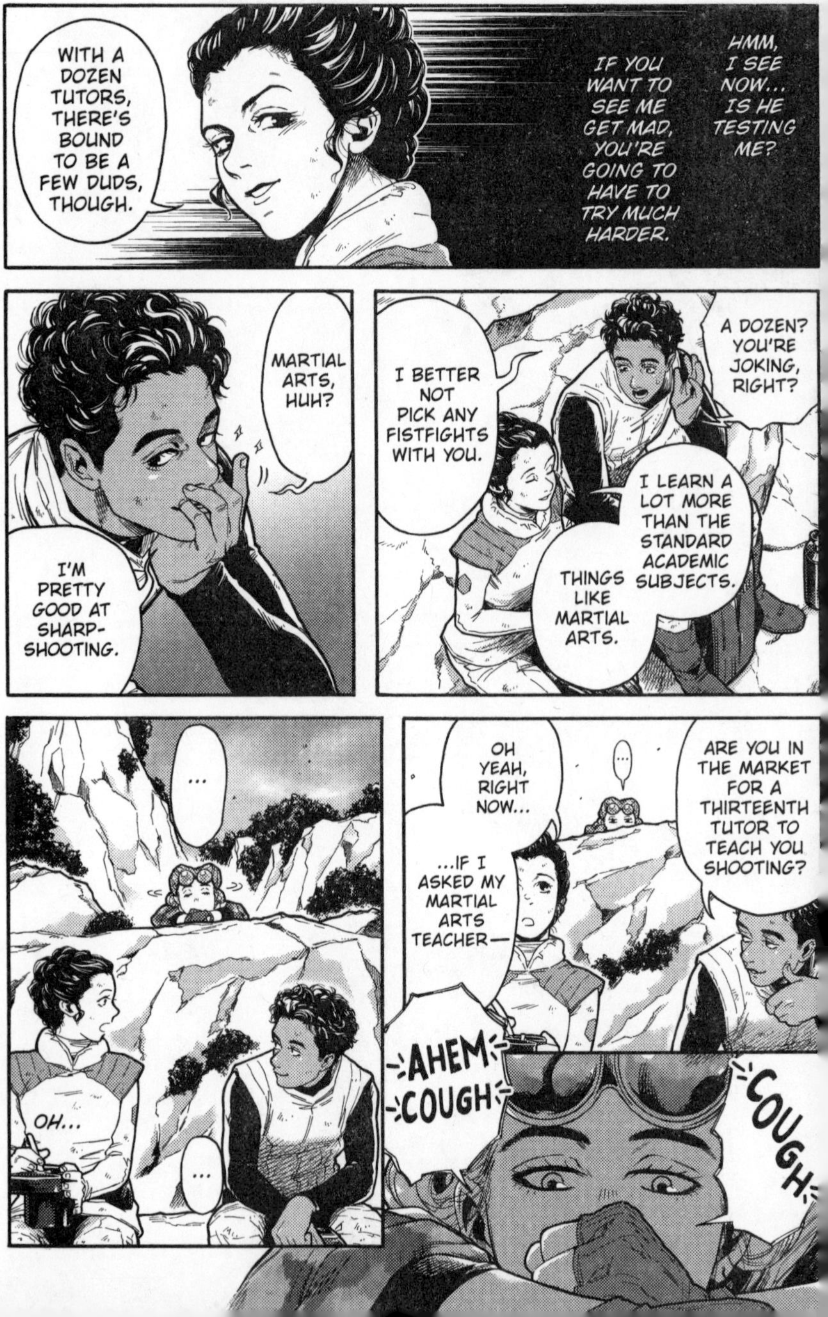
HMM, I SEE NOW... IS HE TESTING ME?
IF YOU WANT TO SEE ME GET MAD, YOU'RE GOING TO HAVE TO TRY MUCH HARDER.
WITH A DOZEN TUTORS, THERE'S BOUND TO BE A FEW DUDS, THOUGH.
A DOZEN? YOU'RE JOKING, RIGHT?
I BETTER NOT PICK ANY FISTFIGHTS WITH YOU.
I LEARN A LOT MORE THAN THE STANDARD ACADEMIC SUBJECTS.
THINGS LIKE MARTIAL ARTS.
MARTIAL ARTS, HUH?
I'M PRETTY GOOD AT SHARP-SHOOTING.
ARE YOU IN THE MARKET FOR A THIRTEENTH TUTOR TO TEACH YOU SHOOTING?
...
OH YEAH, RIGHT NOW...
...IF I ASKED MY MARTIAL ARTS TEACHER—
AHEM
COUGH
COUGH
...
OH...
...

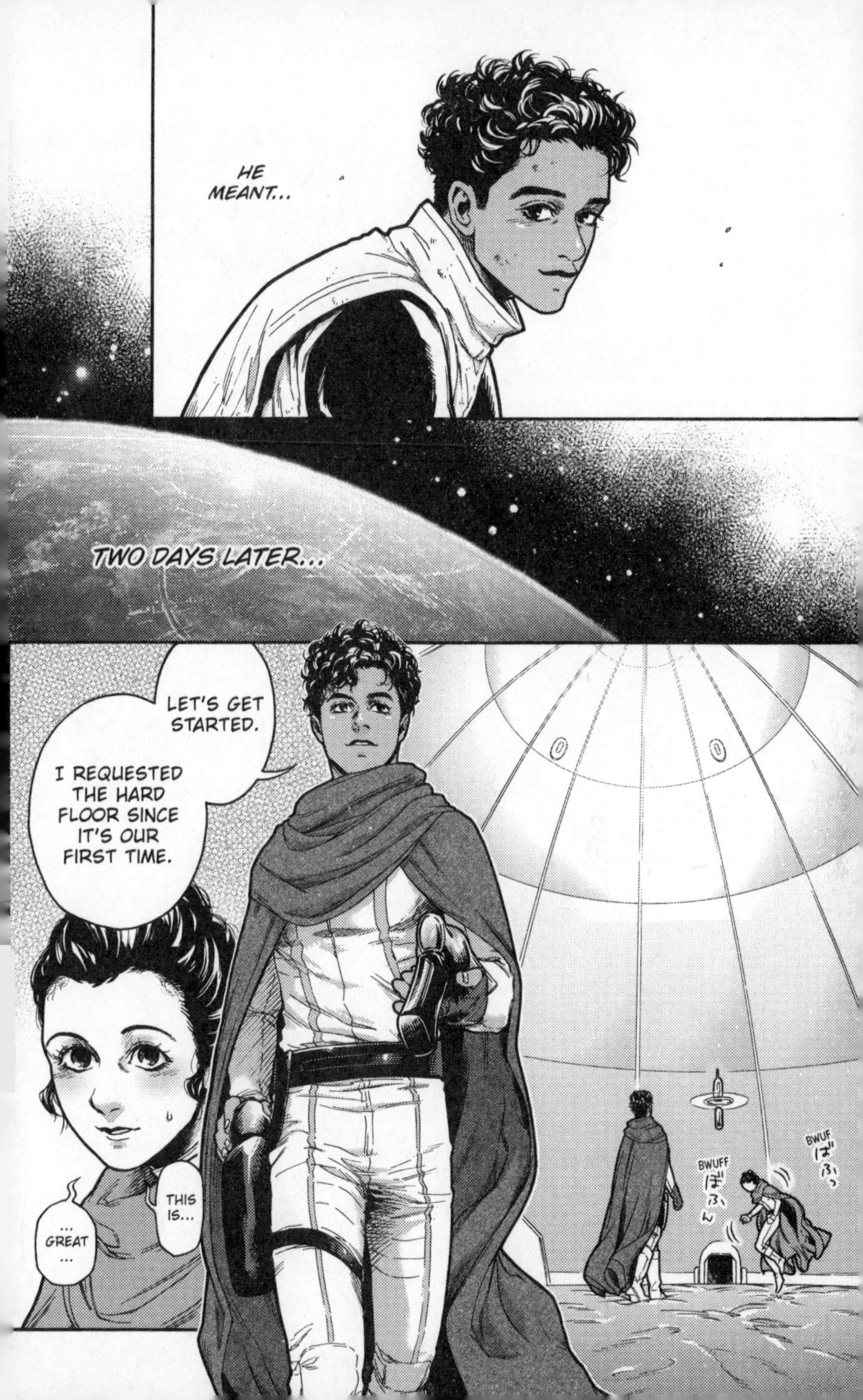
HE MEANT...
TWO DAYS LATER...
LET'S GET STARTED.
I REQUESTED THE HARD FLOOR SINCE IT'S OUR FIRST TIME.
BWUF ぼふっ
BWUFF ぼふん
THIS IS...
... GREAT ...

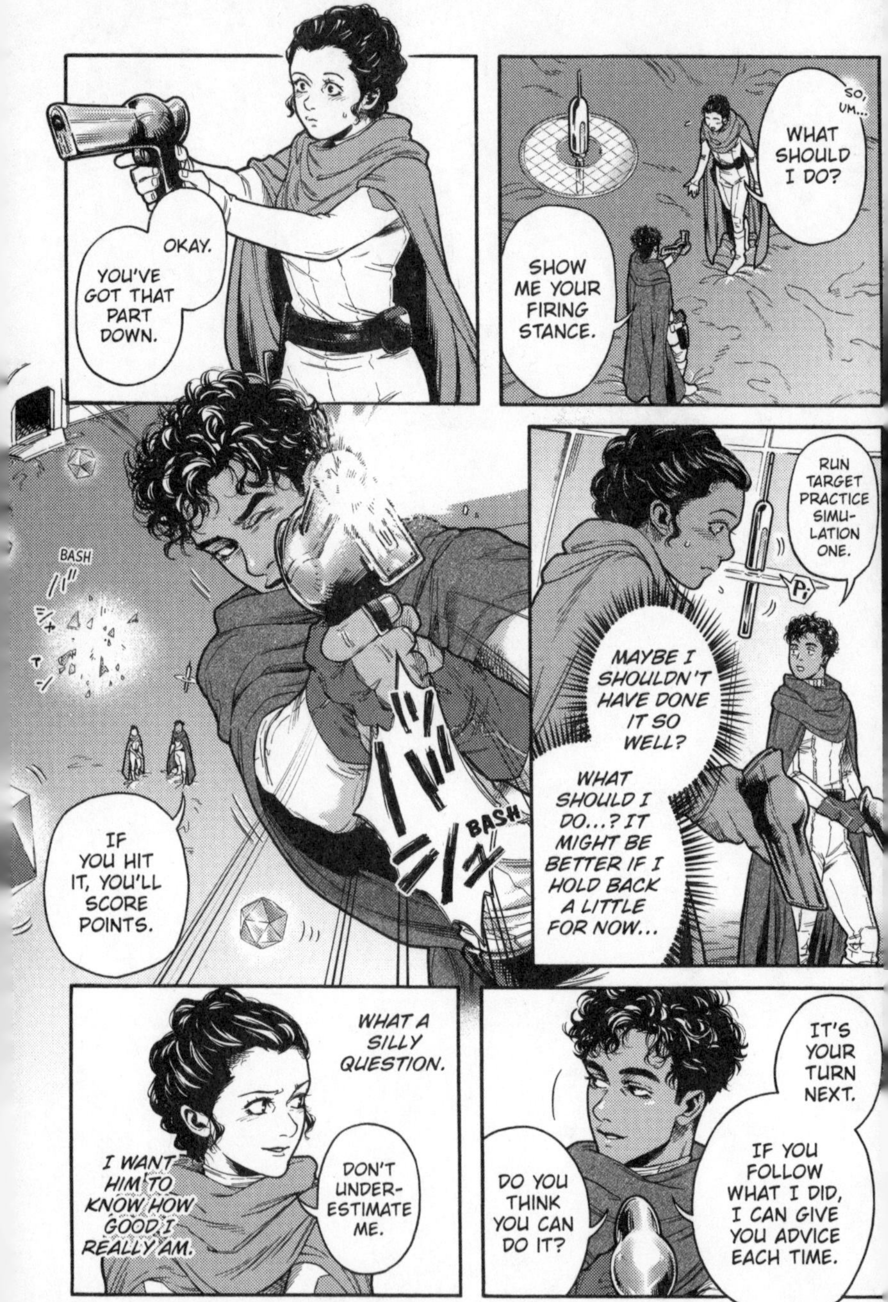
SO, UM...
WHAT SHOULD I DO?
SHOW ME YOUR FIRING STANCE.
OKAY.
YOU'VE GOT THAT PART DOWN.
RUN TARGET PRACTICE SIMULATION ONE.
Pi
MAYBE I SHOULDN'T HAVE DONE IT SO WELL?
WHAT SHOULD I DO...? IT MIGHT BE BETTER IF I HOLD BACK A LITTLE FOR NOW...
BASH
BASH
IF YOU HIT IT, YOU'LL SCORE POINTS.
IT'S YOUR TURN NEXT.
IF YOU FOLLOW WHAT I DID, I CAN GIVE YOU ADVICE EACH TIME.
DO YOU THINK YOU CAN DO IT?
WHAT A SILLY QUESTION.
DON'T UNDER-ESTIMATE ME.
I WANT HIM TO KNOW HOW GOOD I REALLY AM.

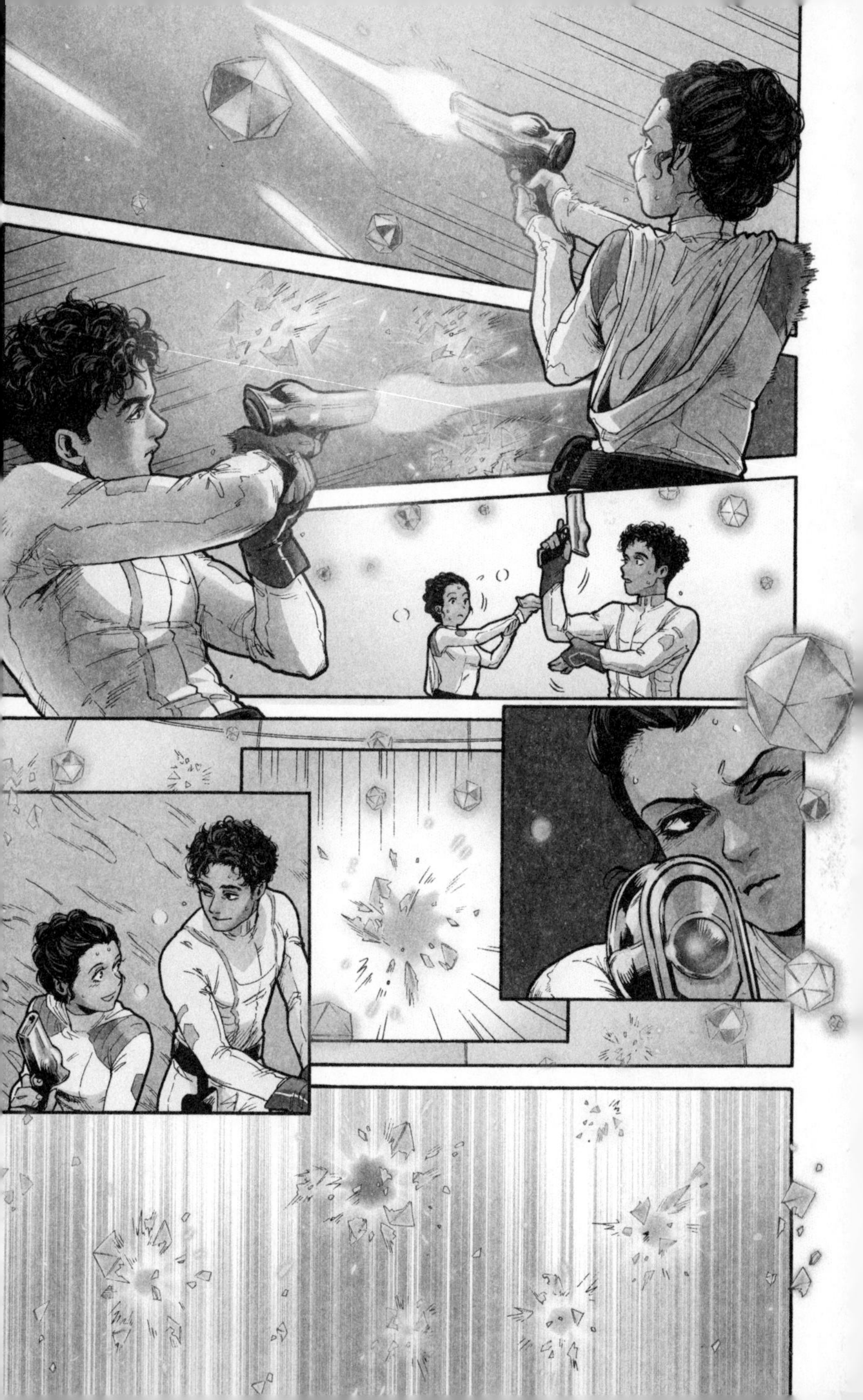

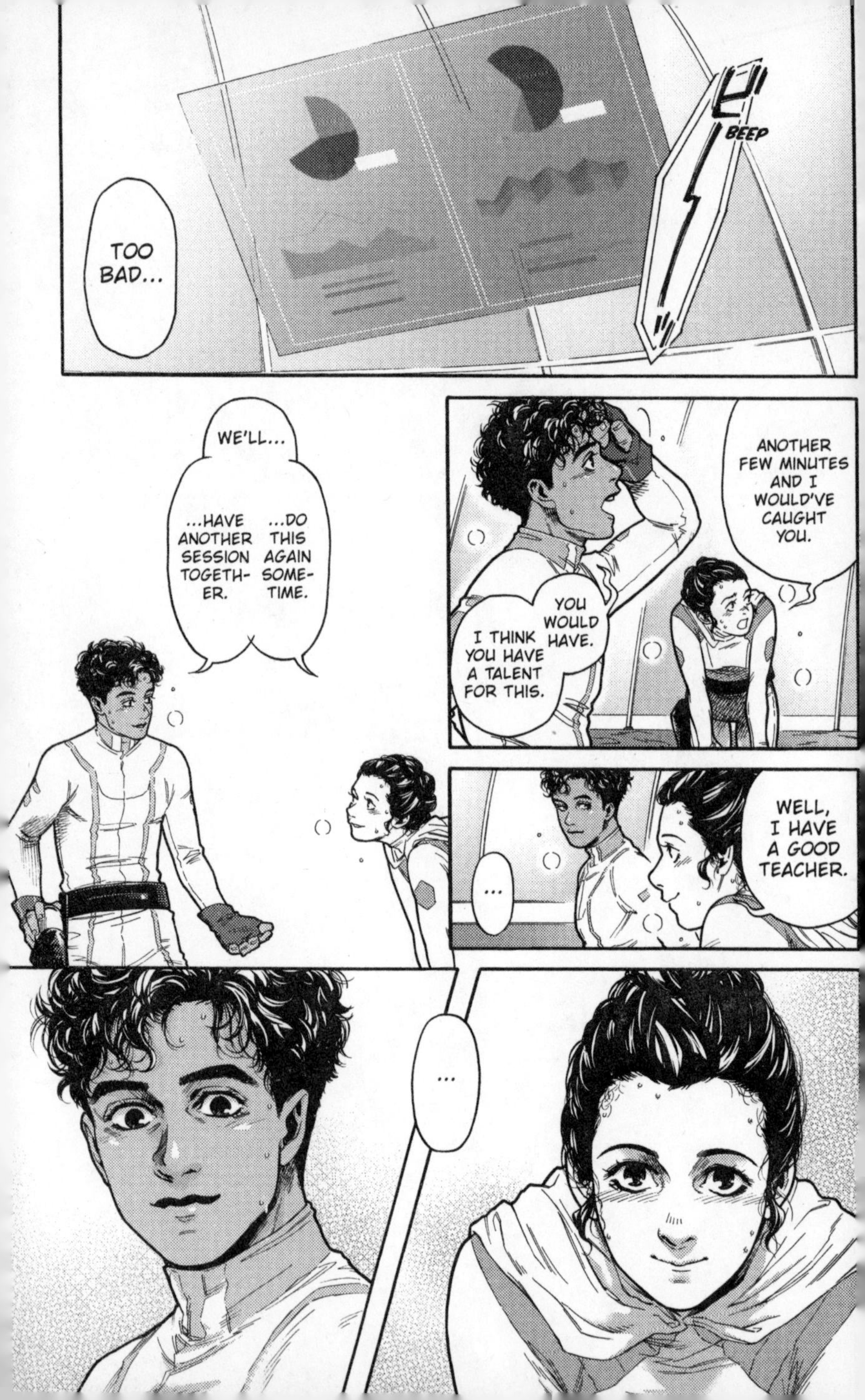
BEEP
TOO BAD...
ANOTHER FEW MINUTES AND I WOULD'VE CAUGHT YOU.
YOU WOULD HAVE. I THINK YOU HAVE A TALENT FOR THIS.
WELL, I HAVE A GOOD TEACHER.
...
WE'LL...
...HAVE ANOTHER SESSION TOGETH-ER.
...DO THIS AGAIN SOME-TIME.
...

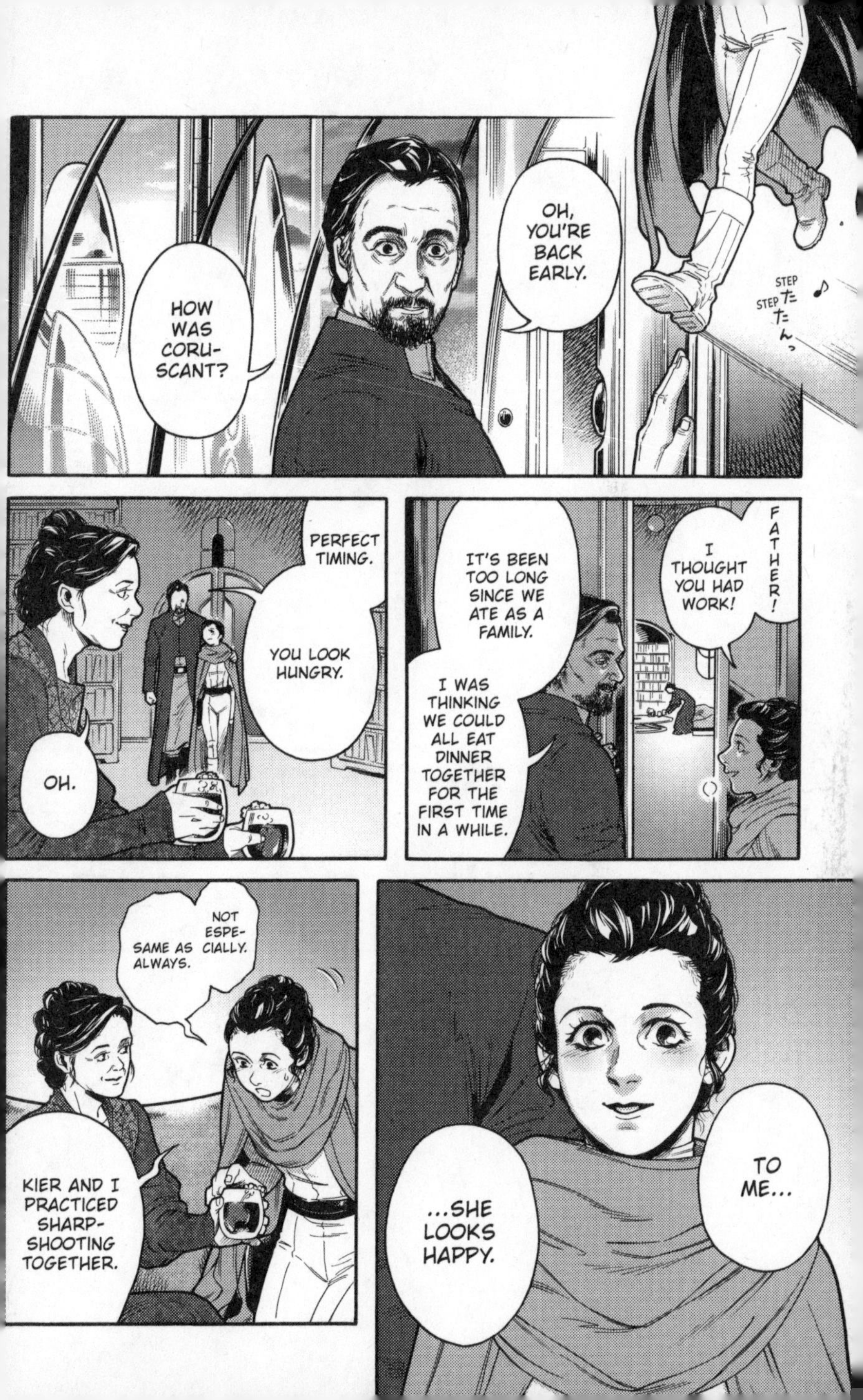
STEP た
STEP たんっ
♪
OH, YOU'RE BACK EARLY.
HOW WAS CORU-SCANT?
FATHER!
I THOUGHT YOU HAD WORK!
IT'S BEEN TOO LONG SINCE WE ATE AS A FAMILY.
I WAS THINKING WE COULD ALL EAT DINNER TOGETHER FOR THE FIRST TIME IN A WHILE.
PERFECT TIMING.
YOU LOOK HUNGRY.
OH.
TO ME...
...SHE LOOKS HAPPY.
NOT ESPE-CIALLY.
SAME AS ALWAYS.
KIER AND I PRACTICED SHARP-SHOOTING TOGETHER.

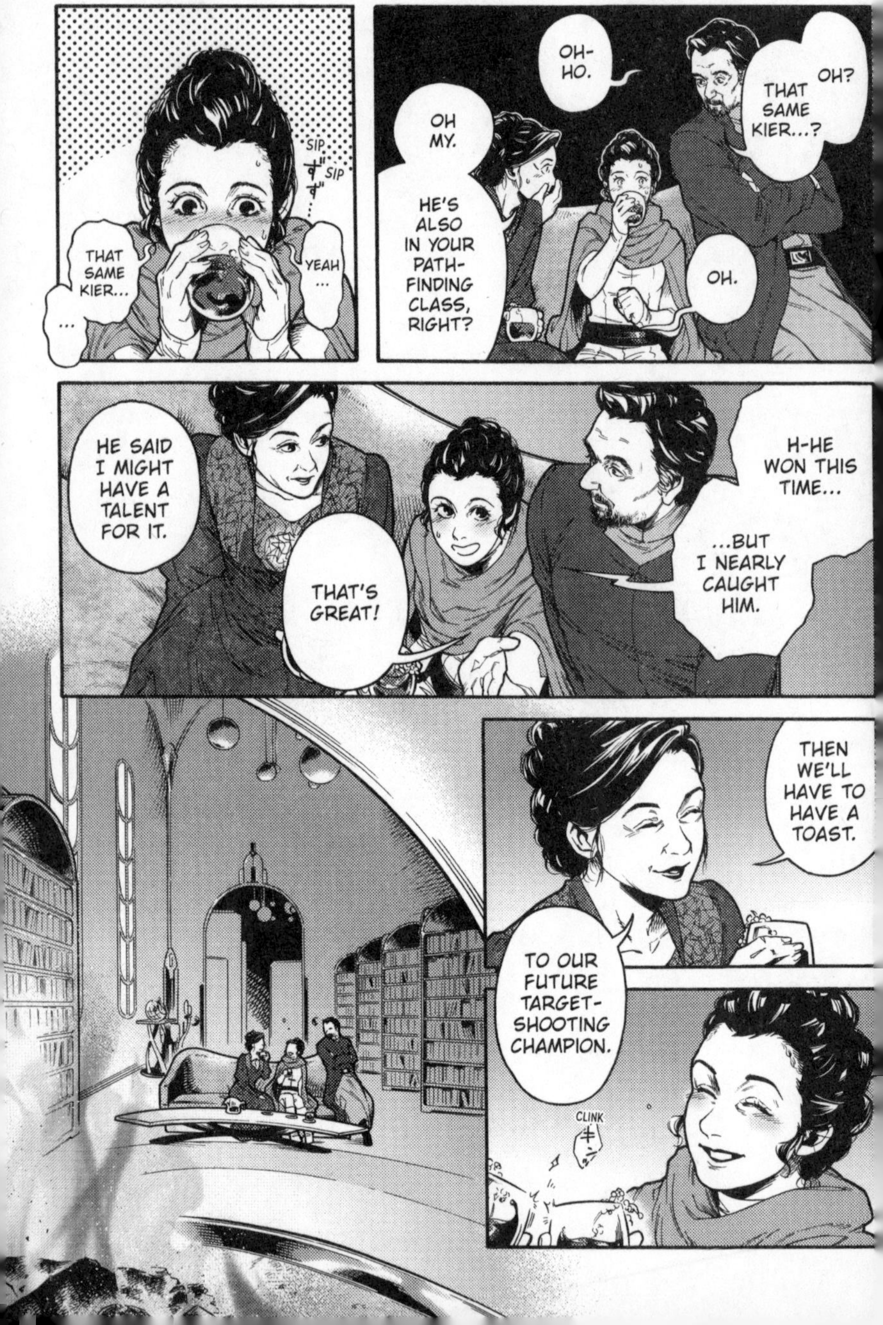
OH? THAT SAME KIER...?
OH-HO.
OH MY.
HE'S ALSO IN YOUR PATH-FINDING CLASS, RIGHT?
OH.
SIP SIP
YEAH...
THAT SAME KIER... ...
H-HE WON THIS TIME...
...BUT I NEARLY CAUGHT HIM.
THAT'S GREAT!
HE SAID I MIGHT HAVE A TALENT FOR IT.
THEN WE'LL HAVE TO HAVE A TOAST.
TO OUR FUTURE TARGET-SHOOTING CHAMPION.
CLINK

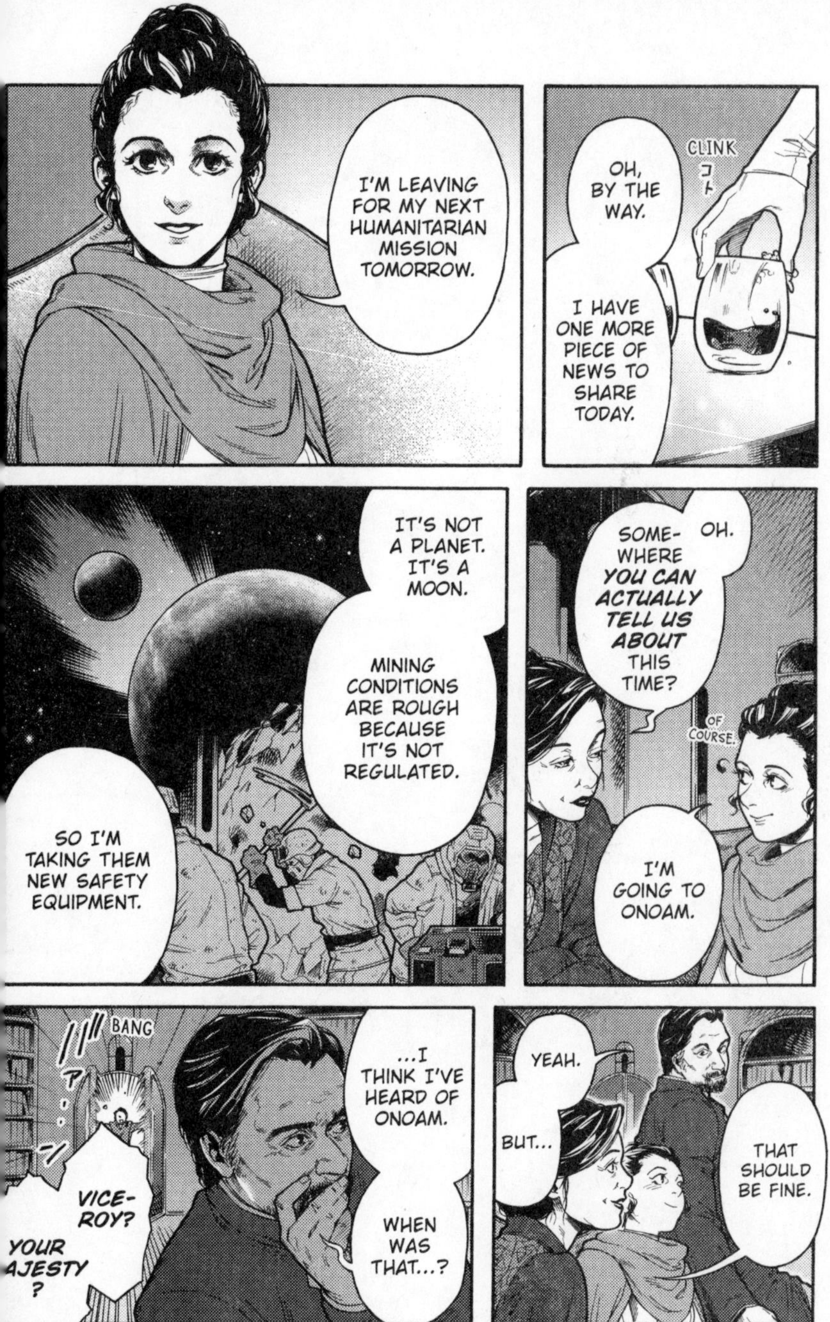
CLINK
コト
OH, BY THE WAY.
I HAVE ONE MORE PIECE OF NEWS TO SHARE TODAY.
I'M LEAVING FOR MY NEXT HUMANITARIAN MISSION TOMORROW.
OH.
SOME-WHERE *YOU CAN ACTUALLY TELL US ABOUT* THIS TIME?
OF COURSE.
I'M GOING TO ONOAM.
IT'S NOT A PLANET. IT'S A MOON.
MINING CONDITIONS ARE ROUGH BECAUSE IT'S NOT REGULATED.
SO I'M TAKING THEM NEW SAFETY EQUIPMENT.
YEAH.
BUT...
THAT SHOULD BE FINE.
...I THINK I'VE HEARD OF ONOAM.
WHEN WAS THAT...?
BANG
VICE-ROY?
YOUR AJESTY ?

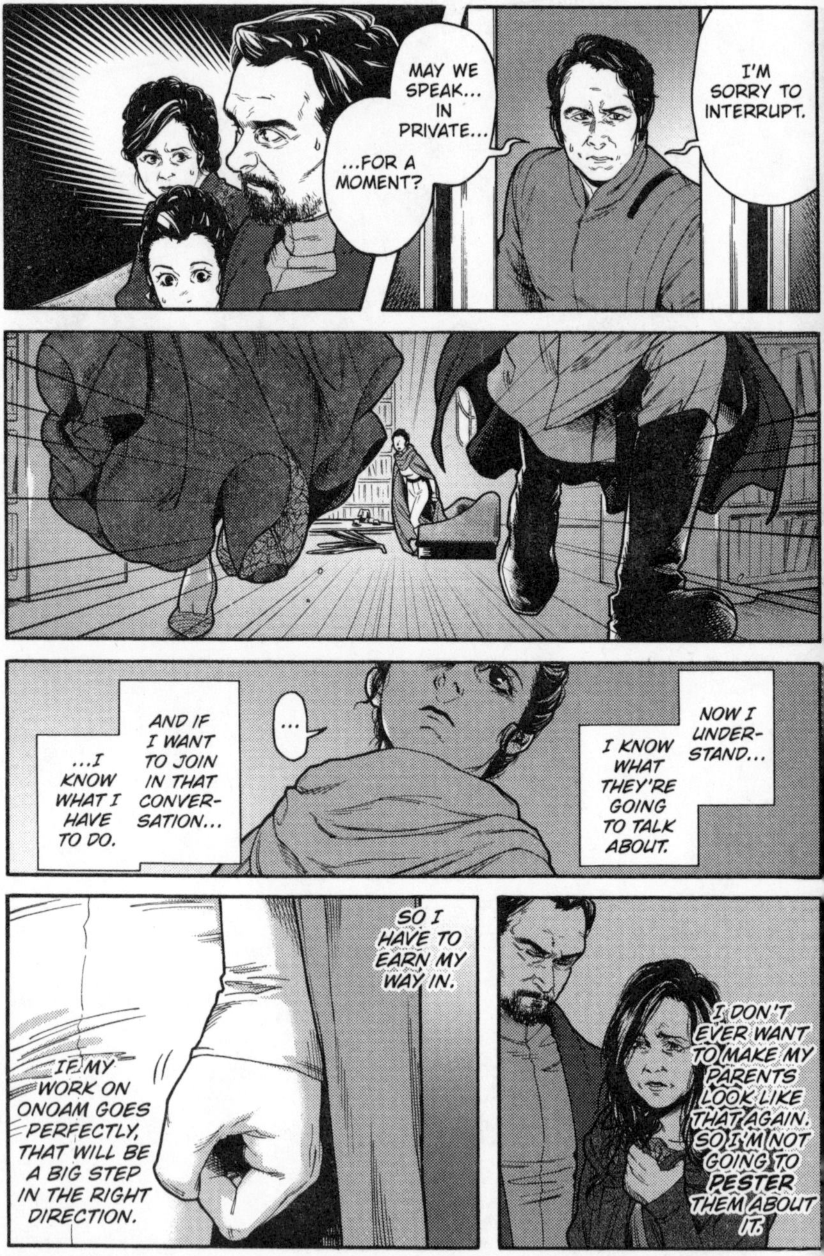
I'M SORRY TO INTERRUPT.
MAY WE SPEAK... IN PRIVATE...
...FOR A MOMENT?
NOW I UNDERSTAND...
I KNOW WHAT THEY'RE GOING TO TALK ABOUT.
...
AND IF I WANT TO JOIN IN THAT CONVERSATION...
...I KNOW WHAT I HAVE TO DO.
I DON'T EVER WANT TO MAKE MY PARENTS LOOK LIKE THAT AGAIN. SO I'M NOT GOING TO PESTER THEM ABOUT IT.
SO I HAVE TO EARN MY WAY IN.
IF MY WORK ON ONOAM GOES PERFECTLY, THAT WILL BE A BIG STEP IN THE RIGHT DIRECTION.

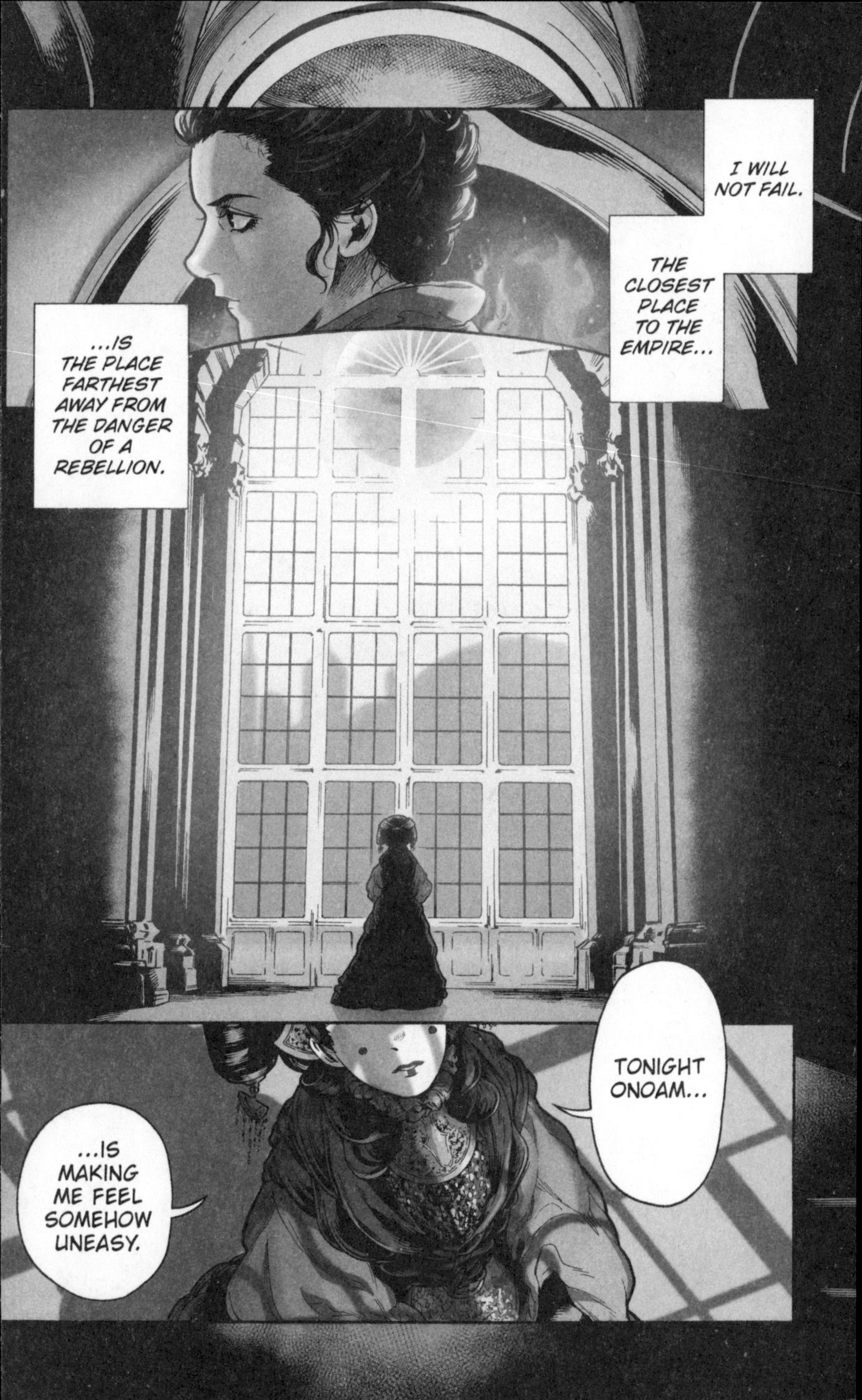
I WILL NOT FAIL.
THE CLOSEST PLACE TO THE EMPIRE...
...IS THE PLACE FARTHEST AWAY FROM THE DANGER OF A REBELLION.
TONIGHT ONOAM...
...IS MAKING ME FEEL SOMEHOW UNEASY.

STAR WARS

LEIA

Princess of

Alderaan

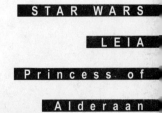

STAR WARS

LEIA

Princess of

Alderaan

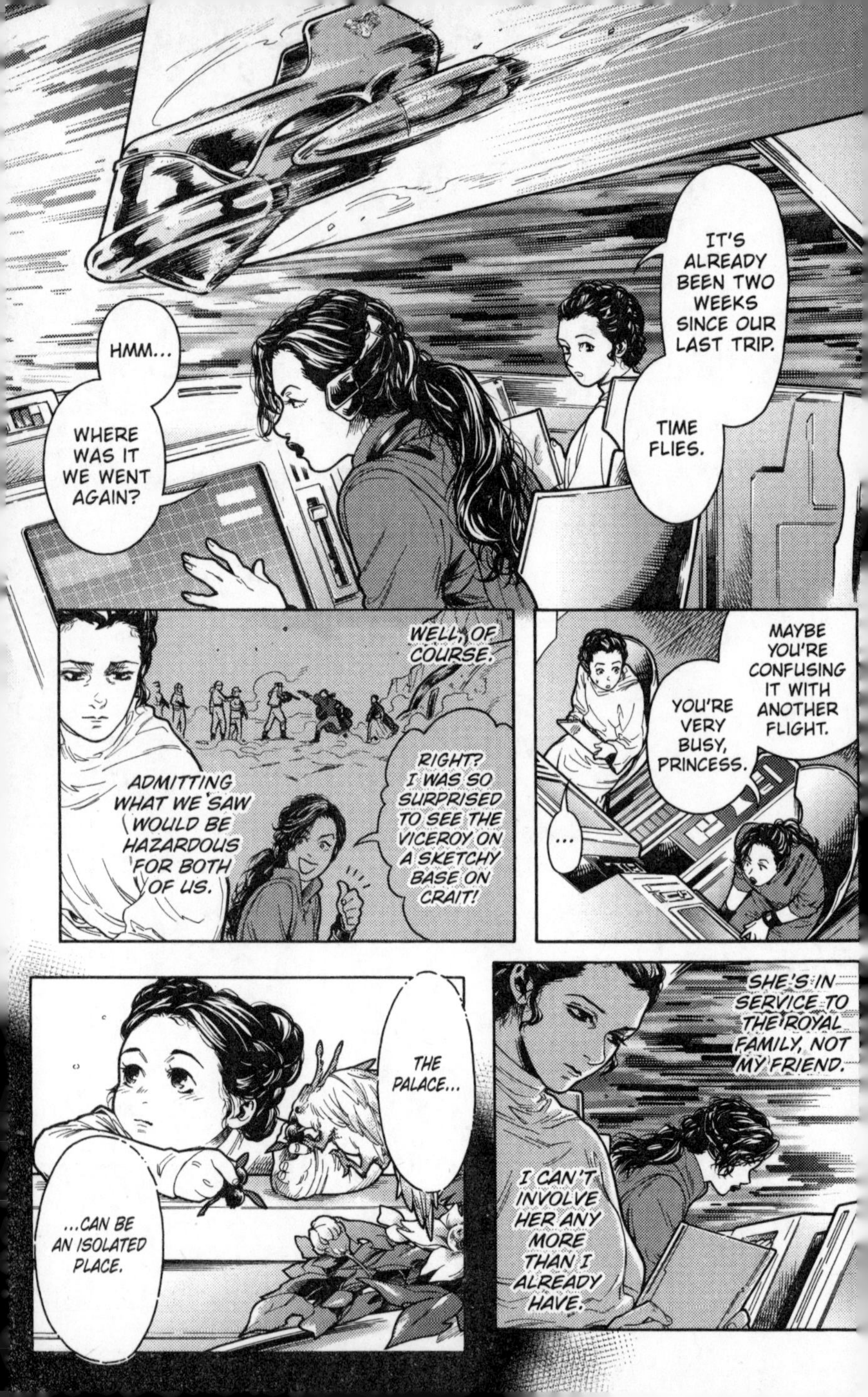
IT'S ALREADY BEEN TWO WEEKS SINCE OUR LAST TRIP.
TIME FLIES.
HMM...
WHERE WAS IT WE WENT AGAIN?
MAYBE YOU'RE CONFUSING IT WITH ANOTHER FLIGHT.
YOU'RE VERY BUSY, PRINCESS.
...
WELL, OF COURSE.
RIGHT? I WAS SO SURPRISED TO SEE THE VICEROY ON A SKETCHY BASE ON CRAIT!
ADMITTING WHAT WE SAW WOULD BE HAZARDOUS FOR BOTH OF US.
SHE'S IN SERVICE TO THE ROYAL FAMILY, NOT MY FRIEND.
I CAN'T INVOLVE HER ANY MORE THAN I ALREADY HAVE.
THE PALACE...
...CAN BE AN ISOLATED PLACE.

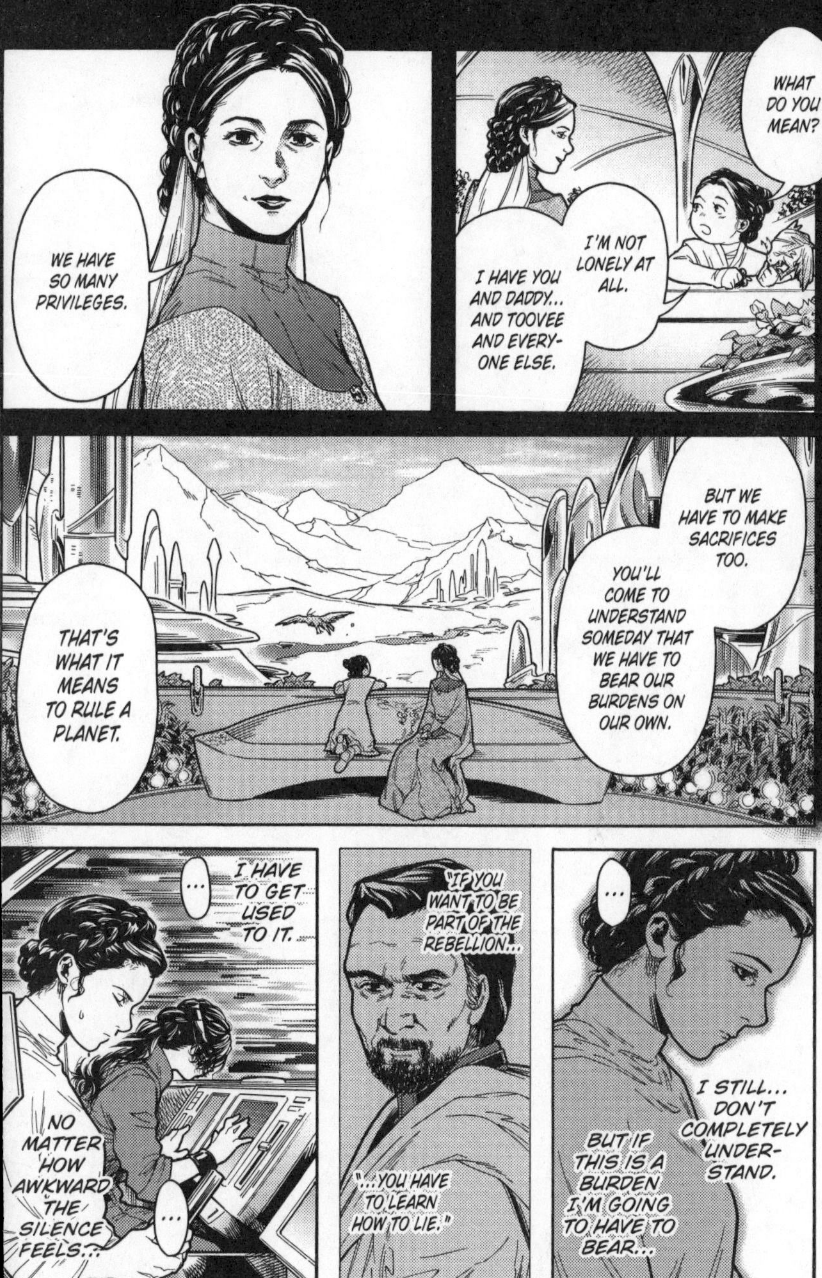
WHAT DO YOU MEAN?
I'M NOT LONELY AT ALL.
I HAVE YOU AND DADDY... AND TOOVEE AND EVERY-ONE ELSE.
WE HAVE SO MANY PRIVILEGES.
BUT WE HAVE TO MAKE SACRIFICES TOO.
YOU'LL COME TO UNDERSTAND SOMEDAY THAT WE HAVE TO BEAR OUR BURDENS ON OUR OWN.
THAT'S WHAT IT MEANS TO RULE A PLANET.
...
I STILL... DON'T COMPLETELY UNDER-STAND.
BUT IF THIS IS A BURDEN I'M GOING TO HAVE TO BEAR...
"IF YOU WANT TO BE PART OF THE REBELLION...
"...YOU HAVE TO LEARN HOW TO LIE."
...
I HAVE TO GET USED TO IT.
NO MATTER HOW AWKWARD THE SILENCE FEELS...
...

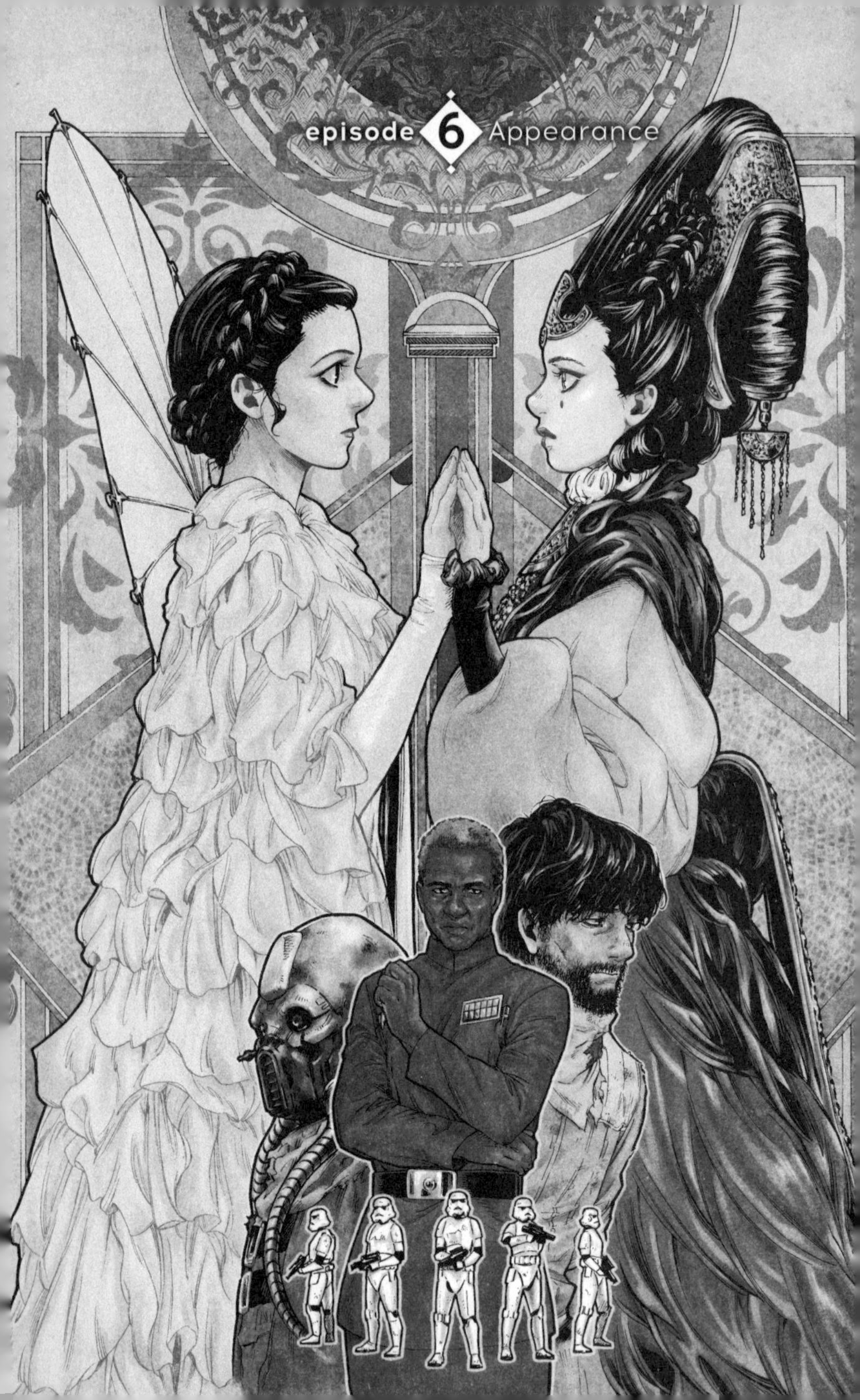
episode 6 Appearance

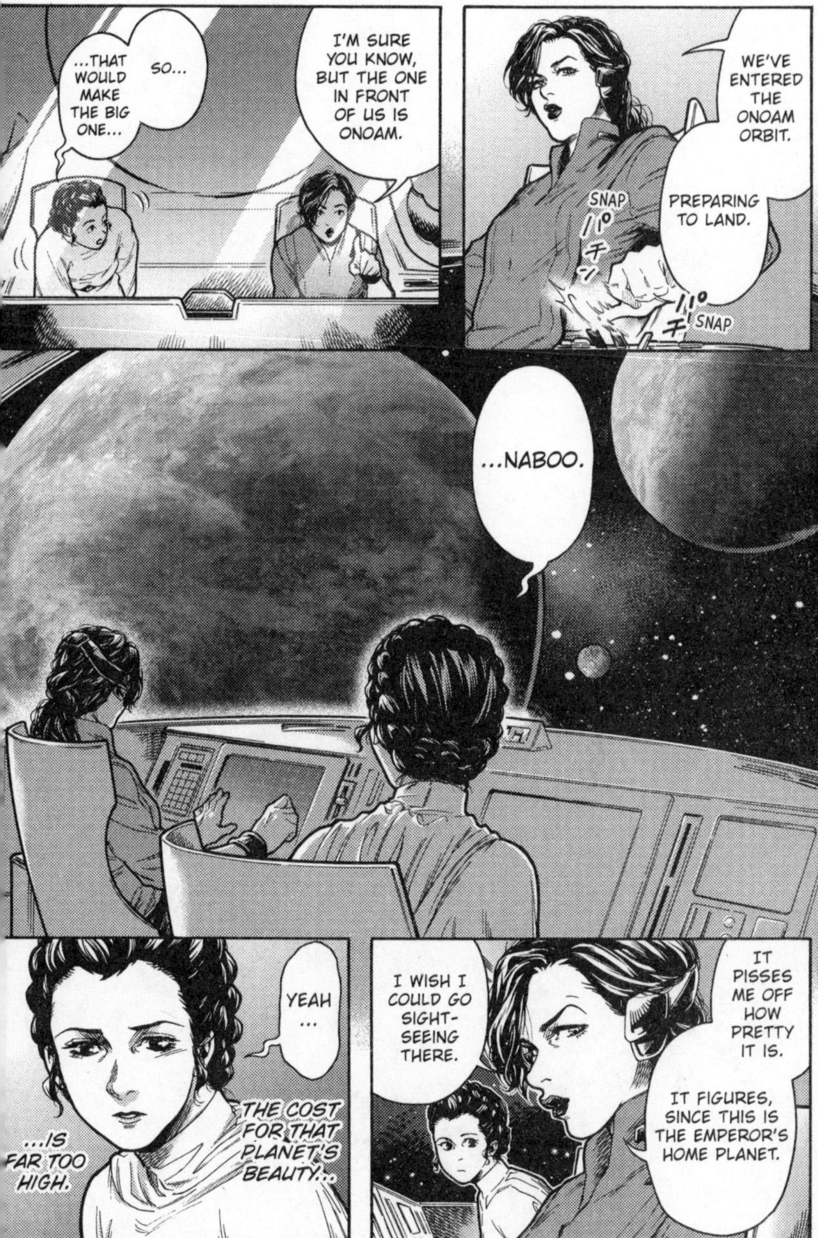
WE'VE ENTERED THE ONOAM ORBIT.
PREPARING TO LAND.
SNAP パチン
パチ SNAP
I'M SURE YOU KNOW, BUT THE ONE IN FRONT OF US IS ONOAM.
SO...
...THAT WOULD MAKE THE BIG ONE...
...NABOO.
IT PISSES ME OFF HOW PRETTY IT IS.
IT FIGURES, SINCE THIS IS THE EMPEROR'S HOME PLANET.
I WISH I COULD GO SIGHT-SEEING THERE.
YEAH...
THE COST FOR THAT PLANET'S BEAUTY...
...IS FAR TOO HIGH.

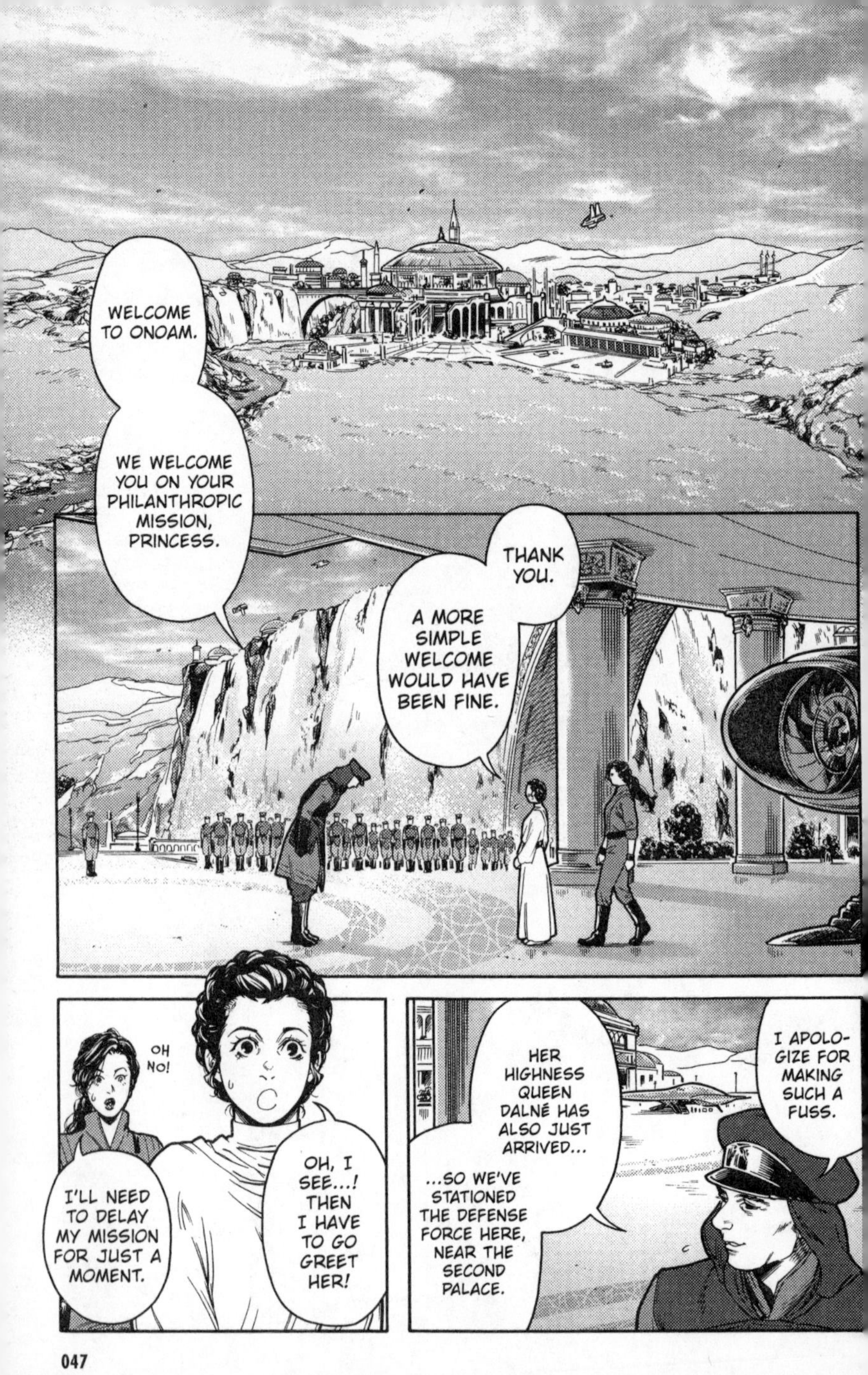
WELCOME TO ONOAM.
WE WELCOME YOU ON YOUR PHILANTHROPIC MISSION, PRINCESS.
THANK YOU.
A MORE SIMPLE WELCOME WOULD HAVE BEEN FINE.
I APOLOGIZE FOR MAKING SUCH A FUSS.
HER HIGHNESS QUEEN DALNÉ HAS ALSO JUST ARRIVED...
...SO WE'VE STATIONED THE DEFENSE FORCE HERE, NEAR THE SECOND PALACE.
OH, I SEE...! THEN I HAVE TO GO GREET HER!
OH NO!
I'LL NEED TO DELAY MY MISSION FOR JUST A MOMENT.

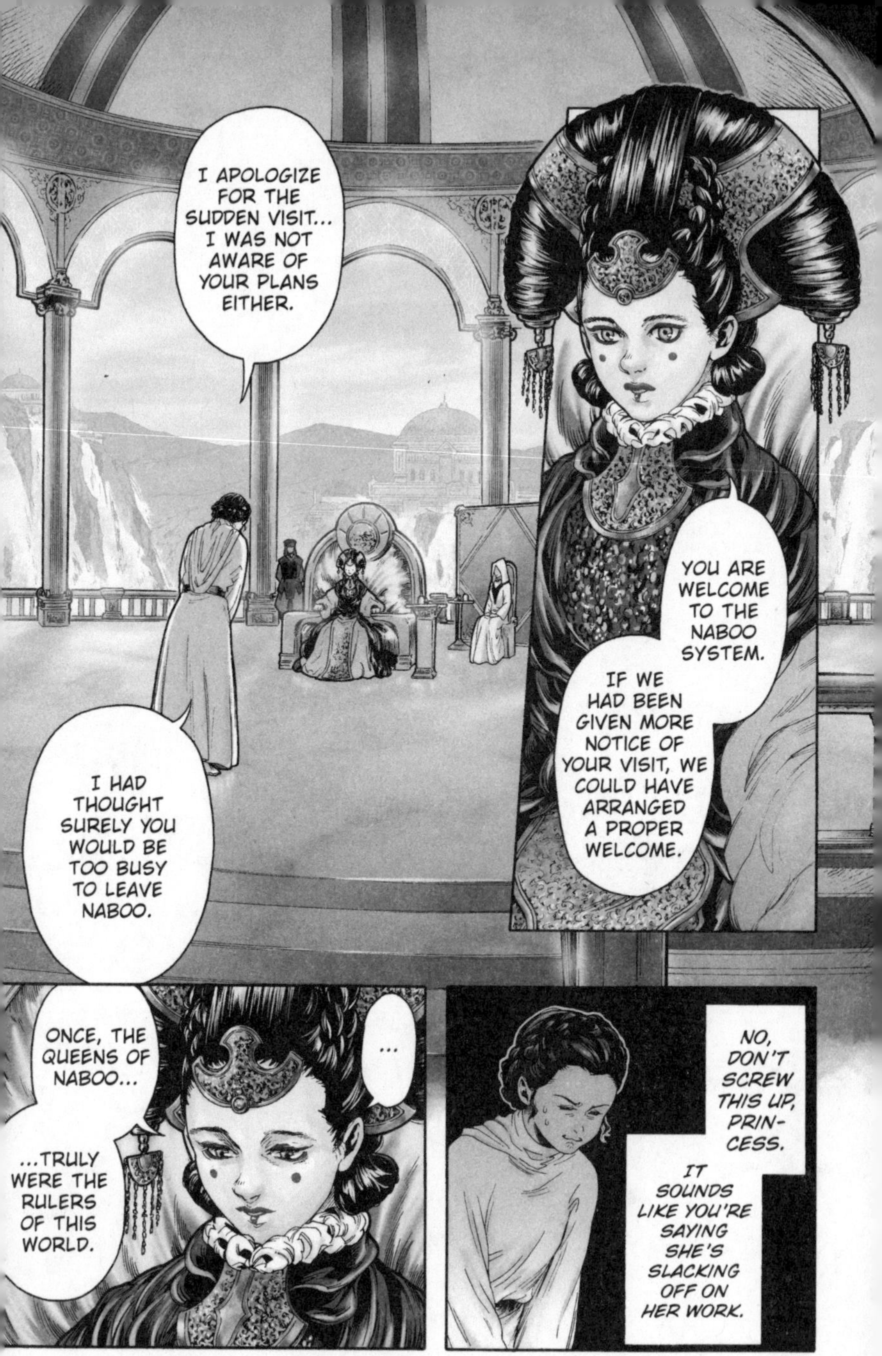
YOU ARE WELCOME TO THE NABOO SYSTEM.
IF WE HAD BEEN GIVEN MORE NOTICE OF YOUR VISIT, WE COULD HAVE ARRANGED A PROPER WELCOME.
I APOLOGIZE FOR THE SUDDEN VISIT... I WAS NOT AWARE OF YOUR PLANS EITHER.
I HAD THOUGHT SURELY YOU WOULD BE TOO BUSY TO LEAVE NABOO.
NO, DON'T SCREW THIS UP, PRIN-CESS.
IT SOUNDS LIKE YOU'RE SAYING SHE'S SLACKING OFF ON HER WORK.
...
ONCE, THE QUEENS OF NABOO...
...TRULY WERE THE RULERS OF THIS WORLD.

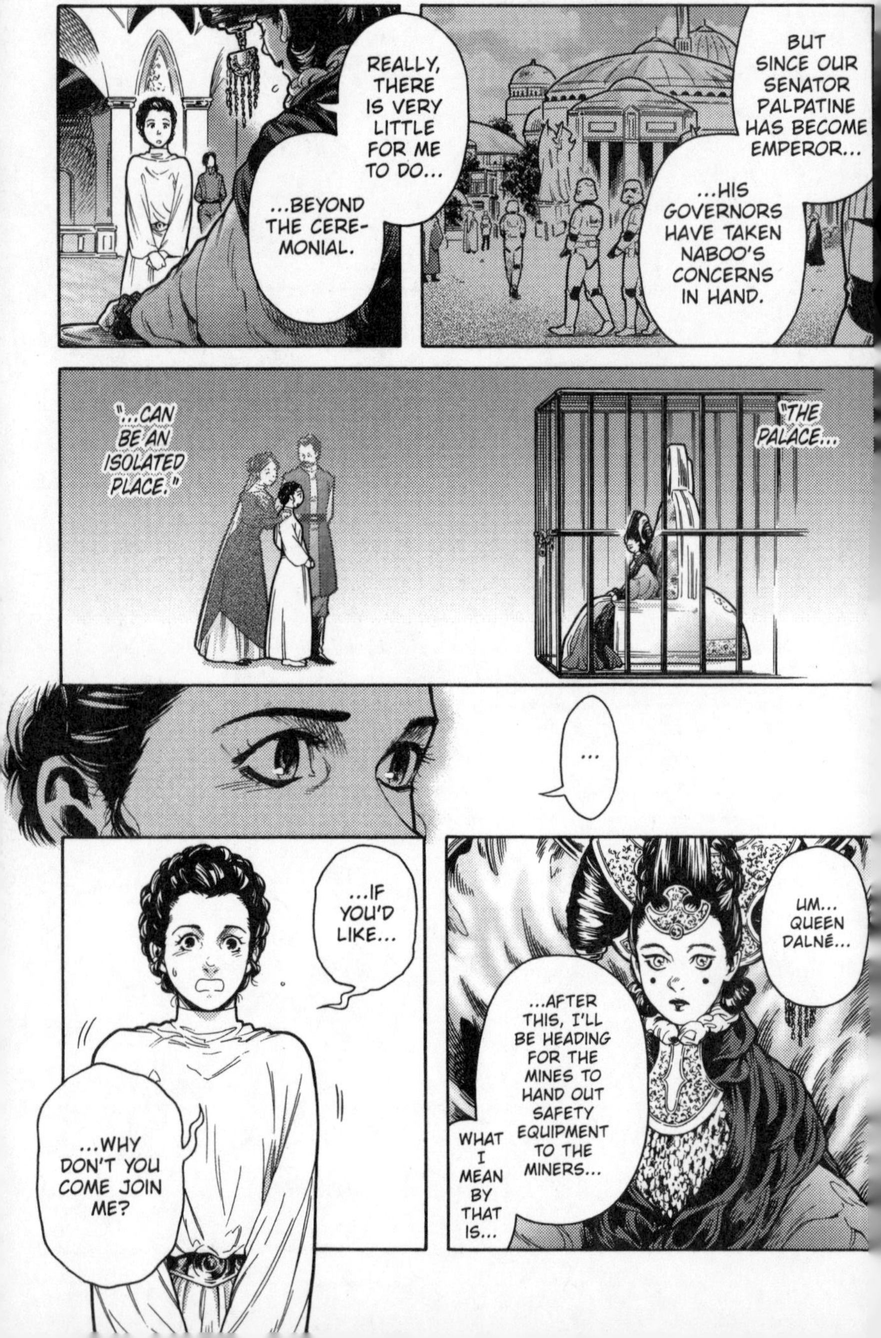
BUT SINCE OUR SENATOR PALPATINE HAS BECOME EMPEROR...
...HIS GOVERNORS HAVE TAKEN NABOO'S CONCERNS IN HAND.
REALLY, THERE IS VERY LITTLE FOR ME TO DO...
...BEYOND THE CERE-MONIAL.
"THE PALACE...
"...CAN BE AN ISOLATED PLACE."
...
UM... QUEEN DALNÉ...
...AFTER THIS, I'LL BE HEADING FOR THE MINES TO HAND OUT SAFETY EQUIPMENT TO THE MINERS...
WHAT I MEAN BY THAT IS...
...IF YOU'D LIKE...
...WHY DON'T YOU COME JOIN ME?

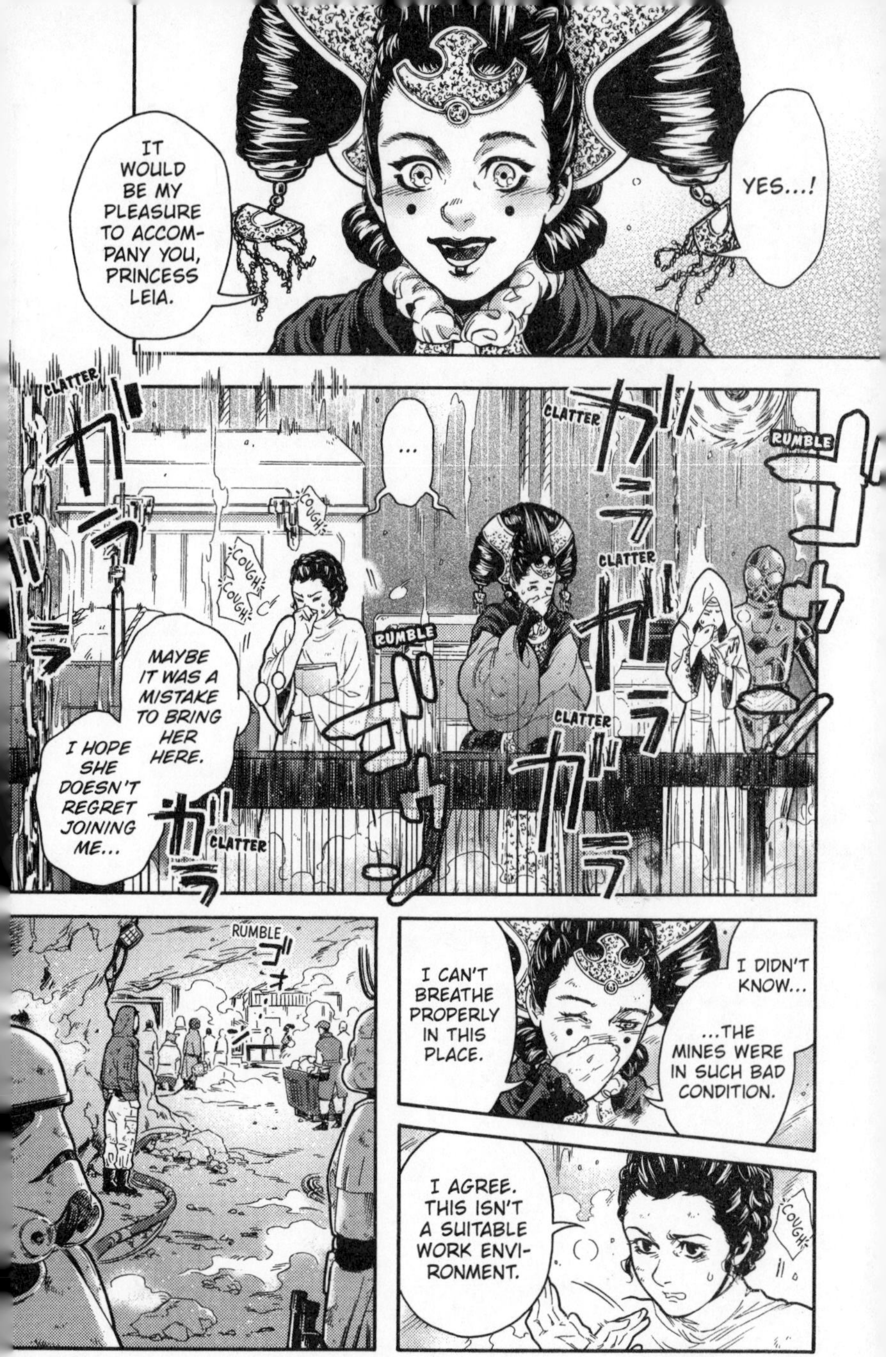
YES...!
IT WOULD BE MY PLEASURE TO ACCOMPANY YOU, PRINCESS LEIA.
RUMBLE
CLATTER
CLATTER
...
COUGH
CLATTER
RUMBLE
COUGH COUGH
CLATTER
MAYBE IT WAS A MISTAKE TO BRING HER HERE.
I HOPE SHE DOESN'T REGRET JOINING ME...
CLATTER
I DIDN'T KNOW...
...THE MINES WERE IN SUCH BAD CONDITION.
I CAN'T BREATHE PROPERLY IN THIS PLACE.
COUGH
I AGREE. THIS ISN'T A SUITABLE WORK ENVIRONMENT.
RUMBLE

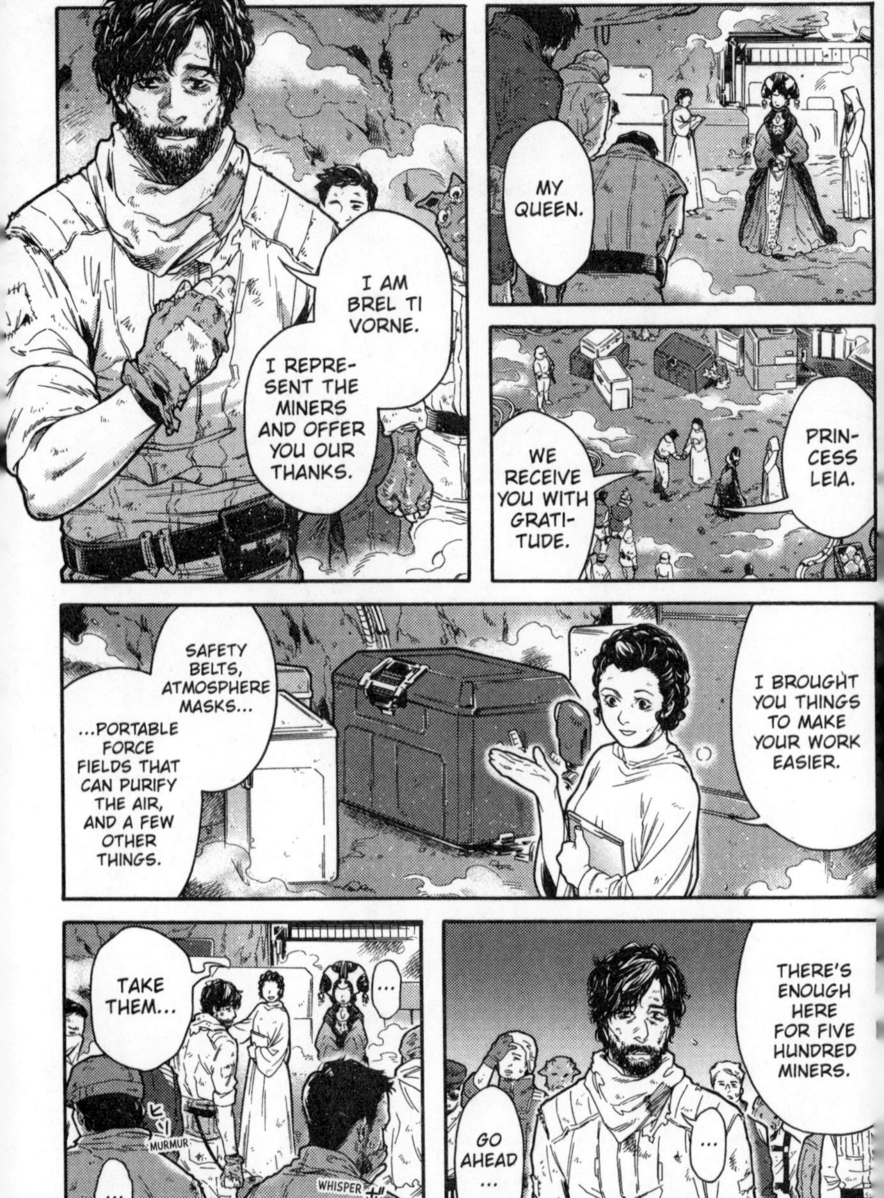
MY QUEEN.
PRIN-CESS LEIA.
WE RECEIVE YOU WITH GRATI-TUDE.
I AM BREL TI VORNE.
I REPRE-SENT THE MINERS AND OFFER YOU OUR THANKS.
I BROUGHT YOU THINGS TO MAKE YOUR WORK EASIER.
SAFETY BELTS, ATMOSPHERE MASKS...
...PORTABLE FORCE FIELDS THAT CAN PURIFY THE AIR, AND A FEW OTHER THINGS.
THERE'S ENOUGH HERE FOR FIVE HUNDRED MINERS.
...
GO AHEAD...
...
TAKE THEM...
WHISPER
WHISPER
MURMUR
...
MURMUR

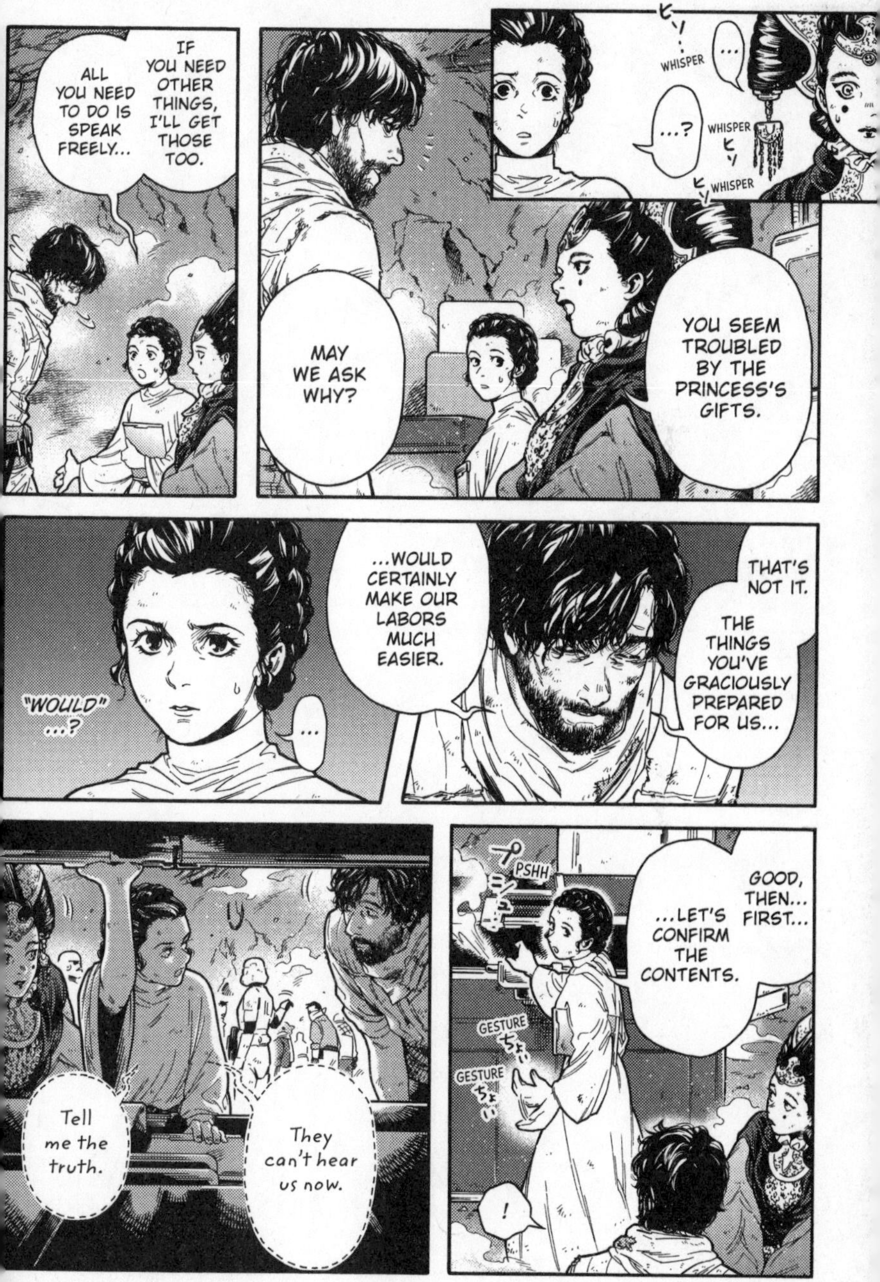
WHISPER
...
...?
WHISPER
WHISPER
YOU SEEM TROUBLED BY THE PRINCESS'S GIFTS.
MAY WE ASK WHY?
IF YOU NEED OTHER THINGS, I'LL GET THOSE TOO.
ALL YOU NEED TO DO IS SPEAK FREELY...
THAT'S NOT IT.
THE THINGS YOU'VE GRACIOUSLY PREPARED FOR US...
...WOULD CERTAINLY MAKE OUR LABORS MUCH EASIER.
...
"WOULD" ...?
GOOD, THEN... FIRST...
...LET'S CONFIRM THE CONTENTS.
PSHH
GESTURE ちょい
GESTURE ちょい
!
They can't hear us now.
Tell me the truth.

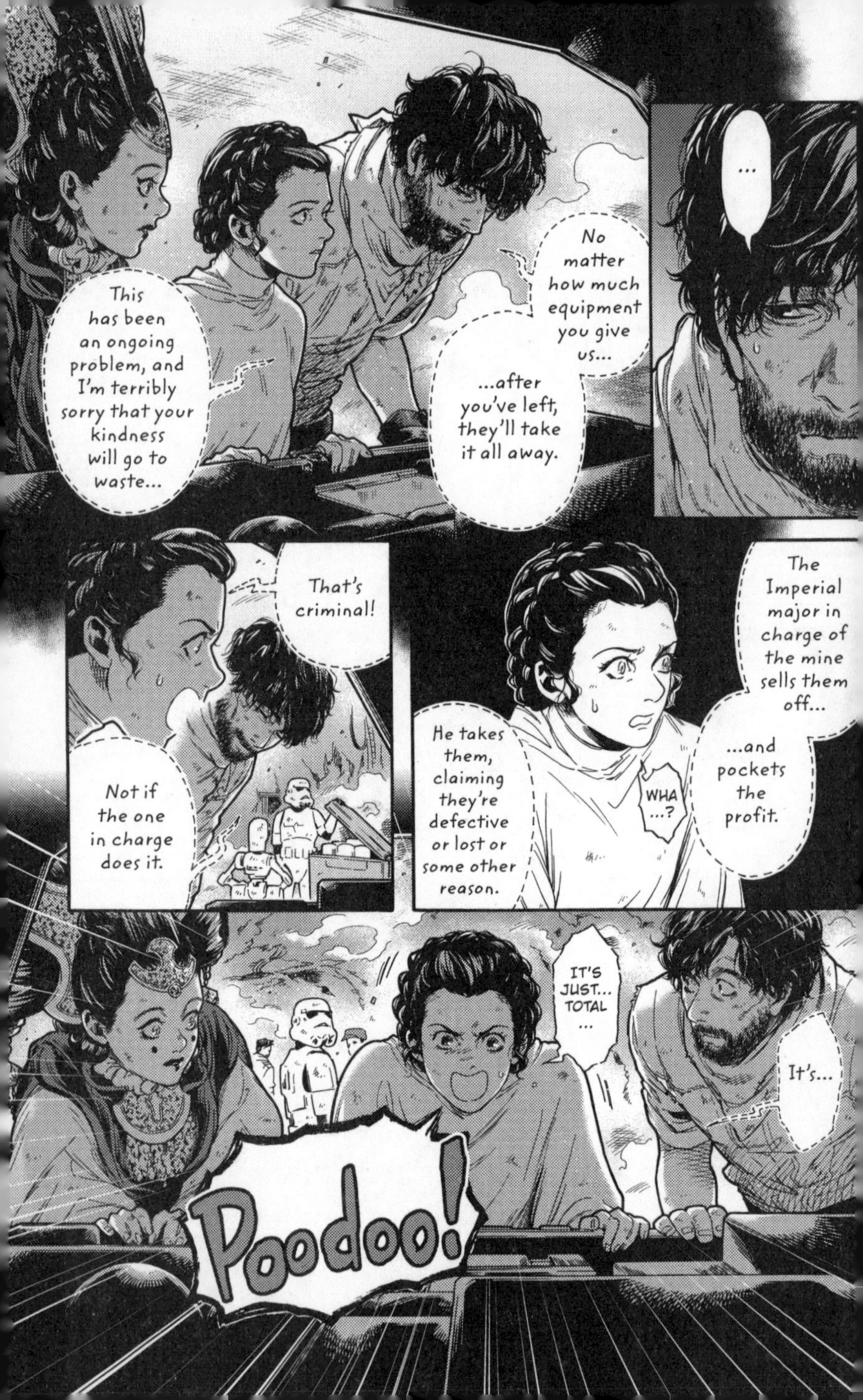
...
No matter how much equipment you give us...
...after you've left, they'll take it all away.
This has been an ongoing problem, and I'm terribly sorry that your kindness will go to waste...
The Imperial major in charge of the mine sells them off...
...and pockets the profit.
WHA...?
He takes them, claiming they're defective or lost or some other reason.
That's criminal!
Not if the one in charge does it.
It's...
IT'S JUST... TOTAL...
Poodoo!

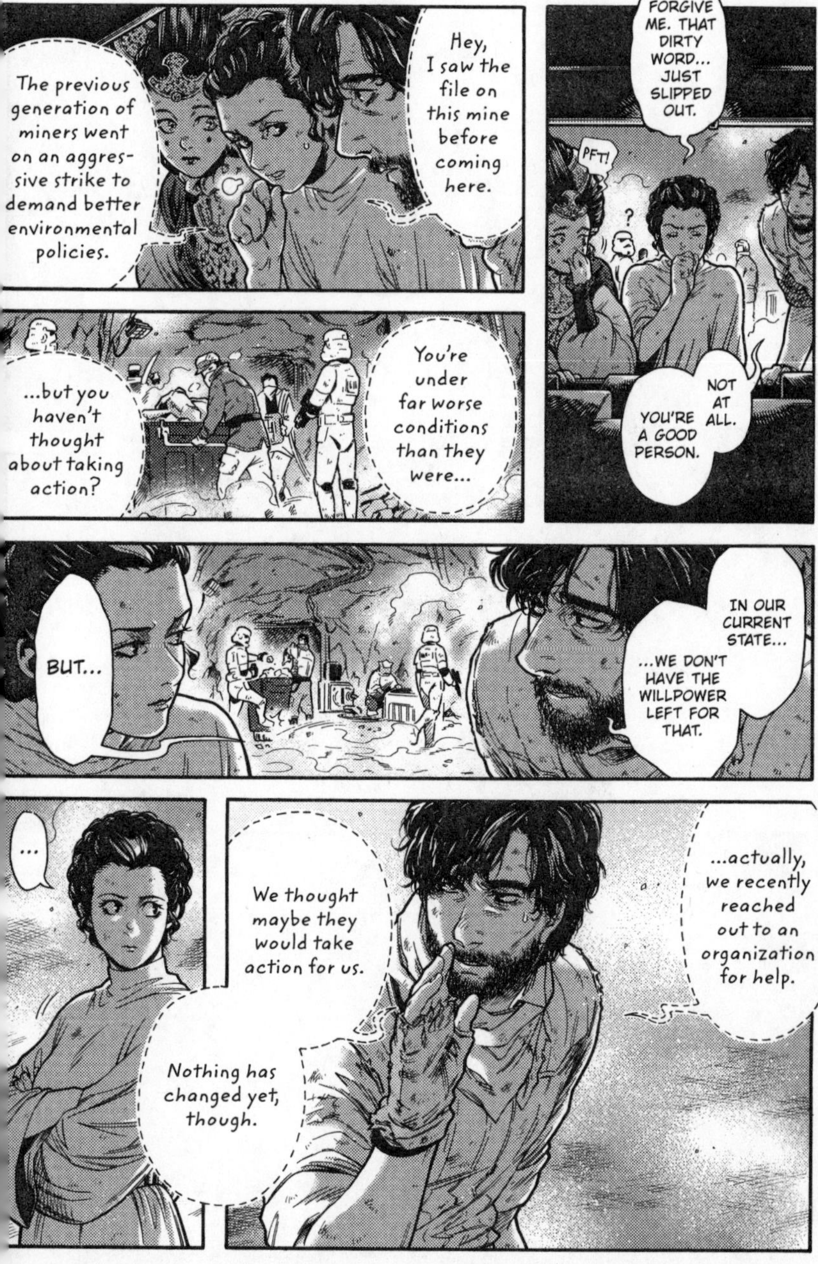
FORGIVE ME. THAT DIRTY WORD... JUST SLIPPED OUT.
PFT!
?
NOT AT ALL.
YOU'RE A GOOD PERSON.
Hey, I saw the file on this mine before coming here.
The previous generation of miners went on an aggres-sive strike to demand better environmental policies.
You're under far worse conditions than they were...
...but you haven't thought about taking action?
IN OUR CURRENT STATE...
...WE DON'T HAVE THE WILLPOWER LEFT FOR THAT.
BUT...
...actually, we recently reached out to an organization for help.
We thought maybe they would take action for us.
Nothing has changed yet, though.
...

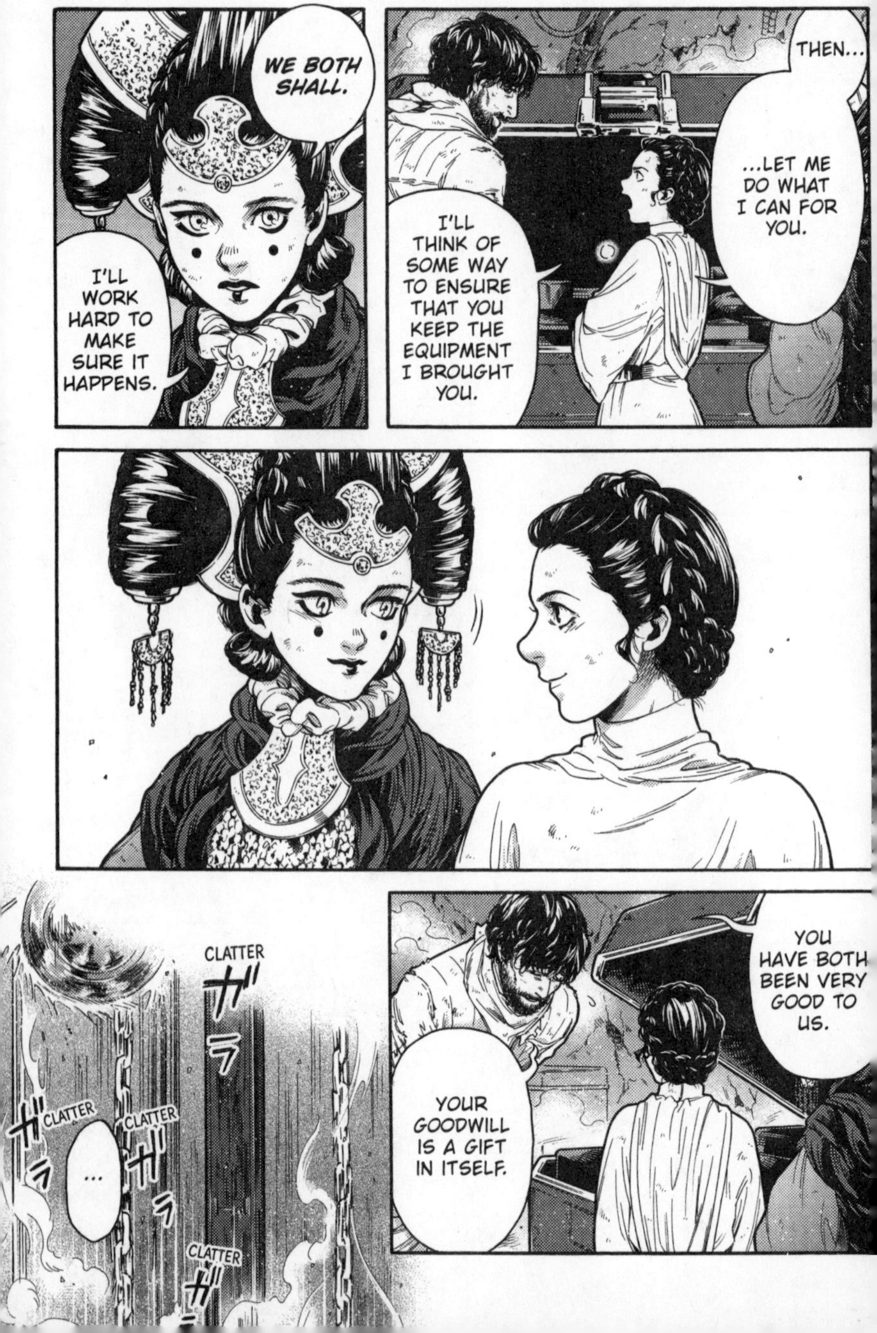
THEN...
...LET ME DO WHAT I CAN FOR YOU.
I'LL THINK OF SOME WAY TO ENSURE THAT YOU KEEP THE EQUIPMENT I BROUGHT YOU.
WE BOTH SHALL.
I'LL WORK HARD TO MAKE SURE IT HAPPENS.
YOU HAVE BOTH BEEN VERY GOOD TO US.
YOUR GOODWILL IS A GIFT IN ITSELF.
CLATTER
ガラ
CLATTER
ガラ
CLATTER
ガラ
...
CLATTER
ガ

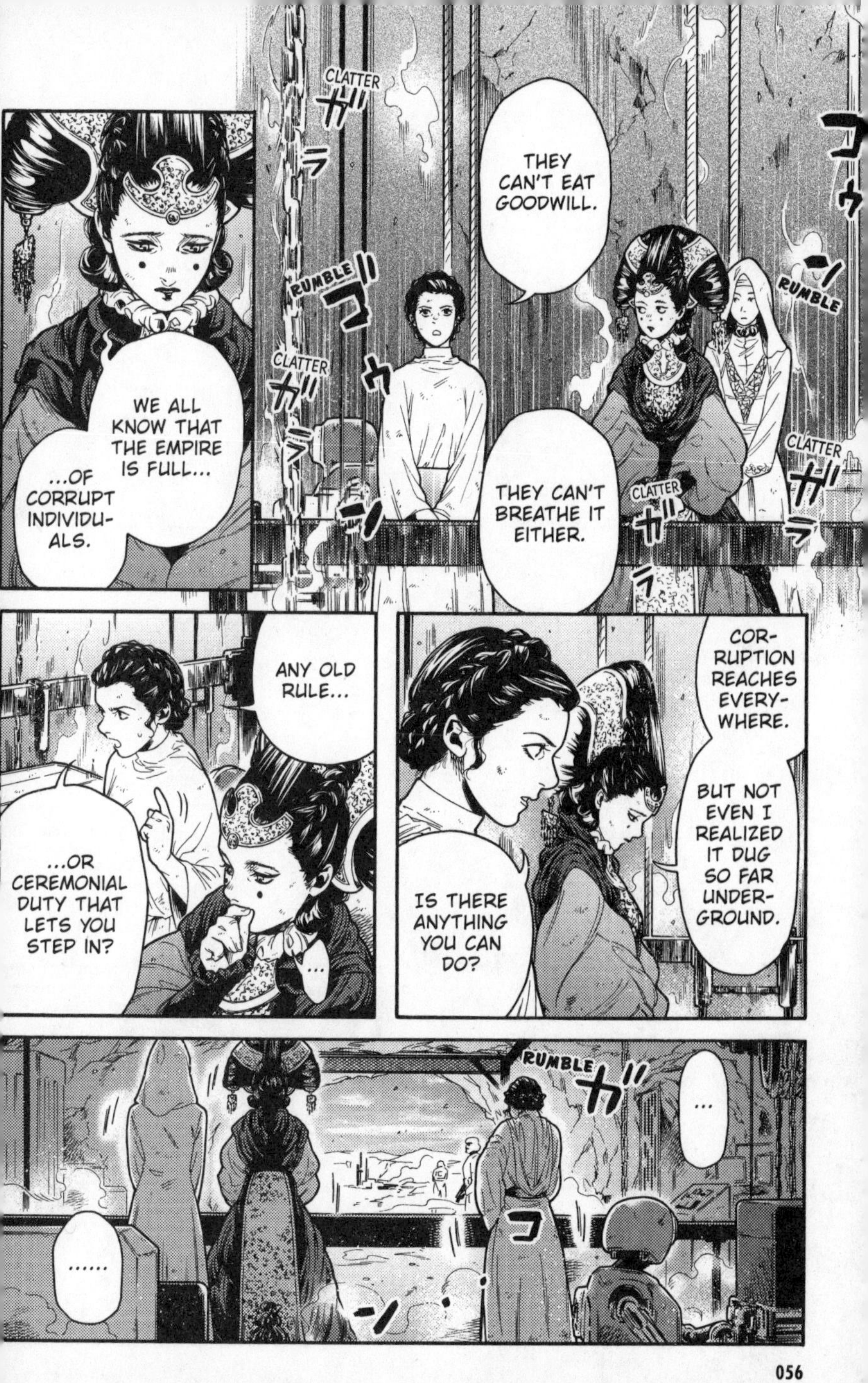
CLATTER
THEY CAN'T EAT GOODWILL.
RUMBLE
RUMBLE
CLATTER
THEY CAN'T BREATHE IT EITHER.
CLATTER
CLATTER
WE ALL KNOW THAT THE EMPIRE IS FULL...
...OF CORRUPT INDIVIDU-ALS.
COR-RUPTION REACHES EVERY-WHERE.
BUT NOT EVEN I REALIZED IT DUG SO FAR UNDER-GROUND.
IS THERE ANYTHING YOU CAN DO?
ANY OLD RULE...
...OR CEREMONIAL DUTY THAT LETS YOU STEP IN?
...
...
RUMBLE
......

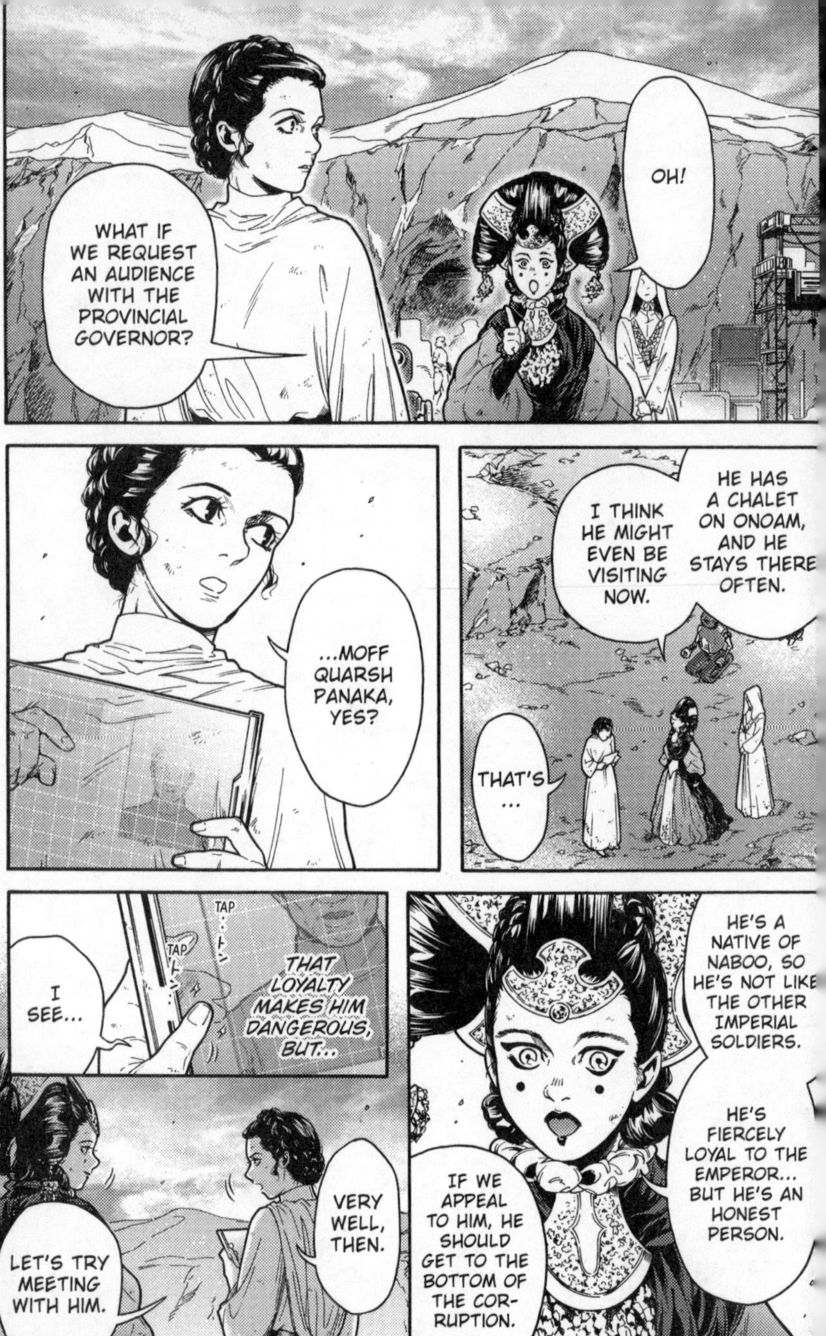
OH!
WHAT IF WE REQUEST AN AUDIENCE WITH THE PROVINCIAL GOVERNOR?
HE HAS A CHALET ON ONOAM, AND HE STAYS THERE OFTEN.
I THINK HE MIGHT EVEN BE VISITING NOW.
THAT'S ...
...MOFF QUARSH PANAKA, YES?
HE'S A NATIVE OF NABOO, SO HE'S NOT LIKE THE OTHER IMPERIAL SOLDIERS.
HE'S FIERCELY LOYAL TO THE EMPEROR... BUT HE'S AN HONEST PERSON.
IF WE APPEAL TO HIM, HE SHOULD GET TO THE BOTTOM OF THE COR-RUPTION.
TAP
TAP
THAT LOYALTY MAKES HIM DANGEROUS, BUT...
I SEE...
VERY WELL, THEN.
LET'S TRY MEETING WITH HIM.

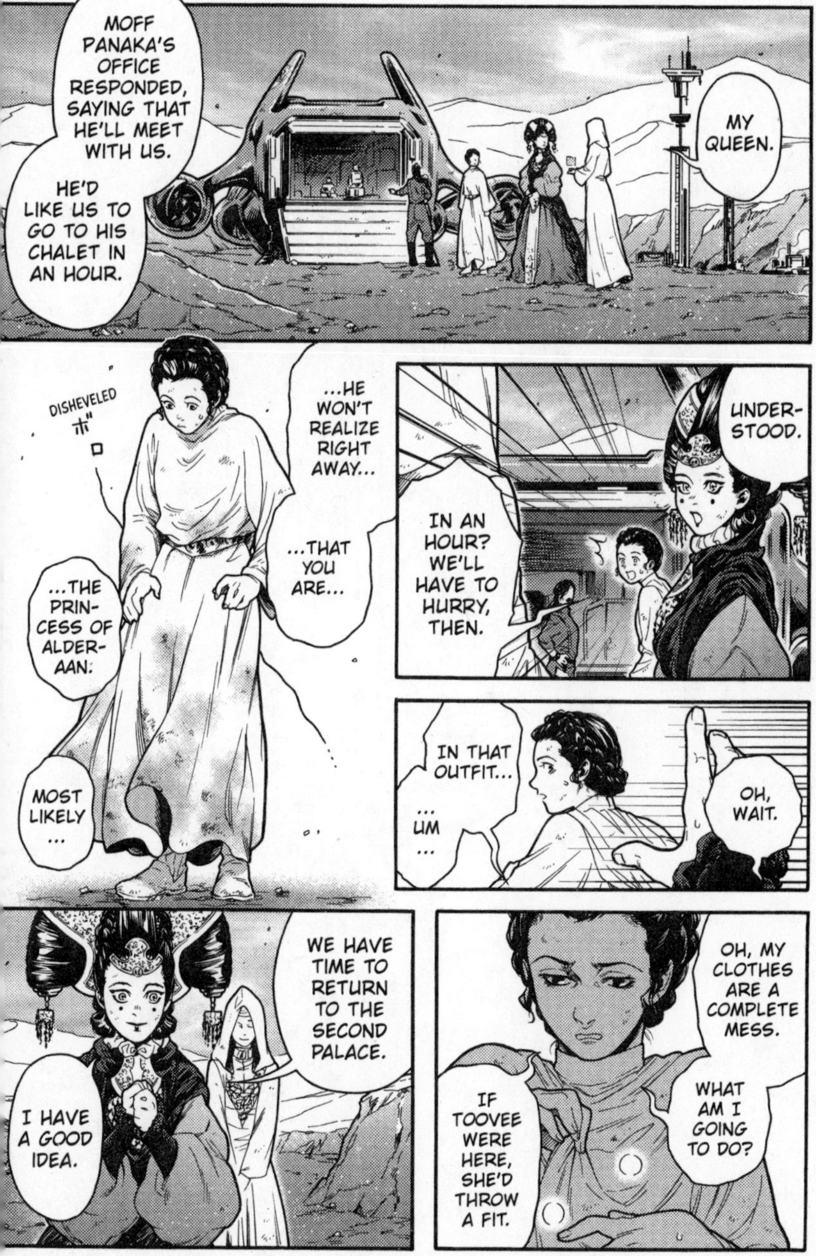
MY QUEEN.
MOFF PANAKA'S OFFICE RESPONDED, SAYING THAT HE'LL MEET WITH US.
HE'D LIKE US TO GO TO HIS CHALET IN AN HOUR.
UNDER-STOOD.
IN AN HOUR? WE'LL HAVE TO HURRY, THEN.
OH, WAIT.
IN THAT OUTFIT...
...UM...
DISHEVELED
ボロ
...HE WON'T REALIZE RIGHT AWAY...
...THAT YOU ARE...
...THE PRINCESS OF ALDERAAN.
MOST LIKELY...
OH, MY CLOTHES ARE A COMPLETE MESS.
WHAT AM I GOING TO DO?
IF TOOVEE WERE HERE, SHE'D THROW A FIT.
WE HAVE TIME TO RETURN TO THE SECOND PALACE.
I HAVE A GOOD IDEA.

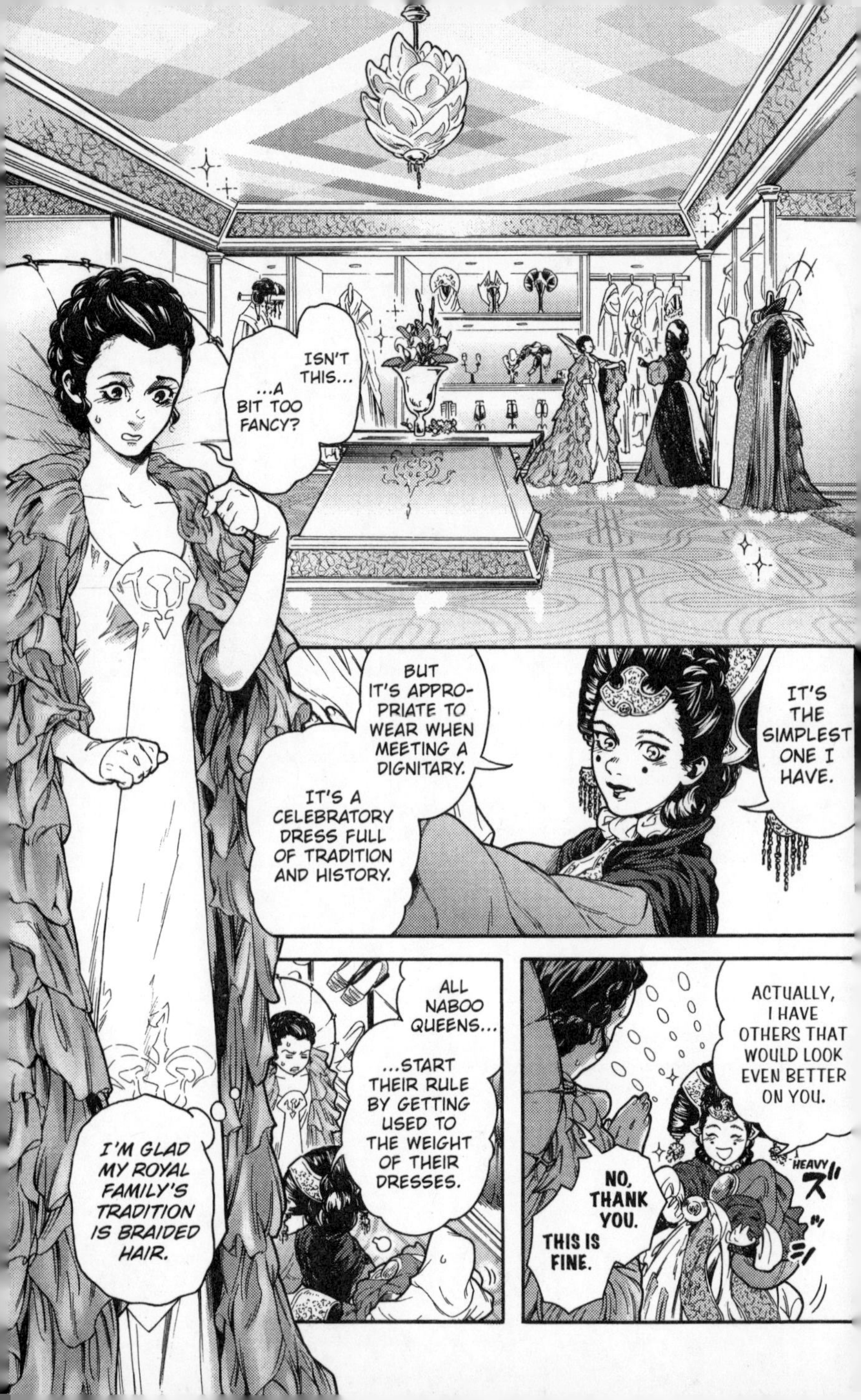

ISN'T THIS...
...A BIT TOO FANCY?
IT'S THE SIMPLEST ONE I HAVE.
BUT IT'S APPROPRIATE TO WEAR WHEN MEETING A DIGNITARY.
IT'S A CELEBRATORY DRESS FULL OF TRADITION AND HISTORY.
ACTUALLY, I HAVE OTHERS THAT WOULD LOOK EVEN BETTER ON YOU.
HEAVY
NO, THANK YOU.
THIS IS FINE.
ALL NABOO QUEENS...
...START THEIR RULE BY GETTING USED TO THE WEIGHT OF THEIR DRESSES.
I'M GLAD MY ROYAL FAMILY'S TRADITION IS BRAIDED HAIR.

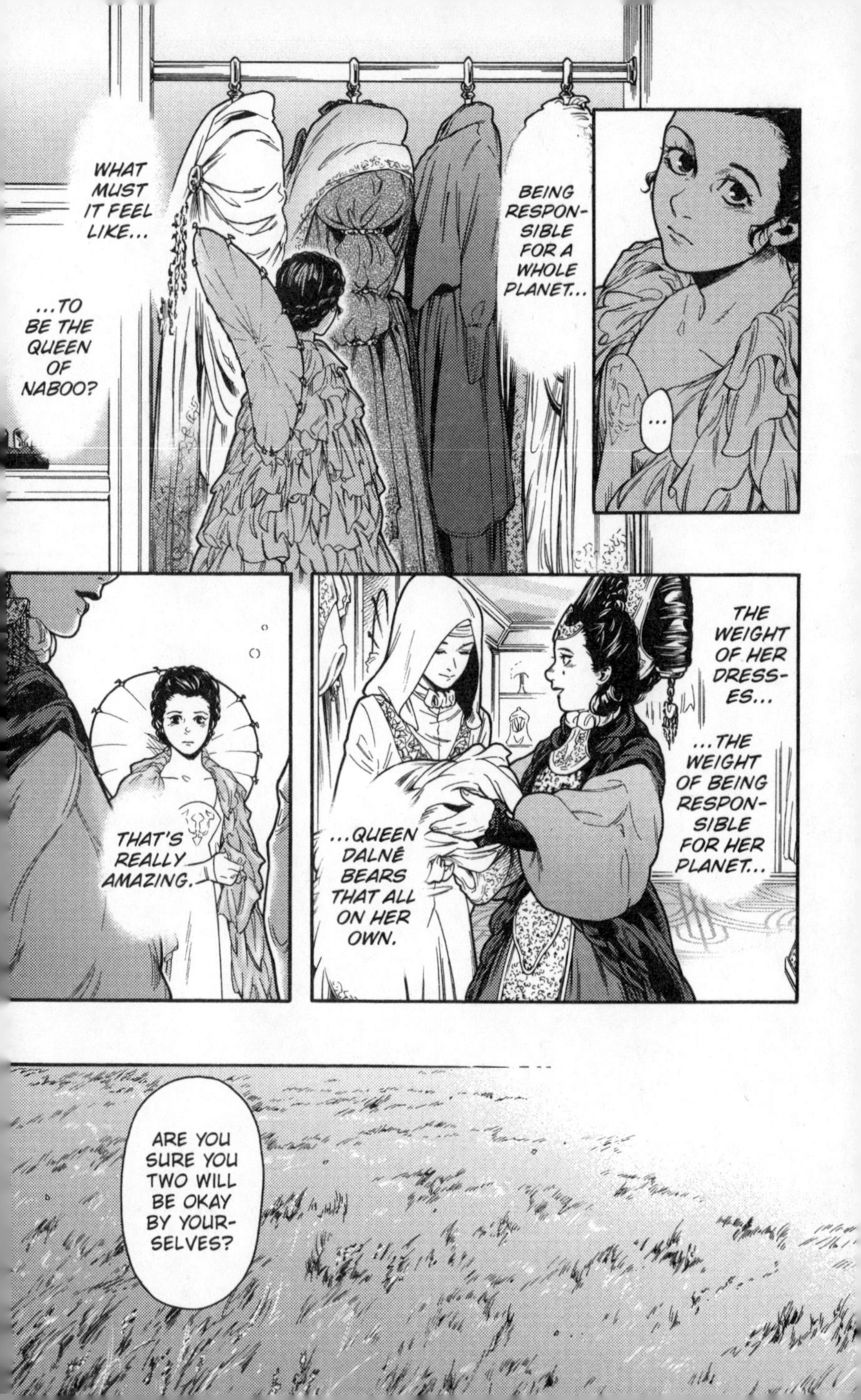
...
BEING RESPONSIBLE FOR A WHOLE PLANET...
WHAT MUST IT FEEL LIKE...
...TO BE THE QUEEN OF NABOO?
THE WEIGHT OF HER DRESSES...
...THE WEIGHT OF BEING RESPONSIBLE FOR HER PLANET...
...QUEEN DALNÉ BEARS THAT ALL ON HER OWN.
THAT'S REALLY AMAZING.
ARE YOU SURE YOU TWO WILL BE OKAY BY YOURSELVES?

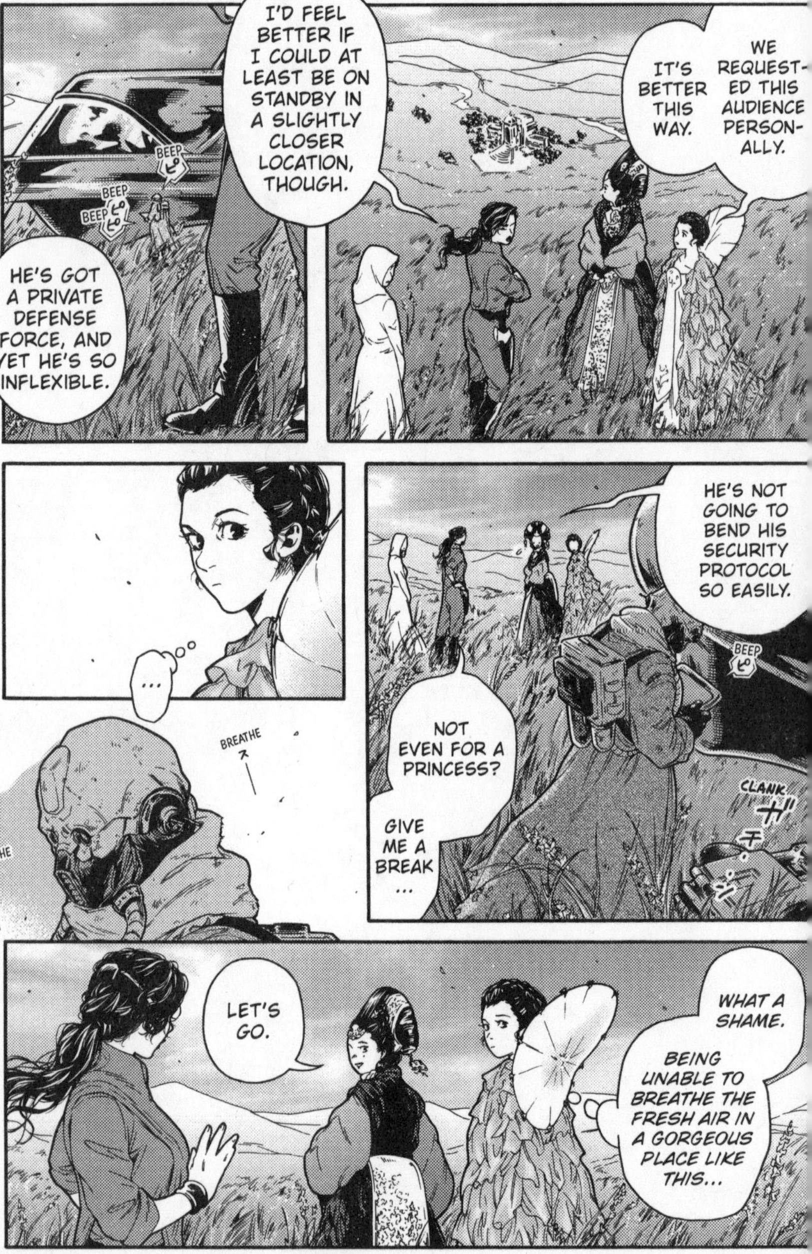
WE REQUEST-ED THIS AUDIENCE PERSON-ALLY.
IT'S BETTER THIS WAY.
I'D FEEL BETTER IF I COULD AT LEAST BE ON STANDBY IN A SLIGHTLY CLOSER LOCATION, THOUGH.
BEEP
BEEP
BEEP
HE'S GOT A PRIVATE DEFENSE FORCE, AND YET HE'S SO INFLEXIBLE.
HE'S NOT GOING TO BEND HIS SECURITY PROTOCOL SO EASILY.
BEEP
NOT EVEN FOR A PRINCESS?
GIVE ME A BREAK...
CLANK
...
BREATHE
BREATHE
WHAT A SHAME.
BEING UNABLE TO BREATHE THE FRESH AIR IN A GORGEOUS PLACE LIKE THIS...
LET'S GO.

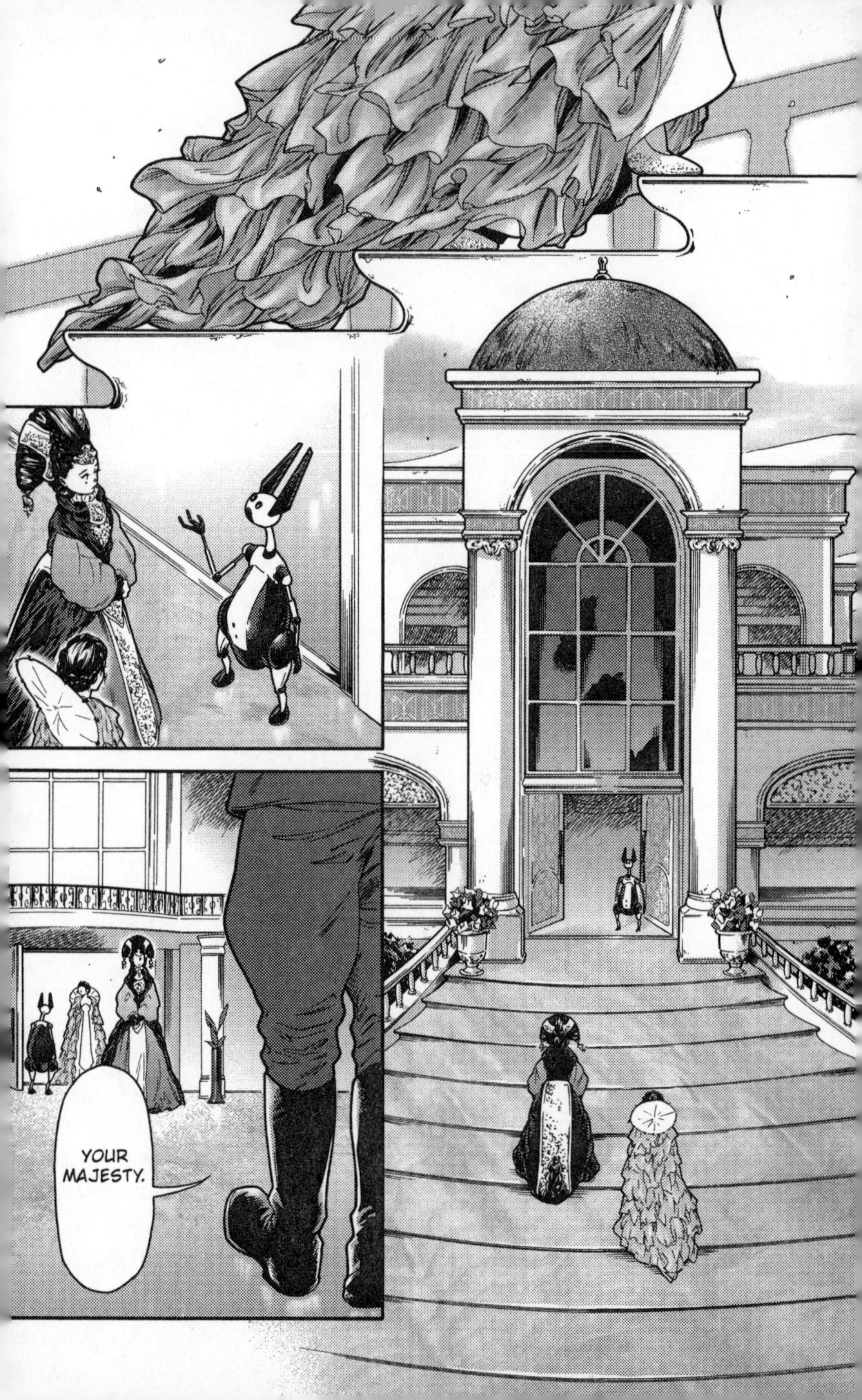
YOUR MAJESTY.

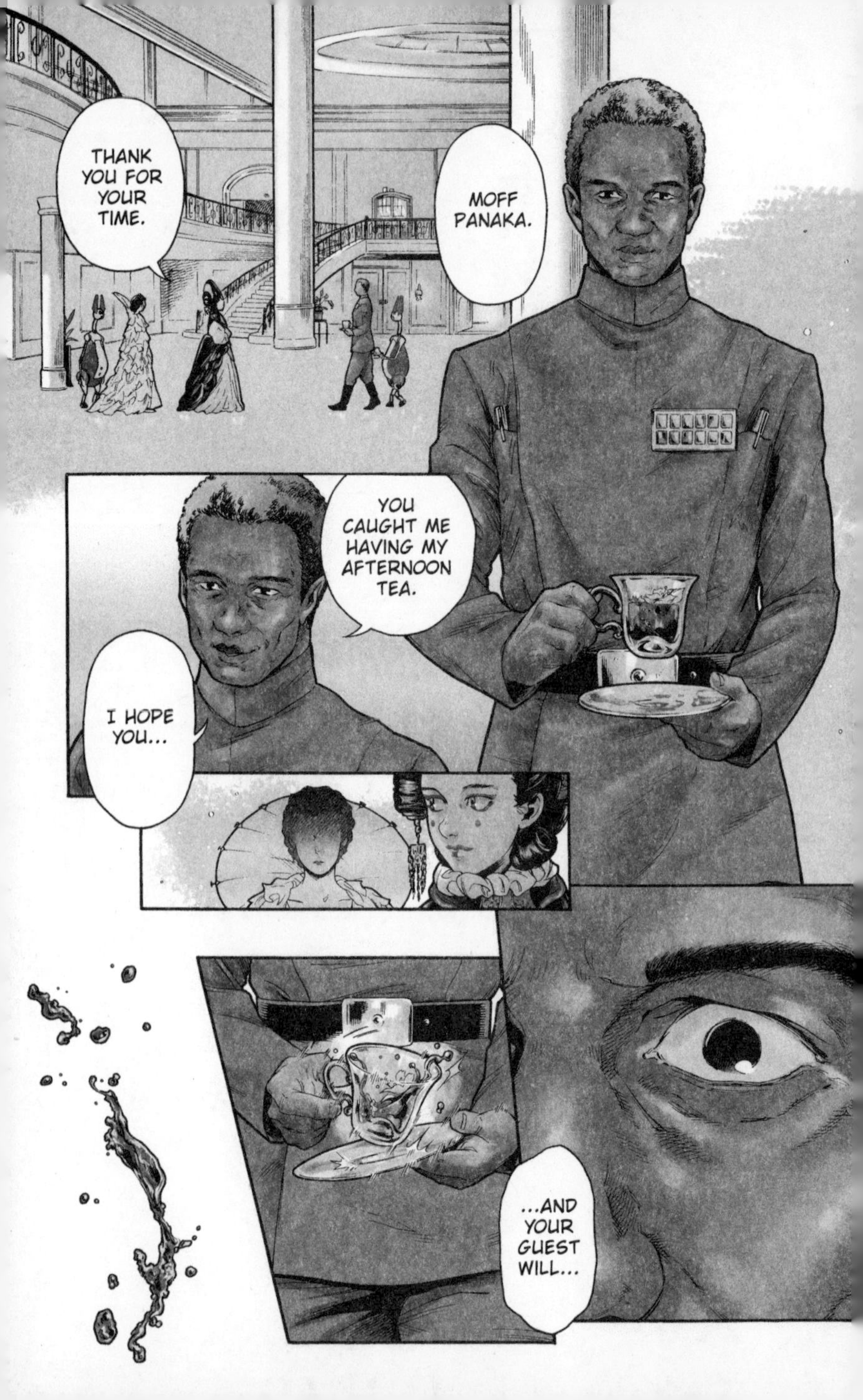
MOFF PANAKA.
THANK YOU FOR YOUR TIME.
YOU CAUGHT ME HAVING MY AFTERNOON TEA.
I HOPE YOU...
...AND YOUR GUEST WILL...

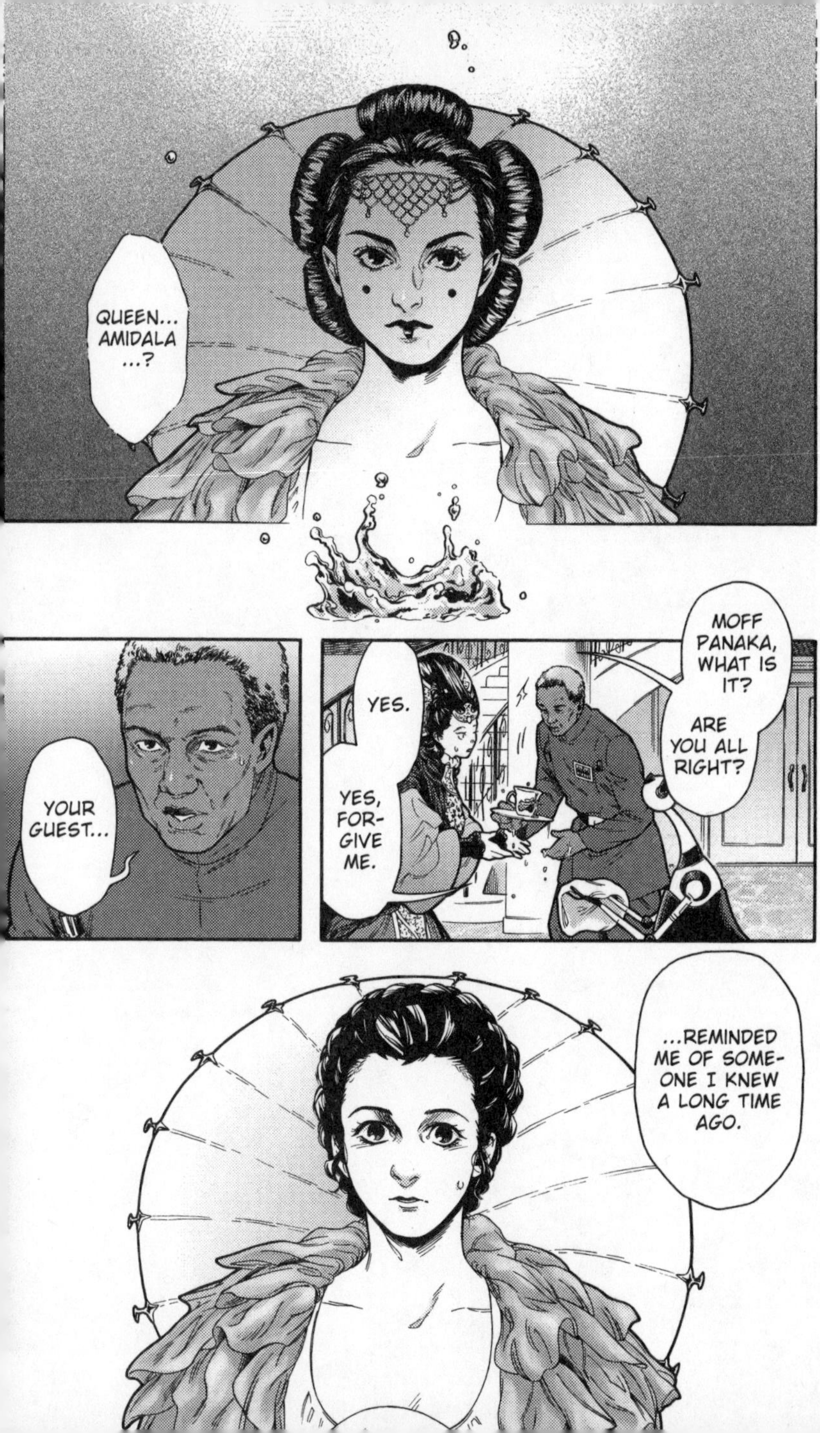
QUEEN... AMIDALA ...?
MOFF PANAKA, WHAT IS IT?
ARE YOU ALL RIGHT?
YES.
YES, FOR-GIVE ME.
YOUR GUEST...
...REMINDED ME OF SOME-ONE I KNEW A LONG TIME AGO.

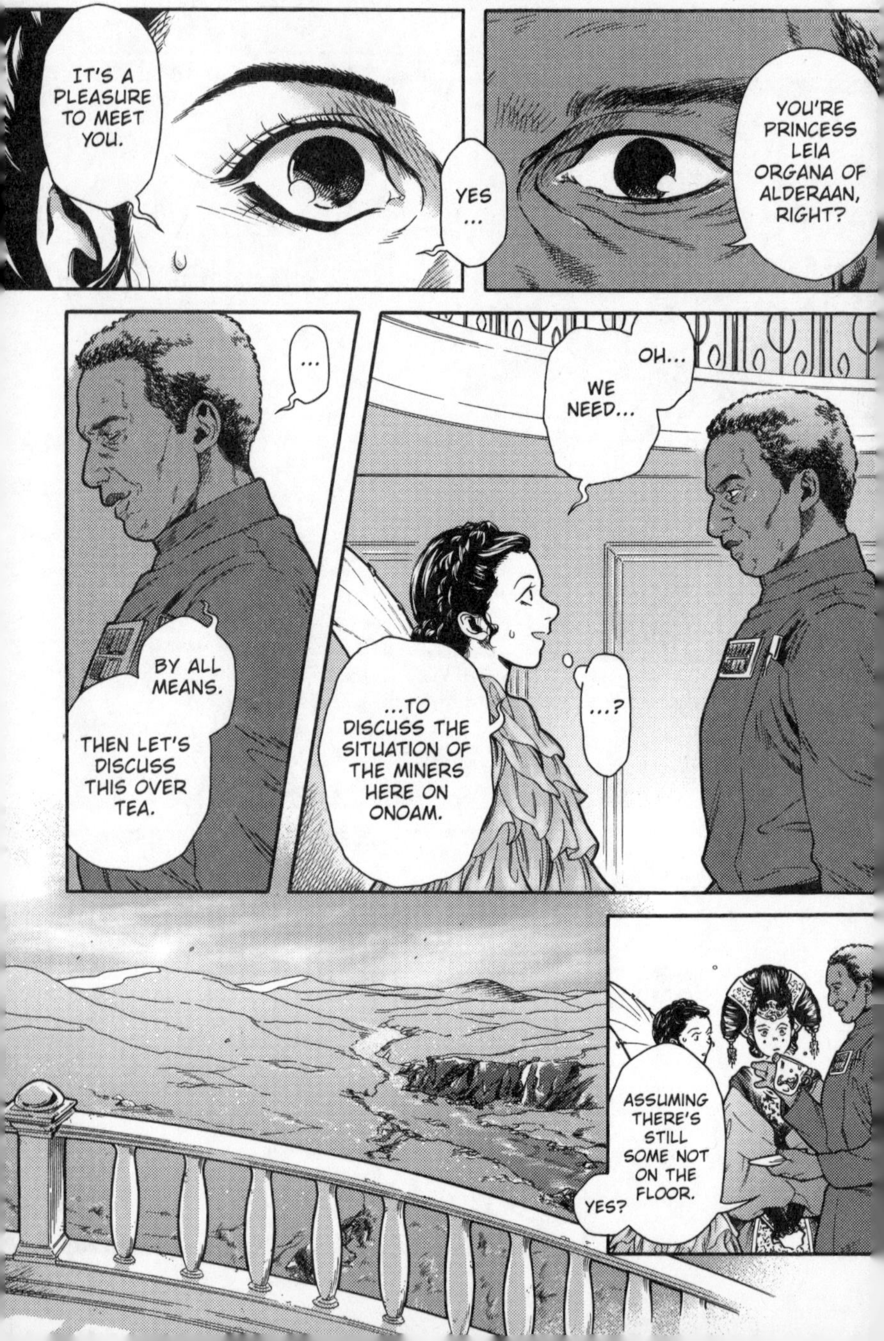
YOU'RE PRINCESS LEIA ORGANA OF ALDERAAN, RIGHT?
YES...
IT'S A PLEASURE TO MEET YOU.
OH...
WE NEED...
...?
...TO DISCUSS THE SITUATION OF THE MINERS HERE ON ONOAM.
...
BY ALL MEANS.
THEN LET'S DISCUSS THIS OVER TEA.
ASSUMING THERE'S STILL SOME NOT ON THE FLOOR.
YES?

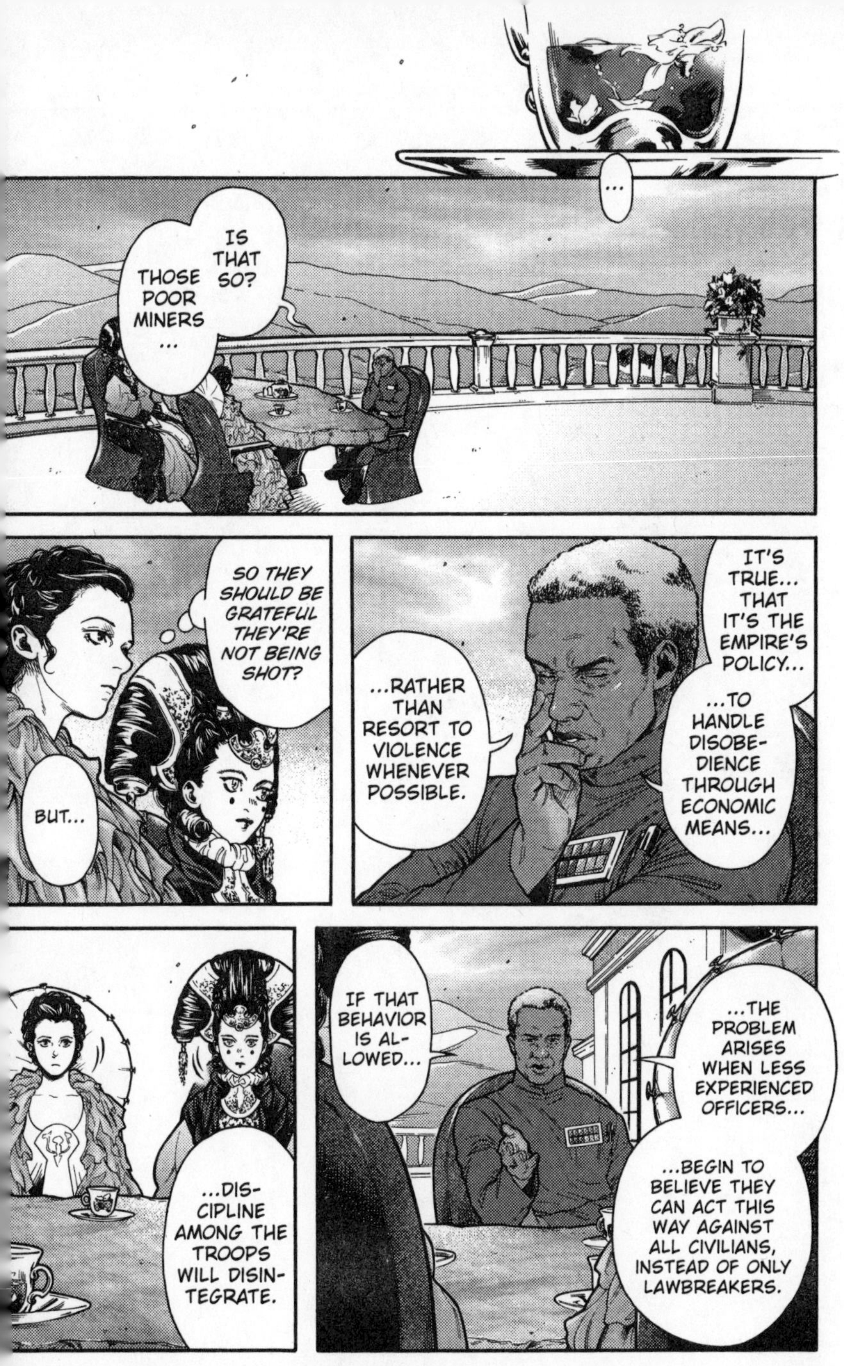
...
IS THAT SO?
THOSE POOR MINERS...
IT'S TRUE... THAT IT'S THE EMPIRE'S POLICY...
...TO HANDLE DISOBEDIENCE THROUGH ECONOMIC MEANS...
...RATHER THAN RESORT TO VIOLENCE WHENEVER POSSIBLE.
SO THEY SHOULD BE GRATEFUL THEY'RE NOT BEING SHOT?
BUT...
...THE PROBLEM ARISES WHEN LESS EXPERIENCED OFFICERS...
...BEGIN TO BELIEVE THEY CAN ACT THIS WAY AGAINST ALL CIVILIANS, INSTEAD OF ONLY LAWBREAKERS.
IF THAT BEHAVIOR IS ALLOWED...
...DISCIPLINE AMONG THE TROOPS WILL DISINTEGRATE.

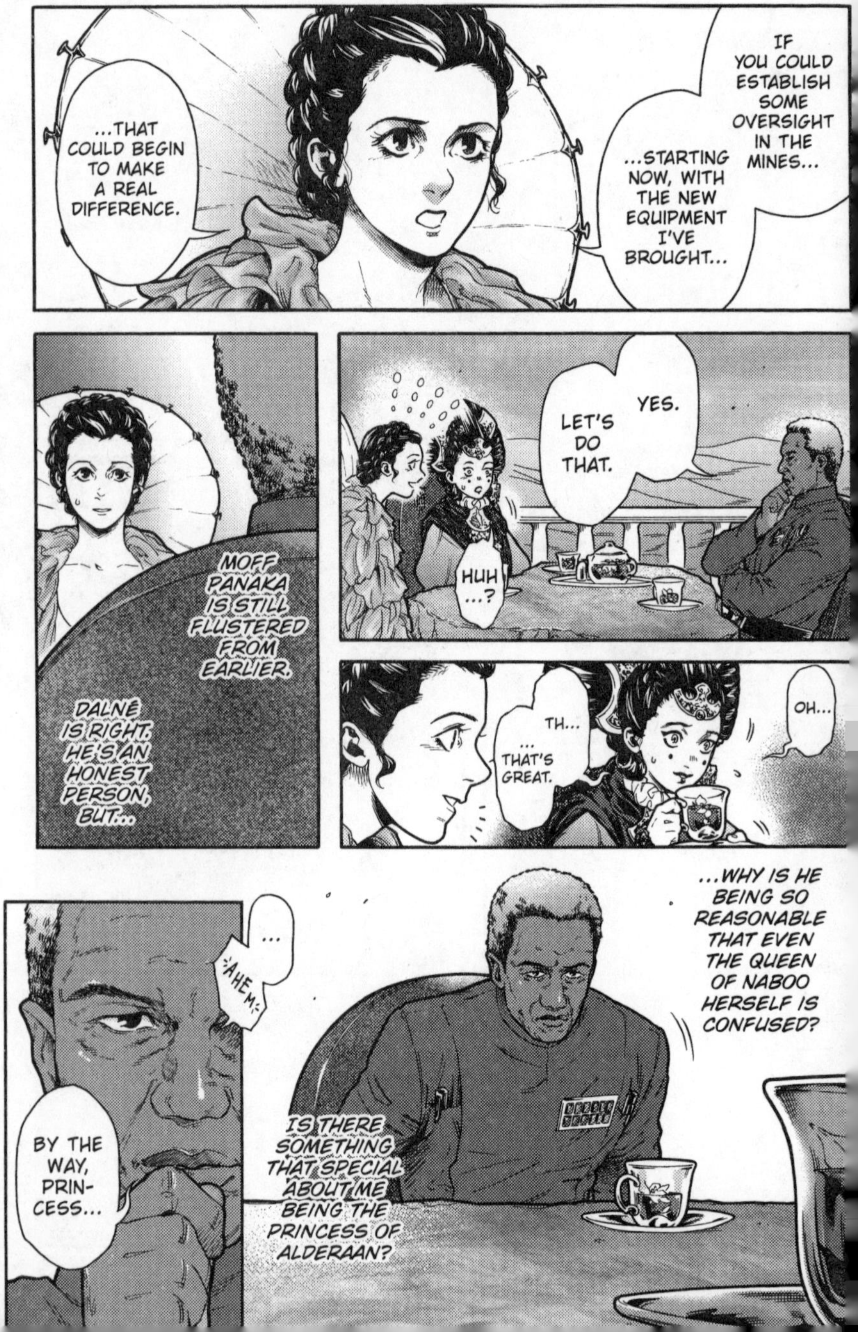
IF YOU COULD ESTABLISH SOME OVERSIGHT IN THE MINES...
...STARTING NOW, WITH THE NEW EQUIPMENT I'VE BROUGHT...
...THAT COULD BEGIN TO MAKE A REAL DIFFERENCE.
YES. LET'S DO THAT.
HUH ...?
OH...
TH... ... THAT'S GREAT.
MOFF PANAKA IS STILL FLUSTERED FROM EARLIER.
DALNÉ IS RIGHT. HE'S AN HONEST PERSON, BUT...
...WHY IS HE BEING SO REASONABLE THAT EVEN THE QUEEN OF NABOO HERSELF IS CONFUSED?
IS THERE SOMETHING THAT SPECIAL ABOUT ME BEING THE PRINCESS OF ALDERAAN?
...
AHEM
BY THE WAY, PRINCESS...

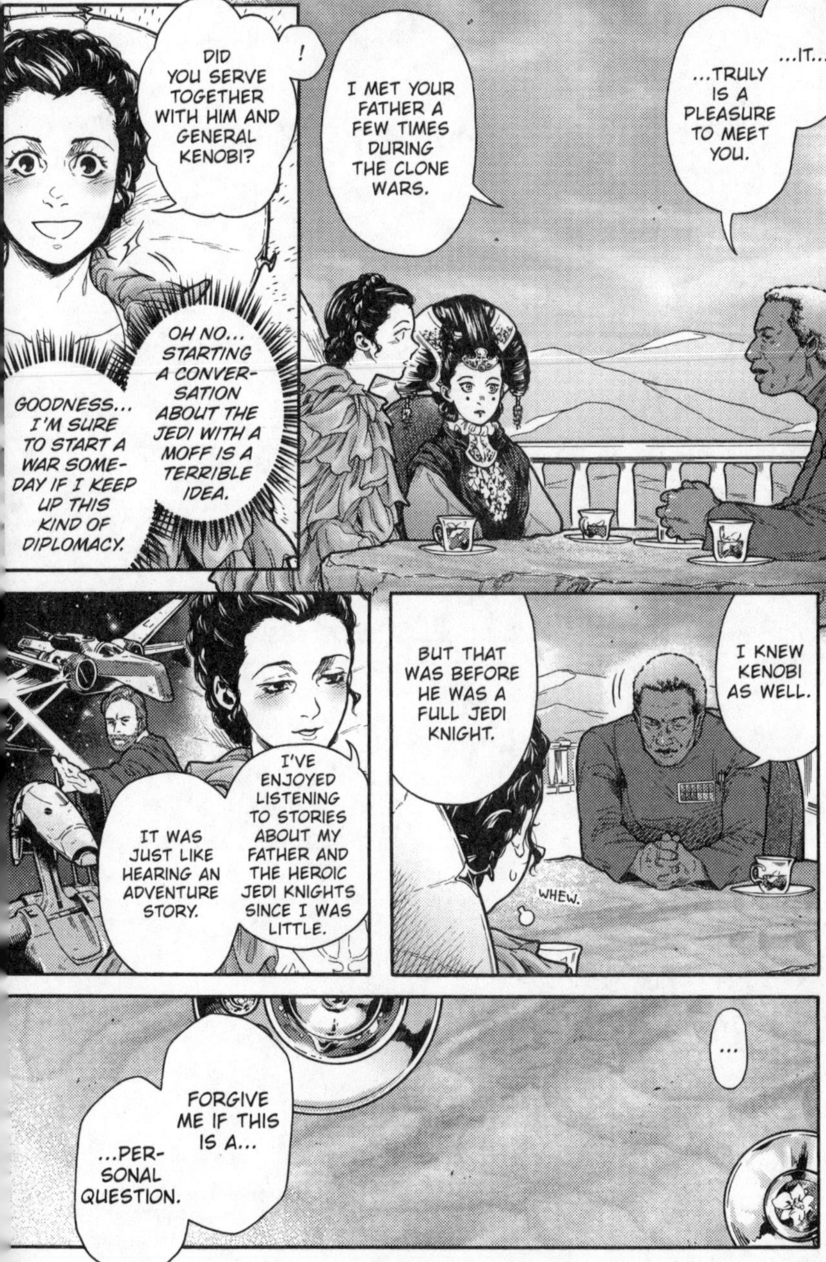
...IT...
...TRULY IS A PLEASURE TO MEET YOU.
I MET YOUR FATHER A FEW TIMES DURING THE CLONE WARS.
!
DID YOU SERVE TOGETHER WITH HIM AND GENERAL KENOBI?
OH NO... STARTING A CONVER-SATION ABOUT THE JEDI WITH A MOFF IS A TERRIBLE IDEA.
GOODNESS... I'M SURE TO START A WAR SOME-DAY IF I KEEP UP THIS KIND OF DIPLOMACY.
I KNEW KENOBI AS WELL.
BUT THAT WAS BEFORE HE WAS A FULL JEDI KNIGHT.
WHEW.
I'VE ENJOYED LISTENING TO STORIES ABOUT MY FATHER AND THE HEROIC JEDI KNIGHTS SINCE I WAS LITTLE.
IT WAS JUST LIKE HEARING AN ADVENTURE STORY.
...
FORGIVE ME IF THIS IS A...
...PER-SONAL QUESTION.

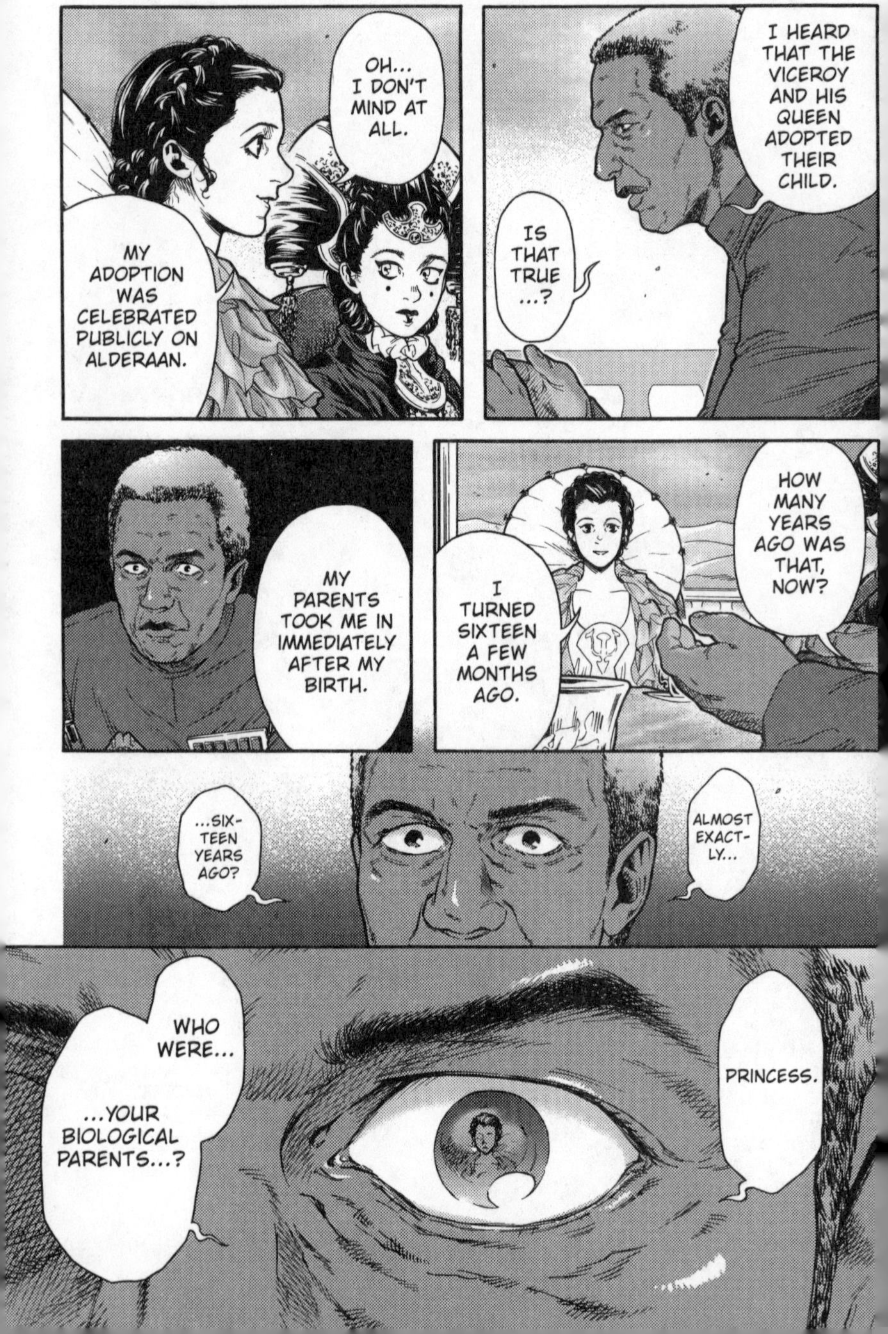
I HEARD THAT THE VICEROY AND HIS QUEEN ADOPTED THEIR CHILD.
IS THAT TRUE ...?
OH... I DON'T MIND AT ALL.
MY ADOPTION WAS CELEBRATED PUBLICLY ON ALDERAAN.
HOW MANY YEARS AGO WAS THAT, NOW?
I TURNED SIXTEEN A FEW MONTHS AGO.
MY PARENTS TOOK ME IN IMMEDIATELY AFTER MY BIRTH.
ALMOST EXACT-LY...
...SIX-TEEN YEARS AGO?
PRINCESS.
WHO WERE...
...YOUR BIOLOGICAL PARENTS...?

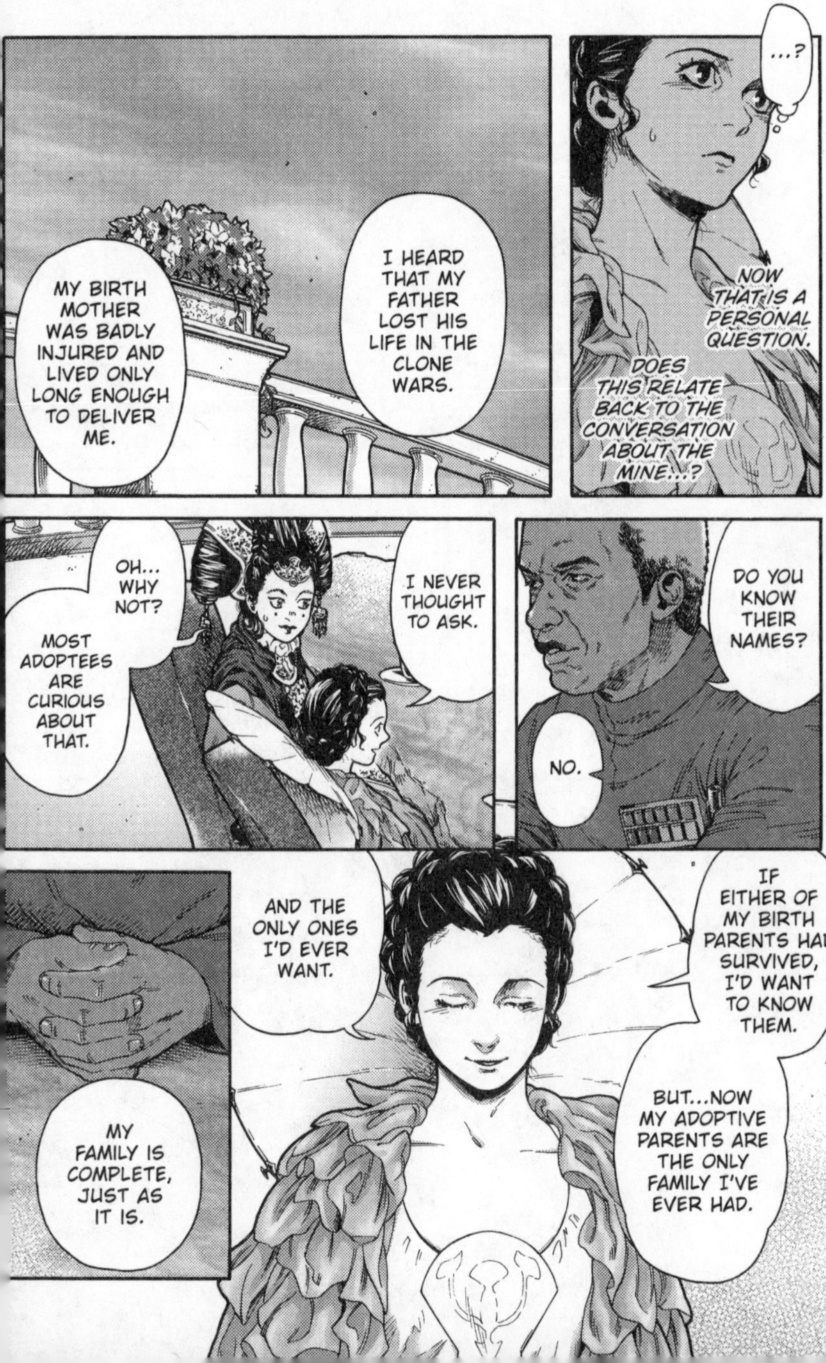
...?
NOW THAT IS A PERSONAL QUESTION.
DOES THIS RELATE BACK TO THE CONVERSATION ABOUT THE MINE...?
I HEARD THAT MY FATHER LOST HIS LIFE IN THE CLONE WARS.
MY BIRTH MOTHER WAS BADLY INJURED AND LIVED ONLY LONG ENOUGH TO DELIVER ME.
DO YOU KNOW THEIR NAMES?
NO.
I NEVER THOUGHT TO ASK.
OH... WHY NOT?
MOST ADOPTEES ARE CURIOUS ABOUT THAT.
IF EITHER OF MY BIRTH PARENTS HAD SURVIVED, I'D WANT TO KNOW THEM.
BUT...NOW MY ADOPTIVE PARENTS ARE THE ONLY FAMILY I'VE EVER HAD.
AND THE ONLY ONES I'D EVER WANT.
MY FAMILY IS COMPLETE, JUST AS IT IS.

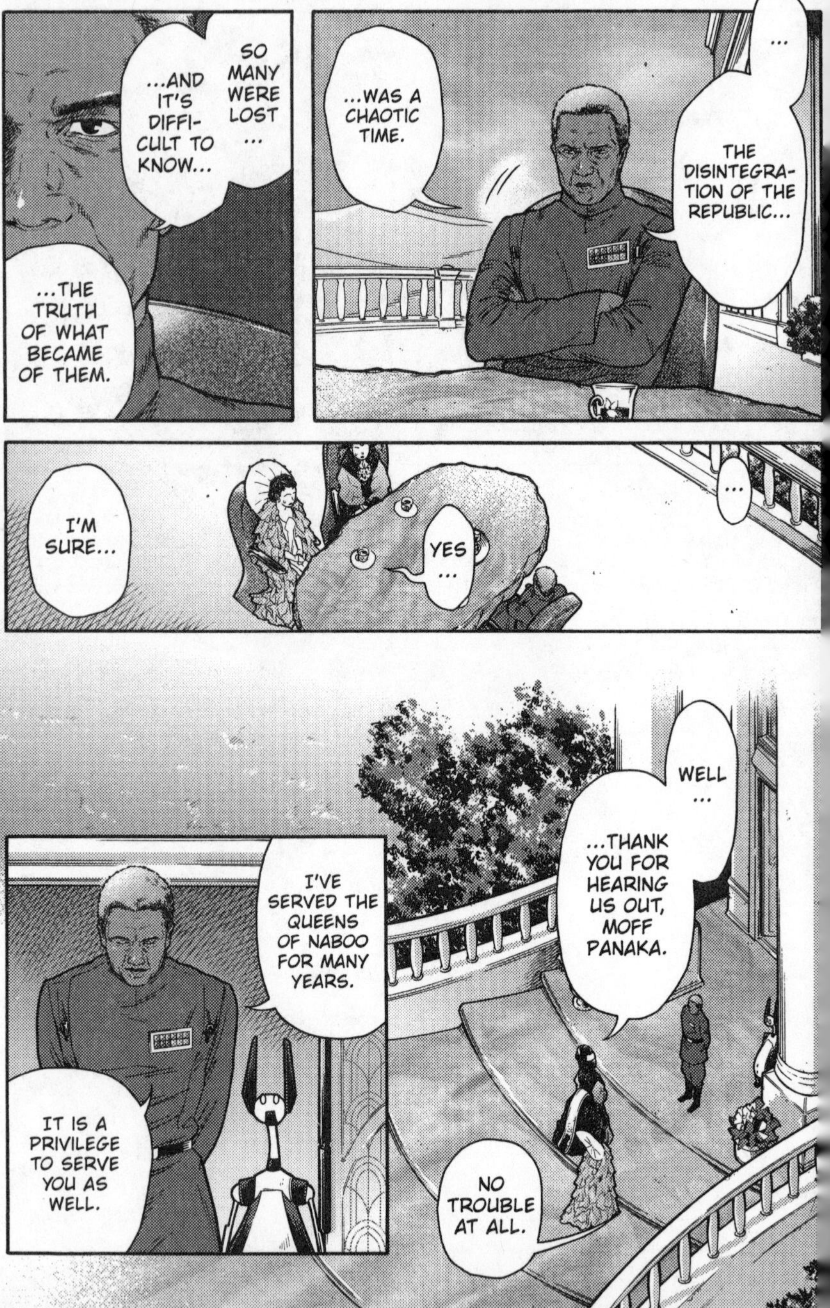
...
THE DISINTEGRATION OF THE REPUBLIC...
...WAS A CHAOTIC TIME.
SO MANY WERE LOST ...
...AND IT'S DIFFICULT TO KNOW...
...THE TRUTH OF WHAT BECAME OF THEM.
...
YES ...
I'M SURE...
WELL ...
...THANK YOU FOR HEARING US OUT, MOFF PANAKA.
NO TROUBLE AT ALL.
I'VE SERVED THE QUEENS OF NABOO FOR MANY YEARS.
IT IS A PRIVILEGE TO SERVE YOU AS WELL.

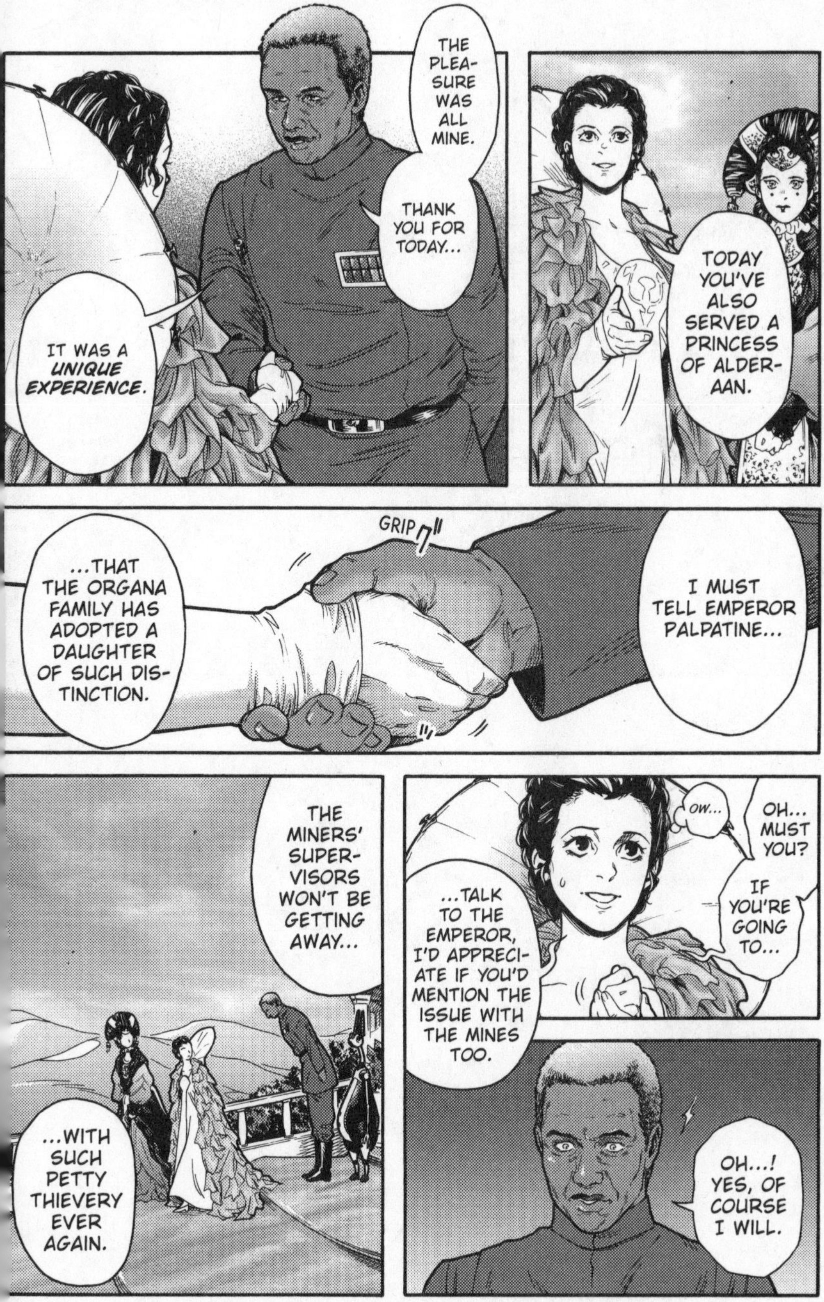
TODAY YOU'VE ALSO SERVED A PRINCESS OF ALDER-AAN.
THE PLEA-SURE WAS ALL MINE.
THANK YOU FOR TODAY...
IT WAS A ***UNIQUE EXPERIENCE***.
I MUST TELL EMPEROR PALPATINE...
GRIP
...THAT THE ORGANA FAMILY HAS ADOPTED A DAUGHTER OF SUCH DIS-TINCTION.
OW...
OH... MUST YOU?
IF YOU'RE GOING TO...
...TALK TO THE EMPEROR, I'D APPRECI-ATE IF YOU'D MENTION THE ISSUE WITH THE MINES TOO.
OH...! YES, OF COURSE I WILL.
THE MINERS' SUPER-VISORS WON'T BE GETTING AWAY...
...WITH SUCH PETTY THIEVERY EVER AGAIN.

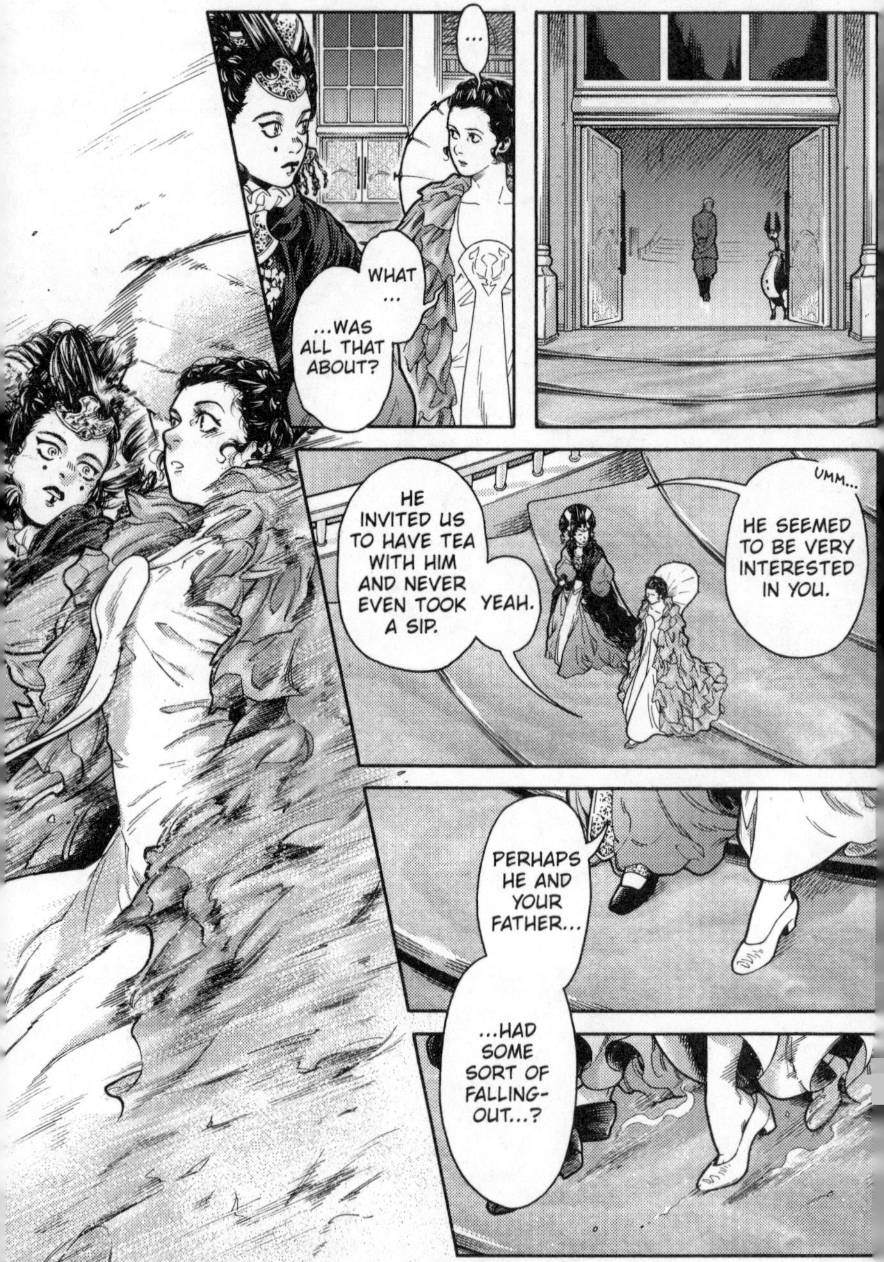
...
WHAT ... ...WAS ALL THAT ABOUT?
UMM...
HE SEEMED TO BE VERY INTERESTED IN YOU.
YEAH.
HE INVITED US TO HAVE TEA WITH HIM AND NEVER EVEN TOOK A SIP.
PERHAPS HE AND YOUR FATHER...
...HAD SOME SORT OF FALLING-OUT...?

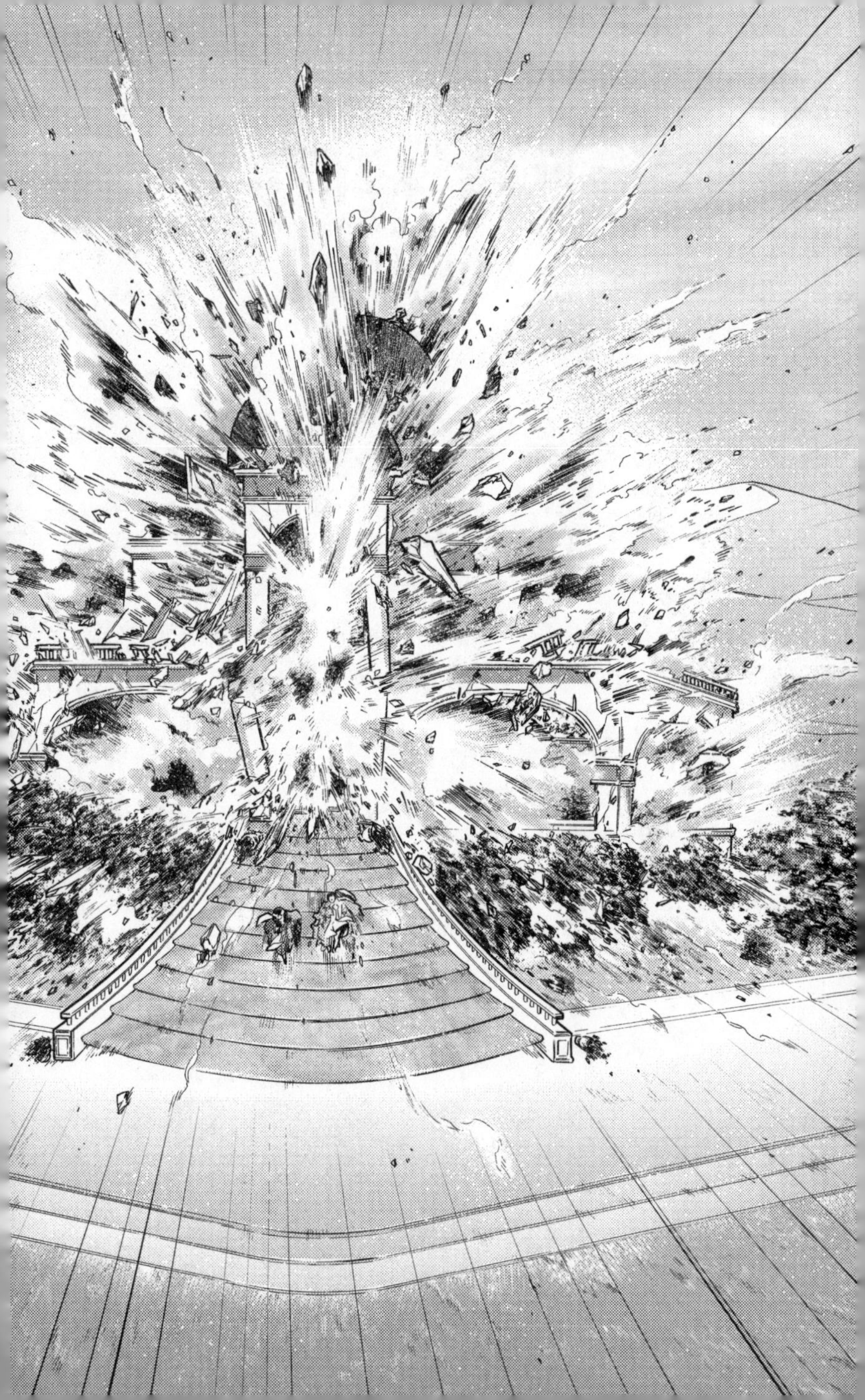

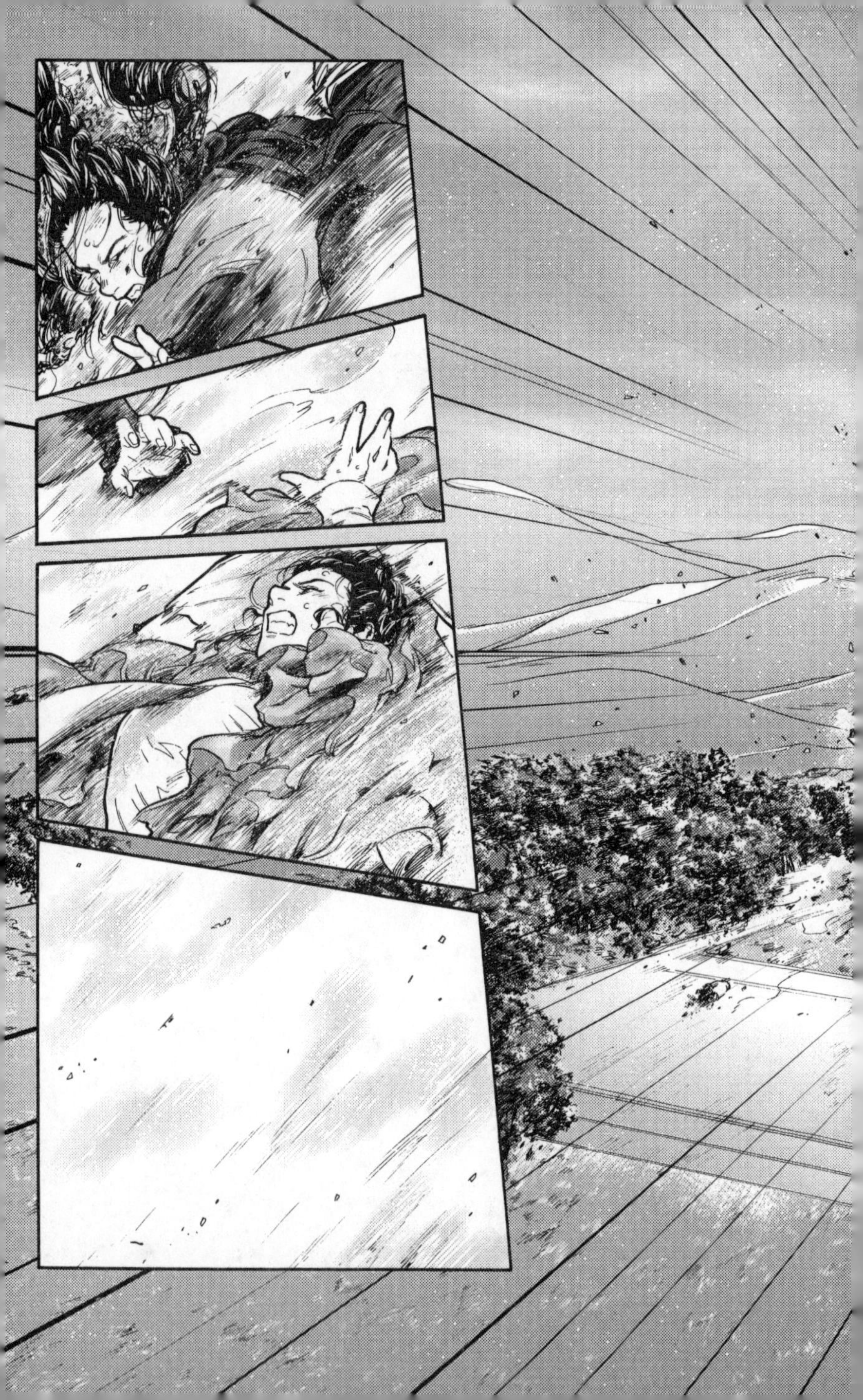

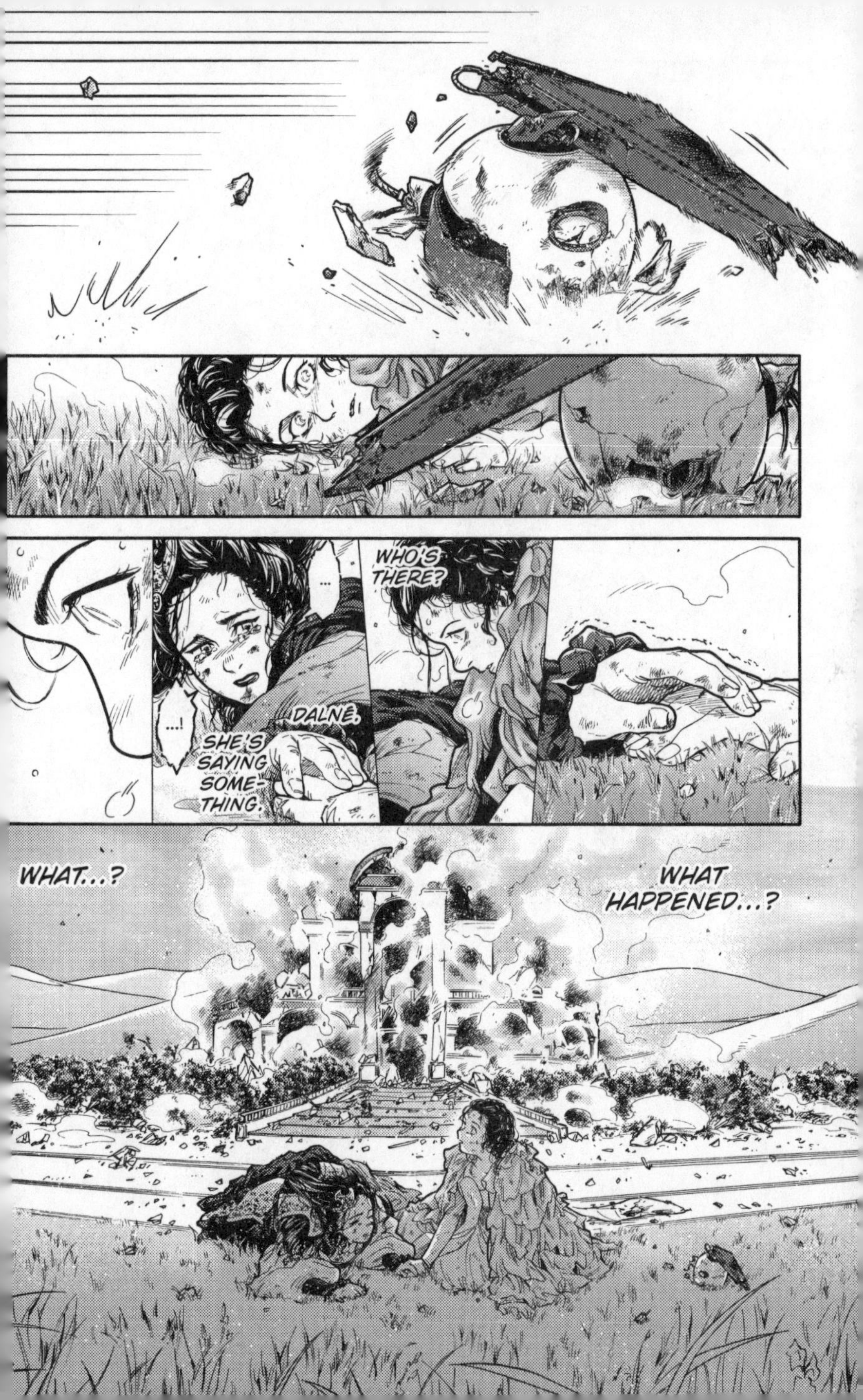
WHO'S THERE?
...
DALNE.
...!
SHE'S SAYING SOME-THING.
WHAT HAPPENED...?
WHAT...?

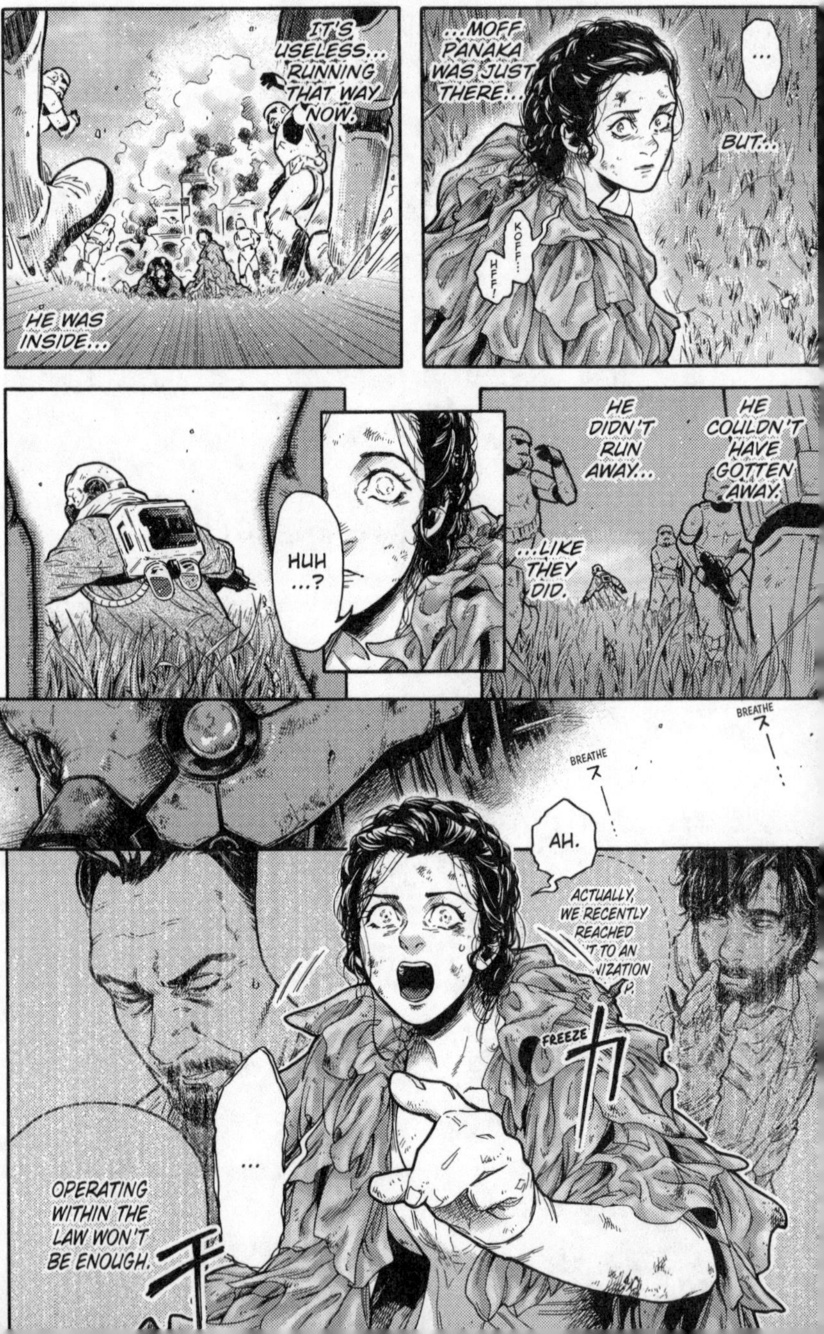
...
...MOFF PANAKA WAS JUST THERE...
BUT...
KOFF... HFF!
IT'S USELESS... RUNNING THAT WAY NOW.
HE WAS INSIDE...
HE COULDN'T HAVE GOTTEN AWAY.
HE DIDN'T RUN AWAY...
...LIKE THEY DID.
HUH ...?
BREATHE ス—...
BREATHE ス—...
AH.
ACTUALLY, WE RECENTLY REACHED
FREEZE カ
...
OPERATING WITHIN THE LAW WON'T BE ENOUGH.

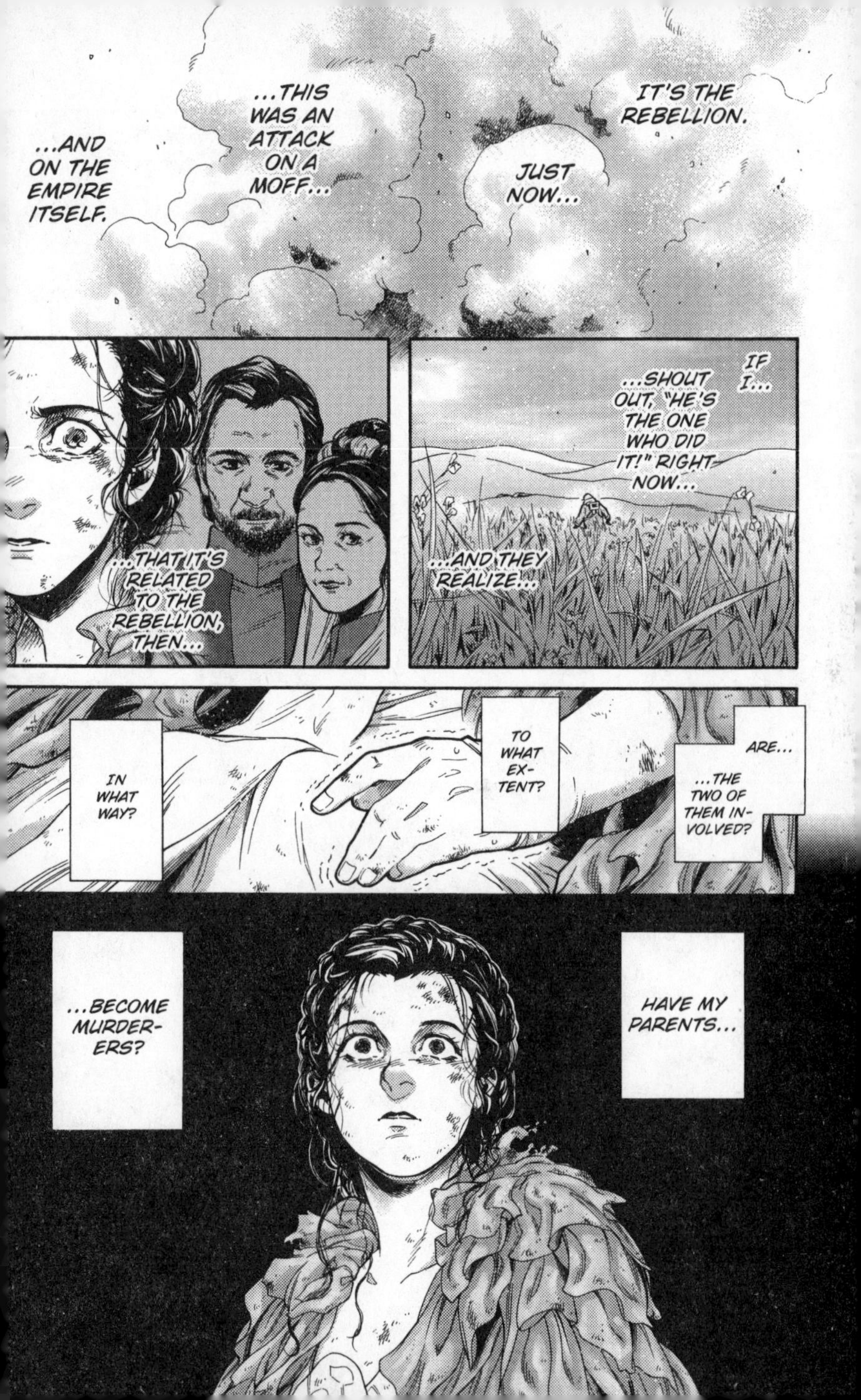
IT'S THE REBELLION.
JUST NOW...
...THIS WAS AN ATTACK ON A MOFF...
...AND ON THE EMPIRE ITSELF.
IF I...
...SHOUT OUT, "HE'S THE ONE WHO DID IT!" RIGHT NOW...
...AND THEY REALIZE...
...THAT IT'S RELATED TO THE REBELLION, THEN...
ARE...
...THE TWO OF THEM IN-VOLVED?
TO WHAT EX-TENT?
IN WHAT WAY?
HAVE MY PARENTS...
...BECOME MURDER-ERS?

STAR WARS

LEIA

Princess of

Alderaan

STAR WARS

LEIA

Princess of

Alderaan

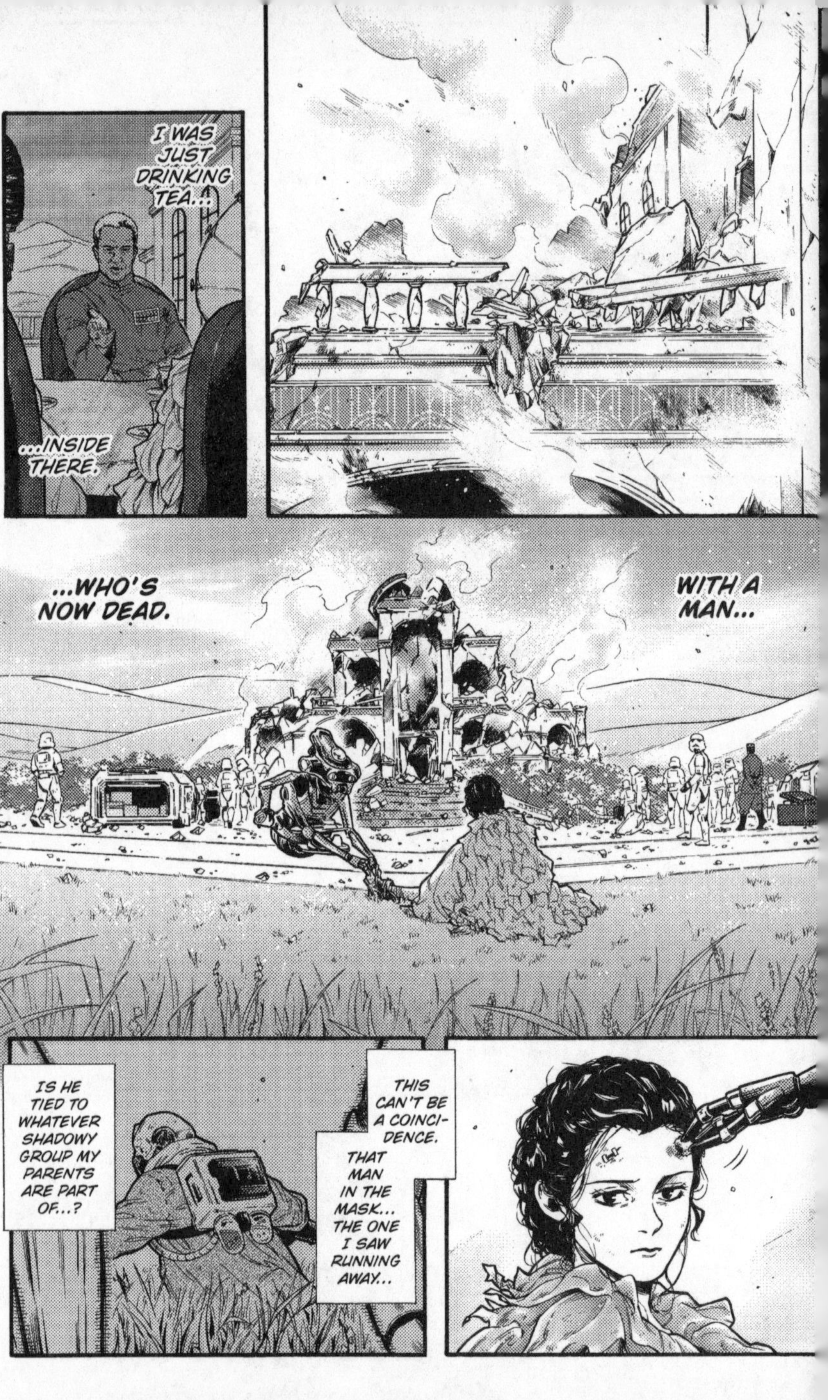
I WAS JUST DRINKING TEA...
...INSIDE THERE.
WITH A MAN...
...WHO'S NOW DEAD.
THIS CAN'T BE A COINCIDENCE.
THAT MAN IN THE MASK... THE ONE I SAW RUNNING AWAY...
IS HE TIED TO WHATEVER SHADOWY GROUP MY PARENTS ARE PART OF...?

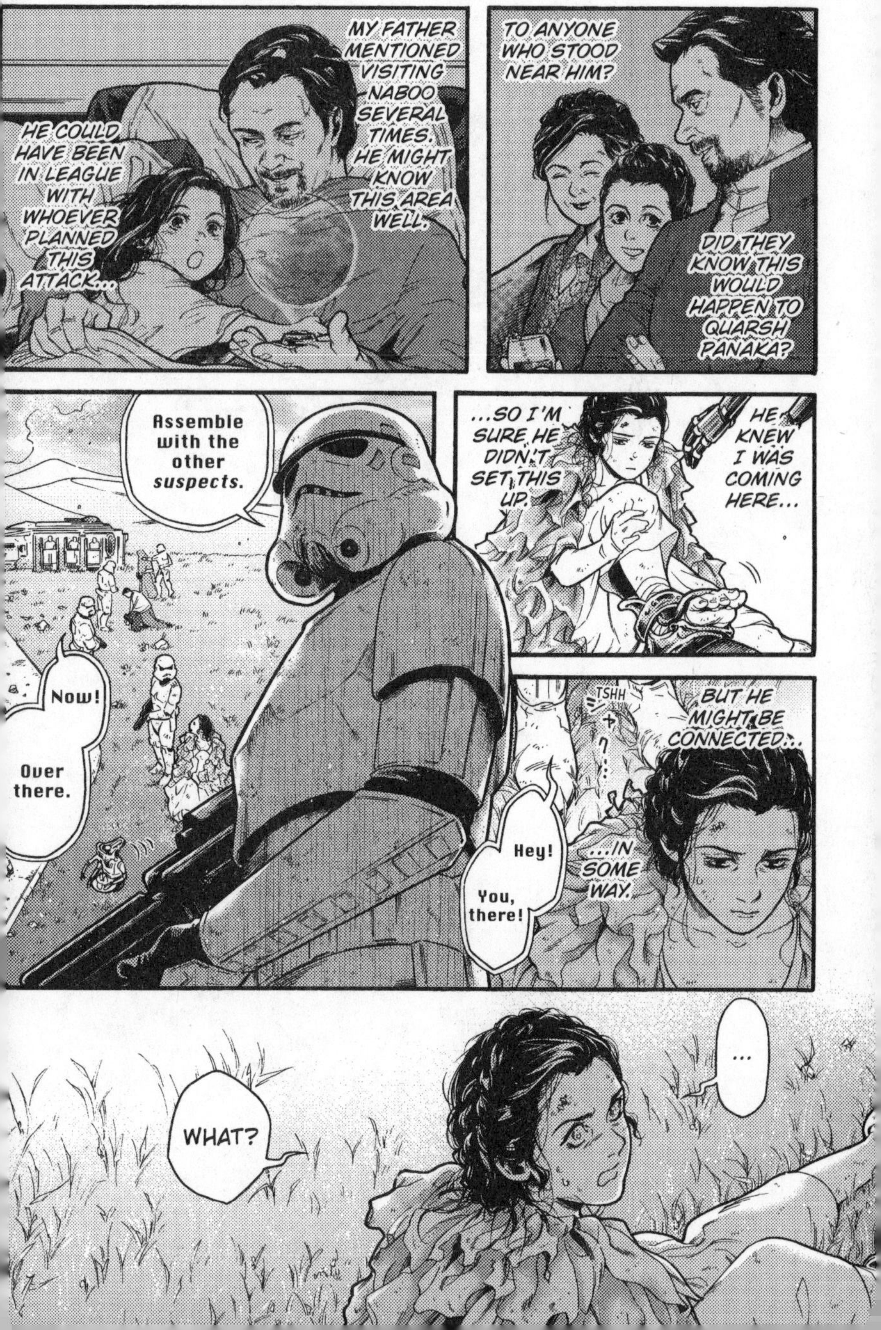
TO ANYONE WHO STOOD NEAR HIM?
DID THEY KNOW THIS WOULD HAPPEN TO QUARSH PANAKA?
MY FATHER MENTIONED VISITING NABOO SEVERAL TIMES. HE MIGHT KNOW THIS AREA WELL.
HE COULD HAVE BEEN IN LEAGUE WITH WHOEVER PLANNED THIS ATTACK...
HE KNEW I WAS COMING HERE...
...SO I'M SURE HE DIDN'T SET THIS UP.
BUT HE MIGHT BE CONNECTED...
TSHH
...IN SOME WAY.
Hey!
You, there!
Assemble with the other *suspects*.
Now!
Over there.
...
WHAT?

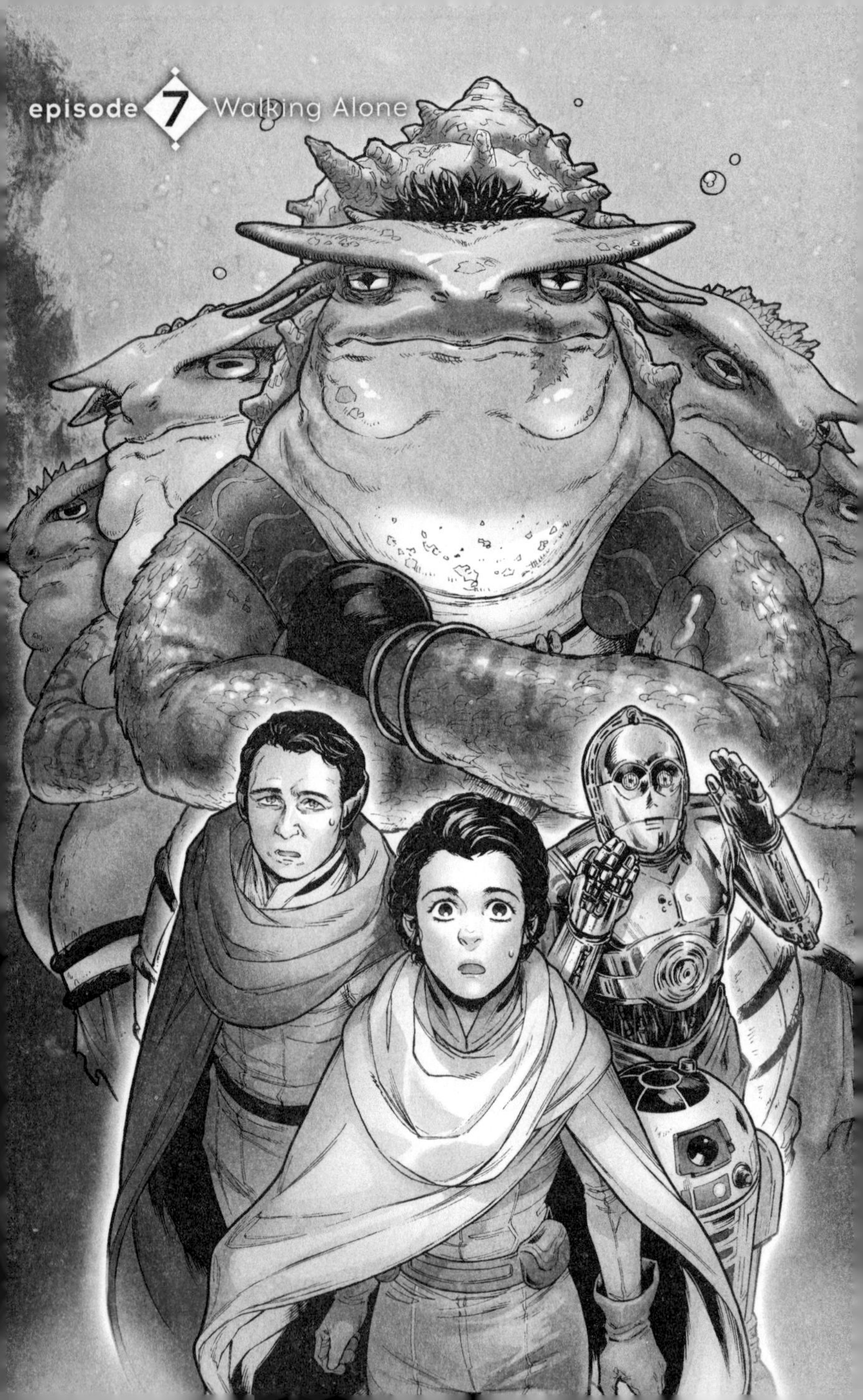
episode 7 Walking Alone

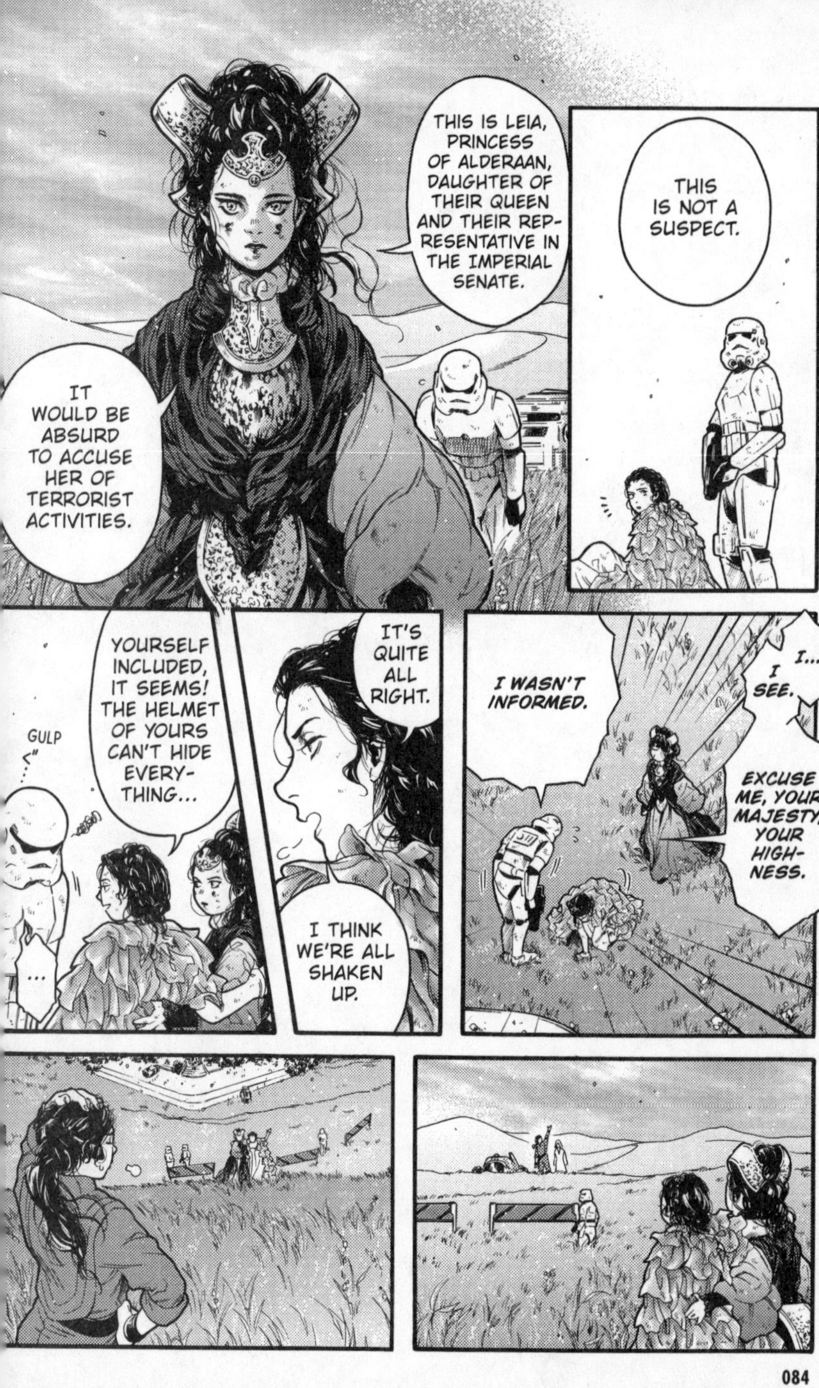
THIS IS NOT A SUSPECT.
THIS IS LEIA, PRINCESS OF ALDERAAN, DAUGHTER OF THEIR QUEEN AND THEIR REP-RESENTATIVE IN THE IMPERIAL SENATE.
IT WOULD BE ABSURD TO ACCUSE HER OF TERRORIST ACTIVITIES.
I... I SEE.
I WASN'T INFORMED.
EXCUSE ME, YOUR MAJESTY, YOUR HIGH-NESS.
IT'S QUITE ALL RIGHT.
I THINK WE'RE ALL SHAKEN UP.
YOURSELF INCLUDED, IT SEEMS! THE HELMET OF YOURS CAN'T HIDE EVERY-THING...
GULP
...

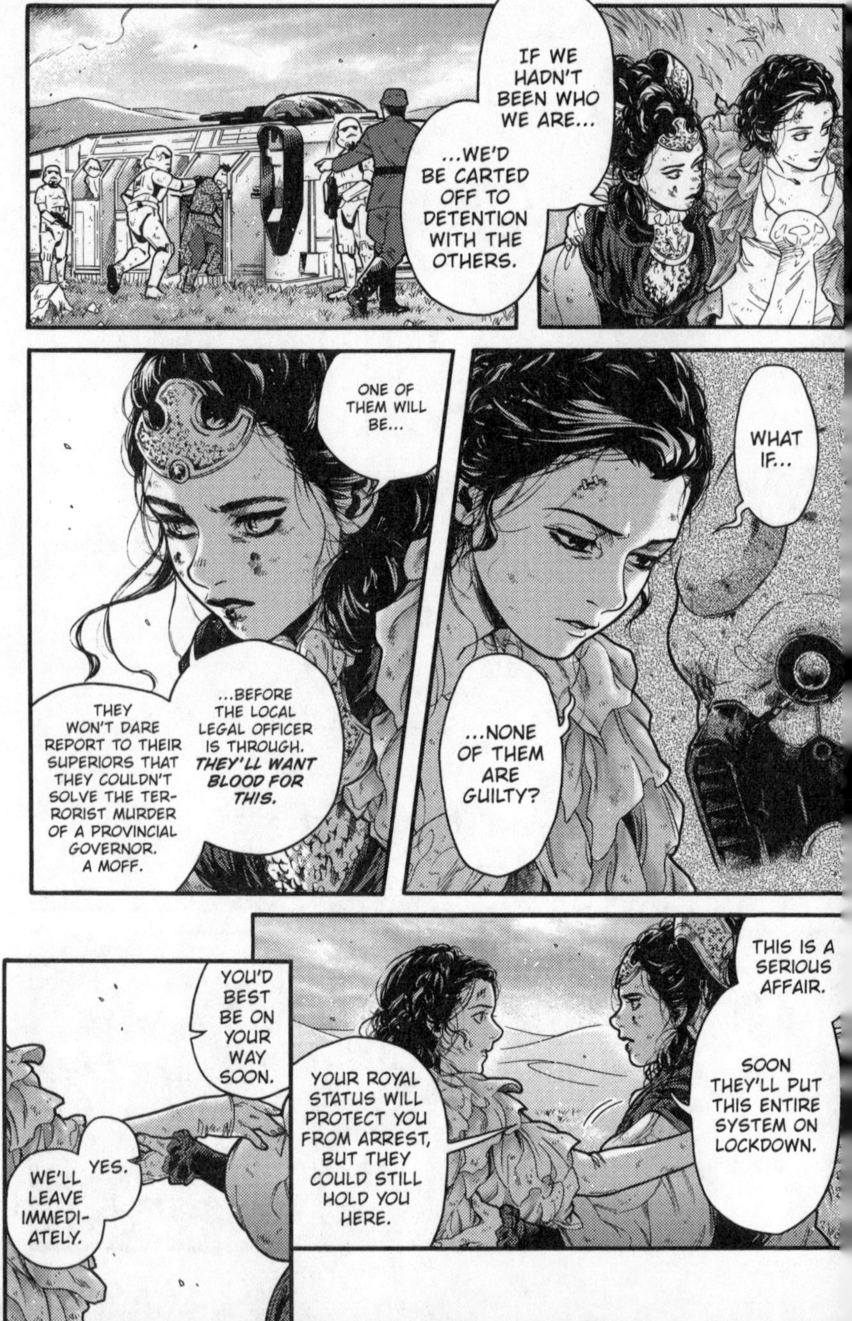

IF WE HADN'T BEEN WHO WE ARE...
...WE'D BE CARTED OFF TO DETENTION WITH THE OTHERS.
WHAT IF...
...NONE OF THEM ARE GUILTY?
ONE OF THEM WILL BE...
THEY WON'T DARE REPORT TO THEIR SUPERIORS THAT THEY COULDN'T SOLVE THE TERRORIST MURDER OF A PROVINCIAL GOVERNOR. A MOFF.
...BEFORE THE LOCAL LEGAL OFFICER IS THROUGH. *THEY'LL WANT BLOOD FOR THIS.*
THIS IS A SERIOUS AFFAIR.
SOON THEY'LL PUT THIS ENTIRE SYSTEM ON LOCKDOWN.
YOUR ROYAL STATUS WILL PROTECT YOU FROM ARREST, BUT THEY COULD STILL HOLD YOU HERE.
YOU'D BEST BE ON YOUR WAY SOON.
YES.
WE'LL LEAVE IMMEDIATELY.

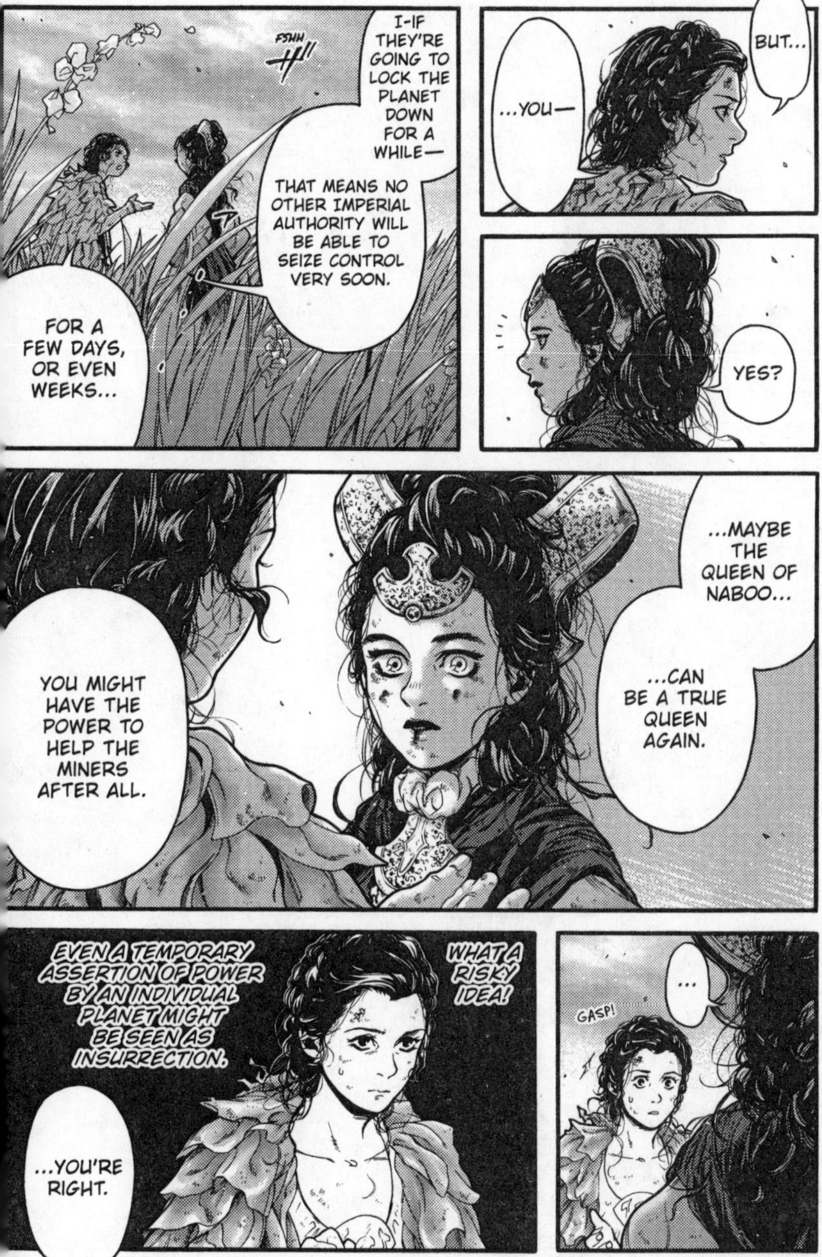
BUT...
...YOU—
YES?
I-IF THEY'RE GOING TO LOCK THE PLANET DOWN FOR A WHILE—
FSHH
THAT MEANS NO OTHER IMPERIAL AUTHORITY WILL BE ABLE TO SEIZE CONTROL VERY SOON.
FOR A FEW DAYS, OR EVEN WEEKS...
...MAYBE THE QUEEN OF NABOO...
...CAN BE A TRUE QUEEN AGAIN.
YOU MIGHT HAVE THE POWER TO HELP THE MINERS AFTER ALL.
...
GASP!
WHAT A RISKY IDEA!
EVEN A TEMPORARY ASSERTION OF POWER BY AN INDIVIDUAL PLANET MIGHT BE SEEN AS INSURRECTION.
...YOU'RE RIGHT.

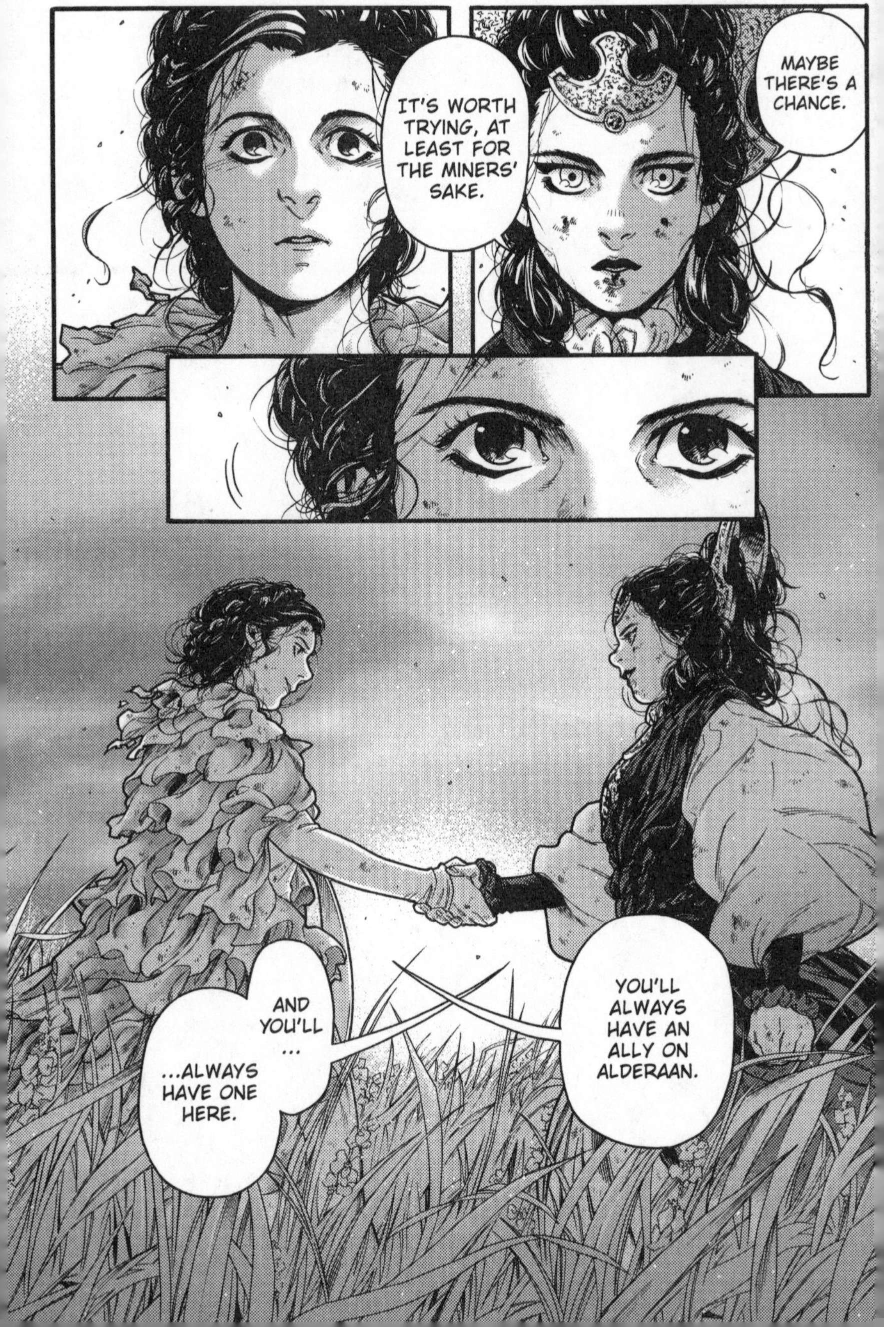
MAYBE THERE'S A CHANCE.
IT'S WORTH TRYING, AT LEAST FOR THE MINERS' SAKE.
YOU'LL ALWAYS HAVE AN ALLY ON ALDERAAN.
AND YOU'LL ...
...ALWAYS HAVE ONE HERE.

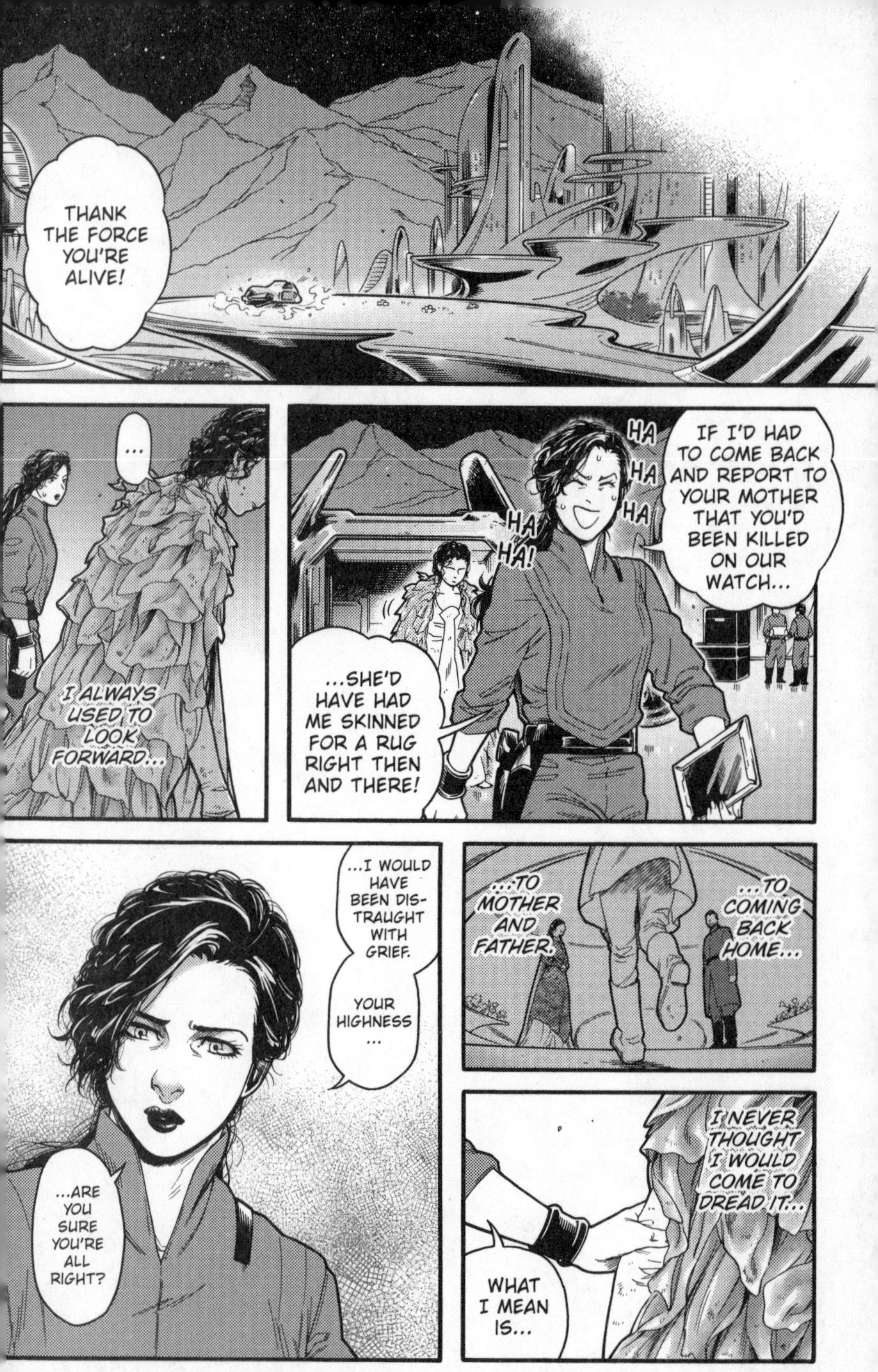
THANK THE FORCE YOU'RE ALIVE!
HA HA HA HA HA!
IF I'D HAD TO COME BACK AND REPORT TO YOUR MOTHER THAT YOU'D BEEN KILLED ON OUR WATCH...
...SHE'D HAVE HAD ME SKINNED FOR A RUG RIGHT THEN AND THERE!
...
I ALWAYS USED TO LOOK FORWARD...
...TO COMING BACK HOME...
...TO MOTHER AND FATHER.
I NEVER THOUGHT I WOULD COME TO DREAD IT...
WHAT I MEAN IS...
...I WOULD HAVE BEEN DIS-TRAUGHT WITH GRIEF.
YOUR HIGHNESS ...
...ARE YOU SURE YOU'RE ALL RIGHT?

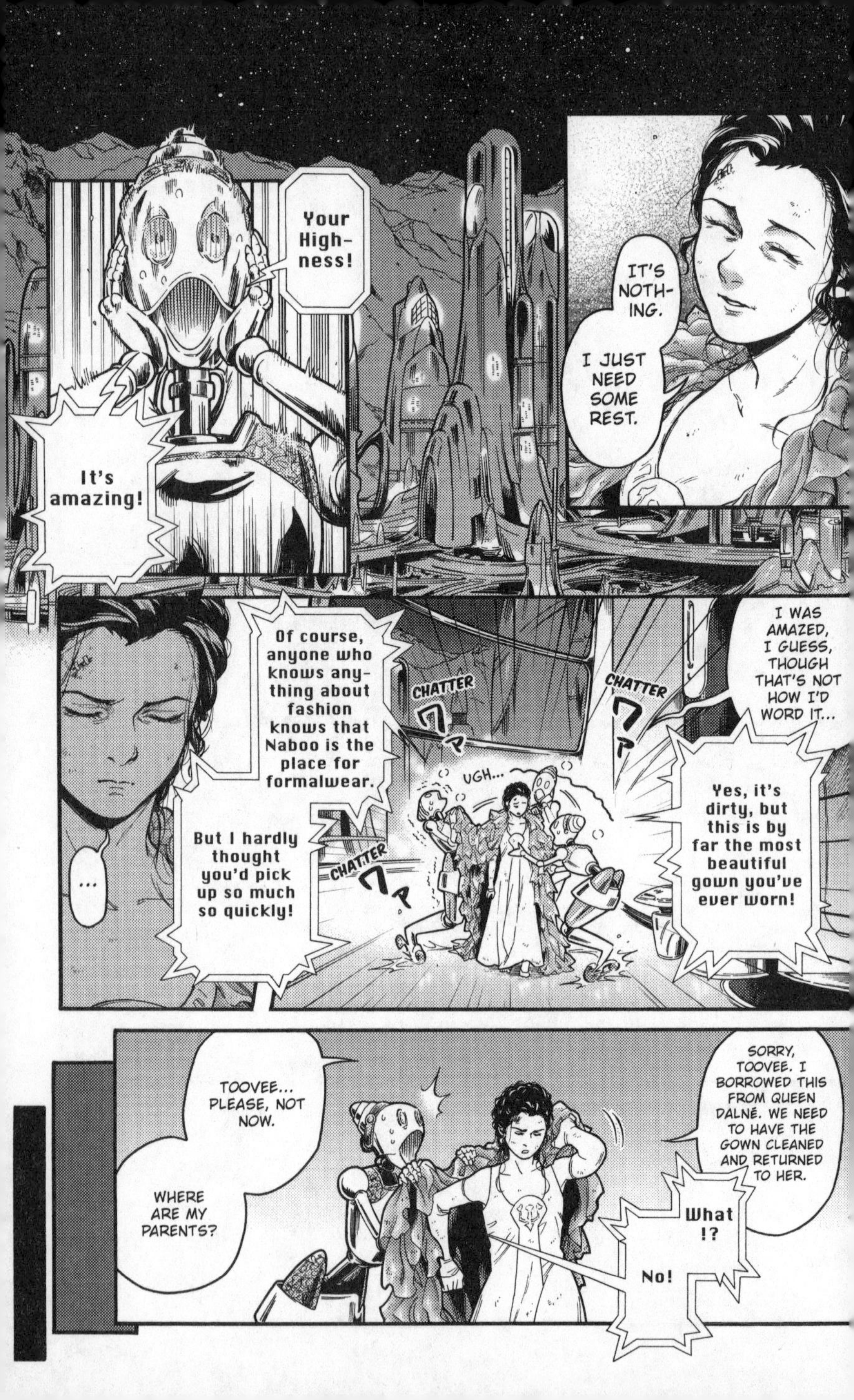
IT'S NOTHING.
I JUST NEED SOME REST.
Your Highness!
It's amazing!
I WAS AMAZED, I GUESS, THOUGH THAT'S NOT HOW I'D WORD IT...
Yes, it's dirty, but this is by far the most beautiful gown you've ever worn!
CHATTER
Of course, anyone who knows anything about fashion knows that Naboo is the place for formalwear.
CHATTER
UGH...
But I hardly thought you'd pick up so much so quickly!
CHATTER
...
SORRY, TOOVEE. I BORROWED THIS FROM QUEEN DALNÉ. WE NEED TO HAVE THE GOWN CLEANED AND RETURNED TO HER.
What!?
No!
TOOVEE... PLEASE, NOT NOW.
WHERE ARE MY PARENTS?

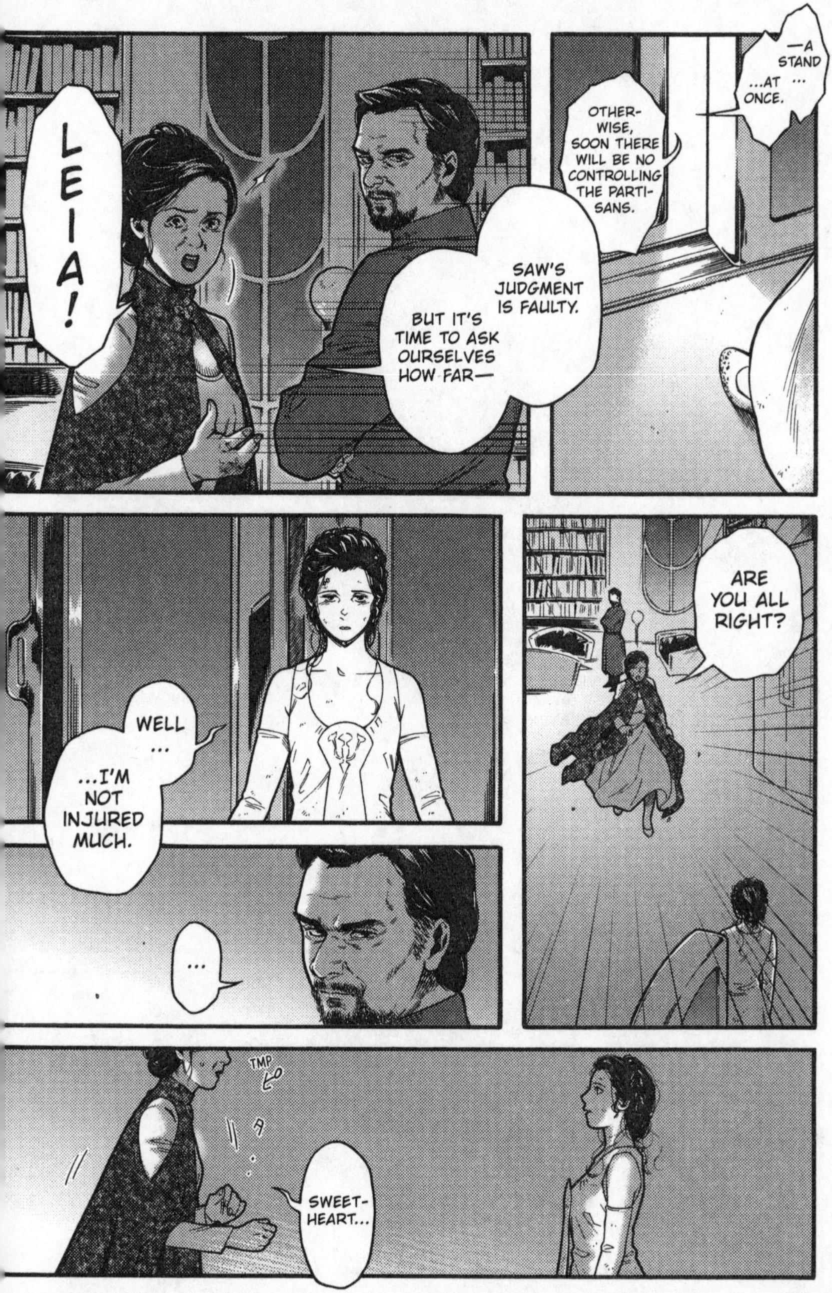
—A STAND ... ...AT ONCE.
OTHER-WISE, SOON THERE WILL BE NO CONTROLLING THE PARTI-SANS.
SAW'S JUDGMENT IS FAULTY.
BUT IT'S TIME TO ASK OURSELVES HOW FAR—
LEIA!
ARE YOU ALL RIGHT?
WELL ...
...I'M NOT INJURED MUCH.
...
TMP
SWEET-HEART...

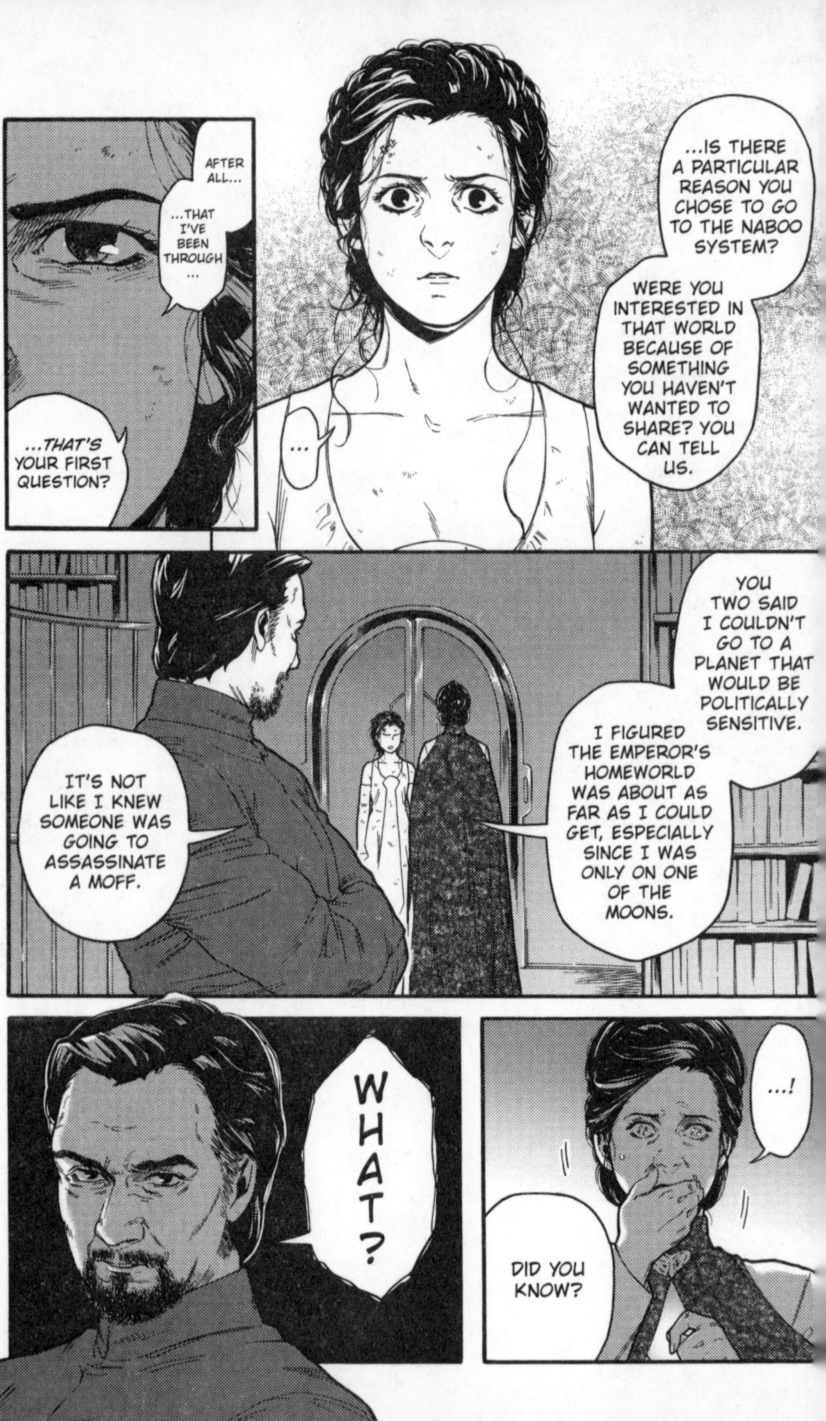
...IS THERE A PARTICULAR REASON YOU CHOSE TO GO TO THE NABOO SYSTEM?
WERE YOU INTERESTED IN THAT WORLD BECAUSE OF SOMETHING YOU HAVEN'T WANTED TO SHARE? YOU CAN TELL US.
...
AFTER ALL...
...THAT I'VE BEEN THROUGH ...
...THAT'S YOUR FIRST QUESTION?
YOU TWO SAID I COULDN'T GO TO A PLANET THAT WOULD BE POLITICALLY SENSITIVE.
I FIGURED THE EMPEROR'S HOMEWORLD WAS ABOUT AS FAR AS I COULD GET, ESPECIALLY SINCE I WAS ONLY ON ONE OF THE MOONS.
IT'S NOT LIKE I KNEW SOMEONE WAS GOING TO ASSASSINATE A MOFF.
...!
DID YOU KNOW?
WHAT?

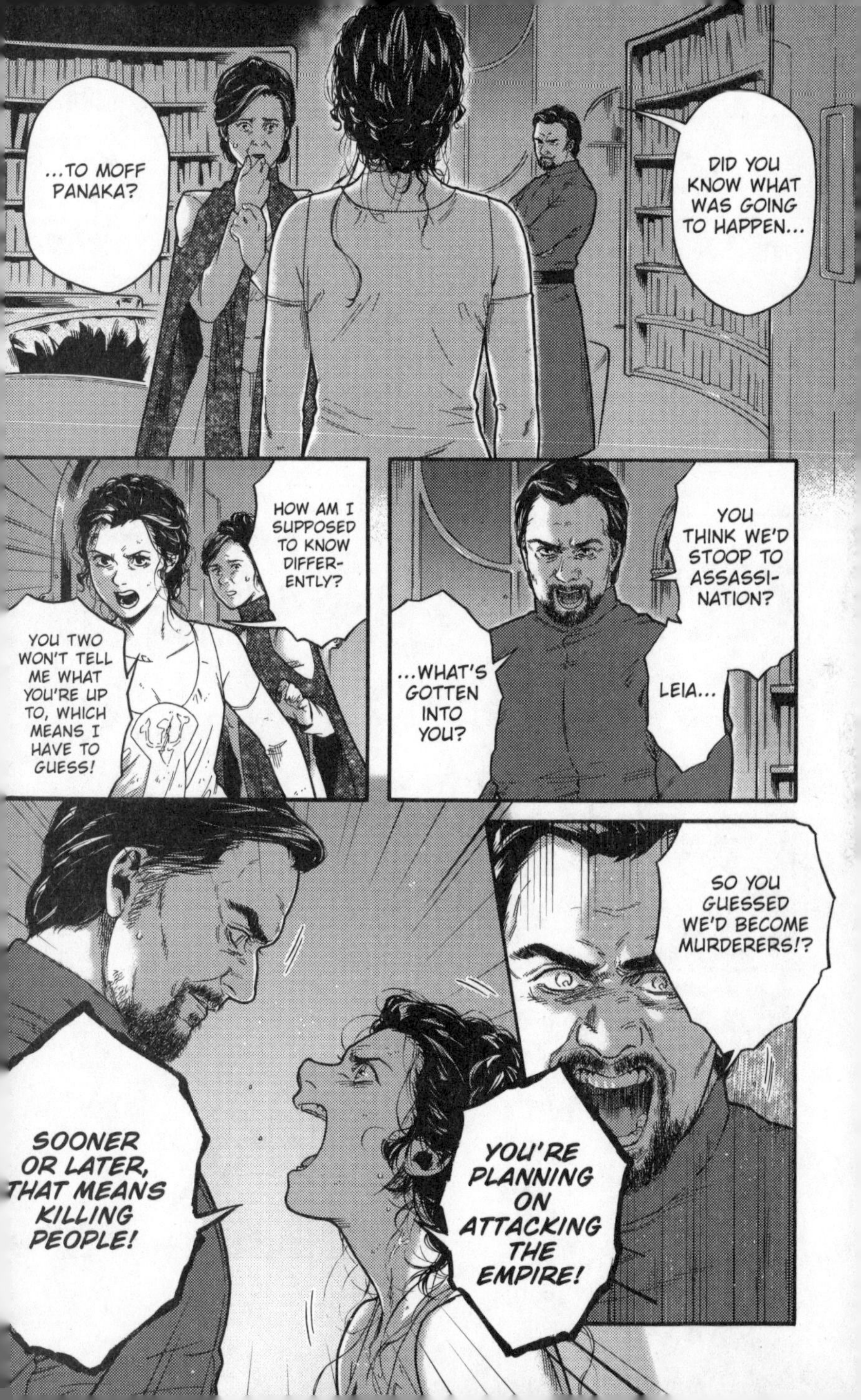
DID YOU KNOW WHAT WAS GOING TO HAPPEN...
...TO MOFF PANAKA?
YOU THINK WE'D STOOP TO ASSASSINATION?
LEIA...
...WHAT'S GOTTEN INTO YOU?
HOW AM I SUPPOSED TO KNOW DIFFERENTLY?
YOU TWO WON'T TELL ME WHAT YOU'RE UP TO, WHICH MEANS I HAVE TO GUESS!
SO YOU GUESSED WE'D BECOME MURDERERS!?
YOU'RE PLANNING ON ATTACKING THE EMPIRE!
SOONER OR LATER, THAT MEANS KILLING PEOPLE!

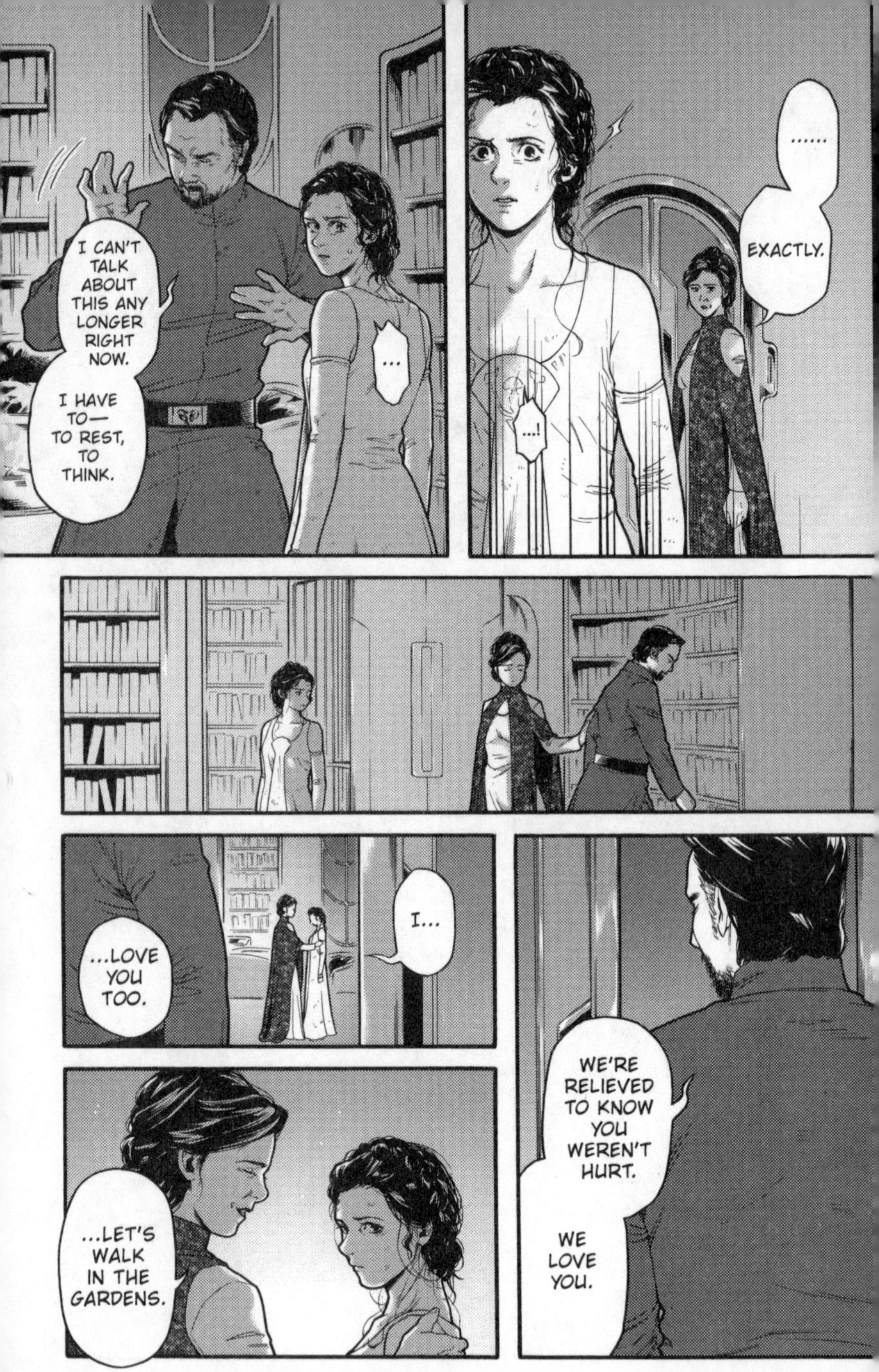
......
EXACTLY.
...!
I CAN'T TALK ABOUT THIS ANY LONGER RIGHT NOW.
...
I HAVE TO— TO REST, TO THINK.
WE'RE RELIEVED TO KNOW YOU WEREN'T HURT.
WE LOVE YOU.
I...
...LOVE YOU TOO.
...LET'S WALK IN THE GARDENS.

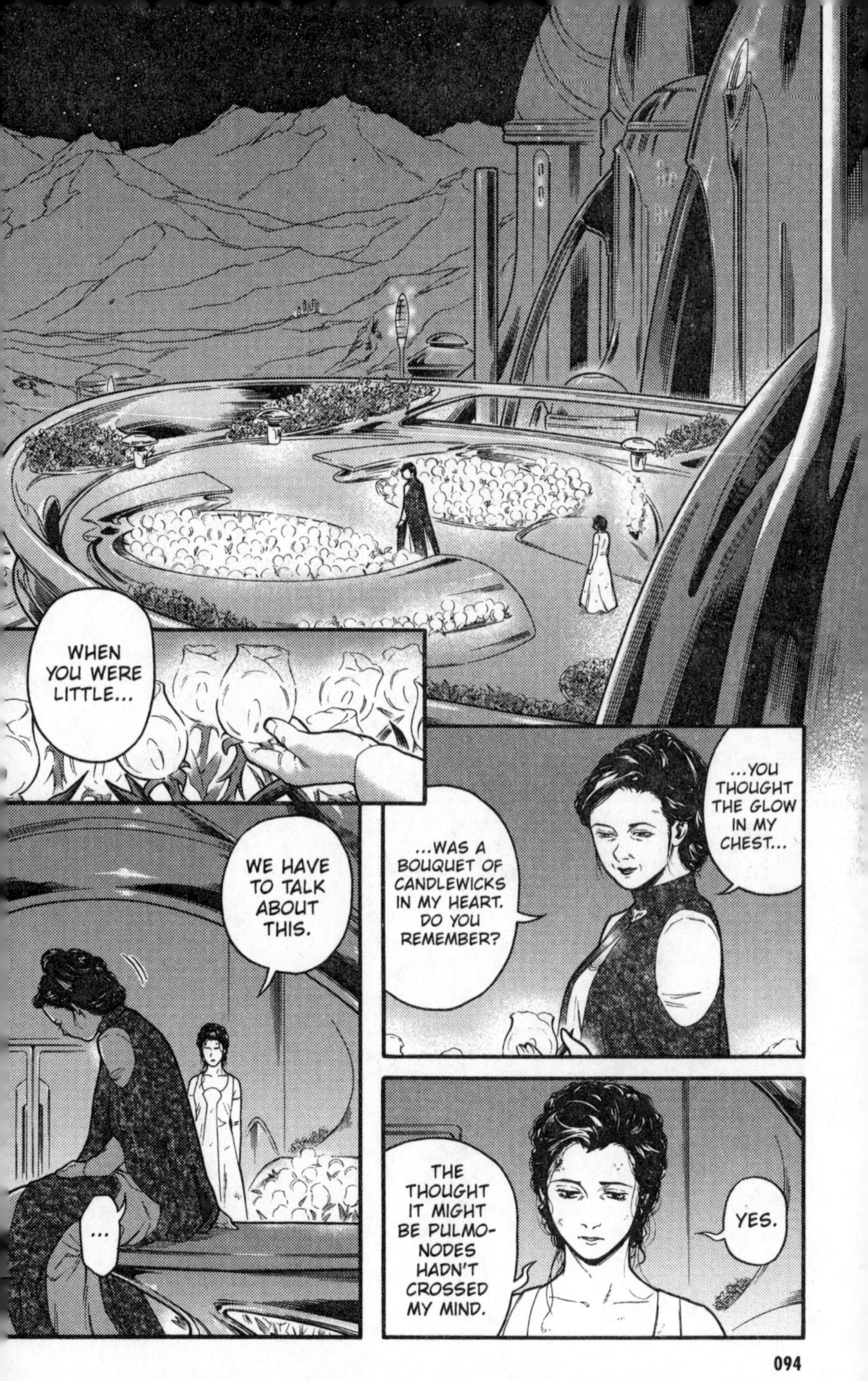
WHEN YOU WERE LITTLE...
...YOU THOUGHT THE GLOW IN MY CHEST...
...WAS A BOUQUET OF CANDLEWICKS IN MY HEART. DO YOU REMEMBER?
YES.
THE THOUGHT IT MIGHT BE PULMO-NODES HADN'T CROSSED MY MIND.
WE HAVE TO TALK ABOUT THIS.
...

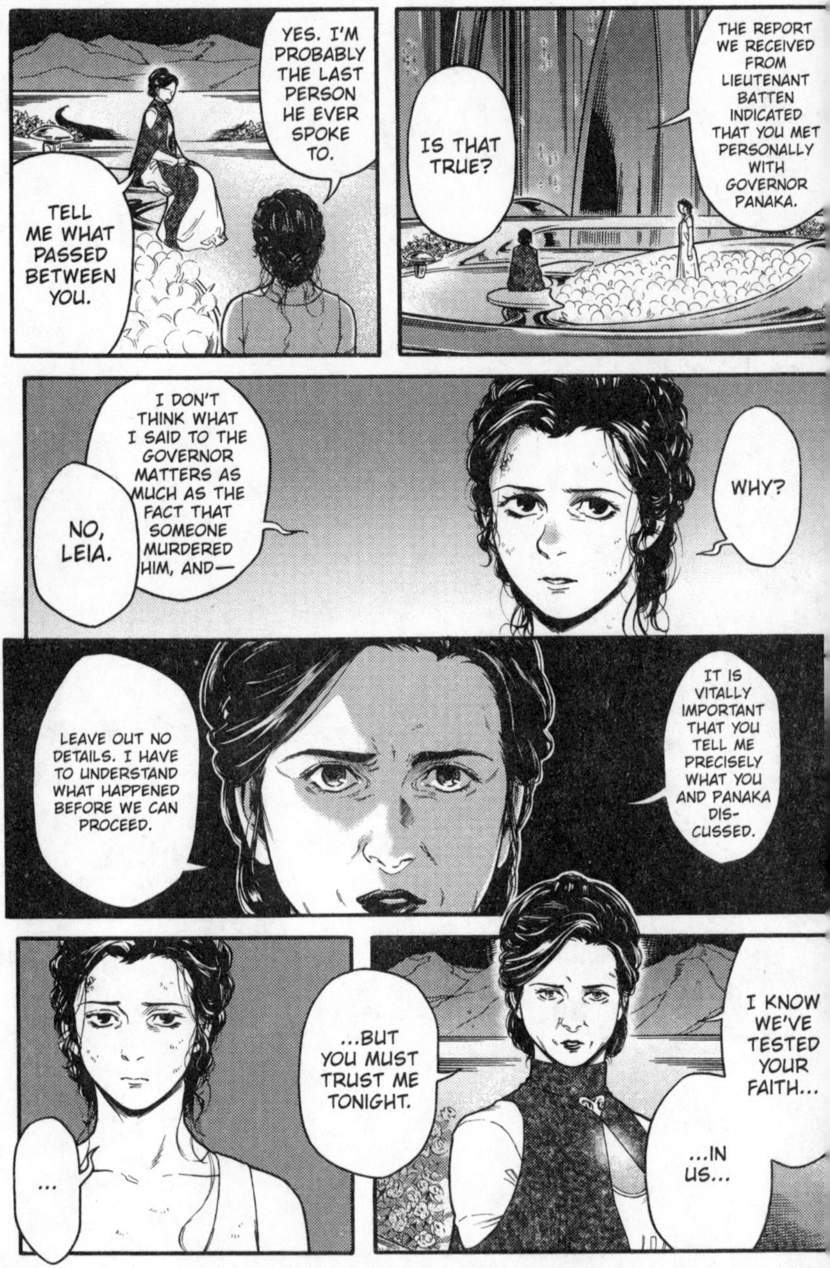
THE REPORT WE RECEIVED FROM LIEUTENANT BATTEN INDICATED THAT YOU MET PERSONALLY WITH GOVERNOR PANAKA.
IS THAT TRUE?
YES. I'M PROBABLY THE LAST PERSON HE EVER SPOKE TO.
TELL ME WHAT PASSED BETWEEN YOU.
WHY?
I DON'T THINK WHAT I SAID TO THE GOVERNOR MATTERS AS MUCH AS THE FACT THAT SOMEONE MURDERED HIM, AND—
NO, LEIA.
IT IS VITALLY IMPORTANT THAT YOU TELL ME PRECISELY WHAT YOU AND PANAKA DIS-CUSSED.
LEAVE OUT NO DETAILS. I HAVE TO UNDERSTAND WHAT HAPPENED BEFORE WE CAN PROCEED.
I KNOW WE'VE TESTED YOUR FAITH...
...IN US...
...BUT YOU MUST TRUST ME TONIGHT.
...

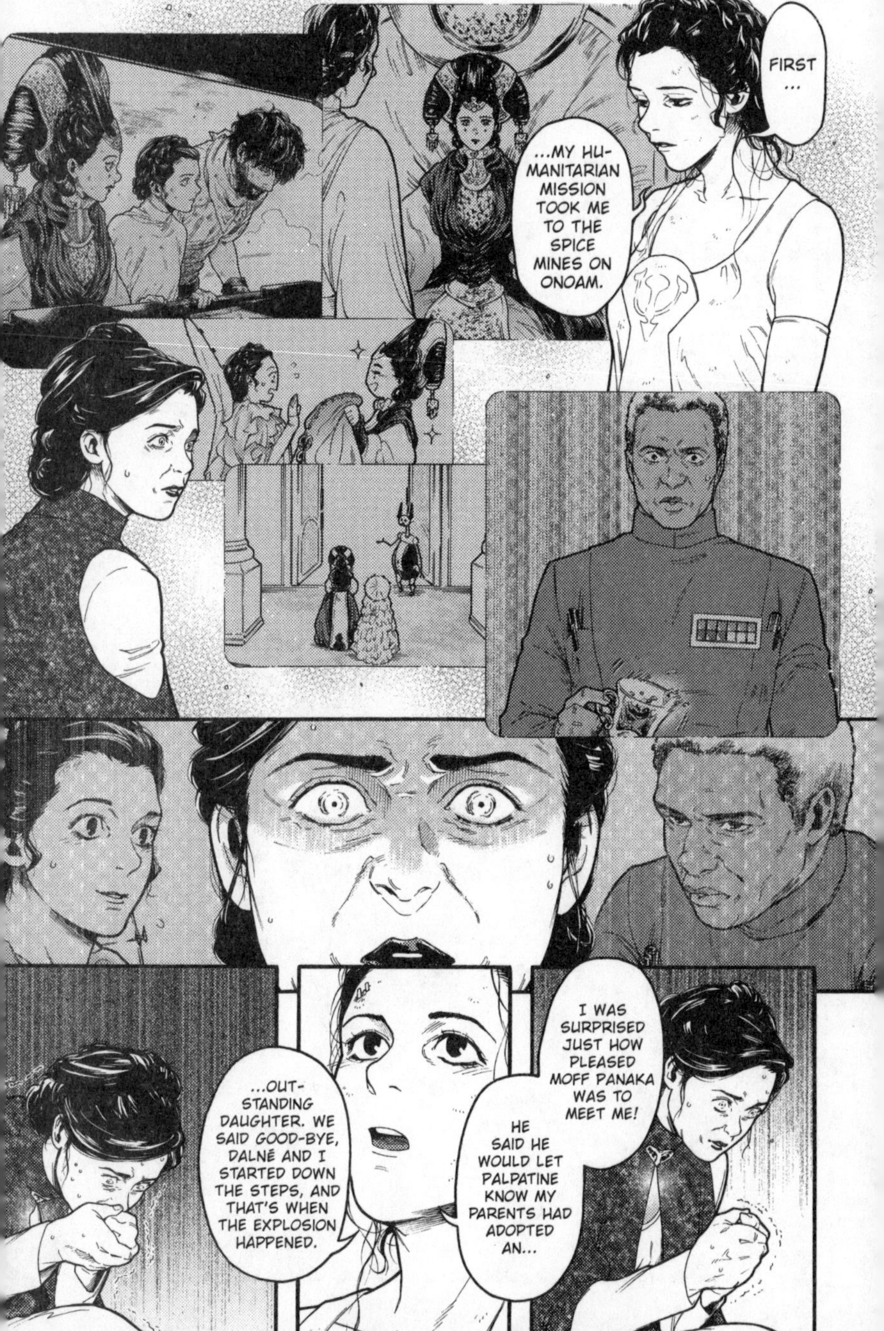
FIRST...
...MY HU-MANITARIAN MISSION TOOK ME TO THE SPICE MINES ON ONOAM.
I WAS SURPRISED JUST HOW PLEASED MOFF PANAKA WAS TO MEET ME!
HE SAID HE WOULD LET PALPATINE KNOW MY PARENTS HAD ADOPTED AN...
...OUT-STANDING DAUGHTER. WE SAID GOOD-BYE, DALNÉ AND I STARTED DOWN THE STEPS, AND THAT'S WHEN THE EXPLOSION HAPPENED.

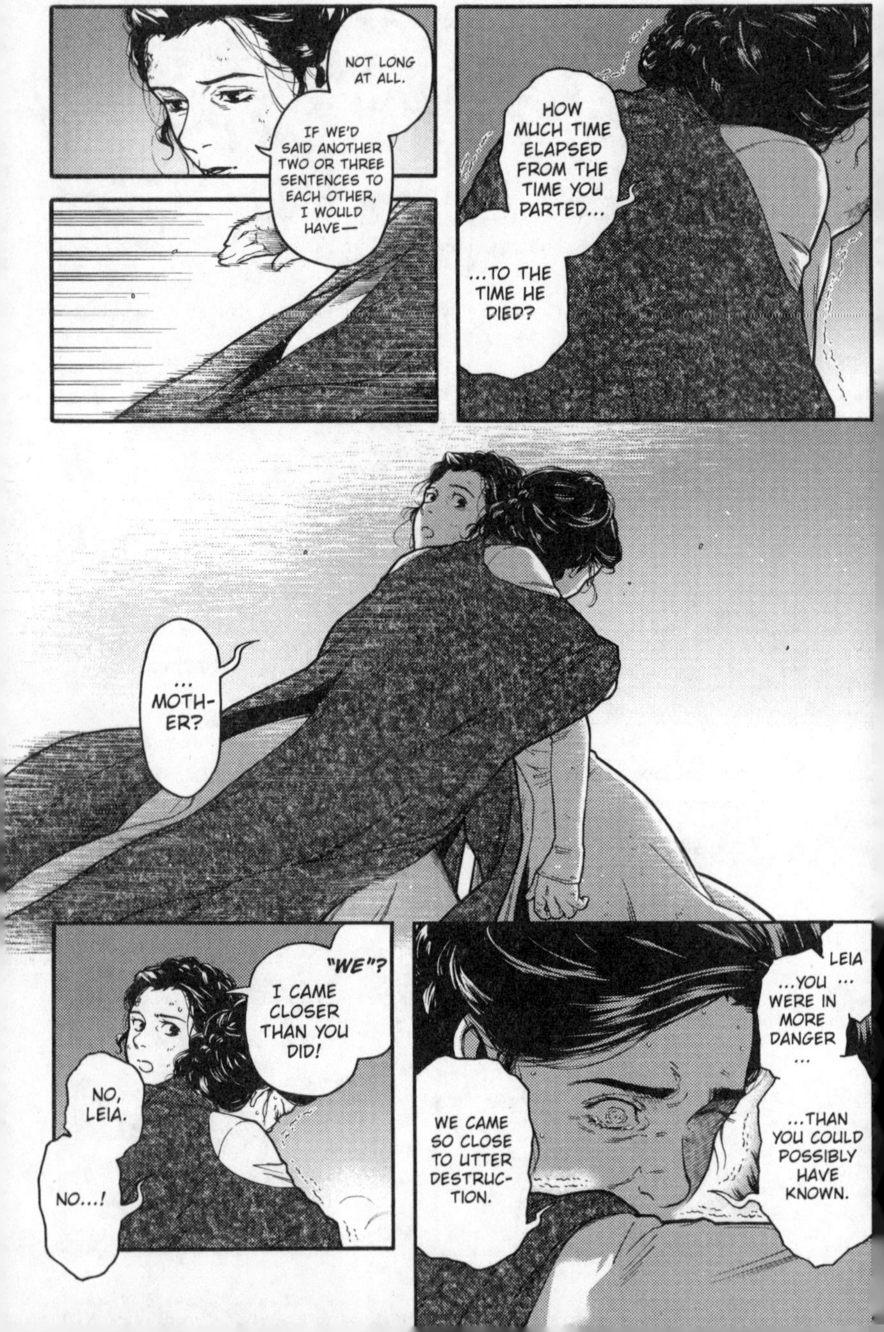
HOW MUCH TIME ELAPSED FROM THE TIME YOU PARTED...
...TO THE TIME HE DIED?
NOT LONG AT ALL.
IF WE'D SAID ANOTHER TWO OR THREE SENTENCES TO EACH OTHER, I WOULD HAVE—
...MOTHER?
LEIA ...YOU WERE IN MORE DANGER...
...THAN YOU COULD POSSIBLY HAVE KNOWN.
WE CAME SO CLOSE TO UTTER DESTRUCTION.
"WE"? I CAME CLOSER THAN YOU DID!
NO, LEIA.
NO...!

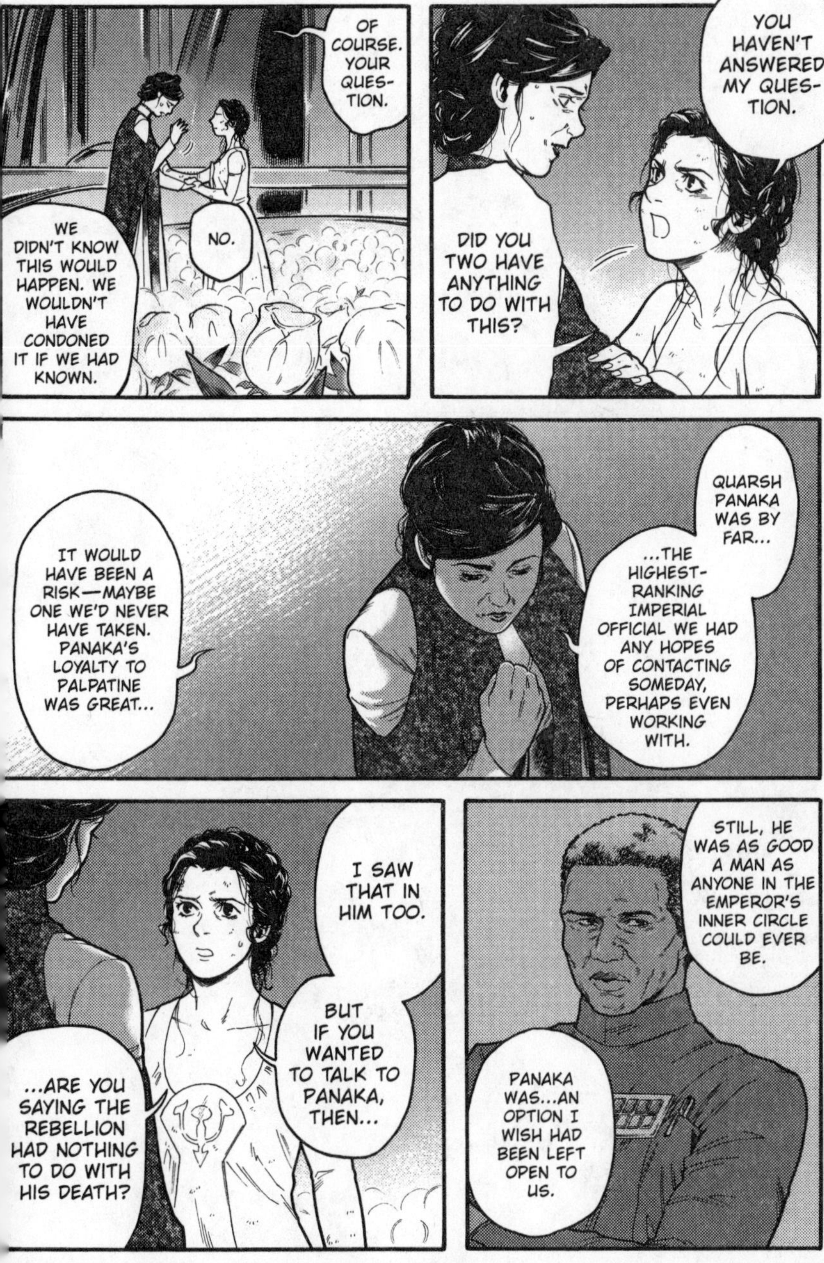
YOU HAVEN'T ANSWERED MY QUESTION.
DID YOU TWO HAVE ANYTHING TO DO WITH THIS?
OF COURSE. YOUR QUESTION.
NO.
WE DIDN'T KNOW THIS WOULD HAPPEN. WE WOULDN'T HAVE CONDONED IT IF WE HAD KNOWN.
QUARSH PANAKA WAS BY FAR...
...THE HIGHEST-RANKING IMPERIAL OFFICIAL WE HAD ANY HOPES OF CONTACTING SOMEDAY, PERHAPS EVEN WORKING WITH.
IT WOULD HAVE BEEN A RISK—MAYBE ONE WE'D NEVER HAVE TAKEN. PANAKA'S LOYALTY TO PALPATINE WAS GREAT...
STILL, HE WAS AS GOOD A MAN AS ANYONE IN THE EMPEROR'S INNER CIRCLE COULD EVER BE.
PANAKA WAS...AN OPTION I WISH HAD BEEN LEFT OPEN TO US.
I SAW THAT IN HIM TOO.
BUT IF YOU WANTED TO TALK TO PANAKA, THEN...
...ARE YOU SAYING THE REBELLION HAD NOTHING TO DO WITH HIS DEATH?

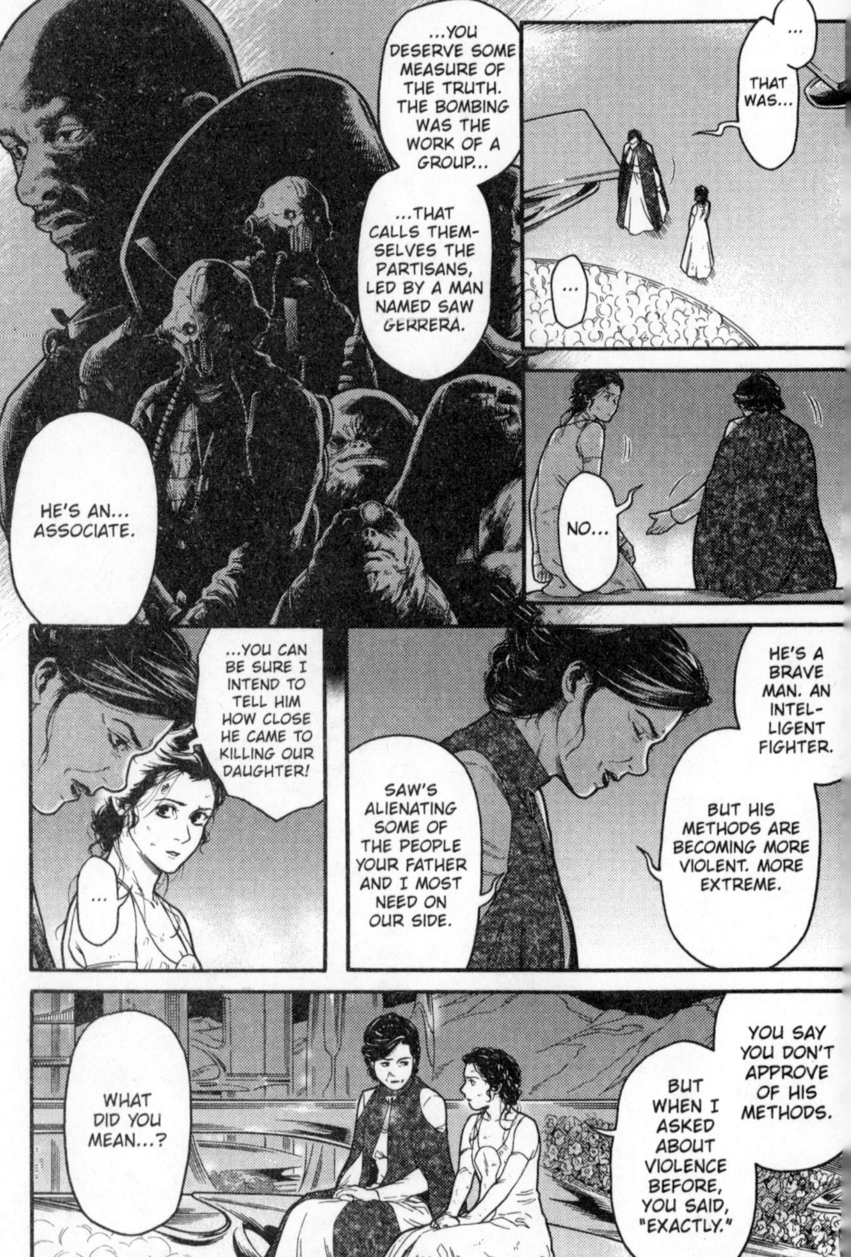
... THAT WAS...
...
NO...
...YOU DESERVE SOME MEASURE OF THE TRUTH. THE BOMBING WAS THE WORK OF A GROUP...
...THAT CALLS THEM-SELVES THE PARTISANS, LED BY A MAN NAMED SAW GERRERA.
HE'S AN... ASSOCIATE.
HE'S A BRAVE MAN. AN INTEL-LIGENT FIGHTER.
BUT HIS METHODS ARE BECOMING MORE VIOLENT. MORE EXTREME.
SAW'S ALIENATING SOME OF THE PEOPLE YOUR FATHER AND I MOST NEED ON OUR SIDE.
...YOU CAN BE SURE I INTEND TO TELL HIM HOW CLOSE HE CAME TO KILLING OUR DAUGHTER!
...
YOU SAY YOU DON'T APPROVE OF HIS METHODS.
BUT WHEN I ASKED ABOUT VIOLENCE BEFORE, YOU SAID, "EXACTLY."
WHAT DID YOU MEAN...?

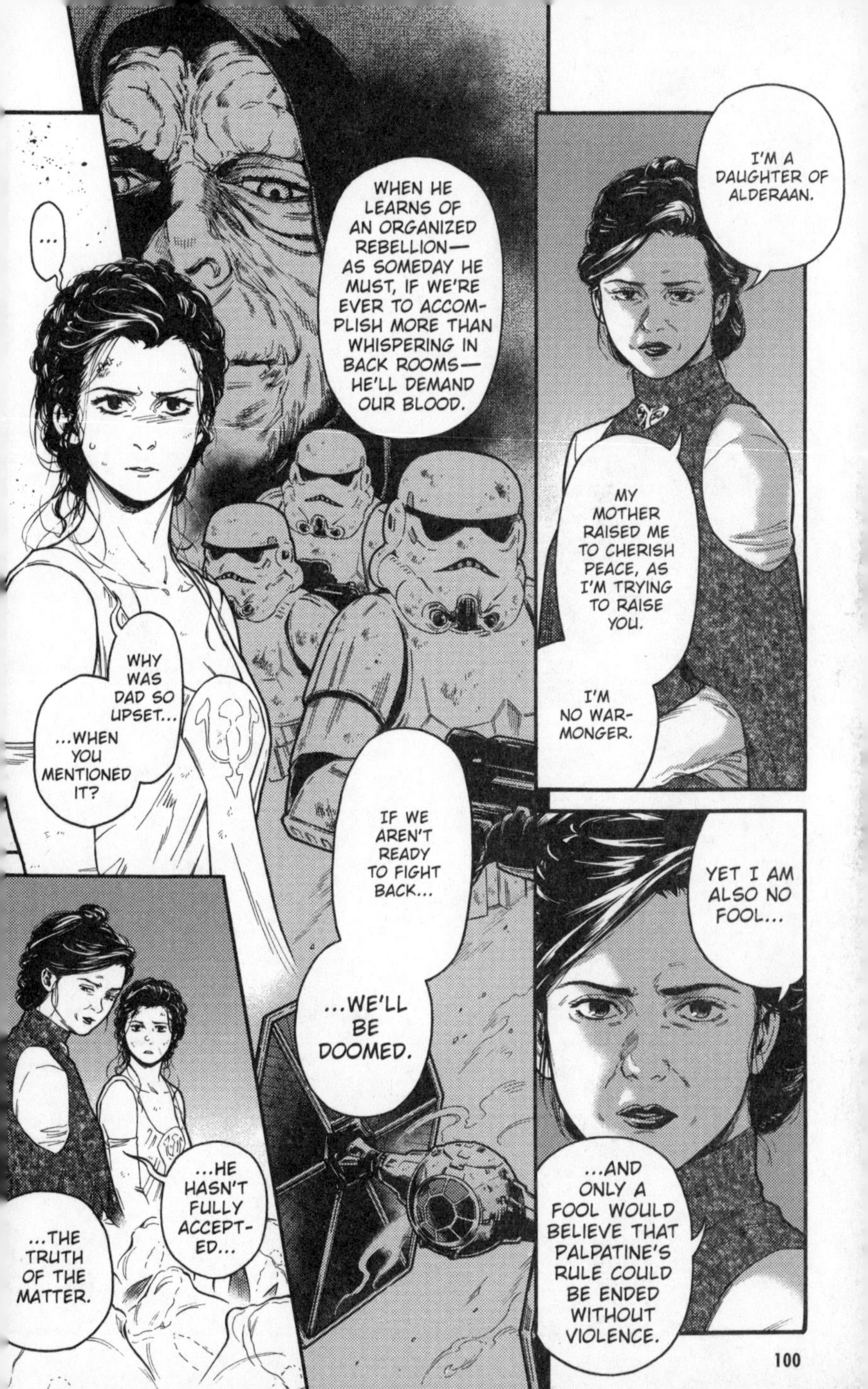
I'M A DAUGHTER OF ALDERAAN.
MY MOTHER RAISED ME TO CHERISH PEACE, AS I'M TRYING TO RAISE YOU.
I'M NO WAR-MONGER.
YET I AM ALSO NO FOOL...
...AND ONLY A FOOL WOULD BELIEVE THAT PALPATINE'S RULE COULD BE ENDED WITHOUT VIOLENCE.
WHEN HE LEARNS OF AN ORGANIZED REBELLION—AS SOMEDAY HE MUST, IF WE'RE EVER TO ACCOMPLISH MORE THAN WHISPERING IN BACK ROOMS—HE'LL DEMAND OUR BLOOD.
IF WE AREN'T READY TO FIGHT BACK...
...WE'LL BE DOOMED.
...
WHY WAS DAD SO UPSET...
...WHEN YOU MENTIONED IT?
...HE HASN'T FULLY ACCEPT-ED...
...THE TRUTH OF THE MATTER.

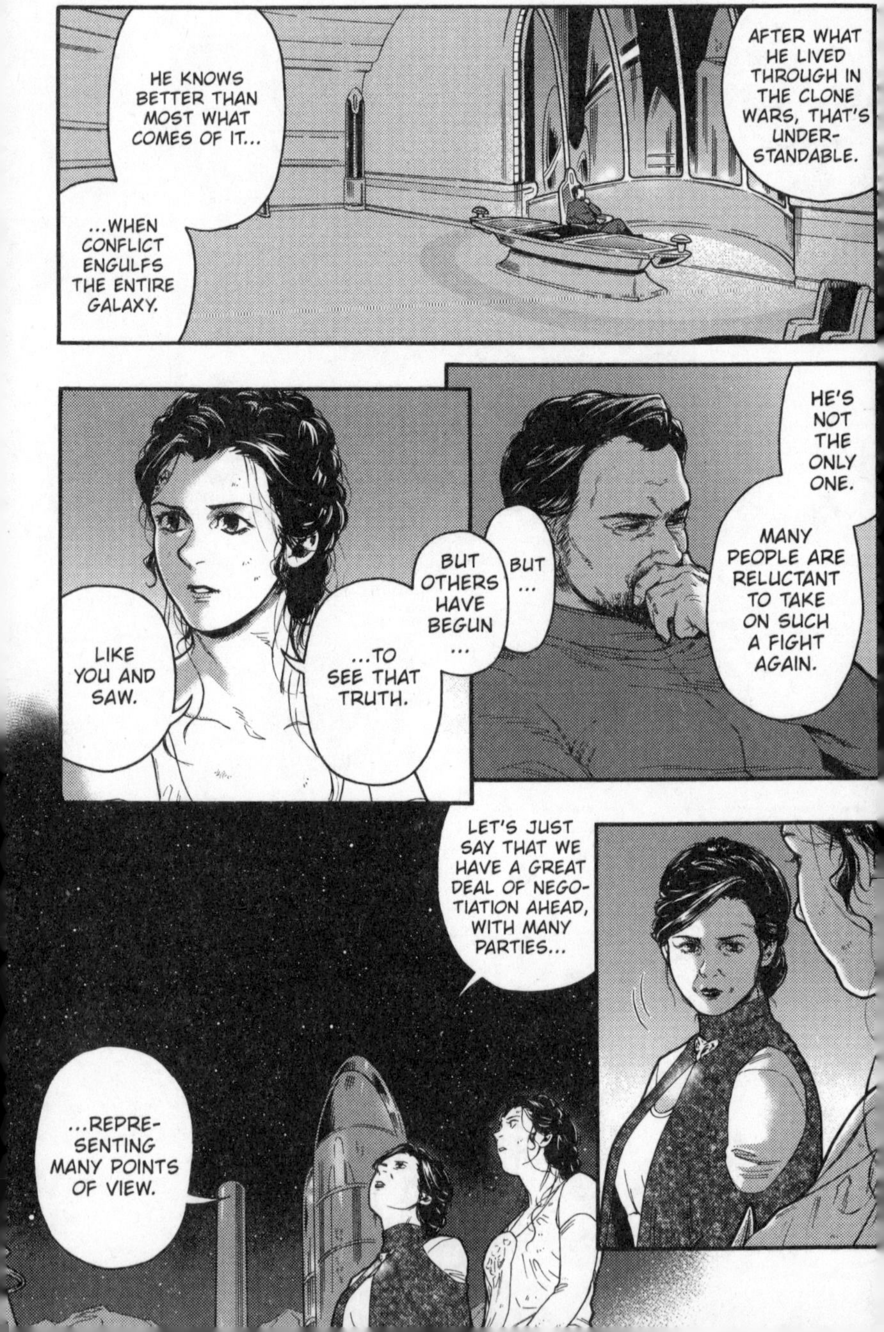
AFTER WHAT HE LIVED THROUGH IN THE CLONE WARS, THAT'S UNDER-STANDABLE.
HE KNOWS BETTER THAN MOST WHAT COMES OF IT...
...WHEN CONFLICT ENGULFS THE ENTIRE GALAXY.
HE'S NOT THE ONLY ONE.
MANY PEOPLE ARE RELUCTANT TO TAKE ON SUCH A FIGHT AGAIN.
BUT ...
BUT OTHERS HAVE BEGUN ...
...TO SEE THAT TRUTH.
LIKE YOU AND SAW.
LET'S JUST SAY THAT WE HAVE A GREAT DEAL OF NEGO-TIATION AHEAD, WITH MANY PARTIES...
...REPRE-SENTING MANY POINTS OF VIEW.

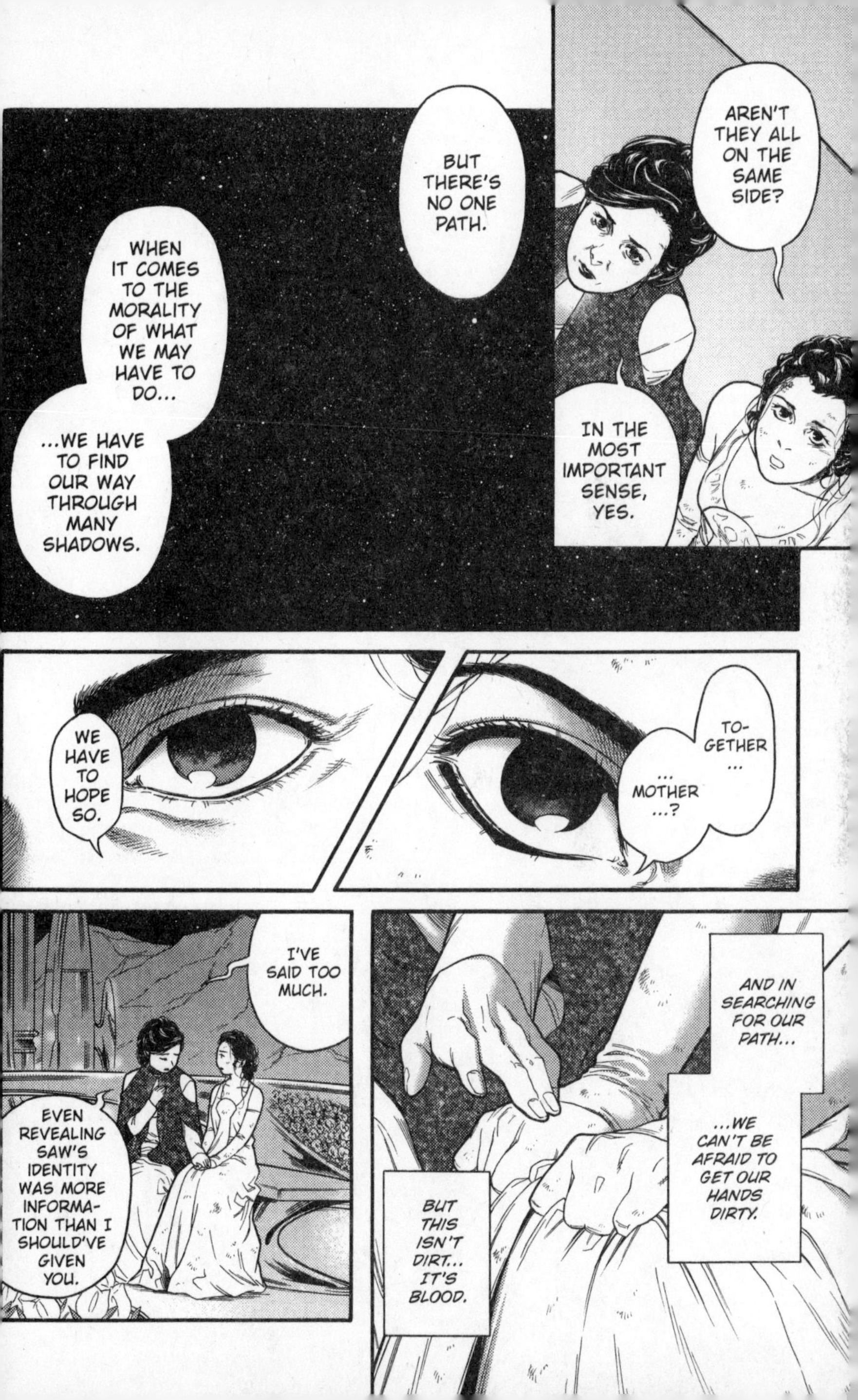
AREN'T THEY ALL ON THE SAME SIDE?
IN THE MOST IMPORTANT SENSE, YES.
BUT THERE'S NO ONE PATH.
WHEN IT COMES TO THE MORALITY OF WHAT WE MAY HAVE TO DO...
...WE HAVE TO FIND OUR WAY THROUGH MANY SHADOWS.
TO-GETHER ...
... MOTHER ...?
WE HAVE TO HOPE SO.
AND IN SEARCHING FOR OUR PATH...
...WE CAN'T BE AFRAID TO GET OUR HANDS DIRTY.
BUT THIS ISN'T DIRT... IT'S BLOOD.
I'VE SAID TOO MUCH.
EVEN REVEALING SAW'S IDENTITY WAS MORE INFORMATION THAN I SHOULD'VE GIVEN YOU.

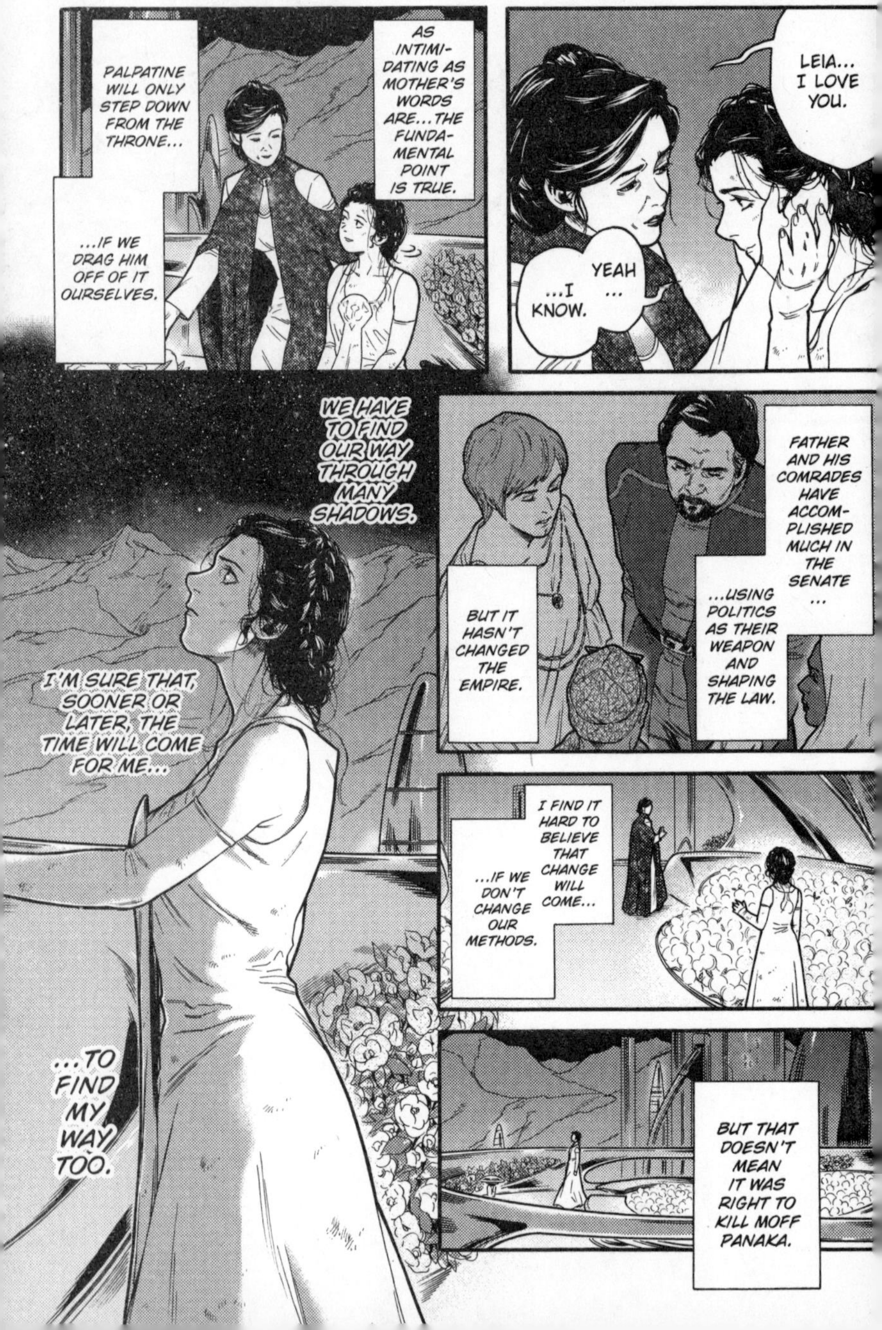
LEIA... I LOVE YOU.
YEAH ...
...I KNOW.
AS INTIMI-DATING AS MOTHER'S WORDS ARE... THE FUNDA-MENTAL POINT IS TRUE.
PALPATINE WILL ONLY STEP DOWN FROM THE THRONE...
...IF WE DRAG HIM OFF OF IT OURSELVES.
FATHER AND HIS COMRADES HAVE ACCOM-PLISHED MUCH IN THE SENATE ...
...USING POLITICS AS THEIR WEAPON AND SHAPING THE LAW.
BUT IT HASN'T CHANGED THE EMPIRE.
I FIND IT HARD TO BELIEVE THAT CHANGE WILL COME...
...IF WE DON'T CHANGE OUR METHODS.
BUT THAT DOESN'T MEAN IT WAS RIGHT TO KILL MOFF PANAKA.
WE HAVE TO FIND OUR WAY THROUGH MANY SHADOWS.
I'M SURE THAT, SOONER OR LATER, THE TIME WILL COME FOR ME...
...TO FIND MY WAY TOO.

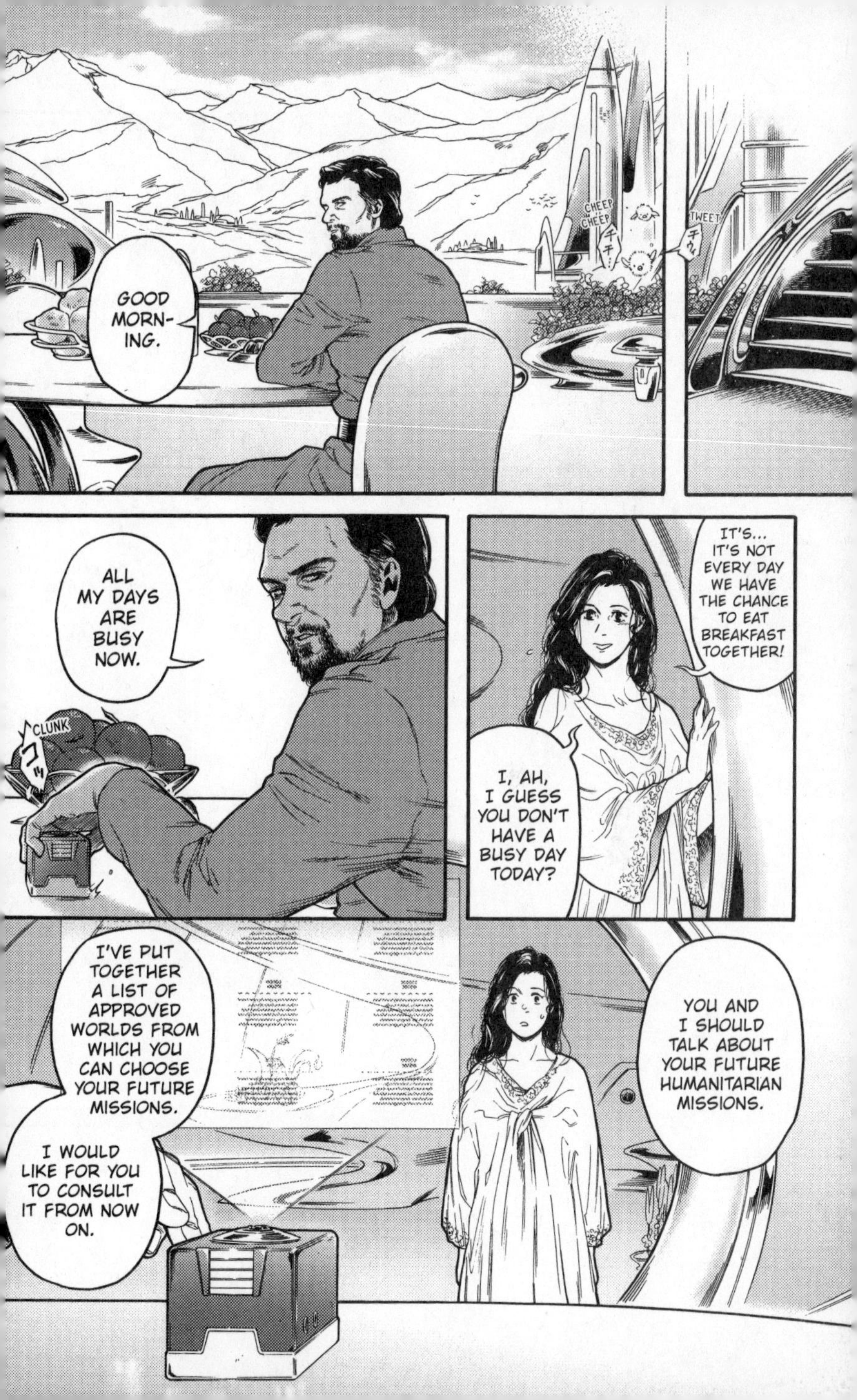

TWEET
CHEEP CHEEP
GOOD MORNING.
IT'S... IT'S NOT EVERY DAY WE HAVE THE CHANCE TO EAT BREAKFAST TOGETHER!
I, AH, I GUESS YOU DON'T HAVE A BUSY DAY TODAY?
ALL MY DAYS ARE BUSY NOW.
CLUNK
YOU AND I SHOULD TALK ABOUT YOUR FUTURE HUMANITARIAN MISSIONS.
I'VE PUT TOGETHER A LIST OF APPROVED WORLDS FROM WHICH YOU CAN CHOOSE YOUR FUTURE MISSIONS.
I WOULD LIKE FOR YOU TO CONSULT IT FROM NOW ON.

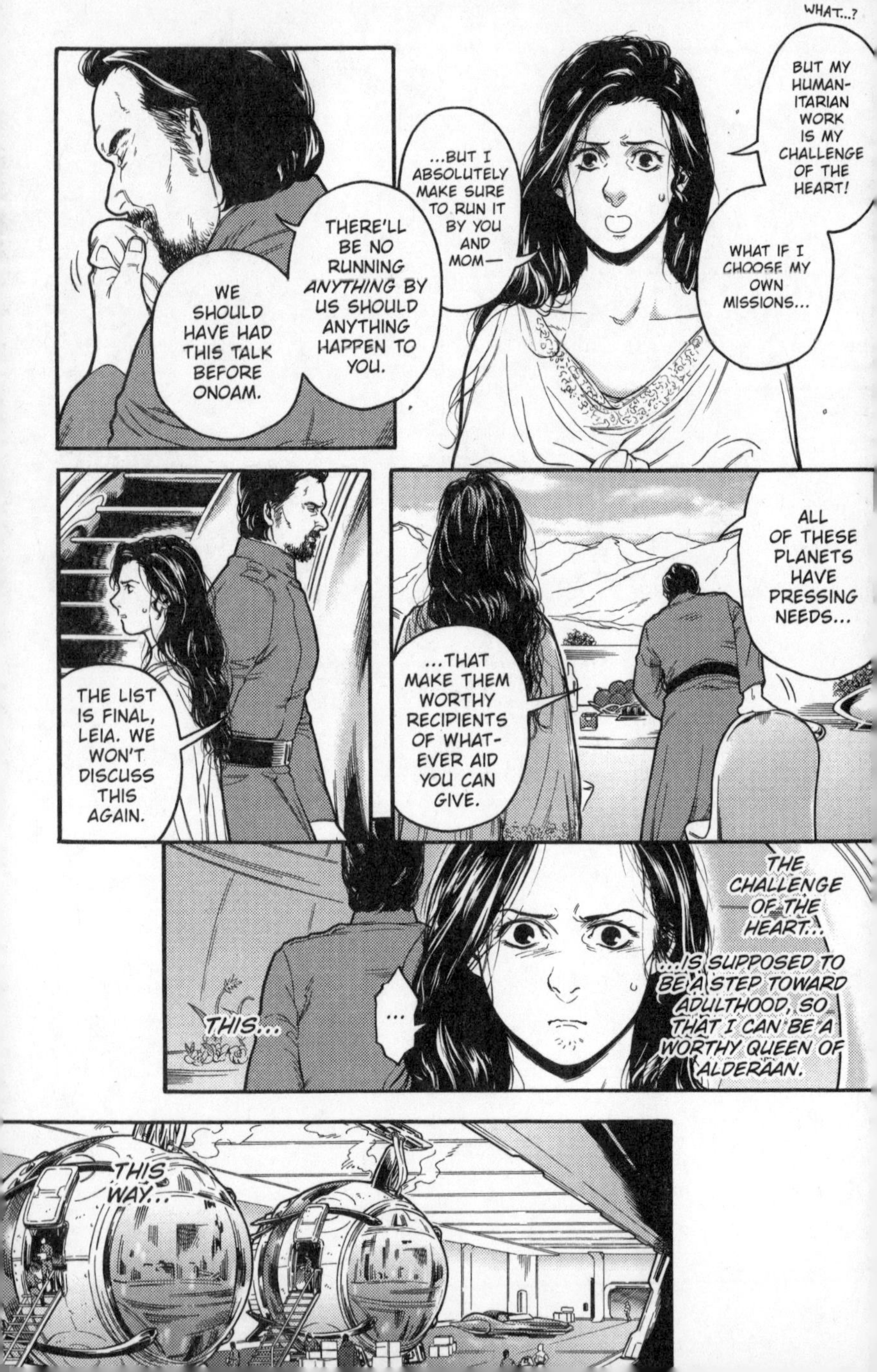
WHAT...?
BUT MY HUMAN-ITARIAN WORK IS MY CHALLENGE OF THE HEART!
WHAT IF I CHOOSE MY OWN MISSIONS...
...BUT I ABSOLUTELY MAKE SURE TO RUN IT BY YOU AND MOM—
THERE'LL BE NO RUNNING *ANYTHING* BY US SHOULD ANYTHING HAPPEN TO YOU.
WE SHOULD HAVE HAD THIS TALK BEFORE ONOAM.
ALL OF THESE PLANETS HAVE PRESSING NEEDS...
...THAT MAKE THEM WORTHY RECIPIENTS OF WHAT-EVER AID YOU CAN GIVE.
THE LIST IS FINAL, LEIA. WE WON'T DISCUSS THIS AGAIN.
THE CHALLENGE OF THE HEART...
...IS SUPPOSED TO BE A STEP TOWARD ADULTHOOD, SO THAT I CAN BE A WORTHY QUEEN OF ALDERAAN.
...
THIS...
THIS WAY...

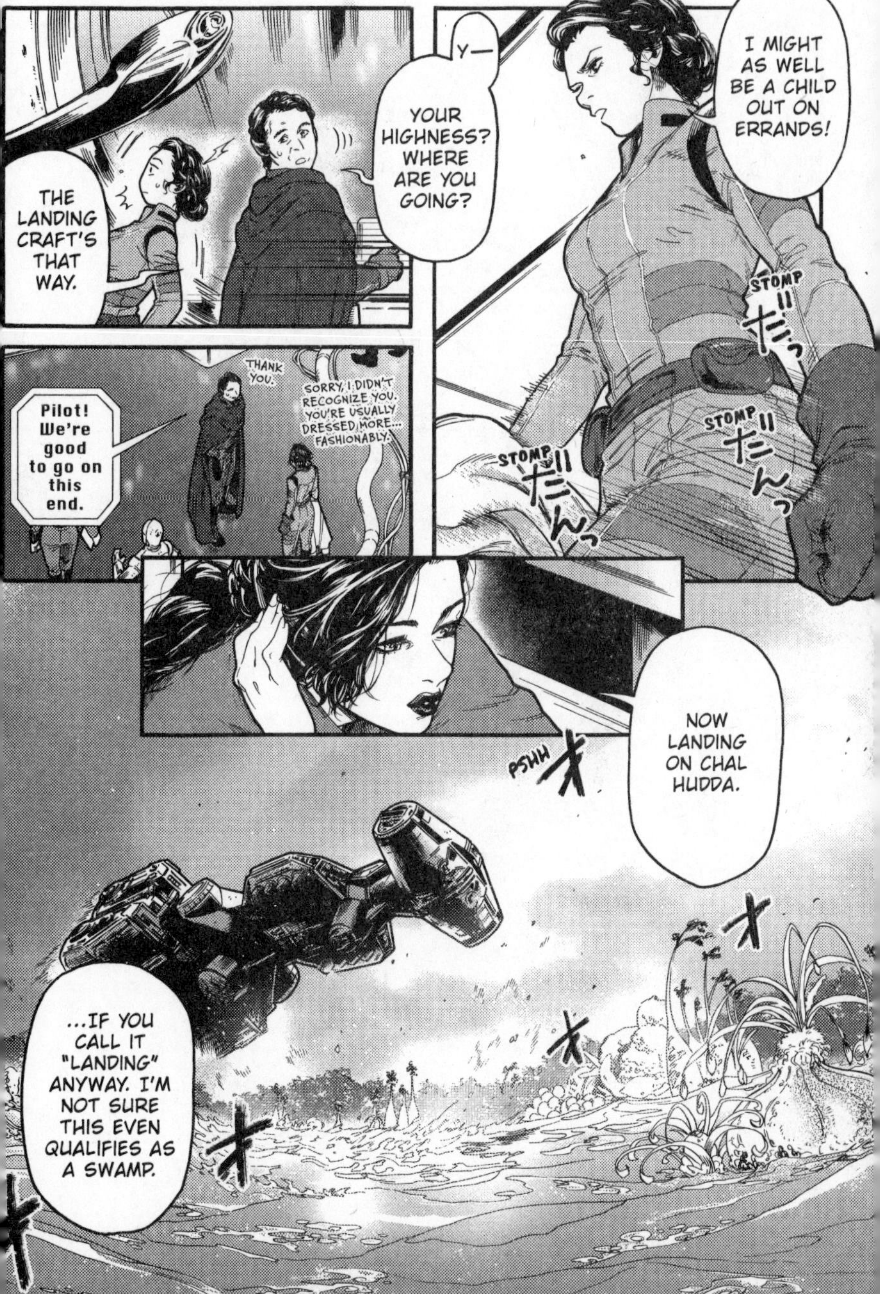
I MIGHT AS WELL BE A CHILD OUT ON ERRANDS!
STOMP
STOMP
STOMP
Y—
YOUR HIGHNESS? WHERE ARE YOU GOING?
THE LANDING CRAFT'S THAT WAY.
SORRY, I DIDN'T RECOGNIZE YOU. YOU'RE USUALLY DRESSED MORE... FASHIONABLY.
THANK YOU.
Pilot! We're good to go on this end.
NOW LANDING ON CHAL HUDDA.
PSHH
...IF YOU CALL IT "LANDING" ANYWAY. I'M NOT SURE THIS EVEN QUALIFIES AS A SWAMP.

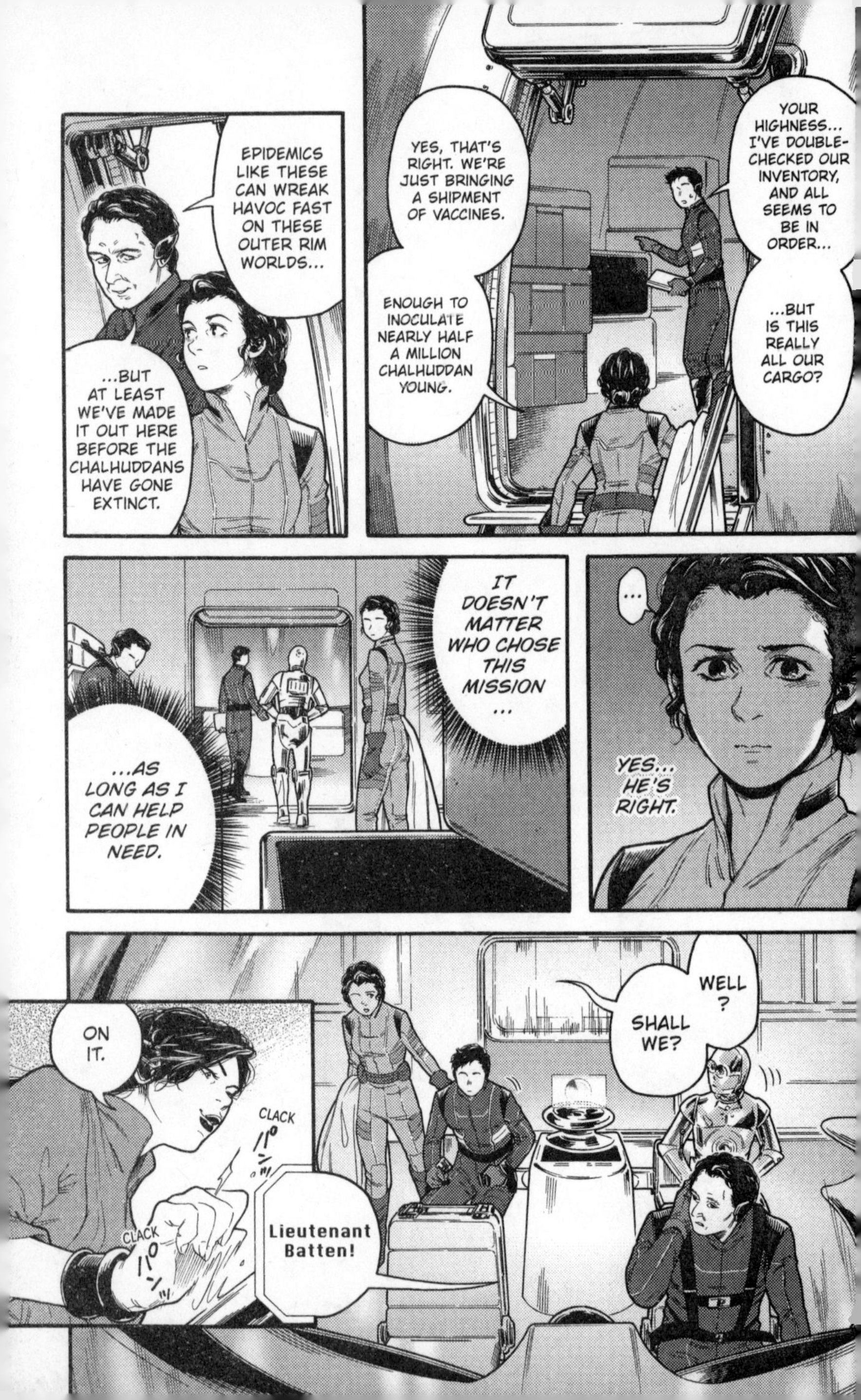
YOUR HIGHNESS... I'VE DOUBLE-CHECKED OUR INVENTORY, AND ALL SEEMS TO BE IN ORDER...
...BUT IS THIS REALLY ALL OUR CARGO?
YES, THAT'S RIGHT. WE'RE JUST BRINGING A SHIPMENT OF VACCINES.
ENOUGH TO INOCULATE NEARLY HALF A MILLION CHALHUDDAN YOUNG.
EPIDEMICS LIKE THESE CAN WREAK HAVOC FAST ON THESE OUTER RIM WORLDS...
...BUT AT LEAST WE'VE MADE IT OUT HERE BEFORE THE CHALHUDDANS HAVE GONE EXTINCT.
...
YES... HE'S RIGHT.
IT DOESN'T MATTER WHO CHOSE THIS MISSION...
...AS LONG AS I CAN HELP PEOPLE IN NEED.
WELL? SHALL WE?
ON IT.
CLACK
Lieutenant Batten!
CLACK

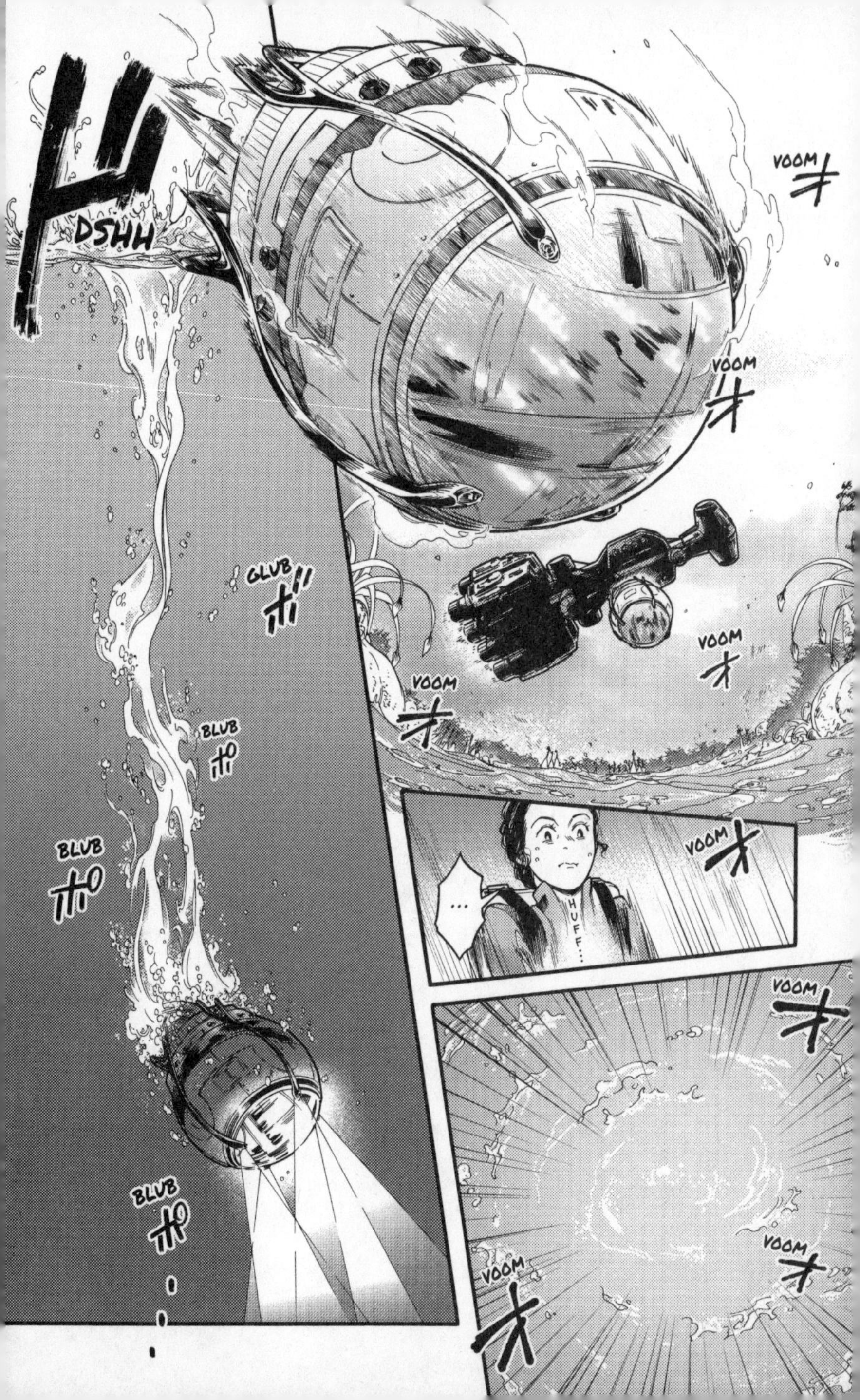
VOOM
DSHH
VOOM
VOOM
VOOM
GLUB
BLUB
BLUB
BLUB
VOOM
...
HUFF...
VOOM
VOOM
VOOM

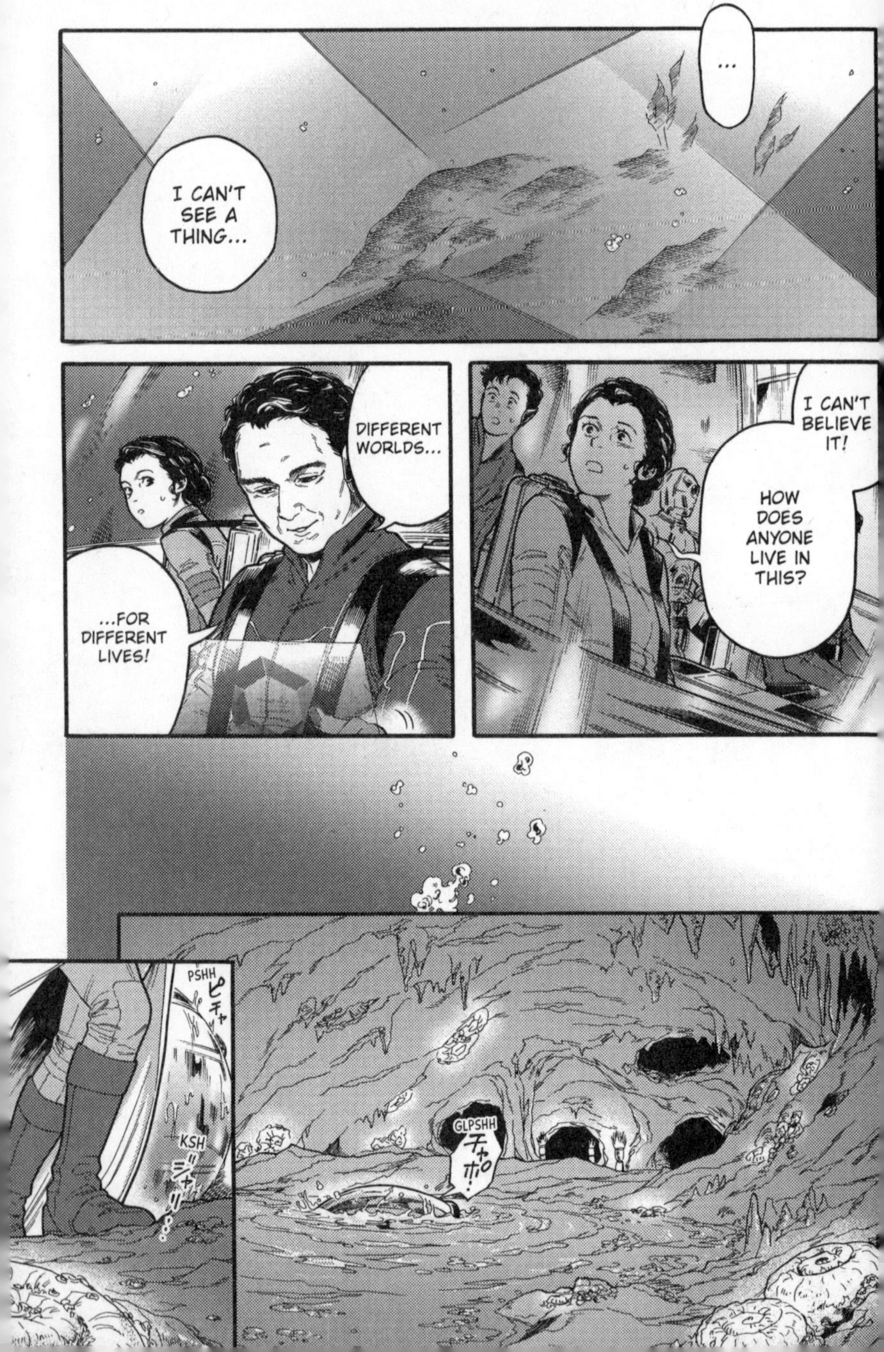
...
I CAN'T SEE A THING...
I CAN'T BELIEVE IT!
HOW DOES ANYONE LIVE IN THIS?
DIFFERENT WORLDS...
...FOR DIFFERENT LIVES!
GLPSHH
チャポ!
PSHH
ピチャ
KSH
ジャリ…

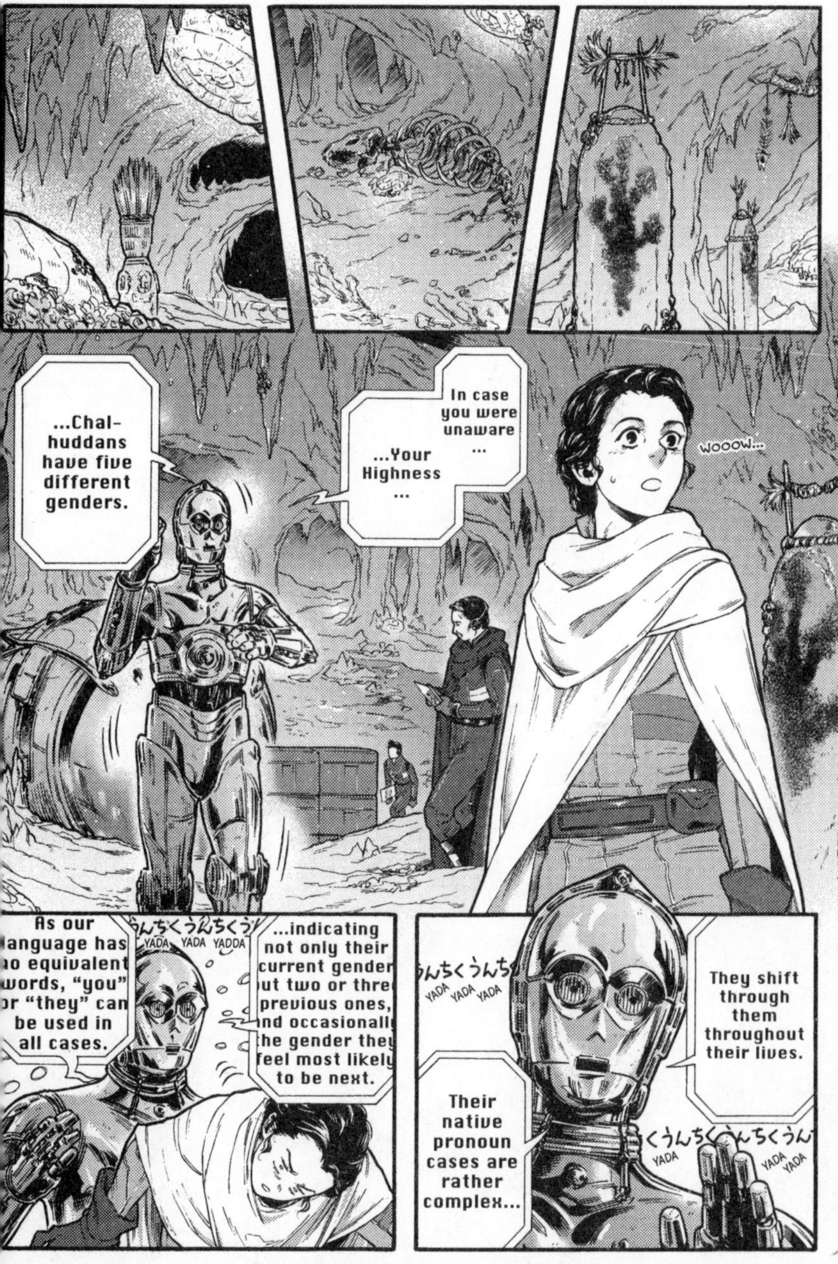

WOOOW...
In case you were unaware ...
...Your Highness ...
...Chal-huddans have five different genders.
They shift through them throughout their lives.
うんちくうんち
YADA YADA YADA
Their native pronoun cases are rather complex...
くうんちくうんちくうん
YADA YADA YADA
...indicating not only their current gende ut two or thre previous ones, nd occasionall he gender the eel most likel to be next.
うんちくうんちくう
YADA YADA YADDA
As our anguage has o equivalent ords, "you" r "they" ca be used in all cases.

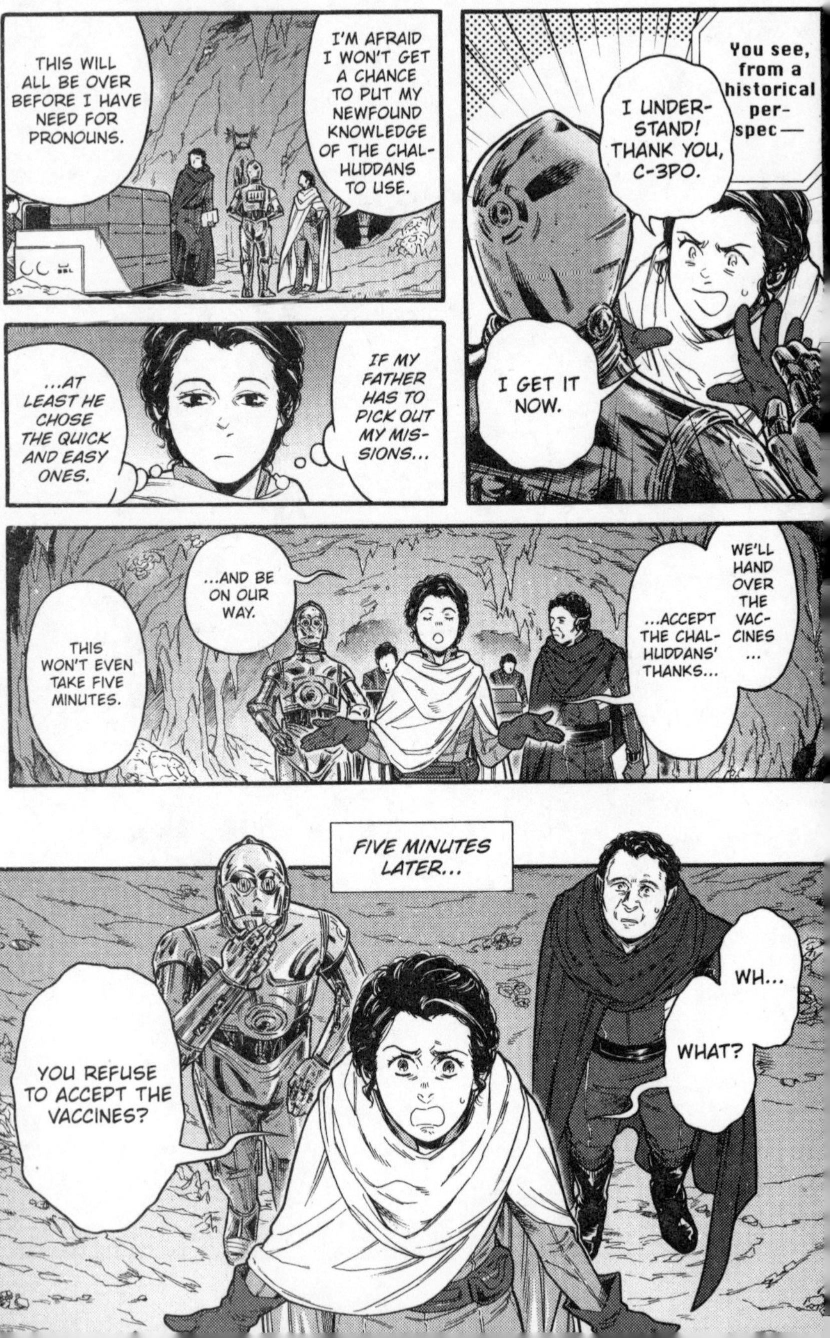
You see, from a historical per-spec—
I UNDER-STAND! THANK YOU, C-3PO.
I GET IT NOW.
I'M AFRAID I WON'T GET A CHANCE TO PUT MY NEWFOUND KNOWLEDGE OF THE CHAL-HUDDANS TO USE.
THIS WILL ALL BE OVER BEFORE I HAVE NEED FOR PRONOUNS.
IF MY FATHER HAS TO PICK OUT MY MIS-SIONS...
...AT LEAST HE CHOSE THE QUICK AND EASY ONES.
WE'LL HAND OVER THE VAC-CINES...
...ACCEPT THE CHAL-HUDDANS' THANKS...
...AND BE ON OUR WAY.
THIS WON'T EVEN TAKE FIVE MINUTES.
FIVE MINUTES LATER...
WH...
WHAT?
YOU REFUSE TO ACCEPT THE VACCINES?

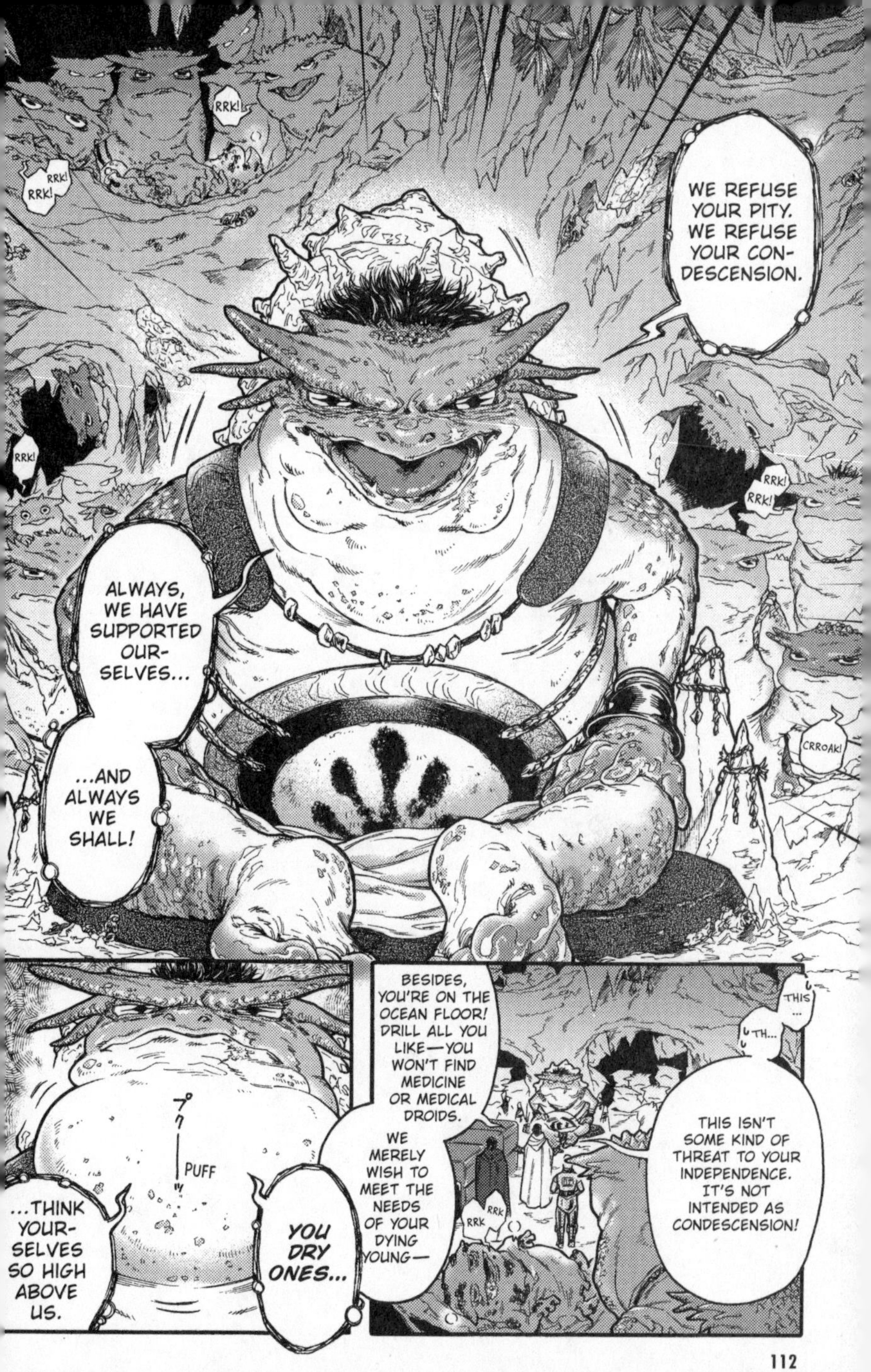
WE REFUSE YOUR PITY. WE REFUSE YOUR CON-DESCENSION.
RRK!
RRK! RRK!
RRK!
RRK! RRK!
ALWAYS, WE HAVE SUPPORTED OUR-SELVES...
...AND ALWAYS WE SHALL!
CRROAK!
THIS...
TH...
THIS ISN'T SOME KIND OF THREAT TO YOUR INDEPENDENCE. IT'S NOT INTENDED AS CONDESCENSION!
WE MERELY WISH TO MEET THE NEEDS OF YOUR DYING YOUNG—
BESIDES, YOU'RE ON THE OCEAN FLOOR! DRILL ALL YOU LIKE—YOU WON'T FIND MEDICINE OR MEDICAL DROIDS.
RRK
RRK
プクー
PUFF
YOU DRY ONES...
...THINK YOUR-SELVES SO HIGH ABOVE US.

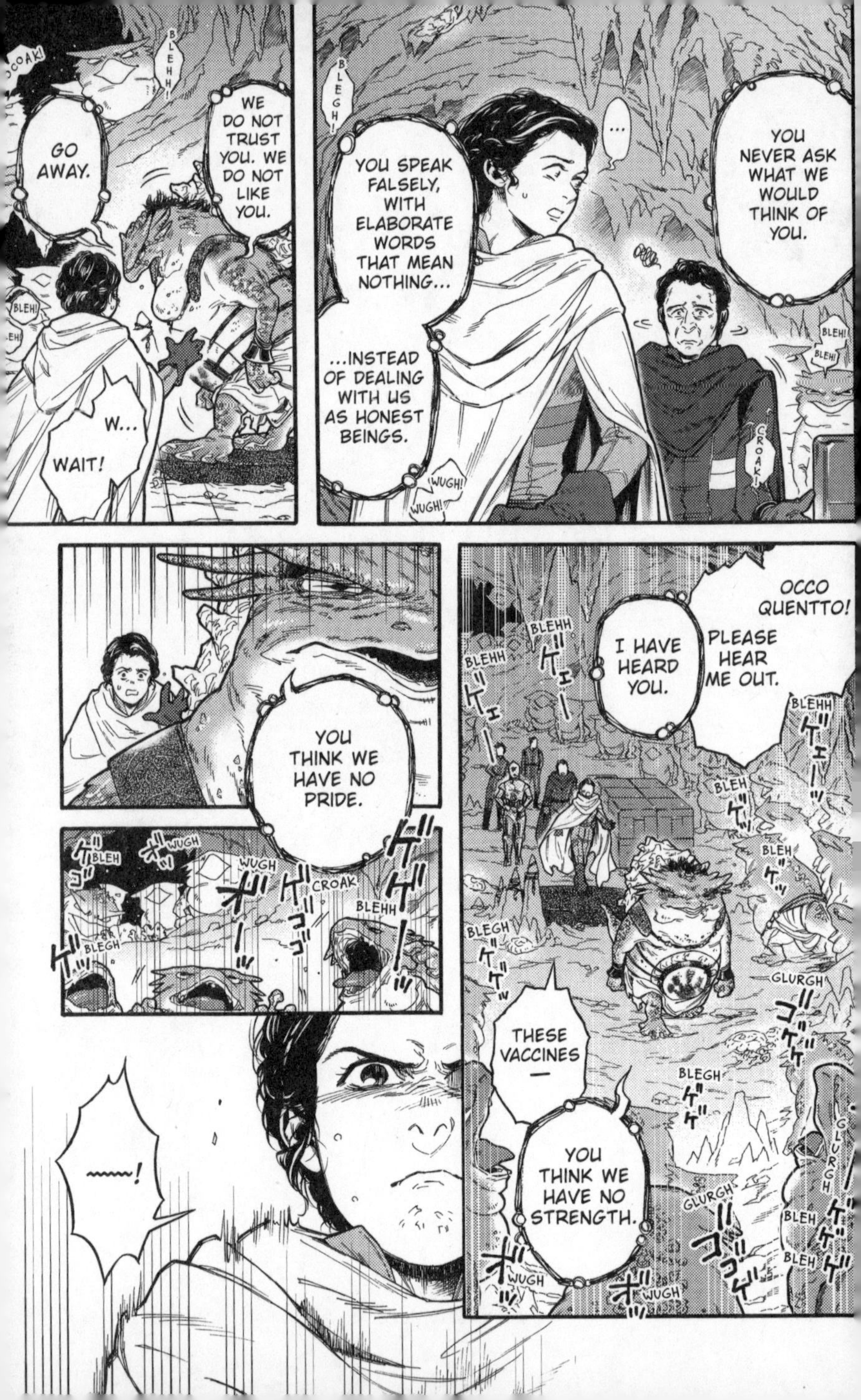
BLEGH
…
YOU NEVER ASK WHAT WE WOULD THINK OF YOU.
YOU SPEAK FALSELY, WITH ELABORATE WORDS THAT MEAN NOTHING…
…INSTEAD OF DEALING WITH US AS HONEST BEINGS.
BLEH!
BLEH!
CROAK!
WUGH!
WUGH!
BLEHH!
CROAK!
WE DO NOT TRUST YOU. WE DO NOT LIKE YOU.
GO AWAY.
BLEH!
BLEH!
W…
WAIT!
OCCO QUENTTO!
PLEASE HEAR ME OUT.
I HAVE HEARD YOU.
BLEHH
BLEHH
BLEHH
BLEH
BLEH
BLEGH
GLURGH
THESE VACCINES—
BLEGH
YOU THINK WE HAVE NO STRENGTH.
GLURGH
GLURGH
BLEH
BLEH
WUGH
WUGH
YOU THINK WE HAVE NO PRIDE.
BLEH
WUGH
WUGH
CROAK
BLEHH
BLEGH
~~~~!
~~~~

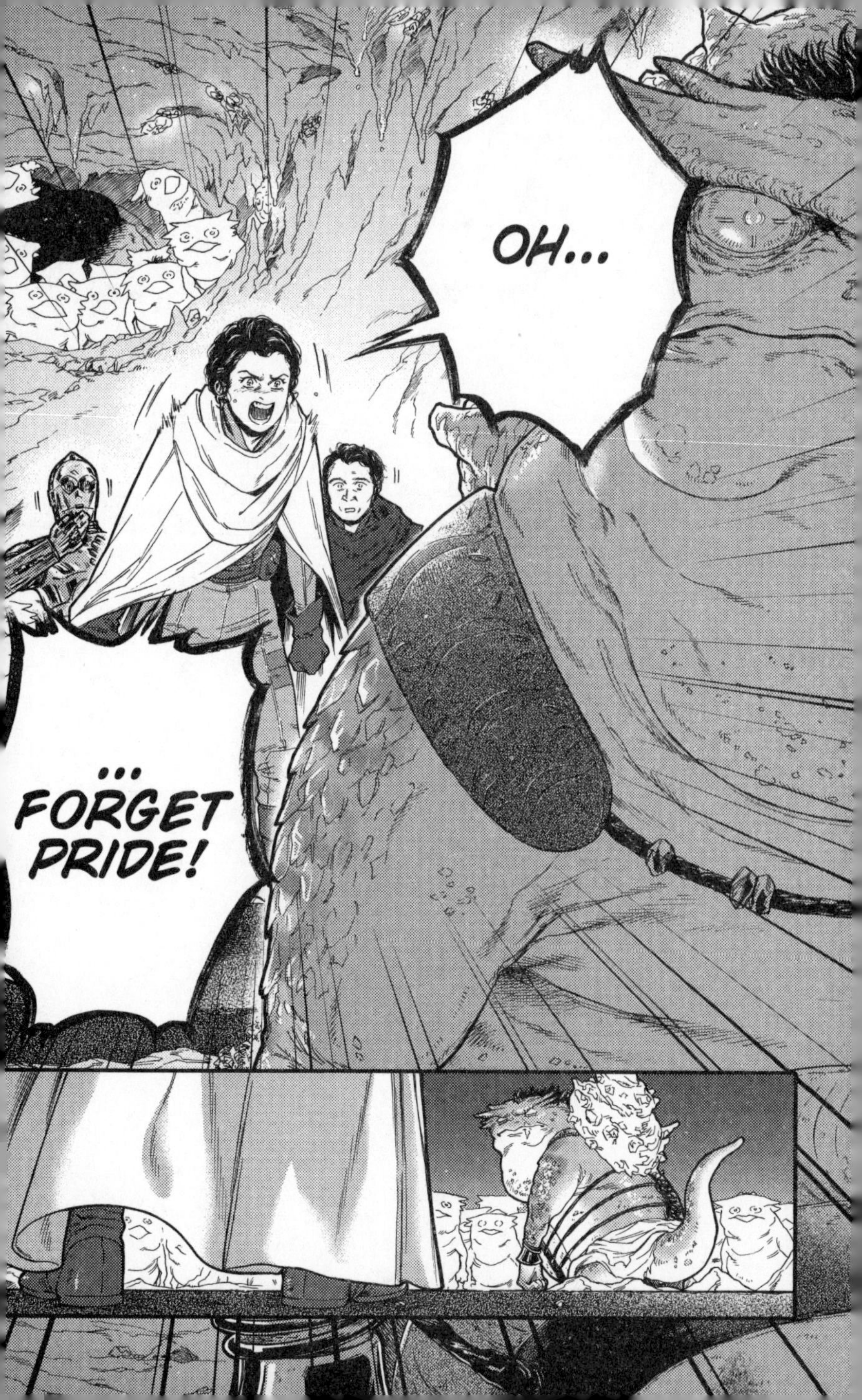
OH...
... FORGET PRIDE!

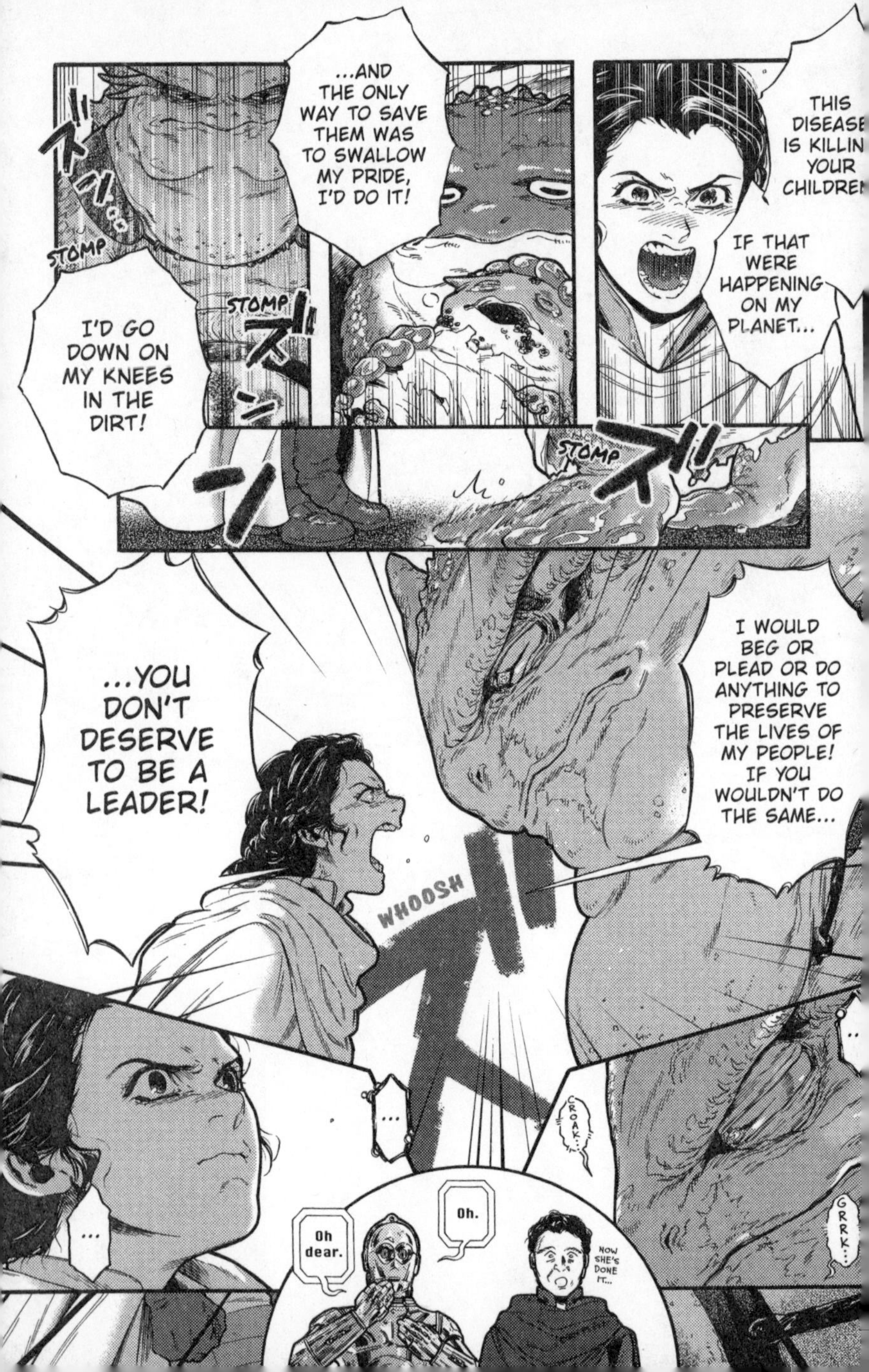
THIS DISEASE IS KILLIN YOUR CHILDREN
IF THAT WERE HAPPENING ON MY PLANET...
...AND THE ONLY WAY TO SAVE THEM WAS TO SWALLOW MY PRIDE, I'D DO IT!
STOMP
STOMP
I'D GO DOWN ON MY KNEES IN THE DIRT!
STOMP
I WOULD BEG OR PLEAD OR DO ANYTHING TO PRESERVE THE LIVES OF MY PEOPLE! IF YOU WOULDN'T DO THE SAME...
...YOU DON'T DESERVE TO BE A LEADER!
WHOOSH
GRRK...
CROAK...
...
...
Oh.
NOW SHE'S DONE IT...
Oh dear.

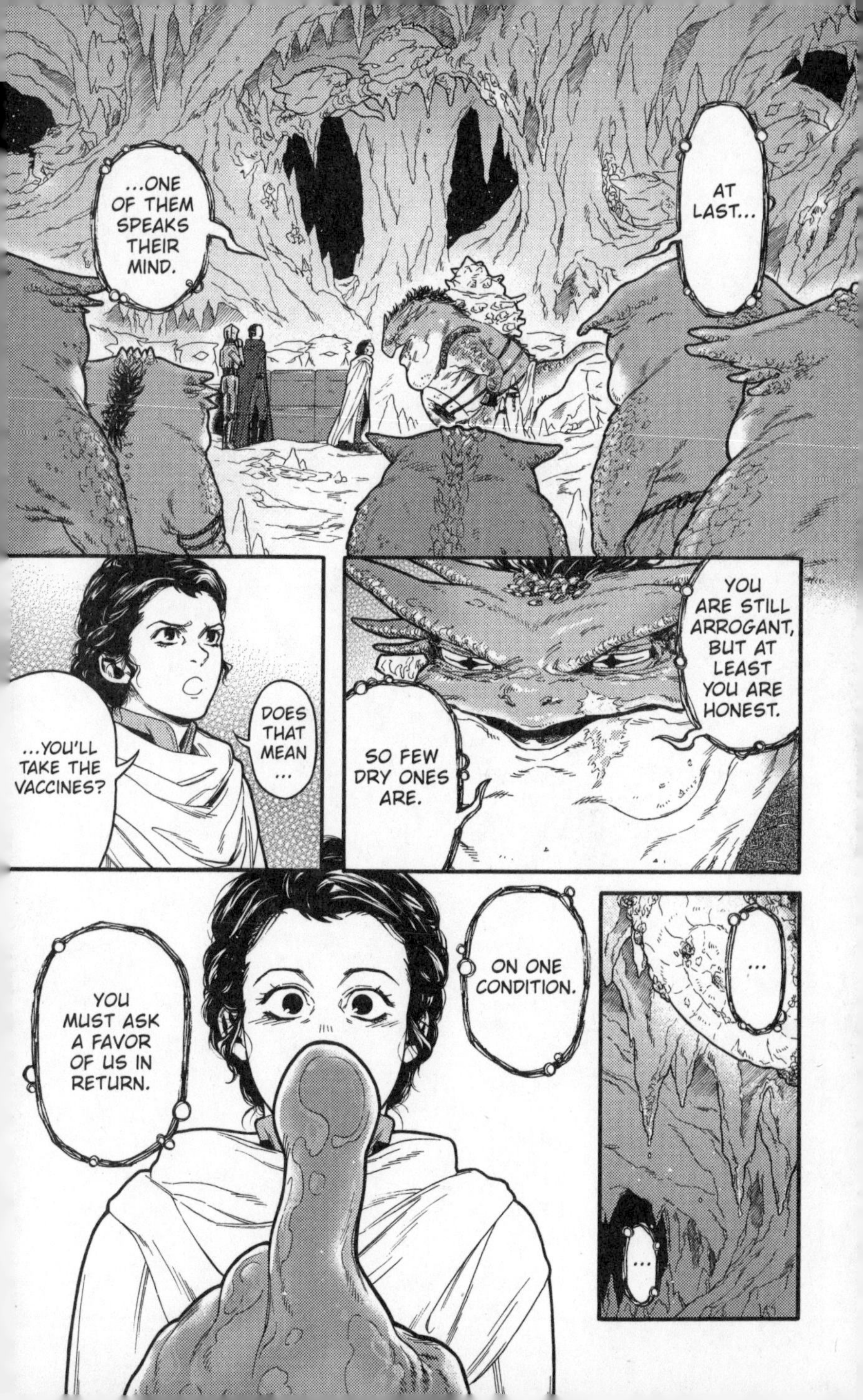
AT LAST...
...ONE OF THEM SPEAKS THEIR MIND.
YOU ARE STILL ARROGANT, BUT AT LEAST YOU ARE HONEST.
SO FEW DRY ONES ARE.
DOES THAT MEAN ...
...YOU'LL TAKE THE VACCINES?
...
...
ON ONE CONDITION.
YOU MUST ASK A FAVOR OF US IN RETURN.

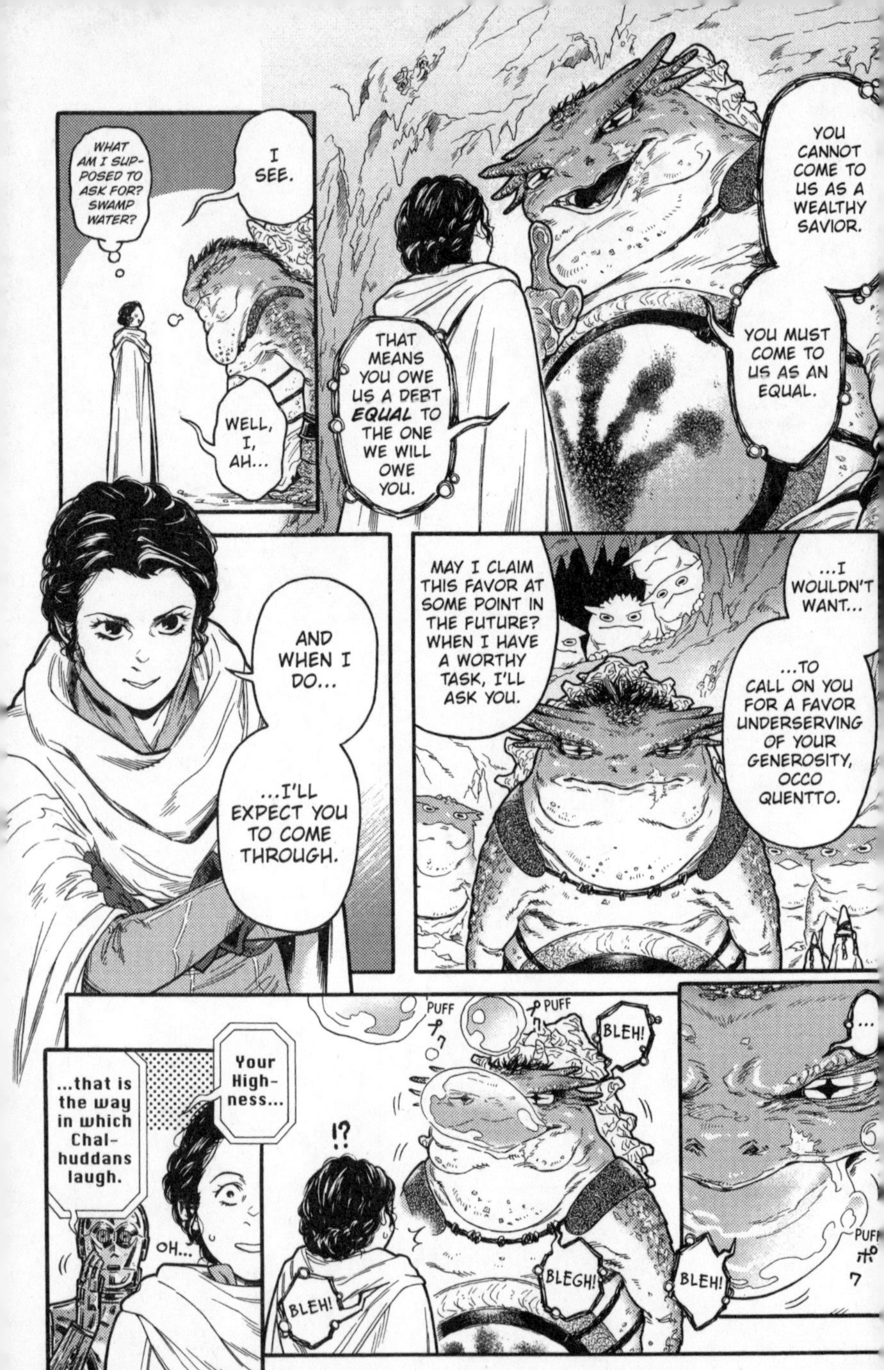
YOU CANNOT COME TO US AS A WEALTHY SAVIOR.
YOU MUST COME TO US AS AN EQUAL.
THAT MEANS YOU OWE US A DEBT *EQUAL* TO THE ONE WE WILL OWE YOU.
I SEE.
WHAT AM I SUP-POSED TO ASK FOR? SWAMP WATER?
WELL, I, AH...
...I WOULDN'T WANT...
...TO CALL ON YOU FOR A FAVOR UNDERSERVING OF YOUR GENEROSITY, OCCO QUENTTO.
MAY I CLAIM THIS FAVOR AT SOME POINT IN THE FUTURE? WHEN I HAVE A WORTHY TASK, I'LL ASK YOU.
AND WHEN I DO...
...I'LL EXPECT YOU TO COME THROUGH.
...
PUFF
PUFF
PUFF
BLEH!
BLEH!
BLEGH!
BLEH!
!?
Your High-ness...
...that is the way in which Chal-huddans laugh.
OH...

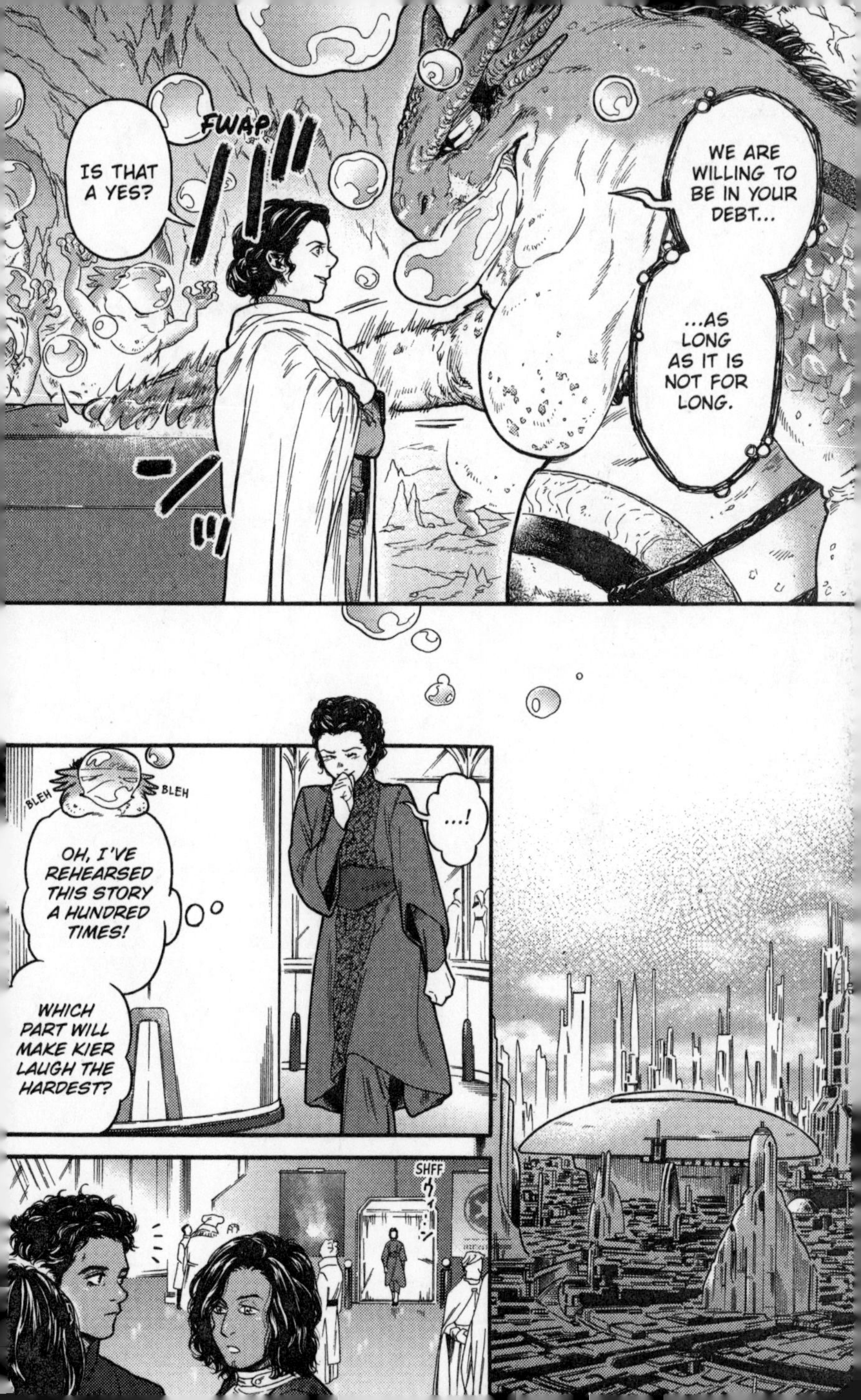
WE ARE WILLING TO BE IN YOUR DEBT...
...AS LONG AS IT IS NOT FOR LONG.
FWAP
IS THAT A YES?
...!
BLEH
BLEH
OH, I'VE REHEARSED THIS STORY A HUNDRED TIMES!
WHICH PART WILL MAKE KIER LAUGH THE HARDEST?
SHFF

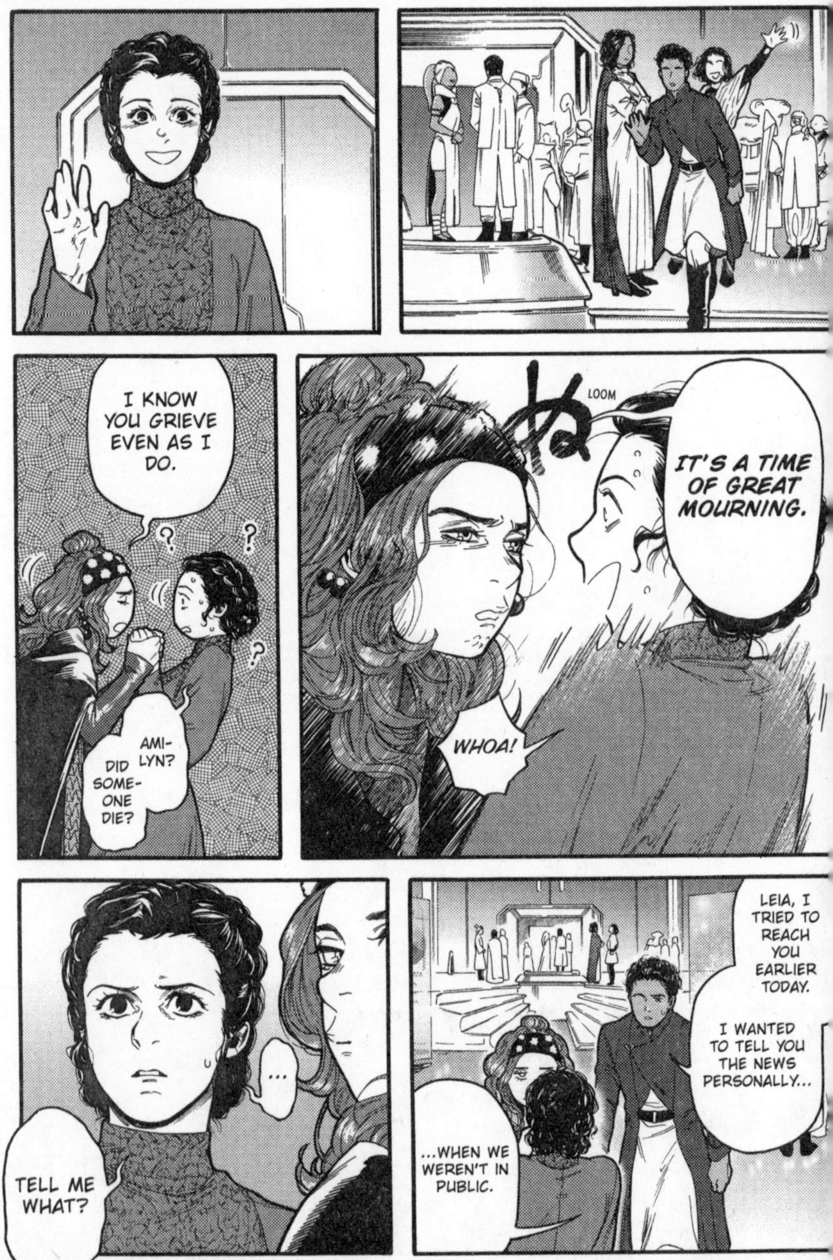
ぬ
LOOM
IT'S A TIME OF GREAT MOURNING.
WHOA!
I KNOW YOU GRIEVE EVEN AS I DO.
?
?
?
AMI-LYN?
DID SOME-ONE DIE?
LEIA, I TRIED TO REACH YOU EARLIER TODAY.
I WANTED TO TELL YOU THE NEWS PERSONALLY...
...WHEN WE WEREN'T IN PUBLIC.
...
TELL ME WHAT?

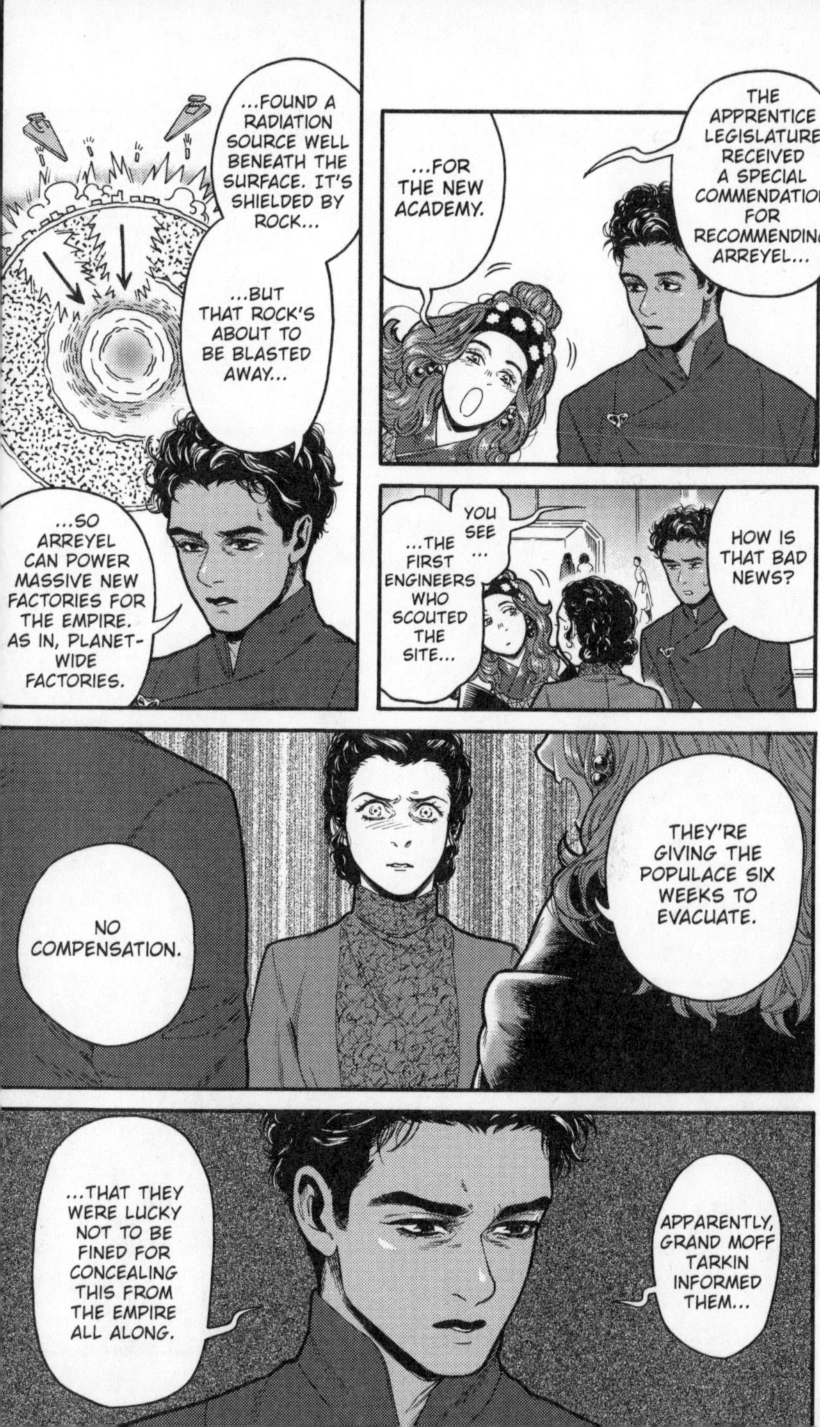
THE APPRENTICE LEGISLATURE RECEIVED A SPECIAL COMMENDATION FOR RECOMMENDING ARREYEL...
...FOR THE NEW ACADEMY.
HOW IS THAT BAD NEWS?
YOU SEE...
...THE FIRST ENGINEERS WHO SCOUTED THE SITE...
...FOUND A RADIATION SOURCE WELL BENEATH THE SURFACE. IT'S SHIELDED BY ROCK...
...BUT THAT ROCK'S ABOUT TO BE BLASTED AWAY...
...SO ARREYEL CAN POWER MASSIVE NEW FACTORIES FOR THE EMPIRE. AS IN, PLANET-WIDE FACTORIES.
THEY'RE GIVING THE POPULACE SIX WEEKS TO EVACUATE.
NO COMPENSATION.
APPARENTLY, GRAND MOFF TARKIN INFORMED THEM...
...THAT THEY WERE LUCKY NOT TO BE FINED FOR CONCEALING THIS FROM THE EMPIRE ALL ALONG.

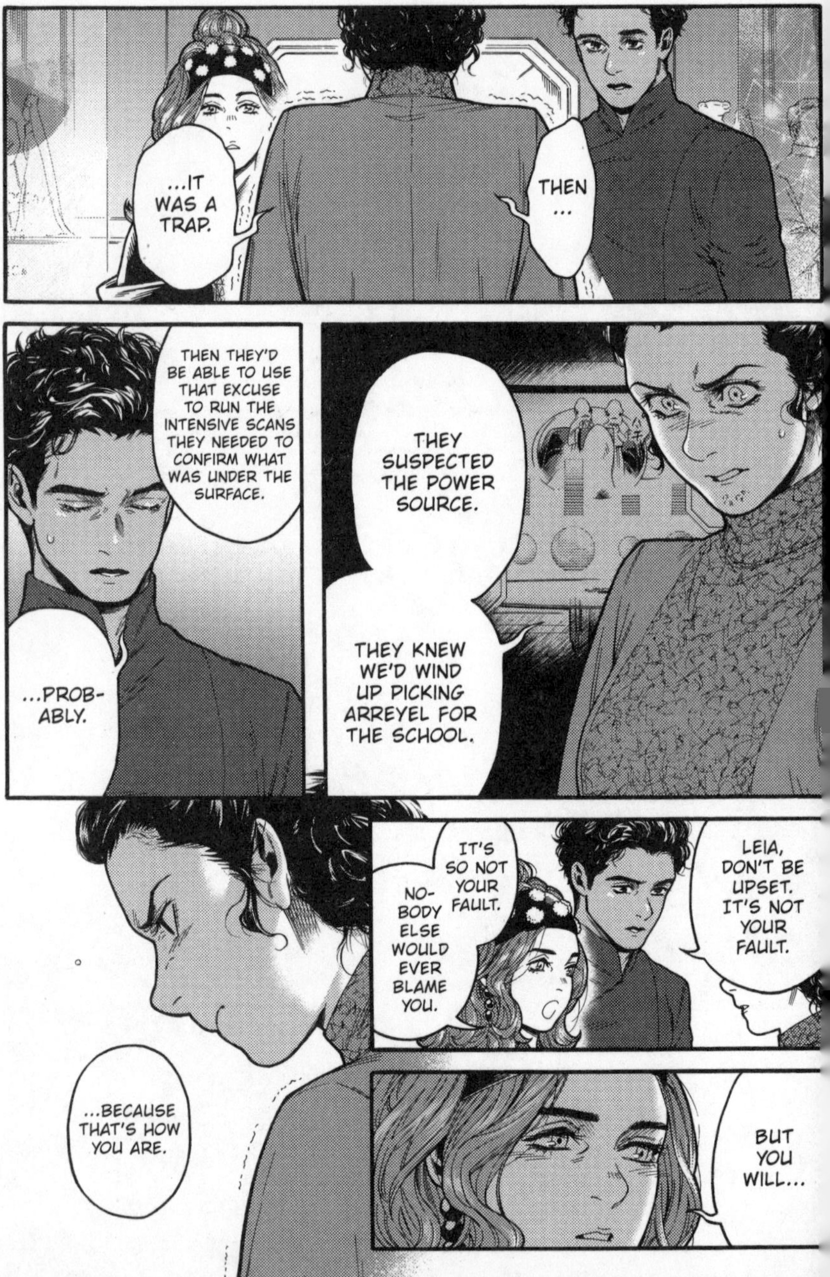
THEN...
...IT WAS A TRAP.
THEY SUSPECTED THE POWER SOURCE.
THEY KNEW WE'D WIND UP PICKING ARREYEL FOR THE SCHOOL.
THEN THEY'D BE ABLE TO USE THAT EXCUSE TO RUN THE INTENSIVE SCANS THEY NEEDED TO CONFIRM WHAT WAS UNDER THE SURFACE.
...PROB-ABLY.
LEIA, DON'T BE UPSET. IT'S NOT YOUR FAULT.
IT'S SO NOT YOUR FAULT.
NO-BODY ELSE WOULD EVER BLAME YOU.
BUT YOU WILL...
...BECAUSE THAT'S HOW YOU ARE.

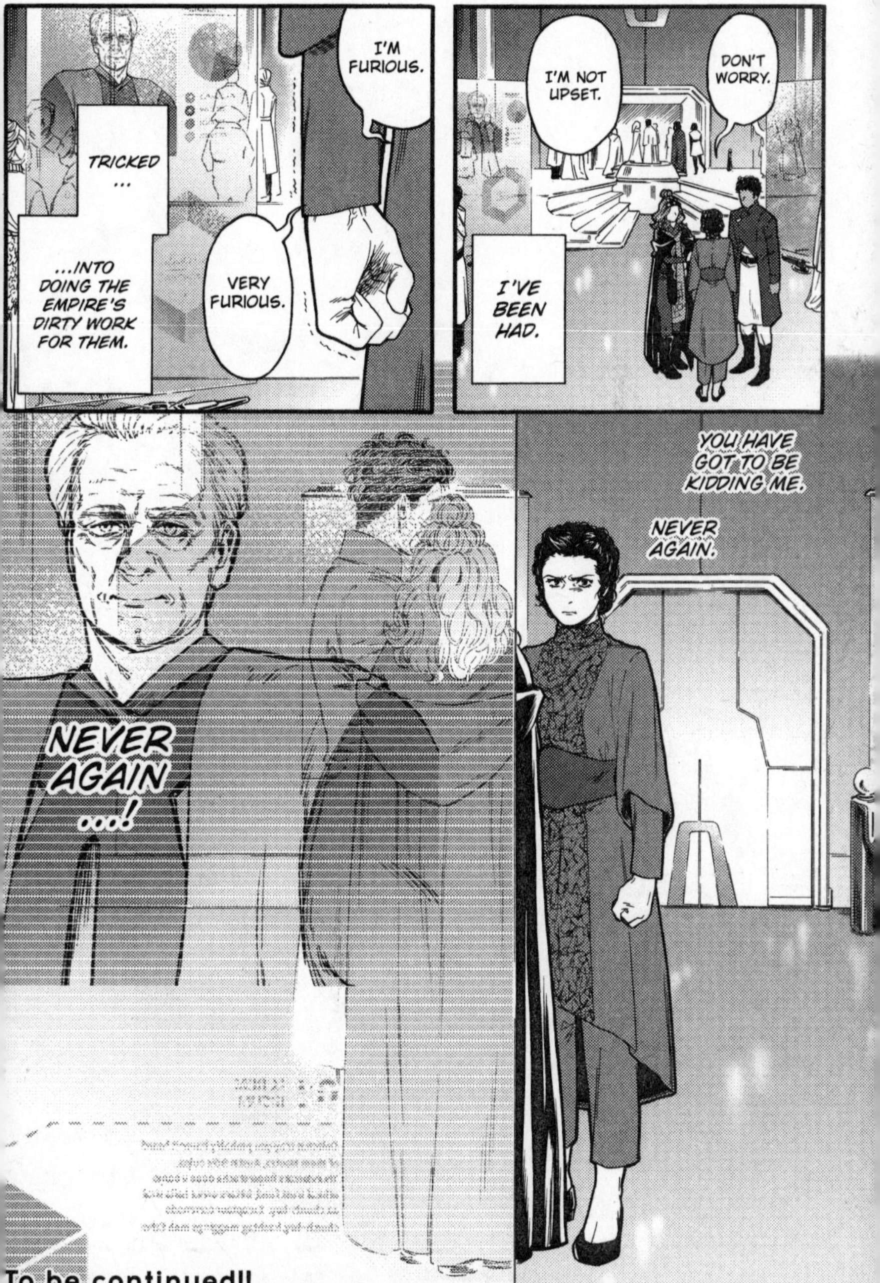
DON'T WORRY.
I'M NOT UPSET.
I'VE BEEN HAD.
I'M FURIOUS.
TRICKED ...
...INTO DOING THE EMPIRE'S DIRTY WORK FOR THEM.
VERY FURIOUS.
YOU HAVE GOT TO BE KIDDING ME.
NEVER AGAIN.
NEVER AGAIN ...!
To be continued!!

SPECIAL

CONTRIBUTIONS

(In Japanese alphabetical order)

Haruichi-sensei received these lovely messages

in honor of the second collected volume's release.

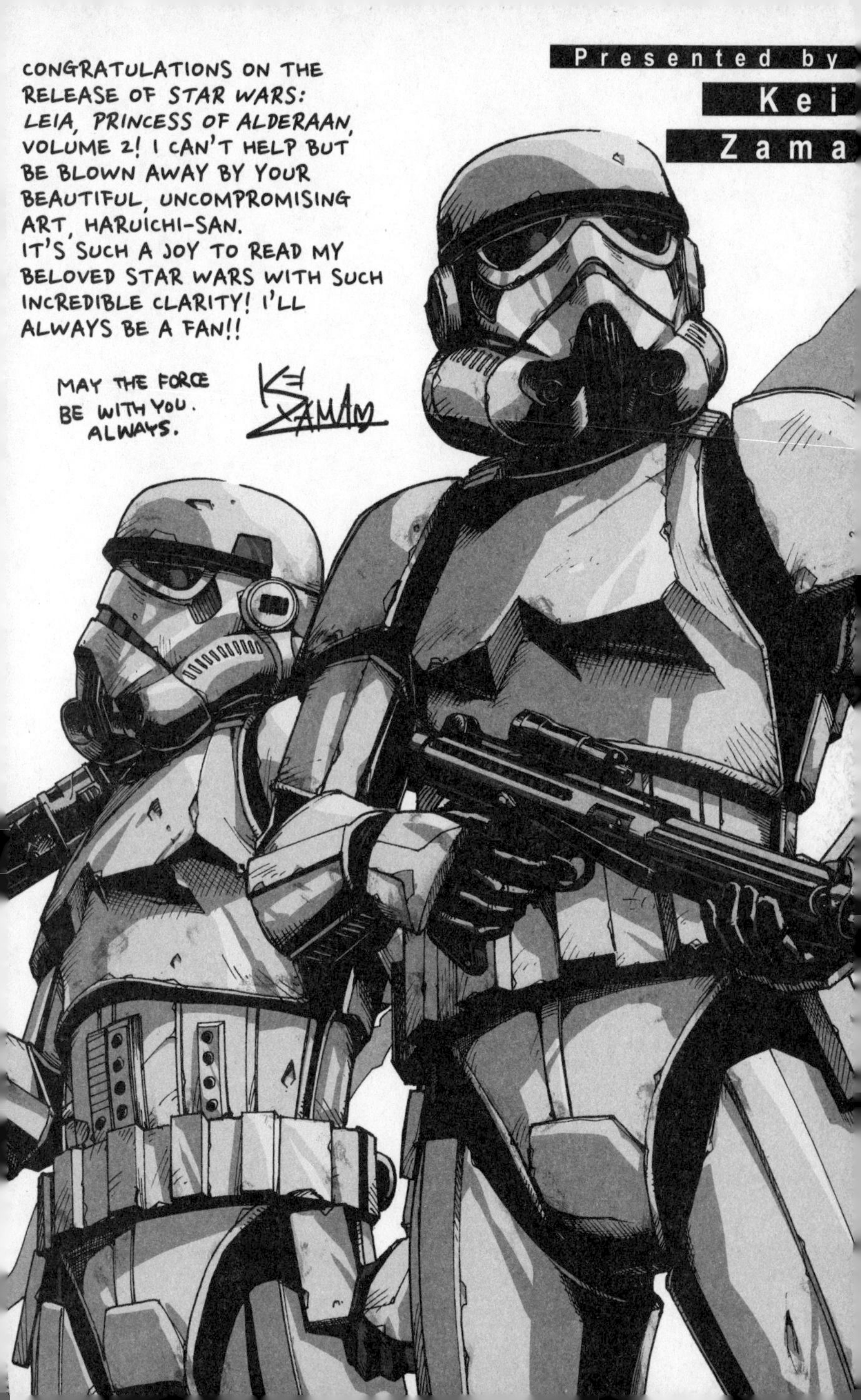
Presented by
Kei
Zama
CONGRATULATIONS ON THE RELEASE OF STAR WARS: LEIA, PRINCESS OF ALDERAAN, VOLUME 2! I CAN'T HELP BUT BE BLOWN AWAY BY YOUR BEAUTIFUL, UNCOMPROMISING ART, HARUICHI-SAN.
IT'S SUCH A JOY TO READ MY BELOVED STAR WARS WITH SUCH INCREDIBLE CLARITY! I'LL ALWAYS BE A FAN!!
MAY THE FORCE BE WITH YOU. ALWAYS.

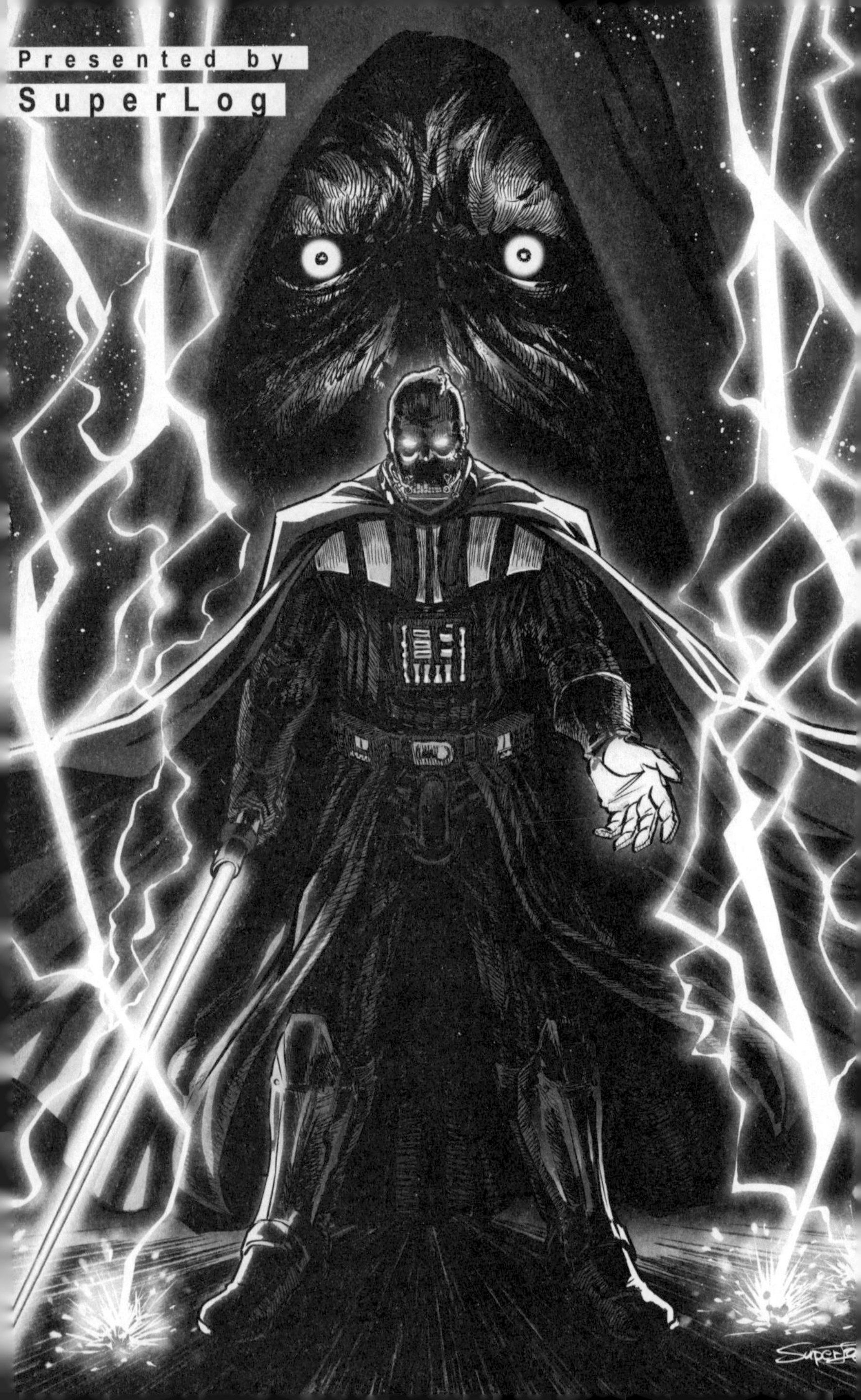

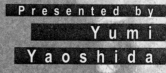

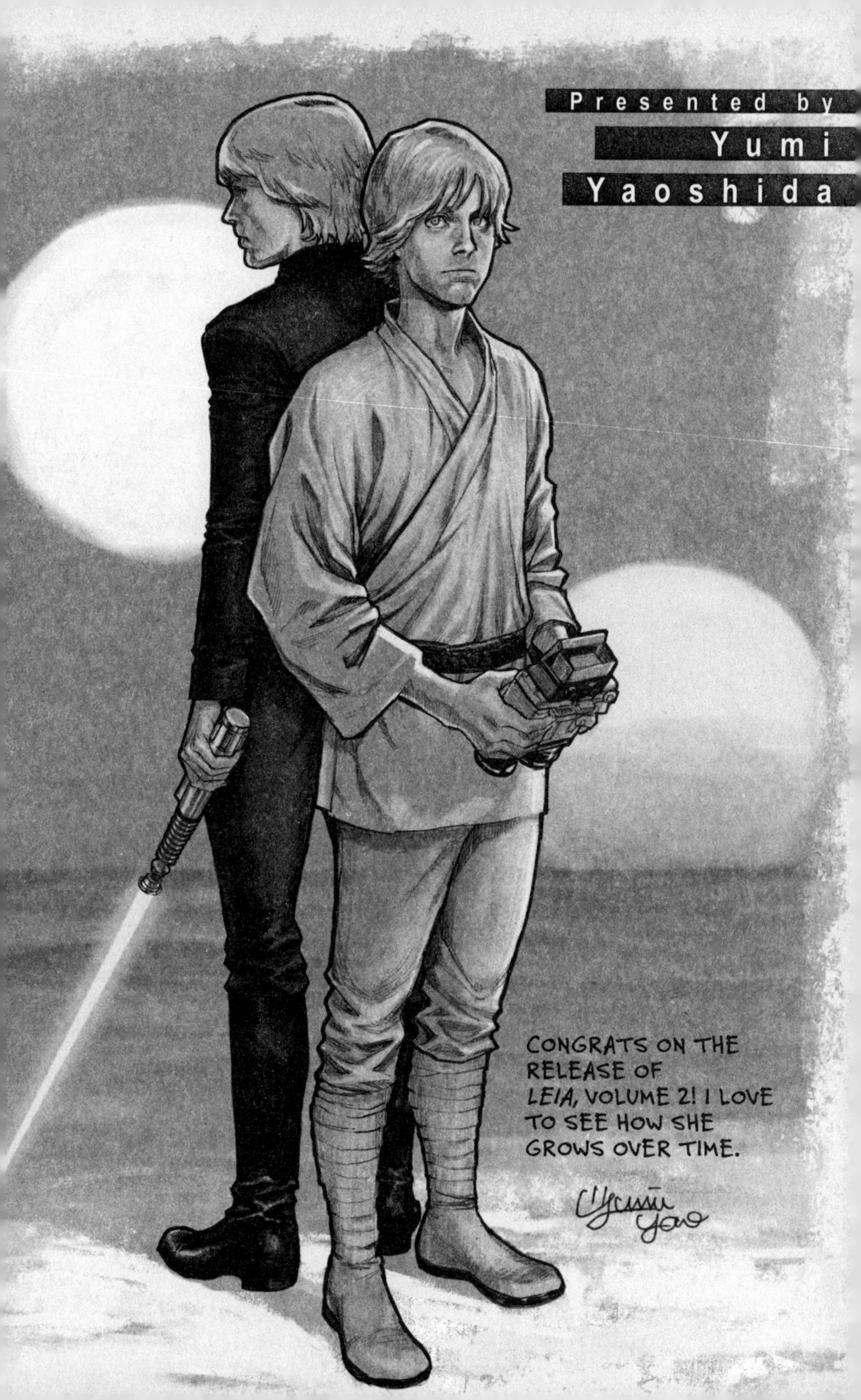

Presented by
Yumi
Yaoshida

CONGRATS ON THE
RELEASE OF
LEIA, VOLUME 2! I LOVE
TO SEE HOW SHE
GROWS OVER TIME.

Presented by
Youhei Penguin

THE STORY OF AMILYN HOLDO FROM *LEIA, PRINCESS OF ALDERAAN* TO *THE LAST JEDI*

After the events depicted in *Leia, Princess of Alderaan*, Amilyn played a public role in the Galactic Senate, while secretly working as a member of the Rebel Alliance. Her friendship with Leia continued, as she took lessons from Leia on how to ride a speeder (*Star Wars Adventures* (2017) #25, IDW Publishing), and when the Galactic Civil War broke out, she left the Empire.

She took on a role as a minister in the Alliance Civil Government, and was on board an Alliance smuggling vessel when an Imperial attack left the ship without a captain. She took control, and when a Star Destroyer caught the ship in its tractor beam, she boldly put up the shields, faced the docking bay, and opened fire, saving the ship and crew. Her exploits earned her the rank of captain in the Alliance Fleet (*Star Wars: Age of Resistance Special*, Marvel Comics).

Later in the war, Amilyn was working deals with criminal syndicates to procure supplies for the Alliance, when she learned that Crimson Dawn was holding an auction of the carbonite-frozen Han Solo, and passed the information on to Leia, who later saved Han (*Star Wars* (2020) #14, Marvel Comics).

Despite the restoration of peace after the New Republic was formed, Imperial remnants soon created the First Order. In order to stand up to this threat, Leia formed the Resistance, which Amilyn promptly joined, taking the rank of Vice Admiral. When Leia was injured, she assumed command of the Resistance, executing a suicide ramming attack to save her comrades that would later be known as the Holdo Maneuver. She was an irreplaceable friend who saved Leia on many occasions throughout their lives and fought with unsurpassed courage for the sake of galactic peace.

SPECIAL THANKS

Editor
Tomomi Uemura
Mika Matsui

Color Artist & Contribution
Yumi Yaoshida

Document
Verse COMICS

Contribution
Kei Zama
Youhei Penguin
AND SuperLog

My FAMILY, Puccho, KUROMI

...AND YOU!!

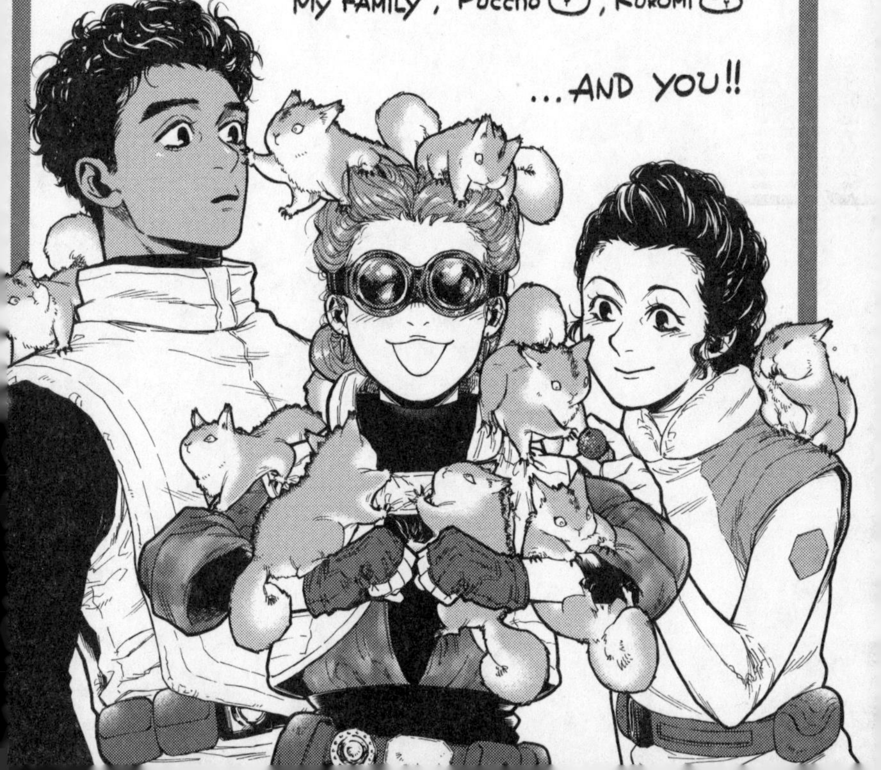

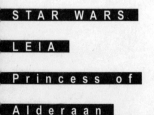

STAR WARS

LEIA

Princess of

Alderaan

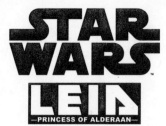

STAR WARS

LEIA
—PRINCESS OF ALDERAAN—

Original Story:
Claudia Gray

Art and Adaptation:
Haruichi

Supplementary Translation:
Stephen Paul

Lettering:
Phil Christie

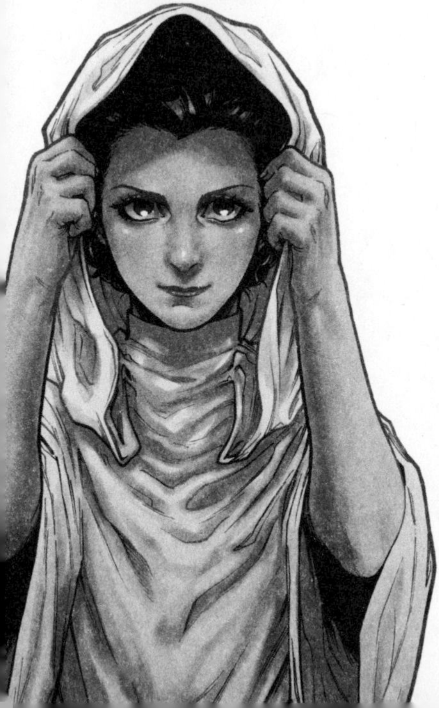

PRINCESS OF ALDERAAN, VOL. 2
© & TM 2021 LUCASFILM
First published in Japan in 2021
by LINE Corporation 4-1-6 Shinjuku,
Shinjuku-ku, Tokyo, Japan.
Produced by LINE Coporation 4-1-6
Shinjuku, Shinjuku-ku, Tokyo, Japan.

Yen Press
150 West 30th Street, 19th Floor
New York, NY 10001

Visit us at yenpress.com
facebook.com/yenpress
twitter.com/yenpress
yenpress.tumblr.com
instagram.com/yenpress

First Yen Press Edition: May 2022

Yen Press is an imprint of
Yen Press, LLC.
The Yen Press name and logo are
trademarks of Yen Press, LLC.

The publisher is not responsible for
websites (or their content) that are not
owned by the publisher.

Library of Congress Control Number:
2020942543

ISBNs: 978-1-9753-4477-1 (paperback)
978-1-9753-4478-8 (ebook)

10 9 8 7 6 5 4 3 2 1

WOR

Printed in the United States of America